ALSO BY ALEXIS HALL

Looking for Group

London Calling
Boyfriend Material
Husband Material
Father Material

Material World
10 Things That Never Happened

Spires
Glitterland
Waiting for the Flood
For Real
Pansies

Winner Bakes All
Rosaline Palmer Takes the Cake
Paris Daillencourt Is About to Crumble
Audrey Lane Stirs the Pot

PRAISE FOR ALEXIS HALL'S LONDON CALLING UNIVERSE

"Brilliance on every single page."

—**Christina Lauren**, *New York Times* and *USA Today* bestselling author

"It's a fun, frothy quintessentially British rom-com about a certified chaos demon and a stern brunch daddy with a heart of gold faking a relationship."

—**Talia Hibbert**, *New York Times* bestselling author

"Every once in a while you read a book that you want to SCREAM FROM ROOFTOPS about. I'm screaming, people!"

—**Sonali Dev**, award-winning author

"FAKE DATING, REAL FEELINGS, BEST JOKES."

—**Olivia Waite**, award-winning author

"Alexis Hall's *Boyfriend Material* perfectly balances laugh-out-loud-while-reading-alone-in-an-empty-room with those-aren't-tears-in-my-eyes-just-allergies."

—**Kris Ripper**, award-winning author

"Alexis Hall is the undisputed master of romantic comedy."

—**Jenny Holiday**, *USA Today* bestselling author

"I'm in awe of Alexis Hall's talent. I don't want the book to end."

—**Cathy Maxwell,** *New York Times* bestselling author

"*Boyfriend Material* is the joyfully queer British rom-com escape book I didn't know I needed."

—**KJ Charles,** award-winning author

FATHER MATERIAL

ALEXIS HALL

sourcebooks
casablanca

Published by Sourcebooks Casablanca, an imprint of Sourcebooks
1935 Brookdale RD, Naperville, IL 60563-2773
(630) 961-3900
sourcebooks.com

Cataloging-in-Publication Data is on file with the Library of Congress.

Printed and bound in Canada.
MBP 10 9 8 7 6 5 4 3 2 1

To all the readers who came with me,
Luc, and Oliver on this journey

PART ONE

SUMMER/AUTUMN

CHAPTER 1

I HAVE, IN FACT, ALWAYS seen the point of children's birthday parties. For children. Not for their adult parents to invite their adult friends to, even if those adult friends don't have kids of their own. Because for adults, children's birthday parties fucking suck. You can't swear. You can't have sex in the toilet. You can't get wasted or high or pass out in the corner. You can't do any of the things that make parties bearable.

Thinking about it, maybe I've just never liked any kind of party ever. I'd always known my mid-twenties fuckboy clubkid phase had been self-destructive. But it had never occurred to me I might have been trying to annoy myself to death.

"You're hating every second of this, aren't you?" said Oliver, making me feel both seen and taken-the-piss-out-of.

"Not at all. I love being surrounded by tiny balls of snot and chaos."

He gave me an amusperated smile. "Children are just in a developmental stage that makes controlling nasal flow difficult. There's nothing to—whoa there." With typically Oliverian expertise, he scooped up an errant child who had somehow acquired a terrifyingly large, terrifyingly sharp pair of scissors. "Those are not for you."

"They are," protested the child, chaotically if not snottily. "I found them. So they're mine."

Deftly separating infant from implement, Oliver flipped the scissors and held them with the blade tucked responsibly against his forearm. "Contrary to popular belief, possession is not, in fact, nine-tenths of the law."

Before Oliver Blackwood's Jurisprudence for Six-Year-Olds could get into full swing, we were interrupted by Ben, of Ben-and-Sophie, one of the many sets of straight married people who had somehow become my friends as a consequence of their having gone to university a decade ago with the man I'm in love with. As usual, Ben was five foot ten of stress and finger paints wrapped in dad jeans and a garishly coloured shirt. "Oh my God," he cried. "Luc, Oliver, have either of you seen Twin A come this way with an actual murder weapon?"

Oliver turned slightly, displaying weapon and twin both.

"Thank fuuuuuuu—goodness." Ben looked at his kid with an expression that was slightly too harried to be stern. "What were you thinking? Where did you even get those?"

Twin A wriggled futilely under Oliver's arm. "They were in the big wardrobe on the top shelf at the back in the box in the other box, but I found them. And then"—he tried to glare at Oliver but couldn't quite turn his neck far enough—"*he* stole them."

"You stole them first," Ben pointed out. "And someone could have been hurt."

"Technically," I said, channelling my inner Oliver, who unfortunately had far worse judgement than the real Oliver, "he just took them without consent."

With a triumphant kick, Twin A disentangled himself from Oliver. "You see. They're mine."

Ben took his hand with parental aggression. "Nothing's yours. You're a child."

"That's not fair."

"Well, life's not fa—" Ben's gaze floated up to Oliver and me. "Shit, I'm turning into my mother."

"Daddy said *shit*," yelled Twin A, pulling free before dashing out of the kitchen. "Mummy, Daddy said *shit*."

"Shit," sighed Ben. "I'd better—" Something bright and fast-moving caught his eye through the kitchen window. "Oh my God, is that Twin B? I think he's got matches."

As Ben parented off, Oliver and I were left alone, listening as the merry babble of kids at a party was cut through by Ben shouting "No, those are for grown-ups" and Sophie adding "You can commit arson when you're older."

"You know," I told Oliver, "I used to be cool before I met you. I did cool stuff."

"Did you?" Oliver raised a bullshit-calling eyebrow. "Because to my recollection, the first time we met, you ignored everybody and spent the evening talking to Priya in the kitchen, the second time we met you were blackout drunk, and the third time—on an actual date—you pretended to speak French to either impress or vex me. I've still not worked out which."

I did that embarrassing thing you do when you've been with someone a long time and you just naturally drift closer to them like the last two Maltesers in a packet. "So what you're saying is that the first time I was busy with my extremely interesting artist friend, the second time I was sexily self-destructive, and the third time I was a man of mystery."

"And look at you now." Surrendering to his inner Malteser, Oliver drew me to him. "Ruined by domestic bliss."

"I know. It's awful. How dare you make me happy."

He stretched up and kissed me in a sweet-and-totally-appropriate-for-a-children's-birthday-party kind of way. "How dare you make me happy back."

I had one of those flashes where you see yourself from a distance or from above or through the eyes of a person you used to be. "Fuck," I said. "We're legitimately disgusting."

"If it's any consolation," Oliver murmured, his eyes all soft and silver and never leaving mine, "I'm about to make you miserable again."

"You're going to say we have to *circulate*, aren't you? Be *sociable*. Support our friends."

"I don't need to. I just baited you into saying it for me." With great ceremony, Oliver plucked a glittering rainbow party hat from a stack of glittering rainbow party hats and strapped it to my head. The elastic settled behind my ears in a way I was immediately worried would make me look like Prince Charles. King Charles. Fuck, we'd been together through two monarchs, and God knew how many prime ministers. "Come on."

He took my hand in a half-affectionate, half-commanding way that, in other circumstances, I would have been extremely into, and led me outside. Where the first thing I noticed about the beautiful August afternoon he'd brought me into was that not a single other adult was wearing a party hat.

Other than me, looking like a prick, the garden also contained a squall of overexcited children, running backwards and forwards in that intense way you do when the world is too big, your legs are too small, and you don't have to worry about taxes, mortgages, or the fact you'll definitely die one day. Dotted amongst them were the usual trappings of a child's birthday: balloons, trestle tables laden with party food, and little clusters of adults in various stages of fuck-giving.

We made our way towards the nearest cluster, which consisted of Jennifer and Peter from the Oliver side of the equation, and the James Royce-Royces from mine. I hoped it said good things about the stability of my relationship with Oliver that not only were my friends becoming his friends, and his friends becoming my friends, but that my friends seemed to be becoming his friends' friends. Or maybe it was just that we'd all dissolved into a mush of thirtysomethings with jobs and responsibilities.

"How've you been?" Oliver asked. "It seems like forever." He was addressing the whole group but had tilted the question just *slightly* towards Jennifer and Peter. And that was why I was glad I'd brought Oliver. Because he knew how to say *Hi, we haven't spoken since your latest unsuccessful round of IVF* without sounding like a complete shit-heel.

"Not bad," replied Jennifer with a very *British* nod. "Busy. Trying to convince a think tank that you can't crack down on human trafficking by criminalising being trafficked."

"While I," added Peter, with his usual dryness, "am illustrating a book about a frog who learns to share his flies with other frogs."

James Royce-Royce, meanwhile, was gazing out into the morass of infancy with the focused rapture he'd once reserved for perfectly roasted pigeons and now reserved for perfectly roasted pigeons and his child. "Just look at him," he cried. "Riding that tricycle like a champion."

Because it was easier than not looking, I looked, and beheld Baby J riding a tricycle in a perfectly adequate way. I had, however, learned not to say anything even remotely resembling that. "Wow," I said, instead. "Look at him go."

"The grace," declared James Royce-Royce. "The panache. The élan."

Baby J turned his handlebars to the left and steered diligently into a sandpit.

James Royce-Royce's expression of adoration didn't falter for a nanosecond. "You see. And now he's exploring."

"He's upside down," said James Royce-Royce. The second James Royce-Royce. The one who was married to the first James Royce-Royce. It was a whole thing.

"Such resilience." James Royce-Royce whipped out his phone and started frantically scrolling. "This is probably an important developmental milestone."

"He's upside down," said James Royce-Royce again.

"He's..." Reality briefly slithered its way through James Royce-Royce's defences. "Oh yes, maybe he does need the *teensiest* bit of assistance." And, like Ben before him, James Royce-Royce parented off to make sure that his wonderful, perfect son was no longer being wonderful and perfect with his head in a pile of sand.

For a moment or two, we were trapped in a kind of stasis, watching James Royce trying to manhandle Baby J into an upright position.

"Wow," I said, out of habit. "Look at him go."

"Which one?" asked Peter, as Baby J—having apparently discovered his inner ostrich—squirmed out of James Royce-Royce's arms and reinverted himself.

"Both?"

After that, we lapsed into a deeper, more awkward silence. And, as a general rule, I wouldn't have relied on James Royce-Royce (the other James Royce-Royce) to be the lube in the social buttfucking because the man was so taciturn that when waiters told him to enjoy his meal, he never accidentally said, "You too."

To everyone's surprise, however, he gave Jennifer and Peter a searching look. "Sorry. Is this awful for you? I think James is going to have baby brain for at least the next fifteen years."

Jennifer shrugged. "It's fine. You see, we had a long discussion about whether we were going to cut all of our friends out of our lives completely or accept that sometimes people might talk about children in front of us."

"I was in favour of cutting you," added Peter. "I mean, what would we lose?"

"You'd lose..." I began, and trailed off partly for comedic effect and partly because I'd need a lot more booze and/or therapy to be able to say spontaneously positive things about myself. "Actually, you're right. You should drop us."

"Well"—Jennifer wasn't quite smiling through the pain, but she was probably smirking around it—"if any more of you have kids, we might. We're beginning to take it personally."

Oliver had that look he got when he was about to unleash his secretly catty side. It was a look that said *You are a bad influence on me, Lucien*, and I loved it. "I'm not entirely sure the twins count as children. I think Sophie must have picked them up in one of her regular deals with the devil."

Some of the strain faded from Jennifer's eyes and she laughed. "As a bonus or a sanction?"

"Probably as a bonus. Not even Lucifer himself could get one over on Sophie."

Except now Jennifer was frowning again. One of those complicated frowns where it was hard to know what she was frowning at and hard to know if she knew either. "Sorry, I'm probably coming across as bitter and resentful."

"We're *all* resentful of Sophie," replied Oliver, even though he definitely wasn't because he didn't have a resentful bone in his body. "She is, after all, a completely terrible human being whom we nevertheless love dearly."

"And besides"—gently, Peter nudged his shoulder against Jennifer's—"we can always spend our twilight years LARPing with Brian and Amanda."

"You're going to do what with them?" I asked. "No judgement, but is that one of those straight people things like swinging? Or swing-dancing?"

"I've never quite worked it out either," admitted Jennifer. "I think it's camping in fancy dress."

"Well, if we'd gone with them this weekend," said Peter, clearly glad they hadn't, "we'd have found out."

Jennifer's expression turned wry again. "We may have to one day. I'm beginning to realise that all those times Brian and Amanda said they hated kids, they genuinely meant it, and so if we ever want to see them again, we might need to do something in a child-free environment."

"Brian and Amanda have never invited us to go LARPing," said Oliver, with a touch of dismay.

"Oliver," I pointed out, "they've met me. Would you invite me to go LARPing? I still haven't figured out what it is, and I know I'd be the literal worst at it."

Oliver's jaw was stubbornly set. "It's still polite to invite people."

"I suspect"—Jennifer had a gleam in her eye that was the offline version of trollface—"the main reason you haven't been invited to go magic camping is Brian and Amanda aren't sure what side you're on."

"What?" I asked. "Like orcs versus elves or something?"

"Like kids versus no kids."

I reminded myself that Jennifer was going through a hard time right now and also that she and Oliver went way back, so she'd paid her needling dues many times over. On the other hand: red alert, panic stations, what the fuck, not ready to think about this right now. "Uhhhh," I said.

Oliver, of course, handled it with aplomb. A massive plomb. A plomb so big it was faintly impractical. "As with many, many other choices in life"—he also had his lawyer voice on—"I think it's rather important not to see children in terms of sides at all."

"That means kids," declared Peter.

"Uhhhh," I said. "Uhhhh."

Thankfully, Oliver was still amply supplied with plombs. "I think you'll find, as with many, many other choices in life, I mean exactly what I said."

"I'm sorry." Jennifer's shoulders slumped. "We shouldn't be taking this out on you. I know it's against your extremely admirable ethics to bitch about people behind their backs, but this is so typical of Brian and Amanda."

It was the wrong moment to feel slightly smug that Oliver would sometimes compromise his admirable bitching ethics when we were alone. But I felt smug about it anyway.

Peter sighed. "It's like they were rooting for us to have problems so we could be on their team. And now we do and we're sad and they've pounced."

"I suspect"—Oliver had replaced *lawyer voice* with *very good friend voice*—"that they're trying to support you in their own way."

"Well, their way sucks," retorted Jennifer, with a childishness I deeply respected. "I know they're mostly saying, 'You don't have to want this,' and that could be a helpful thing to say to some people in some contexts. But the thing is, I *do* want it and I'm not ready to give up on wanting it. It's just, right now, I… I don't know."

"Jenbee…" Peter had his arm around her in that helpless way you do when someone you love is hurting from something you can't control. "This isn't all on you. There's always other options, of which living in a tent with Brian and Amanda is way, way down the list."

The slump had progressed from Jennifer's shoulders to a whole body situation. "I know, I know. There's surrogacy or adoption or… or…kidnapping."

"We could probably grab one of these," suggested Peter, nodding subtly at the pack of young partygoers. "Nobody'd notice until at least four, and by then we'd be in zone six and they'd never be able to find us."

Oliver flicked up a wry brow, and for once, I didn't begrudge him flicking it at someone else. "That's true. Ben and Sophie's friends don't leave Kensington if they can possibly help it."

"We don't even live near a Waitrose anymore," added Jennifer. "They'd be fucked."

Rubbing his hands with faux excitement, Peter started eyeing up the kids in what I want to make very clear was a satirical way. "All right. Which do we get?"

"Not Baby J," said James Royce-Royce. "I'd never hear the end of it."

"And I don't recommend the twins." Wow, Oliver was going with this. There were very few things he wouldn't do to comfort his friends. "They've made me genuinely question my belief in the concept of ontological evil."

"How about that one?" Peter elbow-pointed. "He's been trying to put a manzanilla olive up his nose for the last three minutes. I can't imagine his parents would miss him."

"Hard pass," said Jennifer. "I'd rather go live in the tent."

"Personally," Oliver began, and I felt simultaneously reassured and terrified that he was so ready to have personal feelings about this, "I'd go for the one sitting on the edge of the fountain reading *A Hat Full of Sky*."

Jennifer hugged herself, her eyes lighting up. "Oh, she's perfect. I love kids who hate other kids."

Normally this was exactly the kind of insensitive bullshit I'd have been all over, but I was still trying really hard not to climb into my own head over the whole *Are you and your now unmistakably long-term partner planning for children yet?* thing. Once upon a time, I—along with everyone else who wasn't a heterosexual cis woman—would have been safe from that kind of crap. See, this was the problem with equality. Apparently, if you told a society it wasn't okay to treat one group of people worse than another, it would consider the situation carefully, weigh up its options, and then start treating everyone equally badly.

And the thing was, it's not like me and Oliver hadn't had the conversation. We'd had it multiple times. I just wasn't quite ready to be fantasy-casting my domestic future with other people's kids, so I politely snuck away. All right, I impolitely snuck away, and my friends were too polite to call me on it. Of course, that left me at a loose end at a children's party, which felt a whole lot worse than being at a loose end and *not* at a children's party. For about thirteen seconds I watched an—I was guessing—either highly under- or highly overpaid man in a top hat blasting a stream of shimmering bubbles over the heads of thirty indifferent six-year-olds. Which was a shame because I normally felt bubbles enhanced an event. Then again, in my experience, the events they'd enhanced had involved a pit of half-naked adults on poppers.

"Tarquin"—a voice drifted across the lawn—"stop putting hummus in Petunia's hair."

Oh God, I was in hell. So I did what I always did when I was in hell and went to wallow in misery with Priya. She was sitting on a blanket, surrounded by makeup palettes and brushes and, before I could even get out a "Well, isn't this awful," a little girl had dashed past me, knelt in front of Priya, and declared it was her turn now.

"Sure," said Priya, laconic as usual, but a flavour of laconic that made me feel a bit cockblocked, wallow-in-misery-wise. "What do you want to be?"

"A shark," replied the little girl more decisively than I'd ever replied to anything in my entire life. "Because my brother's scared of sharks."

This felt like a good opportunity to be a grown-up. "That doesn't sound very nice," I tried.

The little girl gave me the *I resent how little you are comprehending me* look I was used to seeing on children. "My brother's not very nice."

"Hi, Luc." Priya was already gathering her shark colours, a mix of blues, greys, whites, and—worryingly—reds. "Also, her face, her choice. What kind of shark do you want to be?"

"A ghost shark who lives under your bed and will bite your hand off if it sticks out of the covers in the night."

"Are you actually trying to give your brother nightmares?" I asked.

"Yes," Priya and the girl said simultaneously, with Priya adding, "*Obviously*."

I eyed her dubiously. "Isn't that a little bit irresponsible?"

Priya grinned like a ghost shark who lives under your bed and will bite your hand off if it sticks out of the covers in the night. "Not my kids. Not my problem."

"I never wanted a brother," explained the little girl tragically. "I wanted a chinchilla."

And so today joined the long list of days in which I failed to quit when I was ahead. "Isn't a brother better than a chinchilla?"

"No," said the little girl and Priya, once again in unison.

"Chinchillas can jump six feet in the air," the little girl went on. "My brother can't jump six feet in the air."

Having assembled her various ensharkening implements, Priya set about applying a base coat of silvery-blue. "I always knew there was a reason I didn't like boys."

"Speaking of not liking boys"—I made what even I could tell was a shit attempt at changing the subject—"where are your girlfriends?"

"Theresa's done the kids thing already. Andi's allergic to children. So they're"—Priya hesitated for a nanosecond—"*shopping at IKEA*, and I'm here."

"It sounds like you got the bad end of that deal."

"Luc, it's fine. I can go to IKEA whenever I want."

I stared at her, wondering who this woman was and what she'd done with Priya. "Are you saying you deliberately chose face painting at a children's party for no money over a long, luxurious, strangely intense trip to IKEA on a Saturday afternoon?"

"You seem to know a lot about my trips to IKEA. But yeah." Priya shrugged. "This is fun. I love kids. I'm one of nature's aunts."

"I wish you were my aunt," put in the little girl, whose new identity as a ghost shark who lives under your bed and will bite your hand off if it sticks out of the covers in the night was taking definite and disturbing shape. "My aunt's Bethany, and she's horrid."

"Why's she horrid?" asked Priya.

"She just is."

Priya winced. "Oh, that's the worst kind of horrid."

"For the record," I said, talking over a child like the classy motherfucker I was, "I'm feeling quite betrayed by this."

"I'll paint you next."

Priya's lack of time for my bullshit was the basis of our entire relationship, and, in theory, I appreciated it. "You're supposed to be the person I complain about other people with. And I can't do that if you're enjoying yourself."

The little girl had been glancing between us in a way that was making it somewhat difficult for Priya to fully realise her ghost-shark vision. "Is he your boyfriend?"

"Nope," said Priya. "We're both mega gay."

"Okay," said the little girl. "Can my ghost shark have blood on its teeth from all the little brothers it's eaten?"

Priya gestured at her vast array of reds. "Way ahead of you, kiddo."

"Betrayed," I repeated.

"I don't know what to say to you, Luc." Without even sparing me a look, Priya started outlining the enormous teeth that would probably make an unsuspecting young boy piss himself later. "I got happy. Deal with it."

Oh fuck, she had, hadn't she?

"And," she added belligerently, "in case you've forgotten, so did you."

"But it didn't make me a better person."

"It hasn't made me a better person either. I've always been fantastic, and I've always liked kids. You just never noticed because you're profoundly selfish."

"Hey," I protested. "That's...entirely fair."

"Besides"—Priya was patron saint of kicking you when you were down—"you're just freaking out because of tomorrow."

I was not. "I am not."

"What's tomorrow?" asked the little girl.

Priya looked very, very serious—like the total dickhead I was pleased to realise she could still be. "Tomorrow, Luc and his boyfriend are doing something huge. Overwhelmingly huge. Life-changingly huge. Nothing will ever be the same again for them after tomorrow."

"It's not that big a deal," I whimpered.

"That's not what you said when you rang me last week. At three in the morning."

"That was last week," I told her. "This is now. Now I have a sense of perspective." I took a deep breath. "And I'm fine."

CHAPTER 2

I WAS NOT FINE. I was the opposite of fine. I was cold, sweaty, nauseous, and, once again, phoning my friends at three in the morning.

Not Priya, though. This was not a *Call me on my bullshit* situation. This was a *Lovingly pretend my bullshit is valuable fertiliser you need for your garden* situation.

"Hi," said Bridge sleepily. "What's wrong?"

I remembered something I should have remembered two panics ago. "Oh shit, you're pregnant."

"I've been pregnant for nine months, Luc. Have you only just noticed?"

"No, I mean, you're pregnant, so I shouldn't be ringing at three in the morning."

"Don't worry," yawned Bridge. "I was up anyway."

"You were not up anyway."

"I was about to be. I'm sure I was about to be. Are you all right?"

Okay, we were in the ethical weeds here. On the one hand, it was wrong to lie to your friends. On the other hand, it was wrong to offload your anxieties onto a pregnant woman. On the other other hand, or perhaps just on more of the same hand, the wrongness had probably begun when I'd reflexively rung the pregnant woman up in the middle of the night. "Yes."

"You're calling me at"—there was a pause as she checked the time—"2:47 on a Sunday morning to tell me you're all right."

"Yes?"

"You're a terrible liar, Luc," said Bridge. And she sounded genuinely hurt. "Also, you shouldn't lie to me."

"I lie to you all the time."

"Yes, but not about things like this. You don't pretend you're okay when you aren't."

I made a valiant effort to be lighthearted. "I do. Otherwise I'd be completely nonfunctional."

"Not to *me*," Bridge replied. And she was right about that. Bridge had never let me play the *it's fine* card, and she wasn't about to start now. "You're trying to protect me because I'm pregnant and that's…that's dehumanising. It's probably misogynistic too."

"Probably?"

"I was giving you wiggle room to spare your feelings. Because I'm a *good friend*."

She was. Although I wasn't totally sure that this particular exchange had been a master class in good-friend-ness on either of our parts. "Bridge, it's not a big deal. You need to look after yourself, and you need to let me pretend I'm a vaguely decent human being who doesn't bother people with his crap when they're trying to have major life events."

"But"—Bridge gave a little wail—"it's not fair to exclude me from your crap just because I'm having a life event. I can't let my life events mess up life. And I've already missed the twins' birthday because my water broke."

At the time, I'd assumed that Bridge's tendency to run late had pushed so hard against my tendency to bail early that we'd completely missed each other. "Oh my God, Bridge, are you okay? Are you in hospital? Did I just call you up to whinge about my problems while you were, I don't know, in labour?"

"I'm not in *active* labour," Bridge protested. "Your water breaking isn't like the movies, where it's all, 'Whoosh, scream, *woowoowoo*, pant, baby.'"

This wasn't the detail that mattered, but I couldn't not. "*Woowoowoo?*"

"That was an ambulance. That was my amazing and accurate impersonation of an ambulance."

Still not the detail that mattered. Still couldn't not. "Wouldn't that be more *neenawneenaw*?"

"Ambulances haven't gone *neenawneenaw* in years. Anyway, the point is, once your water breaks, it's usually a day or two before the actual..."

"*Woowoowoo* bit?"

"Yes."

I still felt kind of crappy about ringing her. "I still feel kind of crappy about ringing you."

"Well, don't. I love that I'm still your person."

"Isn't Oliver supposed to be my person now?"

"Love is love, Luc," she declared, "and persons are persons."

It was becoming increasingly clear that I had made a profound and irrecoverable error with one of my persons. Sadly, my other person was sleeping the sleep of the rational upstairs and probably wasn't about to notice my absence and ride to my rescue. This was my fault and my problem. "Seriously," I tried again. "It isn't a big deal. I had a bit of a freak-out, it's passed, I—"

"Not about tomorrow?" Bridge cried. "You're not having second thoughts about tomorrow!"

"No."

"That's your lying monosyllable. Didn't I just tell you not to lie to me?"

Toppling onto my side, I mashed my face into the sofa cushions. "You know I'm not good with…like, decisions, maturity, responsibility, the future, having tiny lives depending on me, that kind of thing."

"Lucien Havelock O'Donnell, you—"

"Hang on." I briefly unmashed my face. "Havelock?"

"Well, if you're not going to have a middle name, then you…you…get given one."

"No, you don't. That's not a thing. That's never been a thing."

In typical Bridge style, she ignored me. "Lucien Havelock O'Donnell, you are not going to mess this up for me."

Okay, I was officially feeling at least two percent less guilty. "Um, what do you mean, *for you*?"

"I've wanted you and Oliver to do this for years. And since you let us all down by not getting married—"

"Bridge, come on. We did what was right for us."

"But I've always dreamed of going to your wedding."

"You *did* go to my wedding," I pointed out.

"Yes, but you *didn't*."

"And it was the happiest day of my life. Now please go back to sleep and—"

"It's too late. I'm up now."

"You told me you were already up."

"I was lying." It was amazing how sure of herself Bridge could sound even when she was admitting to having done something wrong. "But it doesn't count because it wasn't about something *huge* like 'I'm thinking of not doing something that my *best friend* has wanted me to do for *years* and now I'm trying to not even *tell* her and—'" I became uncomfortably aware that I could hear dragging, moving sounds.

"Bridge…are you putting your shoes on?"

"I'm coming to see you."

I was going to say *But you're pregnant*, but I shelved that particular objection for reasons of dehumanisation and probable misogyny. "Are you?"

"Yes. I'll meet you on the Millennium Bridge."

"You absolutely will not."

"But it's our *thing*. It's what we *do*."

"We did it once. Years ago."

A confused silence briefly echoed down the line at me. "It wasn't."

"It was pre-pandemic. That's years."

"Fuck." Bridge sounded genuinely distraught. "Oh my God, Luc, we're *old*. We lost our youth to a virus."

"I think we'd already lost our youth to not being young anymore."

For the tiniest of moments, I'd thought I'd managed to say something that wasn't horrendously counterproductive. "Then we *have* to do this," Bridge exclaimed. "We have to do it for the people we used to be."

"The person I used to be was an arsehole."

"And I loved that arsehole. I want to see that arsehole again."

"How about," I offered desperately, "I show you that arsehole after you've had your baby."

"It won't be the same."

"It will. Arseholes change very little. It's their whole thing, figuratively and literally."

"I'm calling a cab."

"Don't call a cab. Please don't call a cab."

"I've called a cab."

There was no way this was going to end well. And there was no way it wasn't going to be my fault. "But your water broke."

"And if I start having a baby on the bridge, you can rush me across the city on a madcap drive to the hospital."

"Tell me that's not going to happen."

"Of course it's not going to happen."

"Okay, now you're making me feel like it's definitely going to happen."

"Then"—it was Bridge's triumphant voice—"you'd better come meet me, or I'll be giving birth alone on a bridge at 3:02 in the morning."

"Look," I said. "I know you're an independent woman who can make her own decisions, but this seems like a really, really bad decision."

"Tough. You owe me."

"What do you mean, I owe you?"

"One, you dated Oliver by yourself despite my best attempts to get you together. Two, you flaked on your own wedding that I was really looking forward to. Three, you got a civil partnership for—and I quote—'legal reasons' and didn't even let me be your witness. Four, you're putting the next step of my Luc and Oliver Eternal Happiness Plan in jeopardy."

"Wait," I said. "What? What is this plan?"

"Cab's here. Byeeee."

It was only when I'd been sitting in a cab of my own for about twenty minutes, and had realised I was going to be in it for at least twenty minutes more, that it finally dawned on me that I was no longer in my *leap spontaneously into a taxi like Carrie Bradshaw* era and more in my *live in the suburbs and have a lawn* era. And, thinking about it, the fact that Carrie Bradshaw was my icon of choice for youth, freedom, and troubled singleness meant I was squarely in my *too old for this shit* era. As, ironically enough, was Carrie Bradshaw, if *And Just Like That...* was anything to go by.

After paying the full fifty quid (including tip) it took to get from Havering to Central London in a reasonable time at an unreasonable hour, I scrambled out the cab, mildly relieved that I'd at least got there first and hadn't left my pregnant friend standing around on a windy London landmark when she should have been in bed resting.

While I waited, I stared at the Thames, which—much like me—looked a lot better at night. When, instead of being the sludgy grey sewer of the nation, it became a brilliant mirror of coloured lights and reflected possibilities. Okay. Not much like me at all, actually. And, as I stared, I contemplated all the ways I could have handled this better. I could have not panic-dialled Bridge over something I was beginning to remember was trivial. I could have tried harder to dissuade her from this objectively terrible plan. I could have told Oliver, except that would have been embarrassing, or Tom, except that would have been patriarchal. I could just have been less of a fuckup in general. Always. Like, my whole life.

"Luuuuuc," cried Bridge.

And I turned round to see her emerging, slowly and sideways, from a taxi.

"Oh my God," I said. "You look—"

"Glowing?"

"Like I should not have dragged you out here at three in the morning."

Bridge, with the help of the taxi driver, had finally finished emerging. "It'll be good for the baby. It's fresh air. New experiences."

"It's inside you. What's it going to experience?"

"They experience all sorts of things. Sounds. Vibrations. Music."

"Pollution," I suggested. "Petrol fumes."

"They're going to grow up in London. They'll have to get used to it sometime. Besides"—Bridge forgot about me for a moment and turned to the taxi driver. "Oh, thank you so much. Have a lovely evening." She turned back to me. "Besides, this is important. We can't have a repeat of your wedding. I can't go through that again."

"Bridge," I said, as sternly as I could, given how profoundly in the wrong I was, "it's just a dog. We're getting a dog. People do it all the time, often very irresponsibly."

Her eyes—always fairly wide—widened further. "It's not just a dog. You're expanding your *family*."

My commitment-phobic heart pinned a note saying *It's been fun* to my ribs and did its best to sneak out my arse. "On a scale of one to one," I asked, "how helpful do you think that was?"

"Sorry. I know you get scared and think you're an awful human being who'll be a failure as a dog-daddy, but that little puppy is counting on you."

I gave an actual howl. "Still not helping."

"I'm not trying to help." Having subtly manoeuvred herself into poking range, Bridge took full advantage and poked me. "The last time I tried to help, you didn't get married."

"Which was the right thing to do," I reminded her.

"And the right thing to do now is—" She stopped, looking very briefly pained.

"Bridge?"

"It's fine. Just a contraction."

I stared at her in a way that tried to balance concern for her well-being with concern for how badly everyone would kill me if Bridge had a baby on a bridge.

"Tiny contraction," she told me. "They happen. Still probably got ages before it gets serious."

My look of concern tilted very sharply in the *how badly everyone would kill me* direction.

"What's right for you and Oliver now"—Bridge got straight back on the puppy horse—"is to get a dog. An adorable little dog who will literally be killed if you don't take him home tomorrow and love him."

Jesus Christ. "Nobody's killing puppies. They'll just find him a new owner. A better owner. Who's better."

"And what about Oliver?" demanded Bridge, who'd started poking again now that her definitely-fine-and-not-a-problem contraction had passed. "Are you going to stand in the way of Oliver getting a puppy? Can you imagine how handsome he'd look with a puppy?"

"I've seen him with several puppies," I said. "You have to interact with them before they'll give you one. He looks fine."

This was a lie. He looked great. He looked like a poster trying to encourage you to get a rescue dog.

"You're going to break his heart," declared Bridge. "And kill a puppy."

I collapsed against the railing and covered my face with my hands. "You know, we could have done this over the phone."

"It wouldn't have been as effective. You're getting that puppy, Luc, whether you like it or not."

"I'm pretty sure that's the exact opposite of the advice they give you about dog ownership."

"That's advice for normal people. This is advice for *you*."

"Um," I said. "Thanks?"

"The thing is," Bridge went on, as relentless as a clock counting down the last few seconds of an unwanted puppy's life, "you don't *not want* a puppy. You *want* a puppy. You both want a puppy. You want a puppy so badly you didn't get one over the pandemic so you could be sure you were getting it for the right reasons."

"That was mostly Oliver," I admitted. "I'd probably have just grabbed one from the supermarket in the hope it came with a roll of Andrex."

Bridge made a triumphant gesture. Well, her poking took on

a triumphant air. Then she looked pained again. "Sorry, that was another one. Still fine."

"Pretty sure it's not fine, Bridge."

"It *is* fine. You're trying to change the subject."

"I'm not trying to change the subject. You're having an actual baby."

"Luc." She heaved a sigh, something I'd given her ample practice at over the years. "This is so typical of you. You'll say *anything* to avoid talking about your feelings. You called me up because you were having puppy fears. This is going to remain a puppy fears conversation."

"But," I tried.

"I might," she went on, determined, "maybe, be willing to concede that you and Oliver knew what you were doing about the wedding. This is different."

"How?" I asked, plaintively. "I could be making a horrible mistake. I could be making a horrible mistake with the life of another person…creature…dog."

"Exactly."

I lifted my head from my hands to give her my best *What the fuck?* expression. "What do you mean *exactly*? This isn't an *exactly* situation."

"It's *exactly* an *exactly* situation. When you were freaking out about getting married, it was because you didn't want to get married. You're freaking about getting a puppy because you think you'll be a bad puppy-haver."

"I *will* be a bad puppy-haver," I pointed out. "I'm lazy, I'm selfish, I'm easily distracted, I'm feckless. I don't even know what *feck* is, but I know I lack it."

"You don't lack feck." Bridge paused. "Probably. I'm not sure what it is either."

"Well, clearly it's something people need." I might have been spiralling. "Otherwise we wouldn't have a word for not having it. A bad word for not having it. A word that means if you don't have it, you shouldn't have a dog."

Retracting her poking finger, Bridge gave me a consoling pat instead. "Oliver's got plenty of feck. He's extremely feckful."

That was true. Oliver was feck as fuck.

"And you have other qualities. You're kind, you're loving, you're fun. Puppies need fun. And most importantly, you're prepared to learn. People who go into things expecting to be great at them are usually the...the worst people to be in those things. I mean, do you think I'm expecting to be a great mother?"

"You *will* be a great mother."

"I know, but I'm going to let it happen naturally. I'm not expecting it. That's the point."

I could no longer tell if I felt better or worse for having this conversation. Which, to give Bridge her due, had stopped me worrying about the fact Oliver and I were supposed to pick up a puppy tomorrow. A puppy for whose arrival Oliver had prepared in depth and I had barely prepared in shallows. To be honest, I was probably still in the changing room. For example, of the nine dog books Oliver had purchased, I had read the first three pages of one. And if that was the sort of dog owner I was going to be, what did it say about my readiness for... I mean, what hope did I have of being a good—

"Luc," said Bridge, in a slightly strange voice.

"What?" I asked, still dwelling on my canine inadequacies and the beyond-canine-ownership inadequacies they might or might not imply.

"You know how I said I definitely wasn't going to go into labour?"

I didn't like where this was headed. I didn't like it for myself because this was a horrible situation to have put your best friend in. But, mostly, I didn't like it for Bridge because this was a horrible situation to have been put in *by* your best friend. "You're mentioning that to reassure me it's still the case, right?"

"Well," said Bridge. "Here's the thing."

Oh fuck.

"I think I might be going into labour."

CHAPTER 3

"PARDON?" I SAID.

Bridge had one arm on the railing, the other wrapped around herself. "The contractions are getting stronger."

I stared at her in actual horror. "Are you giving birth on the Millennium Bridge at half past three in the morning?"

"No, I'm going into active labour on the Millennium Bridge at half past three in the morning. I'll only give—ow—birth on the Millennium Bridge at half past three in the morning if you keep asking silly questions instead of getting me to hospital."

For a brief, terrifying moment I forgot how everything worked. "Ambulance?" I suggested.

"Taxi," growled Bridge.

"Oh. Right. Um." The how-working-ness of everything was still…not. My phone had gone from a piece of technology I used every day without thinking to a weird rock with flashing lights on it. "Taxi," I said aloud, because I remembered reading somewhere that saying things aloud helped you to focus on them.

"Ow," said Bridge accusingly.

I finally figured out how to app. The results were not good. "It'll be forty minutes."

Bridge was still doubled over. "I can't be in labour on the Millennium Bridge at half past three in the morning for forty minutes."

"If it helps, at the end of those minutes it'll be ten past four."

"No, it doesn't help."

"Maybe Oliver or Tom could drive—"

"Tom's in Finchley and Oliver's in…wherever you live now. I can't remember, because I'm in labour."

"Havering."

"I'm so glad I have you with me at this precious but difficult moment."

"Maybe it should be an ambulance," I said, watching the approaching-taxi dot on my screen failing to approach.

"Luc, no. There are people getting shot and stabbed and overdosing on ketamine who need those ambulances."

"*You* need an ambulance," I didn't not yell.

"I don't need an ambulance. I need a ride."

The worst thing was that if we'd been about five years younger, we'd probably have known someone with their own transport and the kind of lifestyle that meant they'd be around in Central London at nonsense o'clock in the morning. "Oh, hang on," I said. "I'll call Priya."

To my guilty relief, Bridge was too busy going into labour to have much of an opinion.

"Luc"—Priya picked up on the second ring—"if you're bothering me at 3:41 on a Sunday morning because you're having a panic attack over a puppy, I'll never—"

"It's Bridge. She's kind of maybe slightly in labour?"

"Happy for her. I'll send flowers tomorrow."

She hung up. I rang back.

"Luc, what the fuck?" Priya had an ambient level of *over it* she very seldom deviated from. She was deviating.

"The fuck is," I told her. "She's in labour. She's going into labour right now on a bridge."

"What about Bridge?"

"*On a bridge*. On the Millennium Bridge."

"Why," asked Priya, "is Bridge on the Millennium Bridge at—This is your fault, isn't it, Luc?"

"Yes. Obviously. But we can't get a taxi, so if you're anywhere nearby, can you please get here now because otherwise our friend will have to name her child A3211 after where they were born."

Bridge gave a low cry. "Nooo. I am not calling my child A3211."

From down the phone came the sound of an angry lesbian pulling on her boots. "I am on my way, you fucking, fucking dick."

"I'm sor—"

She'd already gone.

"Okay." I turned back to Bridge, doing my best impression of someone who knew what the fuck he was doing. "Priya's on her way. Should I…I don't know…get some towels or boil a kettle or something?"

"I want to say yes," Bridge told me, "just to see what you'd do."

"There's probably a Tesco's that's open?"

"I don't need towels, Luc. I need—fuck, I've forgotten. I had this written down. Probably it involved not being on a bridge."

It would have been churlish to remind her that this had been her idea. Even though it had totally been her idea. Oh my God, I was the worst friend in the world. "Don't worry, we can google. This is just like that time at university when you were driving me back from that party in Slough and your tyre went out and neither of us had any idea how to replace it, but we looked it up and it was fine."

There was a long silence, partly because Bridge was in the middle of another contraction, and partly because she was mustering a particularly epic boggle. "That wasn't fine. We were in the middle of nowhere, so we were trying to learn how to change a tyre from a YouTube video that kept buffering on a phone with two percent battery and a cracked screen in the dark and none of the bits of the car looked like any of the bits on the video and then you freaked out because you saw a badger and you thought it might have rabies."

"I don't remember that at all. I remember being really calm and collected."

Bridge's boggle became a…whatever was bigger than a boggle. An omniboggle. "You were drunk. You were so drunk."

"Was I?"

"Yes. That's why you don't remember how drunk you were."

This was piecing itself together in ways I didn't like. On the plus side, it was keeping Bridge from either panicking or getting too angry at me. "Why would I have been drunk at a random party in Slough?"

"You'd had a fight with Miles over some play he was in."

"That doesn't narrow it down."

Bridge took another contraction-induced pause. "I think it was one of the Pratchett ones?"

I gave a bitter sigh of reminiscence. "Oh yeah. The ones where he always played Vetinari." It was falling into place. "That's right. He'd been all 'You have to come on Saturday night' and I'd been all 'It's fine, I'll catch the matinee' and then he'd been like 'You care more about our friends than you do about me' and I'd been all 'It's just student theatre,' and he hadn't spoken to me for two days. So when I went to the party anyway, he got super pissed off. So *I* got super pissed, and I ended up talking to some guy in second year about infectious diseases, which is probably how the whole rabies thing got in my head." I was sure I'd had a point when I'd started, but fuck knew where it was now. "Anyway," I concluded valiantly, "what matters is we got in a mess and we got out of it together."

"No, we didn't. You called Priya. And she came to pick us up in her van."

"Truck," I said reflexively.

"Van. It was back when she had the transit."

"And," I continued, even more valiantly, "it worked then and it's going to work now and I'm going to be with you the whole time."

Bridge blinked at me tearfully. "I'm probably just having a lot of hormones right now, but that's the most beautiful thing I've ever heard."

Riding the high of this positive moment, hoping it would eclipse the three different ways this was still all my fault, I unlocked my phone and googled *my friend is in labour what do I do*. "Bridge," I said, "you're fucked. This website is telling me the most important thing is for me to be kind and offer support."

"But you *are* being kind and offering support."

"It also says I should stay upbeat and keep negative commentary or snarky remarks to myself."

She hummed thoughtfully. "You *maybe* shouldn't have started off by telling me I'm fucked then."

"Yeah, I fucked it."

There was a brief pause to acknowledge the fuckedness of it. Then Bridge said, "Look, I really appreciate what you're trying to do, and being kind and offering support is really nice. But is not *one* of the most important things perhaps don't be in the middle of the Millennium Bridge?"

"Not according to the website?"

"Maybe we should let go of the website, Luc?"

"It's also saying you should take a hot bath. Or play a calming hand of cards."

She narrowed her eyes at me. "Are you trying to comfort me by being deliberately useless?"

"Is it working?"

"A bit, actually."

I put my phone away. "Okay, not to ruin my brilliant strategy, but it does *also* say that walking around can help. And we *do* have to get off this bridge, and Priya's coming from the South Bank so"—I offered her my arm in a way that I hoped was kind and supportive rather than downbeat and snarky—"shall we?"

"Certainly, kind sir," trilled Bridge, who wasn't going to let being in the early stages of labour get in the way of a bit. "Ow."

We made our way slowly over the bridge, skirting round the sort of people who were out and about at this time of the night and/or morning, which was to say, people who were working way too hard and people who were working nowhere near hard enough. I mean, like, because they had party lifestyles. Not, like, because they were unemployed or homeless.

"This is all right, isn't it?" I asked. "The walking," I clarified quickly. "Obviously waking you up at three in the morning to have a puppy-related crisis was not all right."

"The walking's good," Bridge declared loyally. "It said on the website. And I think it was on my list too."

"And we've got...um...time?"

"I assume so. The midwife sounded very relaxed when we rang her this afternoon."

I had a feeling if we rang her now she'd be much less relaxed. But, following the advice on the website, I kept that comment to myself.

"Besides," Bridge went on, with the air of someone trying very hard to keep up their own spirits, "it's not like babies just pop out with no warning. If they did that, it would definitely be on the website."

Having friends who were better people than you fucking sucked. I felt fucking terrible. I'd spent sizable chunks of my life developing new ways to feel terrible about new things and this, right here, topped the lot. Took the tea cake. Spaffed on the biscuit. "Bridge," I said. "I'm so sorry. I'm...so, so sorry."

As ever, Bridge poured salt in the wound by being incredibly understanding. “I’m a big girl, Luc.” She paused. “Figuratively. You can’t actually make me do things I don’t want to do.”

“No, but I can… I’m… I shouldn’t help you do the things when they’re…when they’re bad.”

She gave my arm a squeeze. “Of course you should; that’s why we’re friends. A true friend is someone who’ll go along with whatever you’re doing regardless of how awful, dangerous, or stupid it is.”

“A true friend is an enabler with no self-control?”

“Yes.”

“Then good news,” I said, as upbeatly as the website had advised. “I’ve got you covered.”

About five minutes later, we were making our way along the South Bank when we were intercepted by an intense woman with bleached-blond hair. She had her sleeves rolled up on a shirt that looked so artfully ill-fitting that you had to be a very, very specific sort of person to get away with it.

“Hey, Andi,” I said. “I thought you and Theresa were at IKEA.”

She blanked that. “Hey, Luc. Priya wanted me to tell you you’re a complete arsehole.”

“He’s *not*,” replied Bridge with unwarranted loyalty. “He’s looking after me, because he’s my friend.”

Taking control of situations was not my forte. Figuring we were in a bit of a hurry, what with the labour and everything, I had a go anyway. “Look, I deserve this. But we should probably get Bridge to the truck.”

“It’s just up the road,” Andi replied with a studied casualness. “But let’s be clear: You fucked up super bad, and I’m under strict instructions to make you feel super bad about how super bad you fucked up.”

"No," I said, decisively. "That's great. *Super bad* feels achieved. Let's move."

After a short, super-bad-feeling walk, we reached the truck. Priya was leaning against the back bumper, arms folded, looking at me like I'd shat on her pet budgie.

"Say the word," she told Bridge, "and I'll have Andi sling him in the river. Though she be but little, she is fierce."

"I lift," Andi added.

"No," protested Bridge. "Nobody's slinging Luc in the river. He's been *there* for me in my *hour of need*."

"That he caused," said Priya.

"Technically," I pointed out, "Tom caused it."

There was a crashing silence, in which I immediately regretted everything I'd ever done. "Shall I just get in the river?" I asked.

Priya sighed. "No, you should get in the truck. Everybody should get in the truck."

We all got in the truck. It took a while. Seats had to be moved. A giant metal spike had to be secured into the flatbed. And probably a lot of consideration had to be given to exactly how to most safely and comfortably transport a woman who was going into active labour on the Millennium Bridge for reasons that were only a little bit completely my fault. I didn't actually have much sense of what those considerations were other than *Check she's okay*, but I hoped more competent people would be considering them for me.

"Okay," said Priya, drumming her fingers on the wheel. "Where to?"

I jumped on the opportunity to pass the buck to someone else. "Hospital?"

Priya passed it right back. "*Which* hospital?"

"The nearest?"

"Luc, we aren't trying to find a kebab van. Not all hospitals have maternity wards."

Bridge, who was sitting beside me in the back seat, looked up from her phone. "I think St. Thomas's would be best?"

"On it." Leaning forward, Priya fired up Google Maps and got us going. "Be about ten minutes, maybe a quarter of an hour."

"Okay," said Bridge, with slightly too much cheeriness.

"Are you all right?" I asked her.

She grimaced. "This isn't the most comfortable I've ever been. But...but I'm sure I could be less comfortable."

"Just," I suggested, "try to...rest?"

"How am I supposed to rest in the back of a truck when my cervix is dilating?"

"Yeah, Luc?" Priya's eyes flicked to mine in the rearview mirror. "How *is* she supposed to rest in the back of a truck when her cervix is dilating?"

One of Priya's favourite games was forcing me to treat rhetorical questions like they weren't rhetorical. "Um. We could play a game? Does anyone fancy a round of"—I reached out and grabbed the first thing that brushed my mental fingertips—"fuck, marry, kill?"

"I marry Bridge," said Priya, without a second's hesitation, "fuck Andi, and kill you."

"Oh"—Bridge sounded thrilled—"you want to marry me."

"Out of the three people here right now," Priya clarified firmly.

"We're not the marrying kinds," added Andi. "And for what it's worth, I think I'd also marry Bridge, fuck Priya, and kill Luc."

At least Bridge gave the matter some thought. "This is hard because I don't want to hurt any of my friends. But since Priya wants to marry me, I should probably marry her. And since you're gay, Luc, you probably wouldn't want me to fuck you either. So I think I'm also going to fuck Andi and kill you." She made heart hands. "Sorry."

I sighed. "Fine. I'll marry Bridge and kill me too." I looked between Priya and Andi. "And I'll pass on the fucking because I'm dead."

"Does that make me a widow?" asked Bridge. "I don't want to be a widow."

"It also makes you a polygamist," Priya pointed out, "if you marry all of us."

"Oh God." Bridge twitched next to me. "Speaking of marriage, I need to call Tom."

Oh God was right. Tom was going to completely kill me. He'd already married Bridge, was going to skip the fucking part, and would get straight to killing me dead. "Can you tell him I'm sorry?" I asked. "And also that this was totally your idea?"

CHAPTER 4

"YOU DO REALISE," TOM SAID, about two seconds after arriving in the waiting room of St. Thomas's Hospital, "that I work with people who know how to make bodies disappear."

Bridge had, in fact, told him that it was all her idea, but he didn't seem to think that made a difference. And, to be fair, he was right. "I'm really sorry," I said. "Really, really sorry. Really, really, really sorry."

He rubbed his eyes with the weariness of a man who had been dragged out of bed at four-something-horrible in the morning because his wife had gone into labour on the Millennium Bridge because her arsehole best friend had been having a panic attack about a puppy. It was a remarkably specific kind of weariness. "I know you are. But I was kind of hoping you'd got past the stage of thinking that doing a shitty thing and feeling bad about it is the same as not doing a shitty thing in the first place."

"I have." I tried to be all dignified and taking responsibility and everything, but I felt about three inches tall and fourteen years old. "I just… I had a relapse."

"Do you not understand how wrong this could have gone? You could have seriously hurt Bridge."

Everyone in the waiting room, friends and strangers alike, was studiously looking away. Which I guess was better than filming it so they could post it to TikTok, called something like *Wow as a Complete Stranger I Don't Know What's Going on Here but It's Clearly Luc's Fault.*

"She insisted," I protested. "What was I supposed to say? No?"

"Yes. You were supposed to say no."

"I *tried.*"

"You should have tried harder. What the hell is wrong with you?"

"I mean, do you want the list—"

"No, I don't want the list. Look, I"—apparently rubbing his eyes wasn't sufficient to cope with me, so Tom had progressed to rubbing his whole head—"it's not for me to decide who Bridge is friends with or what those friendships look like. But, fuck me, Luc. Being slightly less of a liability than you used to be still makes you a liability."

I had literally no answer for that. Because it was sort of true and sort of not true at the same time, and it didn't seem productive to get into a debate about my personal growth with an ex-boyfriend who was married to my best friend, who we were both extremely worried about.

"Look," he said again, still rubbing, but making a visible effort to not despise me. "I'm...sorry. I'm upset and I'm tired and I need to be with Bridge."

"I never meant to get in the way of that."

"I know. But, somehow, you always do."

I literally had no answer for that either, but I didn't need one because Tom had left.

"Wow," said Andi. "That was the sort of life experience I'm glad I got to see from the outside."

Somewhere out in the ether there was a comeback I could have given that was arch yet humble in a way that would make me seem cool, despite having just received the third-worst dressing-down I'd ever had in my life. Unfortunately, *somewhere* was nowhere near me, so I just said, "Thanks. I feel incredibly comforted."

I was aiming for *playful*, but I must have overshot and landed in *pissy*, because Priya gave me an exasperated look and said, "You know, I was going to say something nice about how Tom didn't really mean it and he's married to Bridge so he must know what she's like, but since you're continuing to handle this whole situation like a dickhead, you're on your own."

"Hang on, why does Tom get a crisis pass but I don't?"

"Because you caused the crisis."

"I just want to say," I said ill-advisedly, "*as a feminist*," I added, even more ill-advisedly, "that putting all this on me is stripping Bridge of, like, agency and shit. She was instrumental in this crisis."

Andi shifted uncomfortably on her blue plastic chair. "I'm beginning to think we should play fuck, marry, kill again."

A woman with one shoe and a swollen ankle, whose partner had gone off to hit up the vending machine, looked over at our little group. "From what I've seen," she said, "I'd fuck her"—she indicated Andi—"marry her"—that was Priya—"and—"

"I know." I flung my hands in the air. "I know."

So, having a baby, it turned out, took a while. And since we'd brought Bridge to hospital, it would have looked some kind of way to drop her and bog off like we were delivering a HelloFresh box. On the other hand, it also felt a bit weird to be bunging up the hospital waiting room for literal hours for an event that didn't typically have spectators. I mean, unless you counted partners and medical professionals. Or, assuming the history I'd learned from TV was accurate, an entire medieval court.

To make matters worse, not only had I fucked up by starting a sequence of events that had inevitably led to my heavily pregnant friend going into labour on the Millennium Bridge at three in the morning, but I'd fucked further up by trapping myself in a waiting room with two-thirds of a throuple I wasn't part of. So while I was stewing internally about six different things at once, Priya was resting with her head on her girlfriend's shoulder looking tired and comfortable and—I tried not to take this personally—contented.

Normally I could at least have distracted myself with my phone, but about an hour ago I'd texted Oliver—my very amazing partner who I lived with and was getting a dog with some time in what was now very definitely this afternoon—the words *Bridge in labour* and *At st thomases*, with no further explanation. So now I was terrified to even look at the damned thing.

So I went to the vending machine and bought nothing. Then having barely got back to my seat, I went to the vending machine again in the vain hope that the selection had magically changed. Then I walked over to the window. Then another window. Then I began to realise quite how surrounded by cheerful NHS posters I was.

Just ask: Could it be sepsis?

I went back to the vending machine. I was pretty sure it wasn't sepsis, and I thought asking now would probably be a bad call.

1 in 8 men will get prostate cancer: Early diagnosis saves lives.

Maybe it was what Oliver would call a cognitive bias, but I felt like I was seeing prostate cancer stuff a *lot* lately. And that wasn't the context in which I usually liked to think about my prostate.

I glanced across the room and saw a group of serious-looking sportsmen who I hoped might offer me some advice about, say, general fitness.

Prostate cancer: It's not a game.

Okay, not that one then.

Lads, get in early…for prostate cancer testing.

I knew I had a lot of personality flaws. Like, a lot of personality flaws. But I'd never, really never, thought hypochondria was one of them. Except I was pretty sure there was a hard limit to the number of times you could be told about prostate cancer without coming to at least *suspect* that you have prostate cancer.

I went to the loo. While I was there, I tried very, very hard not to read too much into the flow of my urine. I did try to ask if it could be sepsis, but I wasn't really sure what the *it* was. And at least if it was sepsis, it wasn't prostate cancer.

Fuck, was I turning into my dad? My dad who definitely did not have prostate cancer. Who had in fact probably left me with a genetic predisposition towards *not* getting prostate cancer. Although also with one towards thinking I had it.

While I was washing my hands, a picture of an uncomfortable-looking baby urged me to **Keep your child safe from rickets,** which was a whole different can of worms because I didn't have a child but I *was* planning to get a dog, and while I didn't *think* dogs could get rickets, I wasn't really sure. What if my future dog got rickets? What if it was my fault my future dog got rickets?

Don't face dementia alone, I was warned on the way back to my seat. And I hadn't been planning to. Although to be fair, I'd also not been planning to **Boost your immunity this winter**, and I maybe should have been because, like, herd immunity was still really important and stuff.

OUCH! Could it be chlamydia?

It could, I thought. It could also be sepsis.

I sat down at last, picked up the rapidly cooling cup of coffee I'd bought on vending machine trip number two, and found myself staring right down the barrel of:

A man dies every hour of prostate cancer in the UK.

In desperation, I picked up my phone, because at this stage Oliver's inevitable string of decreasingly confused and increasingly disappointed messages was going to mess with my head a lot worse than the NHS trying to convince me that I had a small but highly specific range of medical conditions.

Lucien where are you?
Having reread your message I assume you are at St. Thomas's Hospital with Bridget.
Why are you at St. Thomas's Hospital with Bridget?
Having thought about it I assume it's because you were with her when she went into labour.
Why were you with Bridget when she went into labour which seems to have happened some time before 4:30 this morning?
Why aren't you replying to my messages?
Lucien has something happened?
Lucien?
Lucien I tried to call you but it went to voicemail.
Is Bridget all right? Have there been complications?
Are you all right?
Are you and Bridget all right?
Are you still with Bridget?
You forgot your keys.
Lucien I would really like to know what is happening.
I am coming to St. Thomas's now. Please text me if that is not where you are.
Or if it is where you are.
I am coming to St. Thomas's. I will be driving and not able to look at my phone.

Oh God, I was the worst person in the world. I'd run out on my deeply considerate partner at three a.m. because I was worried about a dog, and then sent him a cryptic text over an hour later implying that something bad was happening to two people he cared about. We'd established a while back that marriage wasn't on the cards for us, but at this rate Oliver was going to be downgrading me from *fuck* to *kill*. And I couldn't entirely say I didn't deserve it.

I was just trying to compose a reassuring text that wasn't going to make him plough into a lamppost in frustration when I heard rapid, slightly familiar footsteps approaching down the hallway. And then a tousled, pale-faced Oliver Blackwood with misaligned shirt buttons was in the room. And I was completely fucked. Or possibly completely killed.

"Oliver, I'm..." I started at the same time he said "Lucien, what's wrong?"

"Well." I gazed up at him, trying to compose a reassuring sentence that wasn't going to make him plough into a lamppost in frustration. "Nothing's wrong, really?"

"You're at the hospital."

"Circumstantially. Bridge is having a baby. That's where people have babies. I mean, a lot of people. Not everyone, obviously. And those choices are completely valid."

Oliver gazed back at me, his eyes tired, and at their coolest, most washed-out shade of grey. "While I appreciate this defence of the autonomy of pregnant people, it doesn't explain...anything. Why did you sneak out without waking me up? Why is Bridget at a hospital that isn't the one she planned to go to? Why—" He paused, frowning. Shit, he was putting the pieces together. He knew me too well. "Let me guess: You had a three a.m. crisis about the fact we're getting a dog in approximately eight hours. You instinctively called Bridget, forgetting in your panic that she was heavily pregnant, and by the time you tried to course correct, she was already on the way to meet you. Probably on the Millennium Bridge because Bridget thinks doing something once makes it a tradition."

There was a long silence as I tried to compose a way of saying

Yeah, basically that wasn't going to make him plough into a lamppost in frustration.

"Okay," said Priya, sort-of-not-quite saving me. "That was almost romantic. In a fucked-up way."

Even a drive across London couldn't blunt Oliver's instinctive politeness. Which meant he gave a deeply sincere "Hello, Priya, Andi. I'm sorry you've been so inconvenienced" before turning back to me and adding, "I think we might need to have a conversation."

Normally, I was a big fan of Stern Oliver. Normally, though, I wasn't in a hospital waiting room with my most sarcastic friend and the younger of her two girlfriends.

"Some-one's in trou-ble," sang my most sarcastic friend.

"I'm not in trouble," I retorted. "We're going to have an adult discussion about my flaws."

Priya gave me a look of performative anticipation. "Go on then."

"Somewhere else," Oliver said firmly, before escorting me in a totally non-demeaning way out into the corridor.

We wandered a bit, not saying very much, looking for a good *confront Luc with his failings* spot and eventually settling on a pair of seats bolted to the wall near a very fake potted plant.

I stared at my feet.

"You're sure Bridget's all right?" Oliver asked.

"Yeah. She went a little bit into labour but"—I arse-pulled some unconvincing confidence—"you know it's not like in the movies, where it's 'Whoosh, scream, *woowoowoo*, pant, baby.'"

"Why, Lucien. I had no idea you were such an expert." It was Oliver's dryest voice.

Something stronger than gravity was pulling me down into my seat. Probably shame. "I really do think she's okay. We would have heard if she wasn't."

"I," began Oliver, squeezing the bridge of his nose, "I really don't know what to say."

"That I'm a terrible person? That I should go to my room and think about what I've done?"

"Since we share the same room, Lucien, I think that would just be annoying."

"I'm really sorry?" I tried.

"There's no need to apologise." He paused. "Well, Tom might feel differently. Bridget is pathologically incapable of blaming you for anything."

"Look," I blurted out. It wasn't a particularly apology-compatible blurt, if I was honest. "She's really hard to say no to."

Oliver turned his head towards me, and to my immense relief it was in a reassuring way, not in a *Get your fucking shit together, you utter fuckup* way. "I'm aware of that. Although for what it's worth, one *can* learn to do it."

"*You* can. I can barely say no to those people who call up and ask if you want to change mobile providers."

On anybody else, his smile would have been condescending. I hoped I'd never get bored of Oliver's look of indulgent affection because if I did, I'd be in real trouble. It was the one he needed most often. "Bridget is an adult woman and can look after herself. But I *do* wish you'd talked to me instead."

"She's my best friend," I replied instinctively.

"And..." he prompted.

"And...and"—the words tumbled out in a horrible torrent of inconvenient facts—"I was afraid that if I brought up the dog thing again, you'd be all, 'Lucien, I thought you'd got over being a selfish insecure narcissist, but clearly you're just as bad as you were five years ago. I'm dumping you.'"

Oliver's lips twitched. "That does sound like something I'd say."

"You say it in my head all the time."

"As a barrister, I can confidently inform you that I am not

legally liable for the words or actions of the version of me that lives in your head."

"I know." By this point I'd slid so far down the seat that my shoulders were in my bum divot. "But sometimes he seems so much realer than you. Because you're, you know, so great and everything."

"Lucien, you've been with me long enough, and seen me through so much, you must know that isn't true."

Giving up on the seat as a bad job, I collapsed into a not-exactly-kneeling position in front of him. "You *are* so great and everything."

"And you make me happy. And you will continue to make me happy, whether or not we get a dog, and no matter how many times you wake me up to tell me you're not sure about getting a dog."

"I'm really not sure about getting a dog."

"Yes." His fingers lightly pushed the hair back from my brow. "I gathered that when I woke up without you."

"People who make their best friends get cabs to the Millennium Bridge at three in the morning on a semi-regular basis shouldn't have dogs."

"Those feel like non-overlapping magisteria."

For a moment I could only stare at him. "Stop trying to turn me on in a hospital."

He laughed. "You know as well as I do that managing your neuroses and looking after a pet are different things."

"Are they, though? What if I pass my neuroses onto the dog? What if my neuroses stop me taking care of the dog? What if—"

"You won't, they won't, and there's two of us so we'll deal."

"It's not fair," I muttered, glaring up at him, "when you make things sound simple and reasonable."

"Then," he went on, "you're not going to like what I have to say next. Which is, if you don't want a dog, we don't have to get one."

I didn't like that. I didn't like that *at all*. "But if we can't get a dog, then… Then we can't get a dog."

"Yes," agreed Oliver. "That is indeed what 'not getting a dog' means."

"No, but I mean..." Normally Oliver was much better with euphemism. "Like it would mean we'd never have a dog. And we've been having the 'Do we see a dog in our future?' conversation for a while now."

At last, Oliver cracked my ingenious code. "I know we said that getting a dog would be a good way to test how ready we were for—"

"A dog," I interrupted.

"Exactly. But even if we're not in a...dog-adopting space now, that doesn't mean we never will be."

He'd meant this in a reassuring way, but it was actually one of the last things I needed to hear. "Okay, but...what if it does? I know you want...dogs. And you *should* have dogs. You'd be an amazing... dog owner. And I don't want you to look back on our life together and be all, 'I wish I'd been with somebody who I could have owned a dog with.'"

"I won't," replied Oliver with a certainty you could build a world around. And I wanted so badly to build a world around it.

"You can't promise that."

"I think you'll find I can."

This was getting messy and sticky and uncomfortable in all the ways I didn't like. "Are you sure? Because it's looking a lot like I'm going to keep spiralling into the wrecked pile of unwashed pants I used to be every time we try to do something, you know, challenging or grown up."

"Lucien." Oliver saying *Lucien* in his serious voice made my internal organs want to run away, leaving my skin behind as a distraction.

I blinked up at him in growing dismay. "What?"

"I would very much like it if you stopped pretending that the man I fell in love with is a different person from the man who is currently having a...dog-related breakdown in St. Thomas's Hospital."

"He's not a different person," I demi-wailed. "That's what I'm saying. I can feel myself slipping back—"

"I would also like it if you wouldn't keep pretending you'd *ever* stopped being him. I liked him."

"But he *sucked*. He was a complete mess."

"And so was I. And I still am. And yet here we are."

Okay, this was getting insulting. "Wait, are you saying I haven't changed at all?"

"Of course you've changed," he murmured, stroking my hair in earnest. "Everyone changes. But that doesn't mean you'll never react to an old fear or remake an old mistake."

"And," I asked, "you really think I'll be an okay...dog owner?"

"Yes," said Oliver, answering a different question entirely, "I think you'll be a wonderful dog owner."

"Even though I've had really bad role models, dog-owning-wise? Like, what if we get a dog and then I bail on it the way my dad bailed on...his dog?"

"That won't happen," said Oliver, so firmly it was almost a prophecy.

"But what if—"

"After all these years," he went on, "I am very, *very* used to your flaws. You can be flaky, you can be prone to panic, you can be a little self-absorbed at times..."

"Great pep talk," I told him.

"But you have *never* been somebody who abandons people."

I gave a distressed bleat.

"Abandons *dogs*," Oliver corrected himself obligingly. "You don't have it in you."

I wanted to believe him. I wanted to believe him *so much*. Because Bridge had been right. This wasn't about not wanting a dog. I definitely wanted a dog. Possibly more than one dog. I wanted to grow old with Oliver Blackwood and have dogs with him, and everything I'd said about looking back and regretting hadn't only been about Oliver. Because if we didn't get a dog, if I couldn't even take the first step towards building the life and the family that I'd sort of never quite dared to hope for, then I could say with one hundred percent certainty that I would turn around in old age and say to myself, "Well, you fucked that up, didn't you, you absolute bellend."

So I took a deep breath, put on my waders, and tromped through my own bullshit until, on the other side, I was hugging Oliver way too tightly. And we stayed like that, hugging way too tightly, until a kindly nurse laid a hand on my shoulder and asked Oliver if I was all right and if there was anything he could do for us.

"It's okay," I sniffled, not wanting this NHS professional to think either of us had just been diagnosed with prostate cancer. "We're just getting a dog."

CHAPTER 5

BRIDGE HAD HER BABY JUST after eleven o'clock. She weighed seven pounds, and I had no idea why I knew that, or rather why I'd been told that, because while I was sure it was relevant for health reasons or whatever, I didn't really have a metric to compare it to. It was sort of like when people wanted me to be really interested in the horsepower of their car. Because I don't really know how powerful horses or cars are meant to be.

We all bundled in to wish a tired but happy Bridge congratulations and say things like "Oh, she's beautiful" and "She has your eyes," even though—to be honest—all babies looked the same to me. Sort of small, rumpled, and shouty. Maybe it felt different if it was your small, rumpled, and shouty.

Then Oliver and I dashed into the car so we could dash all the way round London to dash to the dog shelter in time for our appointment. Given the amount of paperwork, home visits, and general checking up we'd been through—none of which had in any way increased my faith in my dog-having abilities—I was pretty sure turning up late would be a dog-jeopardising move.

"I don't know how to say this without sounding passive aggressive," remarked Oliver, "but I do rather wish we'd had a full night's sleep."

He was right. He hadn't known how to say it without sounding passive aggressive. "Hey," I tried, "you don't get to play the this-is-bad-but-I-know-it's-bad-so-it's-okay card. That's *my* card."

"Sorry."

"You're not wrong, though," I told him. Because he wasn't. "I'm seriously worried I'm just going to collapse on top of the dog and drool."

Oliver considered this a moment. "I suppose that is at least a fairly natural dog-parenting arrangement?"

"I think the *collapsing* part might be a bit suboptimal."

"*Suboptimal?*" repeated Oliver, with a tired laugh. "When did you start saying *suboptimal*?"

"You've been a suboptimal influence on me."

Slightly too sleep-deprived to play the using-*suboptimal*-in-increasingly-suboptimal ways game, Oliver gave an affectionate if slightly distracted smile and kept his eyes on the road. I, meanwhile, took advantage of the fact I wasn't driving and tried to get my head comfortable. Turns out, I got it so comfortable that I didn't wake up until Oliver was gently nudging me into consciousness.

"Nnnneruurgh," I said, rising semi-erect like a—actually I'm not going to finish that. "Where are we?"

"We're there."

"Shit."

"What's wrong?"

"Nothing. I think it was just a reflexive *shit*." Levering myself still more upright, I flipped down the sun visor and squinted into the vanity mirror. "Shit," I muttered, less reflexively. "They're never going to give us a dog. I look like a heroin addict."

Oliver undid his seat belt and passed me a bagel he must have bought while I was sleeping the sleep of a selfish bastard. "I've worked with quite a lot of heroin addicts and, like most people, they're a diverse group of individuals. I think what you mean is that you look gaunt, raddled, and interesting. Which is how you've always looked, and it suits you."

"Thank you for the bagel," I said meekly as I unwrapped the wax paper, filling the car with the scent of pickles, mustard, and pastrami. "Really, thank you. This is actually perfect."

He blushed slightly. "Well, I do know you rather well at this point."

To be fair, the fact I'd want to stuff my face with salt and meat the second I woke up after an impromptu all-nighter wasn't exactly a state secret. But that didn't make it any less thoughtful. "What about you?" I asked through a massive mouthful of cured beef.

He waved his own less-delicious-smelling parcel at me. "Hummus, tomato, and rocket."

"Didn't they get to number six in 1973?"

"Yes, with the psychedelic hit 'Plant-Based Groove.'"

Between the food and having the best boyfriend in the universe, I was perking right up. "Shame their second album flopped. In hindsight, *Hail Seitan* wasn't the right title for its era."

"And *Hardcore Quorn* was banned in thirteen countries."

I gave a nostalgic sigh. "Whatever happened to those guys?"

"Hummus and Rocket quit the business, and Tomato died of a tofu overdose. Tragic really."

"I've always said we needed tougher tofu regulations."

Oliver gave me a play-serious look. "Lucien, *surely* you know that every attempt to legislate away the tofu issue has succeeded only in stigmatising tofu users and driving the market underground."

"Oh, fuck me." I let my head thunk back against the seat.

"What's wrong now?"

The *now* was doing a lot of work in that sentence, but I chose to ignore it. "Nothing. I just..." It was kind of hard to roll your eyes at yourself because they were already inside your face. "I, you know. Love you. Like. A lot."

"Come here."

I leaned over the gearstick, and Oliver leaned over to meet me, and we kissed way more lingeringly than made sense when one of us tasted of hummus, and the other tasted of pastrami, and the one who tasted of pastrami was being half choked by the seat belt he'd forgotten to take off. Eventually, we remembered that we were in a car park in Battersea and that, hilarious as the irony would be, we didn't want to get arrested for dogging.

"I love you too," said Oliver, with far less um-ing and like-ing and y'know-ing than I personally considered normal. "Now let's go get Spud."

Much like when we bought our car and, indeed, our house, Oliver dealt with the paperwork, and I sat in an uncomfortable chair watching Oliver deal with the paperwork. I wouldn't say that, out of all the things I could watch Oliver doing, it was the most attractive, but it also wasn't the least attractive. There was something inherently cool and slightly alien to me about someone who looked like they knew what they were doing in an administrative context. Or, for that matter, any context. Probably including sex contexts. Because Oliver flipping me over like he was about to sign me in triplicate hadn't got old in five years of fucking.

Eventually, after long enough to feel like they were taking the piss but not quite long enough that you could say anything about it without looking like a prick, we were allowed to leave. And when we left, we were allowed to take a box with us. And the box was allowed to have a dog in it.

We secured Spud's crate in the back of the car and stood for a moment contemplating the fact that our car had a box in it and the box in the car had a dog in it. I squeezed Oliver's hand.

"We've got a dog," I told him.

"Yes," he replied.

Spud was looking up at us through the little window like an incredibly trusting prisoner. We'd called him Spud because, when we'd first seen him at the shelter, he'd been smaller and rounder, and looked a whole lot like a potato. And, while Oliver had wanted something more subtle, like Edward (as in King) or Maris (as in Piper), I'd wanted to just steer into it. A few weeks further on, he was still small, and still brown, with big dark eyes and an exceedingly waggy tail, but he was notably more animal-shaped.

"I'm fucking terrified," I said.

"Mruff," Spud replied.

"Lucien, it's fine." It was Oliver's *should've been tired of reassuring me by now but somehow wasn't* voice. "People far more irresponsible than us get dogs every day."

"No, they don't. They vet you like whoa."

"Then shouldn't you take the fact that you've been vetted like whoa and they've still let you have the dog as evidence that you can, in fact, look after a dog?"

"I think they probably averaged us out."

"I'm certain they didn't," he said firmly. "If they thought one of us was a danger to the dog, the dog would be in danger, irrespective of the good intentions of the other."

"What if he doesn't like me?"

"Dogs are pack animals. They like the people they live with unless the people they live with are completely terrible. And," he went on before I could make the obvious objection, "despite what you might say and how frequently you might say it, you're not completely terrible."

"I'm a bit terrible."

"Aren't we all." And with that, Oliver carefully shut the door. "Come on. We should get him home."

Watching Oliver with a puppy was, if you can believe it, even better than watching him fill out paperwork. We'd set up a kind of playpen in what was nominally my study, although it was more just the room I sat in when I was meant to be working from home. It had toys and bowls and a blanket, and, once we'd got in, we'd set Spud's box in the corner, letting him come out at his own pace, as the books recommended. Well, as Oliver had informed me the books recommended. Spud's own pace had been "immediately" because, like every dog I'd ever met, he'd taken one look at Oliver and decided he was clearly Best Human. Not that I blamed him. I'd come to a similar conclusion myself, even if it had taken me slightly longer. Initially, Spud had been keen to explore the room, but he'd soon decided he'd rather just explore Oliver, and now the pair of them were folded in a pile of adorableness on the floor.

After what felt like six million years, Oliver looked up from the dog. "You should probably say hello, Lucien."

"Hello, Lucien," I said from the corner. It was safe in the corner. You couldn't accidentally fuck anything up in the corner. Even if it meant you didn't get to pet a puppy. Your puppy.

"Don't confuse him. He's too little to understand irony."

"And boundaries," I added as Spud rose up on his stubby little hind legs to lick Oliver's nose.

"This is normal bonding behaviour."

"You say that, but if I licked your nose, you'd get really cross at me."

Oliver was still nuzzling Spud with the effortless confidence of a natural dog-haver who, finally, after three decades in the wilderness, had been granted the chance to have a dog. "I'm not aware of your ever having tried."

"Well, I can't now. The dog's beat me to it."

"Lucien, unless you have a kink you've been hiding for a very long time, I don't think you want to be in competition with Spud."

He had a point. A bunch of points. On the kink thing, the competition thing, and the bonding-with-the-puppy thing. Gingerly, I approached the dog-and-barrister combo who looked slated to be a major part of my homelife from now on and crouched down next to them.

"Hi, Spud," I said, trying not to sound too much like I was introducing myself to the cool kids at a new school. "I'm the other one."

Spud gave me a look as if to say *Well, they can't all be winners* and went back to love-bombing Oliver like some kind of canine narcissist. I tried patting him, but it increasingly felt like I was in one of those threesomes where the other two clearly wished you'd just leave them to get on with it.

Eventually Oliver decided the dog had lavished enough affection on him. "We should probably encourage him to explore his den a little."

"Sorry?" I asked. "Are you talking to me?"

"No, I was telling Spud we should encourage *you* to explore *your* den."

"Have you hidden any treats in it?"

"I've secreted some French toast under your pillow."

Oliver stood, brushed off his jeans, and went to linger temptingly by the open door to the playpen. "Here, Spud," he said, in an offensively charming singsong voice. "What have we got over here?"

"You sound like you're kerb-crawling for a puppy."

"Do you really think people who solicit sex workers go up to them and do this?" He patted his legs, continuing in what was clearly on track to being his dog voice. "Come on, boy, there's a good boy. Come and see what Daddy Oliver's got for you."

"Oh, Jesus," I yelped. "What are you doing?"

"I'm calling the dog over. Whatever is going on in your head is your problem."

Tail metronoming happily, Spud had already trotted over and, having briefly investigated Oliver's feet, was now inside the playpen unearthing the treats and toys that Daddy Oliver had, with typical fucking everything, tucked away yesterday.

"I think," mused Oliver, watching Spud chewing the toy I'd been repeatedly told not to refer to as the *butt plug*, "unless it's bedtime or there's an emergency, we should avoid closing him in until he's had time to develop positive associations with the space."

"Sure," I said, in the voice of someone who really, really wished he'd read more than zero dog books. "Sounds great."

Oliver gave me the look of a smarter, kinder friend who knew I hadn't done the homework and was doing his best to cover for me with the teacher. "He'll be happy here," he said, "if this is where happy things happen. It's like the opposite of your old flat."

"My old flat was fine," I replied with semi-ironic defensiveness.

"But it had negative *associations*. Which is why when I met you it was a soulless wasteland of underwear and empty pizza boxes."

"Oh yeah. You did see that, didn't you?"

"Once. And then you cleaned it for me, which was breathtakingly romantic. And probably stopped us both dying of typhus."

"Hey," I protested. "I lived in that flat for years and did not die of typhus. Or cholera. Or scarlet fever. Or bubonic plague."

"Yes." Oliver was looking down at Spud, who was nosing under his blanket with his arse in the air, his tail still wagging. "If you'd died of bubonic plague, I'd have been much less inclined to pretend to date you. Or actually date you, for that matter."

"Were we ever," I asked, "*pretending* to date? Really?"

"For the sake of my pride, yes." He frowned, still looking at Spud. "Hmm."

"Hmm?"

"I think he needs to go outside."

And, with that, Oliver swept Spud into his arms and carried

him through the patio doors into the garden, where—continuing to be Oliver in every respect—he'd already prepared a designated toilet spot.

"Um," I said, having followed at a poo-respecting distance, "I feel weird watching this."

"It's very important to watch," replied Oliver earnestly.

"Is it, though?"

"I mean..." Oliver looked briefly flustered. "Not because of the...*event* itself. But we need to be ready to start positive reinforcement the moment he's finished and not, and this is very important, a second before."

"What happens if we're premature in our celebration?"

"Well, then he'll learn to come into the garden, do half a poo in order to receive a reward, and then trail the remainder back into the house to finish in comfort."

"Oliver, this seems really complicated."

"It's not. It'll be fine. We reward him for doing things we want him to do and not for doing things we don't want him to. We just need to be very clear about what things are being rewarded."

Spud was sitting on a patch of grass, looking up at us with a quizzical expression.

"And," I asked, "what if he...doesn't?"

"Then we go back inside and try again in a few minutes."

"Won't he just think that's weird?"

"Probably, but he's a dog, so he's going to have to—oh." Oliver's voice swooped into a register I'd never heard it reach before. "Who's a good boy? Who's a clever boy? Here's a treat for a clever boy. Well done, you. One more? Do you think you deserve one for being such a good boy? Go on then."

To be fair to Oliver, Spud did seem absolutely thrilled, bouncing around like it was his doggie birthday.

"Um," I said. "Yay. Good shit."

"Why don't you give him a treat," suggested Oliver.

I really wanted to, but for some reason, the thought of giving my own dog a treat for doing what we'd wanted him to do felt incredibly overwhelming. So I made excuses. "I think I've missed the window. The all-important treat/faeces window."

"How about," offered Oliver, like he was giving *me* a treat, "you take him next time?"

"How about I keep providing moral support for you?"

Spud was briefly interested in the garden, but it wasn't too long before he remembered Oliver existed and bounded eagerly after him, back into the house.

I trailed along too.

"You do realise," Oliver reminded me, "that I'm in court tomorrow, so you'll be lone-parenting Spud."

Fuck. I had known that. And I had remembered that. I'd just not confronted the full enormity of it until that moment. "I don't think I'm ready."

"You're ready," Oliver told me with so much certainty that I believed him for almost three seconds. "And even if something goes wrong, a difficult fact of being a dog owner is that he *will* relieve himself in our house at some point. Probably more than once."

It was a bit sad how reassuring that wound up being. "You mean it'll be okay even if he shits in my study?"

"Well, probably less so for you, but developmentally speaking, as long as we don't encourage it or frighten him into undesired behaviours, he'll be fine."

"This feels like it's setting me a very low bar."

"And isn't that comforting?" asked Oliver, who already knew the answer. "Now"—he showed me a little notebook—"this is Spud's toilet diary. While we're training, we'll need to record when he goes and what he does."

"Oh my God, I'm writing a poo memoir."

“Technically, it would only be a poo memoir if it was your own poo. This is a poo biography.”

“I am ghostwriting Spud’s poo memoir.”

“Right now,” Oliver pointed out, “*I* am ghostwriting Spud’s poo memoir.”

I sighed. “Is this what you dreamed your life would be? Recording the details of a dog’s bowel moments in a book with a pen tied to it?”

Oliver glanced up from his poo memoir, giving me the sort of look that could still reduce me to emotional custard. “Lucien,” he said very, very seriously, “this is everything I’ve ever dreamed of.”

CHAPTER 6

APART FROM THE TINY, INSIGNIFICANT detail of having a dog in it, the day passed pretty normally. Or at least, it passed pretty normally for Oliver, who went about his lazy-yet-inexplicably-productive Sunday routine exactly as he would have if he *wasn't* suddenly a hundred percent responsible for the survival, comfort, and socialisation of a new living creature. So he prepped his casework for the morning with Spud on his lap, and he read a chapter of *The Man Who Died Twice* with Spud beside him, and made dinner (I was on washing up, which was our usual division of labour for Luc-is-an-awful-cook reasons) with Spud happily eating his own dinner in his little dog-pen.

I, on the other hand, spent the whole day feeling like there was a wasp in the room. Only it was a brown fluffy wasp as long as my forearm that wouldn't sting me but might potentially wee on my shoes. Once or twice, Oliver suggested that I stash some treats in Spud's den, which I dutifully did, knowing full well that tomorrow, when I was on my own, I would totally forget. And then all of Spud's positive associations with his very special doggy space would go up in smoke like our oven that one time I tried to make banana bread.

Between the excitement of a new place and a general puppyish lack of self-control, Spud wound up needing to go to the little dog's room—okay, little dog's designated bit of garden—way more often than I'd expected him to that evening. And every time he did, Oliver treated him like he'd cured cancer just in time for Christmas. Then, afterwards, he'd note down the time and what exactly happened in the Dump Diary. While he was doing all that, I was standing back, trying not to get in the way. In my very slight defence, I *did* think I was learning to spot the signs of a loo-needing puppy fairly quickly—he'd start sniffing the ground and walking in a circle in a way that stood out once you'd started to notice it. I just had no faith in my ability to follow through on those cues in a competent and timely manner. And then our puppy would go from being a well-adjusted, den-loving, outdoor-pooping ball of joy to a neurotic mess living in his own filth somewhere he hated. Fuck. I was going to turn our dog into me. Five-years-ago me, admittedly. But still very much me.

Eventually bedtime rolled around, and Oliver ushered Spud into his pen and clicked the door closed. Spud—busy seeking out the treats I'd hidden—was initially chill with this, especially because we'd been (well, Oliver'd been) shutting the door on him every so often to get him used to it. He was even okay when we left the room because we'd been leaving rooms all day. But around the time I was cleaning my teeth, he realised how brutally we'd betrayed him, which he expressed with a series of heartbroken wails.

I dropped my toothbrush. "Oh my God, he's not okay."

"He's fine," said Oliver, who was making sure the hand towels were all perfectly aligned on their racks. "It's just a little separation anxiety."

"It might be, but he's a puppy. How is he supposed to know we're coming back? For all he knows, we've decided we'd rather be international rock stars than raise a puppy so we've fucked off and he won't see us again until we're in our late sixties and we think we've got prostate cancer for no reason."

"I normally avoid armchair psychoanalysis"—having done

with the hand towels, Oliver had left the bathroom and was climbing serenely into bed—"but there's the tiniest chance you might be projecting."

"Fine. He might not think that exactly because I don't think dogs have a concept of rock music or, like, prostates. He's still going to think we've abandoned him."

"And in the morning," said Oliver, way too calmly, considering a tiny dog was yelping pure trauma on the floor below, "he'll discover we haven't. Over time he'll learn that nighttime is sleep time and we'll be back the next day."

I ditched my toothbrush, much as we had ditched our dog. "Counterpoint: Listen to him."

"Counter-counterpoint: You can't let yourself be emotionally blackmailed by a puppy."

"Objection! Badgering the witness."

Oliver gave me a sleepy look that was just on the right side of indulgent. "You know that isn't how it works. But we *do* need to leave him. If we don't, we'll be making things a lot harder on ourselves in the long run."

"It's quite hard now."

"Well, think how much worse it would be if we never get to have sex again because there's a dog permanently sharing our bed."

Damn that Oliver. Going straight for my Achilles penis. "Is there not some kind of middle ground between 'Never have sex again' and 'Let a dog cry itself to sleep every night'?"

"In the short term? Not really."

I slouched into bed next to him. "This is some Victorian-parenting bullshit."

"And I agree," murmured Oliver, rolling over to face me, "that treating a child like this would be very bad. But, wonderful as Spud may be, he's not actually a human being. Dogs need boundaries and consistency. The more we reinforce those, the happier he'll be."

"He doesn't sound very happy."

"Lucien." He pressed his mouth to mine, meltingly soft. "I love how much you care, even if you're usually pretending not to."

"You've really lowered your standards if you think being upset by a sad puppy is unusual."

"I just mean, you work so hard to hide this side of yourself."

Oliver kissed me again.

And then *again*.

And then his kisses started sort of trailing downwards, in a way I was normally extremely into.

"Oliver," I cried. "Are you trying to sex me right now? Are you trying to sex me to the soundtrack of a distraught dog?"

"I was trying to distract you from the dog who, I repeat, is and will be fine."

I actually pushed my very hot, very smart, very principled barrister boyfriend away from me. "I am not in the mood. I have never been less in the mood. And that includes that one time we both had food poisoning."

"I'm sorry," said Oliver, looking—to his credit—a bit embarrassed. "I'm aware this is difficult for you. I...just... Sorry."

I propped myself up on one elbow, leaned over him, and brought my face to a distance from his face that was only acceptable if you were in a long-term relationship and you'd both recently brushed your teeth—and sometimes, frankly, not even then. "Are you seriously not at all bothered by..." I paused and let Spud, who was still howling mournfully, speak for himself. "*That?* This."

Oliver let out a gentle sigh. "Of course it's not pleasant. But I know it's for the best—for Spud and for us—so I feel the responsible thing to do is see it through."

"What if we just...checked on him?"

"Then he'll be reassured for a few minutes and then feel abandoned all over again when you come back to bed."

Snuggling down on Oliver, I began to suspect I was having a philosophical crisis. "I don't think I believe in being cruel to be kind. I think that's just being cruel."

"And I would normally agree with you," said Oliver, calm again, now he'd given up on misplaced horn. "But this isn't cruel. It's necessary."

"I'm pretty sure that's how cruel people justify being cruel."

"It's the consensus recommendation amongst experts."

"Then...fuck experts."

One of Oliver's eyebrows arranged itself into a condemning arch. "In the current global climate, I'm not sure that's a sentiment anyone should be endorsing."

"Oh, come on. This isn't Brexit or vaccines. This is an adorable puppy who is ours, who we are making unhappy."

"Lucien." It was his rarely used short-on-patience voice. Which he generally only used when he was caring really hard about something that he couldn't fix. "We have three options. We can go downstairs and check on Spud, which will change nothing the moment we come back to bed. We can set a precedent of letting him do whatever he wants, whenever he wants, in which case we will be—and I want to stress this—extremely irresponsible dog owners. Or we can continue with our current course of action."

Okay. He was doing a rhetoric. And I knew he was doing a rhetoric. I'd been with Oliver for long enough that I understood how he thought, and I knew how he argued, and I could even, sometimes, on a very good day, beat him at his own game. This was not, given it'd started with my friend going into labour on the Millennium Bridge and ended with my dog going through the stages of grief in my study, a very good day.

The problem was, Oliver was technically right. Leaving Spud to cry his little doggy heart out was the best thing to do if we were thinking about our long-term futures as people who wanted a well-trained pet. And we *did* want that. Especially because if we couldn't train our pet properly, it probably meant we'd suck at all kinds of other responsible family stuff, and that said bad things about our ability to look after a…after any other dogs we might want to get in the future. Except I also wanted to stop feeling sad, like, right now. And I wanted Spud to stop feeling sad. And I wanted Oliver to stop feeling sad, too, which I was pretty sure he was, behind the rationality, tough love, and closing arguments. Unfortunately, I couldn't say that without sounding like an arsehole. Like I cared more about my own comfort than Being a Responsible Dog Owner. This was the downside of having a partner who'd honed his debating skills at Oxford and the bar when I'd honed mine at three in the morning *in* a bar.

So I sighed and rolled over, muttered a noncommittal "I suppose," and tried to sleep.

For the second time in less than twenty-four hours, I was sneaking out of bed while Oliver was asleep. It was, honestly, kind of annoying how good at sleeping he was. I mean, even when I didn't have a vocally miserable canine to contend with, my own brain had long ago decided that sleep was a privilege I didn't always deserve. Of course, the fact that Oliver got up early, worked hard, went to the gym, ate fresh vegetables by choice, kept a regular schedule, and didn't look at his phone in bed, while I did the opposite of those things, might have had something to do with it.

Anyway, I'd tried. I'd tried really hard. But I fought the puppy and the puppy won. I just wasn't whatever-personality-trait-it-took-to-sleep-through-a-crying-dog enough to sleep through a crying dog.

The second I set foot in the study, Spud went from traumatised wailing to happy ruffing so fast that I couldn't decide if I felt loved or faintly manipulated. Which, honestly, Oliver and my mum aside, was my general experience of relationships.

"I'm a fucking bellend," I told Spud, who wagged his tail cheerily at me.

Fucking bellend that I was, I knelt down and opened his pen, and he rushed into my arms like a princess rescued from a castle. For whatever reason, while he'd coyly licked Oliver's nose, he decided to lick my entire face. And, on the one hand, it was probably incredibly unhygienic, especially since he nearly got my eyeball. But on the other, I kind of felt like a real dog owner. Because you had to really care about your dog to be okay with his saliva literally on your face holes.

"I'm taking that as a compliment," I said. "But I'm still wiping it off."

Which I did, as quickly as I could, using the sleeve of my T-shirt.

Spud's excitement at my return didn't quite win out over his obvious tiredness, and after a few minutes of sniffing round me to make sure I was all there, he curled up in my lap and started making snuffly, sleeping noises.

"Okay." I attempted a reassuring whisper. "You know we're still here, and now you're unconscious. So Daddy Luc"—oh my God, I couldn't believe I'd just said that, although I also didn't entirely hate it—"is going back to bed."

I gently transferred my bundle of puppy back into the pen, clicked the door closed as quietly as possible, and then tiptoed out of the study. I got one foot over the threshold when I heard the first tragic "Arroou?"

Fuck. Why hadn't I listened to Oliver?

Half turning, half out of my mind from sleep deprivation, I decided that the best plan was to reason with a dog. "It's all right. I'll just be upstairs. Oliver and I will be with you again in the morning."

"Arroou?"

"I promise." With hindsight, it was quite a nuanced cultural concept to expect Spud to understand. "Look," I tried instead. "You just have to get used to this."

Spud did not look like he wanted to get used to this.

"You're not allowed to come into the bedroom because then I'll never be able to have sex again."

"Ruff!"

"No not *ruff*. *Arroou*. Very *arroou*."

"Ruff!"

"Great," I said. "Since you're feeling so *ruff*, I'm going to bed."

"Arroooooou."

Double fuck. How-slash-why did I keep doing this to myself? I went back, opened the pen, and sat down next to Spud. "I'm only staying until you're asleep."

Spud smooshed right up against me.

I patted his little head, right between his little mismatched ears. "Just so you know, I wouldn't rather be living the life of an eighties rock star than looking after you."

"Mrrfhhh."

"I'm not going anywhere. Even if I temporarily go somewhere."

"Mrrfhhh."

"Unless I die or something. Or Oliver dumps me. Because in that situation, the dog courts would one hundred percent give custody to him."

Spud's fur was silky under my fingers.

I closed my eyes for, like, half a second.

CHAPTER 7

"LUCIEN."

My first thought was that Oliver's morning breath was really, *really* bad. My second thought was that his voice sounded weirdly far away. My third, fourth, and fifth thoughts were that my arm was numb, my neck was killing me, and I was sure I had carpet marks on my face.

"You do realise," Oliver was saying, "that attempting to preserve our sex life by keeping the dog out of our bedroom will be somewhat undermined if you move into the dog pen?"

"Mrrffhhh," I groaned.

"Ruff," said Spud, nuzzling closer.

I rolled over and squinted up at Oliver. He was already showered and dressed for work, which meant shiny shoes and a three-piece suit, while I was in my pants, on the floor, with—I was slowly coming to realise—one of our hidden dog treats stuck to my arse.

"Well." Oliver actually put his hands on his hips. I wouldn't say he was looking at me disdainfully, but I'd definitely seen more dainful expressions on him. "At least you weren't in hospital this time."

"Ruff," said Spud.

"And you"—Oliver gazed sternly down at our dog—"shouldn't encourage him."

He turned crisply around and disappeared into the hallway. I wobbled to my feet and followed, Spud trailing close behind me.

I found Oliver in the kitchen eating bircher with the ferocious concentration of a man who wanted to pretend nothing was wrong.

"I'm really sorry," I said.

"Mruff," agreed Spud.

"It's fine," Oliver replied to both of us. It blatantly wasn't.

With a picking-a-scab instinct, I circled right back to: "He was *really* sad. And I couldn't sleep."

"You made your bed, Lucien. And to your credit, you also lay in it."

I tried my most disarming smile. "You've been working on that one since you woke up, haven't you?"

He half smiled back, but it was pretty fucking grudging. "I'm genuinely not angry with you," he admitted at last. "And I know you're somewhat afraid of responsibility. But you can actually do this. *We* can actually do this. But we have to do it right, or we'd be better off giving the dog up entirely."

"Hey." Crouching down, I put my hands over Spud's ears. Which confused him, but he was willing to go with it. "Don't say that in front of him."

"He's a dog. He's not going to understand."

"He might pick something up from…from…your tone of voice. Or the vibes. The vibes might be bad."

In what felt like a pointed challenge to my vibe-related dog concerns, Oliver put his spoon and empty mason jar into the dishwasher and opened the cupboard that I had *definitely remembered* was the one we were keeping the dog food in. The second he opened the pouch of nutritionally balanced puppy food, Spud bounced out from between my hands and scampered over to Oliver, tail *dodoinging* like one of those springy doorstops you get in old people's houses.

"He doesn't seem traumatised," said Oliver with a smugness I felt was at best ten percent warranted.

There'd been no way I was winning this conversation last night. And there was no way I was winning it this morning. And the fact I'd started thinking in terms of winning and losing was probably a bad sign. Not, like, in a relationship-ending sense. But in an argument-ending sense.

Leaving Spud with Oliver, I creaked upstairs in the hope a hot shower would make my body feel more like a body and less like a coat hanger.

It didn't particularly.

I was just sitting in my towel, hoping to drip-dry because normal towelling motions had become a Doctor, Doctor joke about how it hurt when I did this, when Oliver knocked on the door.

"Come in," I said.

To his credit, he didn't comment on the fact I was sitting morosely on the toilet lid, looking damp and uncomfortable. "I've fed Spud and taken him outside."

"Did you make a note of it in the Log Log?"

"I did," replied Oliver, without blinking. "As should you, the next time he goes."

"I will."

"Will you?"

Damn, he knew me too well. "At this moment in time, I fully intend to."

Stepping into the still-misty bathroom, Oliver dropped a kiss on my forehead. "I'm not expecting miracles. I'll see you this evening."

Frankly, Oliver's willingness not to expect miracles was probably a large part of the reason we were still together. As was the fact that he was an excellent judge of when I was sitting on a toilet wrapped in a towel in a way that was actually a *problem* or in a way that meant it was fine for him to go to work.

This was a fine-for-him-to-go-to-work towel-wrapped toilet sit. So when Oliver left to do exactly that, I didn't collapse into a pile of goo on the floor. Well, I mostly didn't collapse into a pile of goo on the floor. I *was* still pretty knackered on account of my dog-related moral crisis, meaning I was up way earlier than I would normally be.

I left my towel on the bathroom floor, then went back to put it neatly on the towel rack, and then dove into the soft, faintly me-and-Oliver-and-fabric-conditioner-scented cloud of duvets and pillows. My eyes closed blissfully. My back began to unkink itself. All my cares and worries began to float off like balloons at a child's birthday. My dog began barking downstairs.

Shit. I had a dog.

I peeled myself back out of bed and lurched onto the landing. Spud was sitting at the foot of the stairs, behind the dog-proof gate we'd—Oliver'd—installed, and staring up at me in a way that made me really understand where the phrase *puppy dog eyes* came from.

"I'm here," I said.

Spud's tail thumped the floor behind him.

"I just need to—" I suddenly realised I was completely naked in front of Spud. And I suppose, technically, Spud was completely naked in front of me as well, but it still felt weird. "I'm going to put some clothes on," I explained. "Don't worry and don't poo anywhere."

"Ruff," promised Spud.

And, you know what? I took him at his word.

As far as I could tell, our house had so far remained a dog-shit-free zone. Unfortunately, between playing with Spud, getting breakfast, and being a lazy arse, I'd managed to stay in the pants-and-T-shirt stage of getting ready until about two minutes before my meeting. Panicked, I ran upstairs and realised that literally every single one of my shirts was in the wash. Or more precisely in a wet knot inside the washing machine, where they'd been sitting ever since I'd promised I'd unload it two days ago. I was in no way too proud to just pull a worn one out of the laundry, but sadly the whole reason that it had been my job to unload the washing machine was that it had been Oliver's job to load it. Which meant *that* job had been done in a timely fashion, and the laundry basket was now sitting accusingly empty.

Fortunately—well, fortunately-ish—I was *also* not too proud to steal clothes from my more organised, more sensibly dressed boyfriend. So I raided Oliver's closet for one of his impeccably chosen, immaculately ironed shirts that he always remembered to put away properly. It was a tasteful pink herringbone, too tight in the chest and too short in the arms for me, but fuck it. Any shirt in a storm.

I threw a jacket over it to cover the arms part of the problem and genuinely spent a good two to three seconds debating whether I needed to put trousers on before deciding…*nah*. I didn't have the excuse of the pandemic anymore, but being able to go to meetings in your underwear was a universally recognised working-from-home perk.

By five minutes past nine, I was at my desk, with my computer booted up, my camera on, and my ring light in place, with Spud frolicking around behind me, very confident in his not-being-abandoned-ness. I wasn't even the last person to show up. That was Rhys Jones Bowen. It was always Rhys Jones Bowen.

"Okay, Alex," I said, figuring I'd fill the time while we were waiting. "Try this one. Doctor, Doctor—"

My screen suddenly filled up with Dr. Fairclough's face. "Yes?"

"Um, no. I'm doing a Doctor, Doctor joke for Alex."

"If you need to see a doctor," said Alex, "I know an excellent one in Harley Street."

I squinted at him. He seemed to be sitting in an actual throne in front of a vast marble fireplace. This, on its own, wasn't unusual because that was what working from home looked like for Alex. But he was also wearing a green velvet frock coat and a cravat. "Why are you dressed like Mr. Darcy?"

"Oh." Alex looked down at himself in mild surprise. "Forgot about the clobber. Fearfully funny story. Turns out they're shooting one of those costume thingies in the second ballroom, and I'm helping out by being extra."

There was nothing about that I couldn't believe. "Doctor, Doctor," I repeated.

"Yes?" said Dr. Fairclough.

"Still a joke," I explained.

Alex got that concerned look he often got at about this stage of the joke-telling process. "Luc, I know I'm sometimes a bit of a duffer comedy-wise, but I don't think just saying the word *doctor* over and over again qualifies as a joke."

"Doctor, Doctor," I tried for a third time, "I've broken—"

"Are you sure"—this was Barbara Clench, who was currently on holiday somewhere sunny and was now filling my screen with a brightly coloured mocktail and a disapproving expression—"that humour is an effective use of work time?"

Alex, at least, defended me on this one. "Oh, don't be a sourpuss. Finish your joke, Luc."

"Doctor, Doctor," I said.

"Yes?" said Dr. Fairclough.

"I've broken my arm in three places," I continued.

She gave an irritated blink. "I'm not a medical doctor, O'Donnell, I'm an entomologist."

"Gosh," exclaimed Alex. "It's bally sporting of you to be at a meeting with a broken arm. Did it happen recently?"

"No," I said, "because it's a joke."

"Stiff upper lip's all well and good, old man, but you need to be careful with this kind of thing. I had a friend who broke his arm, and he died."

"Did he get an infection?" asked Dr. Fairclough.

Alex shook his head. "No. Eaten by an alligator."

I gritted my teeth and tried not to ask myself why I kept doing this, because it never stopped me. "Doctor, Doctor—"

"Yes?"

"—I've broken my arm—"

"And we're dashed sorry for you."

"—in three places—"

"I really think we should be doing something more productive."

"'Well, don't go back to those places,'" I finished, utterly exhausted.

"What?" said Alex.

I gave the deepest sigh I had given since the last time I'd told Alex a joke. "Doctor, Doctor, I've broken my arm in three places. 'Then don't go back to those places.'"

Silence on a Zoom call was the worst-possible silence.

"And that's a joke?" asked Alex.

"Yes."

"*Why?*"

This was not, and had never been, worth it. "Okay. First of all, the Doctor, Doctor format is a well-known joke structure, based around the premise that the first speaker is a person with a medical complaint, and that the second speaker is a doctor giving them advice."

Dr. Fairclough popped up again. "That wasn't at all clear from context. It was far more natural to assume you were reporting a single speaker." She went still and quiet just long enough I thought her connection had frozen, then added, "Perhaps you could use some kind of hand signal. Or modulate your voice. Or adopt a system of hats."

"I'm not adopting a system of hats," I just-short-of-yelled. "I don't even have a hat." Well, technically I did have *a* hat, but it had a vulva on it so wasn't really appropriate for a professional Zoom call.

"So"—Alex was holding up one finger thoughtfully—"in this joke, the imaginary patient says, 'Doctor, Doctor.' Then is it the doctor or the patient who says the next bit?"

"*Obviously*, it's the patient who's broken their arm in three places."

"Well, one doesn't like to assume," Alex replied. "Doctors have ailments too. *Medice, cura te ipsum* and all that."

"Nobody is curating anybody's ipsums. The patient says, 'I've broken my arm in three places—'"

"Oh, I'm sorry to hear that." Rhys Jones Bowen had finally managed to connect. "Very dedicated of you to be coming into work anyway."

"Yes," I said. "Yes, it is."

"Sorry I'm late, chaps, chapesses, and chapnonbinary people," Rhys Jones Bowen continued. "I had a bugger of a time getting on the Wi-Fi. Forgot the password, you see."

"Would you not just connect automatically?" I asked, ill-advisedly.

Rhys Jones Bowen shook his head. "Oh no, Luc. As social media and data security manager"—Rhys Jones Bowen's suite of responsibilities had expanded after GDPR came in—"it's important for me to set an example."

Since the pandemic, we'd had a lot of Zoom meetings. Honestly, this one was going better than most. We were also, by my count, reaching the point where Dr. Fairclough would consider herself to have exceeded her allocation of time spent interacting with human beings before noon.

Dr. Fairclough's face appeared in the centre of the screen, pushing the rest of us into a little sidebar. "I consider myself," she said, "to have exceeded my allocation of time spent interacting with human beings before noon. Therefore, I shall convey the information I have convened this meeting to convey, we will briefly discuss it, and we will conclude. Any questions?"

"What's that on the wall behind you?" asked Alex.

If someone had said that to me, I'd have assumed they were talking about a monster or a spider and whipped around to look. Dr. Fairclough, though, wasn't scared of monsters, and her only problem with spiders was that arachnids fell outside her field of study. "It's a print of a VW Beetle," she explained. "I am currently engaged in a romantic and sexual relationship. We have had a slight miscommunication about my interests." She paused again, for about a third of a second. "Does anyone have any questions pertinent to the format of the meeting?"

To my intense relief, nobody had any questions pertinent to the format of the meeting. Or any questions they had mistakenly decided were pertinent to the format of the meeting.

"Good," said Dr. Fairclough. "Our patron is dead."

In hindsight, it was not my finest work moment to respond to this news with, "What? The Earl of Spunkwhistle?"

"Spitalhamstead," Barbara Clench corrected me, either out of respect for the dead or because—as she'd told us in several long email chains—she found the Spunkwhistle thing both childish and inappropriate.

Alex's face reflected its usual confusion. "Gosh. It seems like a lot of earls are dying recently. I hope there hasn't been a revolution."

"I think if there was a revolution," I said, as diplomatically as I could, "you would be among the first to know."

"Jolly kind of you, Luc. Still, it's a deuced queer thing because I was at an earl's funeral only the other day. Friend of the family. Excellent fellow, absolute riot." He paused, frowning. "I mean, not so much now, obviously."

"Can we focus on one earl at a time, please?" asked Barbara Clench.

And, somehow, my status as third-least professional person in the room was dragging me back on Team Barbara. "When did this actually happen?"

"Last Friday," said Alex. "Lovely ceremony. Very tasteful."

I just about managed not to face-palm on camera. "No, when did the earl die?"

"About two weeks ago," replied Alex and Dr. Fairclough simultaneously. "But," Dr. Fairclough went on, "I've only recently been informed. The estate has shown a shocking lack of regard for our research into and reintroduction of ecologically vital strains of coleoptera."

Something was nagging at me. "Alex," I asked. "This earl friend of yours..."

"Hilary?" Alex volunteered. "Yes?"

"Where was he earl of again?"

"Spitalhamstead, I think. Though one knows such a lot of earls these days, it's a little hard to keep track."

That was what I'd thought. "So you were at the funeral of our patron then?"

Alex looked genuinely offended. "Certainly not. I wouldn't skip out on old Hilary for a work do. What kind of chap do you think I am?"

"No, I mean Hilary was—"

"Luc," interrupted Rhys Jones Bowen sternly, "this isn't the time to be badgering Alex about his dead friend. We've just lost our patron—which is very sad but also very worrying. And I really think we need to be talking about that."

Ordinarily, Dr. Fairclough paid zero attention to the non-insect-related parts of running CRAPP. But at the end of the day she was an academic, which meant that the one thing she could bring herself to care about as much as her research was *funding* her research. "I agree," she said. "This leaves the future of the Coleoptera Research and Protection Project uncertain. I do not like the future of the Coleoptera Research and Protection Project being uncertain."

"By uncertain"—there was no sign of Barbara Clench's mocktail at this point—"do you mean we might lose our jobs?"

"Oh, I hope not," piped up Alex. "What would I do with my weekends?"

Dr. Fairclough used her second blink. "I understand that this is a shock, but I need you all to retain a sense of proportion. Our jobs are far less important than long-term soil aeration."

"Of course," said Barbara Clench with a level of sarcasm I was jealous of and everyone else was oblivious to. "Let me rephrase. What is the likelihood that the earl's death will lead to C.R.A.P.P."—Barbara always said *See Arr Ay Pee Pee*, and always said it so you could hear every dot—"having to end its vital work and also lead, secondarily, to us all losing our jobs?"

"Unknown," replied Dr. Fairclough.

And probably, if it had been left up to her, the call would have been over, which would have sucked for the slim majority of us who needed to work for a living. "Okay," I put in quickly, "but can you speculate?"

Dr. Fairclough was still radiating end-meeting energy. "Logically, there are three possibilities. Either he has provided for us in his will and we can continue as normal, or his heir will provide for us and we can continue mostly as normal. Or they will not, and our research will cease and the species we protect will go into an irrevocable decline, leading ultimately to the complete collapse of agriculture and the extinction of the human species."

"Shit," I cried.

"Yes." Dr. Fairclough gave a brisk nod. "The stakes are, in fact, existential."

"No, I mean—"

Spud had spent the call doing puppy things in the pen and around my feet, but now he was doing the very specific kind of puppy thing which I'd learned came just before he did the puppy thing that we on no account wanted our puppy to do indoors.

I leapt to my feet. "I need to take my dog outside."

If there was any response, I didn't hear it because I'd jumped up quickly enough to yank my headphones out of the computer. With the wire trailing behind me, I scooped Spud up, wrestled open the patio doors, and plonked him in the designated shitting area.

He looked up at me in some confusion.

"You know what to do," I told him. "You were doing it yesterday with Oliver repeatedly. Don't pretend you've forgotten or that this is weird."

Spud kept looking at me like I'd lost my mind.

I sighed. "Just poo, will you? I'm in a meeting."

"Ruff." Spud thumped his tail on the ground happily.

"Look, if you don't go in the next thirty seconds, I'll have to take you back inside."

"He's not got a watch." A small, familiar, deeply irritating voice drifted over the garden fence. It was followed by a small, familiar, deeply irritating face. Both belonged to Next Door's Kid. "Also, you're talking to a dog. Dickhead."

In my heart of hearts, I knew it was beneath me to trade insults with an eleven-year-old. "Better than talking to you," I said. "Bum-face."

"That's not a real swear."

"Well, you're not a real..." Fuck. I'd already fucked it.

"Not a real what?" asked Next Door's Kid, even more smugly than his normal baseline of smugness, which was, let's be clear, unbearable.

"A real..." Every second that passed without my coming up

with a creatively devastating answer was just confirming his assessment of my dickheadedness. "A real bum-face."

"I'm a bum-face," he said slowly, "but not a real bum-face?"

I should have just gone with *is too*. It was a classic for a reason. As it was, I had no option but to double down on Schrödinger's bum-face. "Yes."

"Dickhead."

"You can't just keep saying *dickhead*."

"Dickhead."

"Why are you like this?" I asked.

Next Door's Kid sneered over the fence. "Why are you like *that*?"

"Years of trauma. What's your excuse?"

"Adickheadsayswhat?"

"What?" I replied, fatally.

He had a laugh like a machine gun. A really annoying machine gun.

"One of these days"—I actually wagged my actual finger—"I'm going to tell your parents exactly what a slimy, vicious, obnoxious little piece of—oh my God. Spud." My voice went up into that range that people use for talking to dogs and children who aren't arseholes. "Look at you. Who's a good boy? Who's the best boy?" I reached into my jacket pocket and produced a small rain of treats. "What a wonderful…um. Bowel movement?"

"You're weird," declared Next Door's Kid.

"Yeah, well. I'd rather be weird than…than"—I gestured—"you. Come on, Spud."

A singsong of *dickhead* followed us back inside. I wouldn't say it had become my life's ambition to one day win an argument with that particular eleven-year-old, but it was creeping onto my bucket list, bringing the total number of items on it to one.

I threw myself back into my computer chair, letting Spud scrabble onto my lap. To my complete lack of surprise, Dr. Fairclough had already left the meeting.

"—decent chap," Alex was saying. "And a decent chap wouldn't just leave a chap to twist in the wind. Ah, hello, Luc."

"Welcome back, Luc," said Rhys Jones Bowen. "Did your dog have a nice poo?"

"There've been better poos," I said, thinking of Next Door's Kid.

Rhys Jones Bowen nodded sagely. "Don't worry, there'll be plenty more where that one came from."

"Before we conclude," said Barbara Clench, "can I make a formal request that nobody attend any future meetings in their underwear?"

I looked down at Spud, my bare legs, and my hedgehog boxers.

Fuck.

A few minutes after one—Oliver's lunchtimes were a little unpredictable when he was in court, and it wasn't like he could text me from the…the…the sitty-downy bit where the lawyers go—my phone buzzed, and I looked down to see a classic *Withnail and I*–era picture of Richard E. Grant.

Nice dick, I replied. Then I coaxed Spud up into my arms, learned very quickly how hard it can be to find a flattering selfie angle while also wrangling an overenthusiastic puppy, and took an at least moderately okay-looking picture to send back to him.

His response was near-instantaneous. You're both adorable.

It was not, however, stand-alone.

Has everything been okay?

Have you been remembering to keep hiding treats in the pen?

Has he gone to the toilet yet?

If he did, did you remember to make a note of it?

If he hasn't, we probably don't need to be concerned yet but it's worth keeping an eye on.

Yes mostly yes and I'll do it now, I typed when I could get a text in edgeways. It can be a poo retrospective.

After a little less than half a second, Oliver texted back, Thank you.

I got distracted by next doors kid being an absolute shut while spud was shutting

*shit

*shitting

Spud keeps poking the phone

There was a slight pause. Oliver was, by nature, a long-form texter. I really don't understand why you have such a problem with Colin. He's a perfectly pleasant boy.

This stung. It wasn't the first time Oliver had said neutral to positive things about Next Door's Kid. The fucking traitor. No hes not. He keeps calling me a dickhead

Perhaps he's going through a phase.

A phase of calling exactly me a dickhead

He's probably testing boundaries because he perceives you as an authority figure.

Oliver no one has perceived me as an authority figure in my entire life

Another Oliver-length texting pause. Or maybe he was getting food on his lunch break, which I hoped he was.

I hope, I texted, you're getting lunch

On my way to get a wrap.

I thought about sending a "love you," but I'd told Oliver I loved him only yesterday, and I had a reputation to uphold. So I sent a heart emoji instead, and felt like a different sort of dickhead. Oh God, Next Door's Kid had been right.

"Come on, Spud." I deposited him back on the floor. "It's your lunch time too."

He bounced after me into the kitchen and bounced even more when he saw me pulling down a pouch of puppy noms. It felt weirdly validating every time I made him happy, which seemed to happen a lot for reasons of dog. In a complicated world, it was nice to have a relationship where I could get regular positive reinforcement by doing very simple actions. Which raised some uncomfortable questions about exactly who was being trained here.

Once I'd put the bowl down in the puppy pen and Spud had stuck his face in it, I went and did my due diligence with the Journal of the Poo Year.

6:47, Oliver's entry began, *urine and some stool of good consistency and healthy colour*.

Underneath it, I wrote, *10ish? Did poo. Maybe wee?*

My phone buzzed.

By the way, Oliver was telling me, as lovely as you're looking in your coquettish hedgehog boxers you should probably wear trousers to meetings. You never know when you might have to stand up.

Good tip, I sent back. Timely.

CHAPTER 8

DURING OUR LUNCHTIME TEXTS, I'D told myself I'd let Oliver know about the whole *might be losing my job thing* when he got home. When he got home, I told myself I'd let Oliver know about the whole *might be losing my job thing* after dinner. After dinner, I told myself I'd let Oliver know about the whole *might be losing my job thing* before bed. Except now I was in bed, and I was fucked. Fucked in the emotional sense, not in the fun sense.

Or, I reasoned as Oliver was brushing his teeth, I'd been deeply unselfish. Because he'd had a hard day in court—apparently it wasn't so great when the defendant showed up wearing the exact clothes he'd been caught on CCTV in—and he deserved to play with our new puppy without being burdened by a problem that still might not lead to me losing the only job I'd been able to hold down since Miles left.

Or, I reasoned as Oliver climbed in next to me, that was complete bullshit and I was being a coward. After all, what was the worst that could happen? I'd tell him the situation and he'd be supportive and insightful, and I'd have to…deal with my feelings and stuff. And I didn't want to do that because it was very, very important to me that working at CRAPP sucked and I hated it. If that turned out to be less than entirely true, I honestly wasn't sure I'd psychologically recover.

At least Spud had calmed down. Maybe me spending the night in the pen had helped him understand that we'd always be here for him, even after we'd left the room. Maybe Oliver, and all his dog books, had been wrong.

"Oliver," I said. "I've got somet—"

"Arroooooou," said Spud, from below. For a little dog, he had a set of lungs on him. "Arroooooou."

"Fuck."

Oliver nestled his bookmark neatly into *The Man Who Died Twice*. "Were you about to tell me something?"

("Arroooooou.")

"No." I buried my head under the pillow.

"Are you sure?" he asked. "Because normally when you've something important to say, you put it off all day and then hint vaguely at it once we're in bed."

"That's..." I flailed for a devastating put-down, briefly considered calling him *bum-face*, and then settled on, "very insightful. And annoying."

("Arroooooou.")

"Yes"—somehow, even through the pillow, I could tell when Oliver was smiling—"I realise caring about your feelings is one of my worst traits."

"It really is."

"I'll try to do better in future. But, for now, what's wrong?"

"Arr-arrr-aroooooooooooou!!"

This kind of conversation was hard enough when there wasn't a sad puppy downstairs. Which meant it wasn't technically a lie when my mouth, with the tacit consent of my brain, said, "It's Spud."

"I did actually think about that."

Reaching into his pyjama pocket—apparently I was in a long-term relationship with the kind of man who wore the kind of pyjamas that had pockets—Oliver produced a little plastic drug bag.

And, for a moment, I thought he'd gone for the extremely unbarristerly solution of getting stoned off our tits.

To be honest, I'd have been up for it.

"Happy second day of having a dog," said Oliver, dropping a set of blue rubber earplugs into my hand.

I appreciated the thought, but… "You know it's not the noise that's the problem, right?"

"I do, but it'll be easier if you can't hear him."

"Arr-arrr-aroooooooooooou."

"I'm not sure," I tried, "I want to make it easier to ignore my crying dog."

Oliver sighed. "And that's very kindhearted of you. But ignoring your crying dog is the best way to stop your dog from crying."

"Okay, but—" I was floundering. Not having read all or indeed any of the dog books was putting me kind of on the back foot here. "Isn't that, like, teaching him toxic dogsculinity? Aren't we just training him to repress his feelings?"

Any thought I'd had that Oliver was being heartless evaporated when I saw the look in his eyes, all compassion and sorrow. "Lucien," he said, running his fingertips along the line of my jaw, "I am so pleased we took this step together. But this is supposed to be our space. Our time. If it's going to become the place where we worry about Spud, I don't think that's going to work for me. Not long term."

"Arrooooooou."

When he put it like that, it wasn't going to work for me either. I made a semi-committal *I suppose* kind of noise and tried the earplugs. On a very literal level they worked. I couldn't hear Spud or much of anything else. But all that meant was that I went from listening to my dog arooooouing his heart out, to imagining my dog arooooouing his heart out. Which, if anything, was worse.

Oliver leaned over to kiss me good night. Then, despite having just given me earplugs, he said something.

"What?" I asked, not completely sure how loud I was being.

He said the something again. It was clearly meant to be a comforting something. So I just nodded and nestled into my usual trying-to-sleep position in Oliver's arms.

"Lucien," said Oliver the following morning. "This isn't sustainable."

Spud and I poked our heads out of the blanket nest that I'd built for us. "I know. I just..."

Except I couldn't think of a *just*.

There was a longish, not-great silence while Oliver gazed down at me with an expression that made me really miss anger.

"I'm running late," he concluded.

Oliver had never run late in his life. But part of the reason for that was that he always felt like he was running late. And he always felt he was running latest when he was upset.

"Oliver," I tried. "I—"

"Please take care of Spud. He'll need feeding and taking outside. I'll see you this evening."

At which point, my amazing barrister boyfriend strode out of the house, trailing sadness like a piece of toilet paper stuck to his otherwise immaculate shoe. Toilet paper sadness that I had stuck there.

"Ruff," said Spud, sticking his tongue in my ear.

"Not the time," I told him.

And I must have sounded firm because he made a discouraged "Mruff?" and looked away. Which made me feel doubly shitty because while the universe had presented me with a situation where I could have a not-sad dog or a not-sad Oliver but couldn't have them both be not-sad at once, I apparently had the power to make them both not-not-sad as much as I liked.

In an effort to be a slightly less rubbish dog owner, I fed

Spud—much to his delight—and took him outside—much to his delight—and then, hoping to win back some Oliver points, filled in the Defecation Chronicle (*7:05 did a poo and some wee, looked normal I think*).

Despite not having any meetings at all that day, I put on trousers so I could feel at least a little bit professional while WFHing. We were a couple of weeks post–Beetle Drive, and I had a fair bit of work to do chasing up people who were dragging their feet on donations. Work that I mostly managed to do, although the whole business with the earl was still preying on my mind (no updates), as was the business with Oliver (no updates, not even at lunchtime) and Spud (updates entirely toilet- and treat-related).

By about two I'd had enough of pretending to be a serious grown-up who knew how to compartmentalise. So I flopped down on the sofa and FaceTimed my mum. Or, at least I tried to FaceTime my mum. What I actually FaceTimed was a wall that greeted me with a boisterous "Luc, m'boy."

"Hi, Judy," I said to the wall. "Could you maybe turn the iPad round? And," I added, after receiving an intense close-up of her left nostril, "move it slightly farther away?"

Eventually, Judy managed to get a manageable visual. "Odile'll be here in a minute or two. She's just in a rather sticky situation at the moment."

"Oh my God." I jolted upright out of a sense of duty. Because I knew the one time I didn't, my mum would be genuinely dead. "Is she okay?"

"Honestly, not so much. She's perilously close to chucking it in entirely."

My heart gave a nervy thwip. "Wait? What?"

"You know how it is. You get to a certain point, and it just doesn't seem like it's worth carrying on. It's like you've tried everything and you can barely imagine a way forward."

My heart un-thwipped itself. This did not sound like Mum. Or rather it did but only in a very specific context. "Is she having trouble with Wordle again?"

"How's it going, Odile?" Judy yelled.

"Do not distract me," Mum yelled back, despite clearly being in the same room. "This is important. I am hanging by a thread here."

"How many guesses have you got left?" I asked.

"One. This is life and death."

I resigned myself to temporarily communicating with my mum by shouting through an octogenarian. "Can I help?"

"Non. Nobody can help me. I must do this alone."

"Mum," I said. "I'm actually having a bit of a freak-out about, like, my relationship and my dog and shit. So could we maybe… I don't know how to say this in a way that doesn't sound ungrateful, but could we maybe focus less on guessing five-letter words and more on, say, me?"

"But her streak, man," cried Judy. "Her streak!"

"No, no, no," declared Mum, immediately appearing in shot. "My son is more important. Although"—she grinned slyly—"if you happen off the top of your head to know a five-letter word that goes something-*o*-something-*e*-*r*, that would be very helpful. Alternatively, it will destroy me entirely. It will depend if you are right or not."

Surreptitiously, I googled *today's wordle solution* in another tab. "It's *cover*."

"Could be *mover*," suggested Judy. "Or *lover*. Or *hover*."

"It's *cover*," I said. "Trust me."

Mum gave me the *I know what you did* look that I knew too well from childhood. "*Luc*, you did not use the Googles."

"No," I lied.

Begrudgingly, almost defiantly, Mum typed the answer in. "You were correct, mon caneton, but I wish you to know that I do not feel good about this victory. Now. What did you need your maman for?"

"It's"—I shifted uncomfortably—"it's about the dog."

Her eyes widened. "The dog?" she cried. "Oh no. Is he dead? He is dead, isn't he? Luc, you should have said that your dog was dead. That was much more important than the Wordle."

"He's not dead. He's right here." I pointed at Spud, who, to be fair, was nose down and half asleep in the crook of my arm.

"That is your dog?" asked Mum. "I thought it was a potato."

"Why would I be cuddling a potato?"

"As your mother"—she gazed loftily at the ceiling—"it is not my place to judge."

This was hard to process. On the one hand, I'd rather my mum didn't think I regularly got on video calls with an emotional support potato. On the other hand, it was nice to know that, if I did, she'd be there for me. "This is Spud," I explained.

"So it is a potato?"

"No, we called him Spud."

"Why?"

"Because when he was very little, he looked like a potato."

"He still looks like a potato."

"He does not," I insisted, "still look like a potato."

"Luc, are you sure that is a dog and not a potato?"

"Yes. He's got ears. How many potatoes have ears?"

"They have eyes."

A thought dripped into my brain like ice water. "Mum, are you winding me up?"

"Maybe a little bit." She grinned unrepentantly. "Though, honestly, he does look like a potato."

"You're going to give him a complex."

"Don't worry," Judy joined in. "Dogs are very resilient animals."

"It is very sweet, though," Mum added, "the way you care about your puppy. It is like the meme."

On a global scale, a lot of extremely bad things had happened in the last few years. But on a personal scale, none of them quite beat my mum discovering the internet. "Which meme?"

"You know the meme. Where there is the man and he does not want the dog but then the family, they go against his wishes and get the dog anyway, and this causes a breakdown between the man and his family, which I think is why they are not in the meme. But then, through the pain and loneliness, the man turns to the dog and he finds the solace."

I was silent for a long moment. "That is the bleakest take on the Dad and Dog meme I have ever heard."

"It's a very moving story, Luc, about a man who finds companionship in his lowest moment. Also," she went on thoughtfully, "it has a deep and tragic irony because the family chooses the dog over the man, and then the man chooses the dog over the family."

Somehow, like always, Mum had chaos-gremlined her way into being insightful. "Funny you should mention that," I said. "Because I might be in a photo without Oliver in it."

Mum nodded understandingly. "None of the photographs have you or Oliver in them. They're all pictures of the dog."

"No, I mean, a metaphorical life photograph."

"Are you seeing things in a funny way again?" asked the woman who'd interpreted the Dad and Dog meme as a searing domestic drama about loss and healing. "I have known Oliver for a long time now, and I do not think he is the kind of man who would make you choose between him and a puppy."

"And if he is," added Judy, "you should divorce him. That's what I did every time."

I couldn't tell if Mum and Judy's inability to stay on topic for six seconds together made this conversation much easier or completely impossible. "How many times is that?"

"Two or three? Lost count."

I had follow-up questions. But they were probably best left unanswered. "I don't think he's asking me to choose. Not really. If anything, Spud is."

"Go with the dog," Judy told me with generational authority. "A dog'll never let you down."

"I don't think Oliver is going to let me down either."

"That's what I thought about my fifth husband. Then he went and took up backgammon."

Definitely best left unanswered. "Everything's fine," I denialled. "It's just Spud gets really sad when we go to bed, and Oliver won't let him into our room. Which means I have to go downstairs to stop him crying—"

"Why is Oliver crying?" interrupted Mum.

"The *dog* is crying."

She made a Gallic gesture. "That does make more sense."

"So anyway, I've spent the past two nights on my study floor looking after Spud, which means I'm not with Oliver. And that's sort of the opposite of being in a relationship with someone."

"Want my advice?" asked Judy, one hundred percent rhetorically. "Ditch the bugger."

"But I really like Spud," I protested, squeezing him just a little bit tighter. "This was a big step for me, and I don't want to unstep it."

Judy shook her head. "Not Spud. Oliver. A man who won't let a dog sleep on the bed isn't a man at all."

"Okay, but I really, *really* like Oliver. And I don't think either of us want Spud sleeping on our bed for the rest of his life. We have other things we want to do in bed."

"Luc," put in Mum, "if you are talking about sex, you can say *sex*. It is like *gay*. It is not a bad word."

I sighed. "Fine. Oliver and I don't want Spud sleeping in the bed because that'll make it harder for us to have gay sex in it. Happy?"

"Oui."

"Will it?" asked Judy. "Is there a logistical issue I'm not aware of?"

"No," I replied very, very quickly. "It's just neither Oliver nor I want to have sex in front of a dog."

"Why not? Dog won't mind."

"*I* will mind."

"I do see his point, Judy." Mum came to what, on a good day, might have been my rescue. "I would not want to have sex in front of a dog either. I had sex in front of Mick Jagger once and that was bad enough."

Not my rescue, then. Some previously unknown pit of hell. "Back to me?" I suggested.

And, mercifully, Mum went with it. "You know I love you, mon caneton, but I think you may be making a molehill out of a teacup. It has only been two days, after all."

"Yeah, but Oliver says if I keep messing this up, we'll have to get rid of Spud."

"Did he say exactly that?" It was the gentle voice Mum used when she was navigating my bullshit. "In exactly those words?"

"Well, no," I admitted. "But Spud needs discipline and consistency and boundaries and…and everything. And I'm not doing that."

"There is more than one way to skin a dog, Luc."

I put my hands protectively over Spud's ears. "Not the right phrase, Mum."

"You know I love Oliver too," Mum said. "But you are a person who makes molehills out of teacups, and he is a person who thinks it is his way or the autoroute. And that can be good because you will stop each other becoming complete arseholes."

"Thanks, Mum."

"I am complimenting you. I am saying you are not complete arseholes."

"That implies that I'm at least some part of an arsehole."

She shrugged. "Everyone is some part of an arsehole sometimes. But this thing with you and Oliver, he is not going to leave you just because you have a different philosophy on dog owning."

"I would," said Judy.

"Yes"—Mum glanced at her—"but Luc would not go out with you because he is a gay and you are very, very old."

Judy slapped her chest proudly. "Geriatriccore. Old-girl aesthetic. Hashtag stillgotit."

"I don't have a philosophy on dog owning, though." I yanked the conversation back on track. "I don't know what I'm doing."

"And, Luc, neither does Oliver. He is just better at covering it up than you are."

"No but..." I squelched into a quagmire of my own inadequacy. "He's, like, read all the dog books and things."

"So what?" said Judy. "Never read a book in my life, dog or otherwise." She snapped her fingers. "Michael of Kent, here, girl."

And, sure enough, Michael of Kent bounced into view, hopped into Judy's lap, and awaited further instruction.

"Good girl." Judy pulled what appeared to be about a third of a chicken out of her pocket and fed it to Michael of Kent.

"Also"—Mum swivelled the camera away from the Judy/Dog/Chicken triad—"you do not have to be a barrister to read a book."

"No, but you have to be, like, not lazy and hopeless."

"You are not hopeless," Mum told me. "And you are only lazy because it is easier."

"Yeah. By definition," I pointed out.

Mum struck a pose of smug wisdom that, to be fair, was at least moderately earned. "Ah, but is it easier now, mon caneton?"

Was there anything worse than the person you'd explicitly called for advice giving you the advice you'd explicitly called for? In the grand scheme of things? Probably. In the moment? Definitely not.

CHAPTER 9

"OH DEAR," SAID OLIVER, COMING into the kitchen. "Am I being punished?"

I dumped a can of chickpeas into a pan of summer vegetables that were supposed to be roasted but looked more charred and shrivelled. "No. I'm making you dinner. Because I love you"—my voice was getting faster and smaller as I went on—"andalsoweneed-totalkaboutsomestuff."

"Who are you and what have you done with Lucien O'Donnell?"

"Very funny." Tossing a can of tomatoes after the chickpeas, I squinted into the depths of my sad and soggy veg. "What does a simmer even look like?"

Oliver peered over my shoulder. "Not like that." He reached past me and turned the hob up and, once the tomato juice had started bubbling, back down. Then he gave me the softest peck on the cheek and asked, "How was Spud today, by the way?"

"Good," I said, nodding. "You can check the Shit List if you like."

He gave a low chuckle. "I do actually trust you. Now if you're okay to keep an eye on that, I'm going to change out of my work clothes."

Privately, I always kind of liked the moment just before Oliver changed out of his work clothes. When he looked all buttoned-up and serious but just on the edge of becoming *not* buttoned-up and serious. But my personal fantasies weren't quite a reason to make the man I love sit around all evening in an uncomfortable shirt. Well, not unless it was a special occasion.

I kept an eye on the vegetables while Oliver nipped upstairs, although I wasn't really sure what I was supposed to be keeping an eye on them *for*. I gave them a halfhearted stir and watched in culinary despair as one of my aubergine fingers fell into two limp halves held together with a stringy skin that used to be purple.

Still, it was the thought that counted.

Figuring it wasn't about to get any better, I dished up two bowls of vegan gunge, scattering coriander over the top like a cushion over a stain on the sofa. As I carried them through to the dining room, I heard a "Who's a good boy?" from the study, and then Oliver emerged in full *At Home with the Blackwoods* mode. Which was to say, he was wearing a slightly more comfortable shirt and slightly less formal trousers.

"I think it's a good sign," he said, "that Spud's already going into his pen voluntarily."

I plonked Oliver's bowl in front of him. "He's hiding from my cooking."

"Well, that still means he views his pen as a place of security."

"Do *you* need a pen?"

Oliver gently forked up a lump of what might have been pepper, might have been courgette, or might have been a bit of undissolved stock cube. "No no, this is lovely. Thank you."

"It's not lovely," I said, "it's disgusting. We both know it's disgusting."

"It's lovely that you tried."

I wasn't sure what it meant that I didn't find that patronising. Maybe it was the raw sincerity with which Oliver said it. Or maybe it was just that having a realistic sense of each other's weaknesses was an important part of an adult relationship. At least I hoped it was because I had a lot of weaknesses to have a realistic sense of. "We could still get a takeaway."

"Certainly not. You made this. We're eating it."

"Okay, now I feel like *I'm* being punished."

"If so"—Oliver smiled across the table—"it's entirely self-inflicted. Now what was it you wanted to talk about?"

I squirmed. "Umm, it might actually be a couple of things."

"I assume one of them is to do with you sleeping on the floor the past two nights. I'm a little worried I don't know what the other is."

"It's not a big deal," I said, casually dismissing my medium- to long-term employment prospects in order to focus on a dog. "There's a chance CRAPP might be falling over."

Oliver's smile was neatly put aside in favour of just the right level of *here for you but not freaked out*. "I'm surprised to hear that. I thought the Beetle Drive went well this year."

"It did. But most of our funding came from the earl, and he's sort of...snuffed it."

"Sort of?" Perhaps he was following my lead, but Oliver let his smile creep back just fractionally. "You mean he's only snuffed it a little bit?"

Okay, that hadn't been the right time to hedge. "No, he's definitely snuffed it all the way. Died. Had funeral. Buried. Full Solomon Grundy Weekend experience."

"I'm sorry."

I shrugged. "I barely knew him."

"But he was quite a character."

"I mean, as far as I can tell, his only interests were sex workers and dung beetles."

One of Oliver's eyebrows twitched wickedly. "So a typical British peer?"

"Apparently he died on a bouncy castle with three strippers."

"So"—Oliver's eyebrow remained wickedly in place—"a typical British peer."

I loved Mean Oliver, and Oliver knew I loved Mean Oliver, which meant this was probably a deliberate attempt to cheer me up.

"It's also possible," I went on reluctantly, "he didn't leave a will. And if that's the case, we might be kind of fucked."

"It's very unlikely." Oliver had surrendered on the vegetable front, and I'd capitulated without a fight. He gathered up the bowls and took them into the kitchen, where he loaded them immediately into the dishwasher because of course he did. "This isn't my area of specialisation, but even if he died intestate, his heir will probably let things carry on as they are. Deliberately dismantling the life's work of a dead relative would be...how can I put this? A look."

Having followed Oliver in the least puppylike way I could manage, I leaned against the doorframe. "Thanks for putting that in layman's terms for me."

"Anytime," he said, smirking.

God, how had I slept two nights on the floor without this man, without his eyebrows, and the eyes beneath the eyebrows, and his smirking and the lips that did the smirking, and his hands, and his arms, and... Okay, now I was just listing body parts I'd denied myself access to.

"Listen," I tried. "About..."

There was a pattering of paws, and the tiny, fuzzy elephant in the room poked his head between my feet.

"About him," I finished.

"Mruff?" said Spud.

And I knelt down to scratch him behind the ears, where he liked it best.

"Hello, Spud." Oliver came over to join in the puppy scritching. "Have you been a good boy today? A good boy for Daddy Lucien."

Daddy Lucien was sounding way less unnatural than I'd expected it to, but I protest-too-muched anyway. "*Oliver.*"

"Sorry." He hid his laugh unconvincingly behind a cough and continued gently ruffling Spud. "Were you a good boy for Commitment-Phobic Dog Owner Lucien O'Donnell?"

I rose in order to escape Oliver's entirely justified mockery and took up a serious pose with my arms folded seriously. "Oh, shut up. He was a good boy. He was and is the best boy. And that's sort of what I wanted to talk about."

"I don't care how good a doggo he is," said Oliver, working more gravitas into the word *doggo* than I thought was humanly possible, "he's not sleeping in our bed, and you can't stay downstairs forever."

"I know. But I do actually think there's a compromise here."

Oliver and Spud both looked up at me, Oliver with a touch of impatience, Spud just, well, like a dog. "We've been over this. He needs to learn and we need to be firm."

"Right. But I've been doing some reading—" I broke off because Oliver looked unflatteringly surprised. "Hey. I can read."

"Yes, but you usually choose not to."

"Is this about my literacy or our dog?"

"Both, it seems."

"Okay, well," I ploughed on, "one of the books, the one with the puppy on the front—"

"Lucien, they all have puppies on the front."

"The puppy on the front doing this." I raised a hand in imitation of a puppy giving paw. "And that book says that not wanting your dog to be sad is normal and sensible, and it's okay to do things to make him less sad."

"I've read all the puppy books, and none of them recommend sleeping on the floor in your study."

Oliver could get unhelpfully stubborn when you told him you

wanted to try, as Mum put it, the autoroute. "No, but it says it's okay to let the puppy sleep in its den in your room for the first few days or weeks."

"That might be what one book says, but it's not the—"

"Don't say 'It's not the consensus.'"

It wasn't normal for him, but Oliver was looking almost petulant. "Well, it's not."

"Okay, but—"

"What's more likely"—now he was crossing from petulant to argumentative—"that this one person has discovered an otherwise unknown technique for training a puppy without doing any of the emotionally difficult parts, or that everybody else is right and the book that happens to agree with you is wrong?"

I was beginning to get a sense of what Oliver was like in court, and it wasn't a sense I particularly wanted to get more of. "I don't think it's really a right-or-wrong situation," I told him, depressingly aware that he was better with words than me.

"Of *course* it's a right-or-wrong situation. I do not want to be the kind of dog owner who can't control their pet because they didn't have discipline when it counted."

Honestly, I'd been hoping this conversation would take more of a *Why gosh, Lucien, you're completely correct; how could I have been so foolish?* direction. But hoping wasn't the same as expecting. The worst of it was, I could almost hear the ghost of David Blackwood in Oliver's voice. The never-quite-unlearned lesson that hurt was good for you.

"Come on," I said to Oliver and Spud both. "Let's at least take this out of the kitchen."

We went through to the study, and I opened the patio doors so that Spud could play in the garden, while Oliver sat on the step and I stood beside him, halfheartedly chucking a ball in Spud's general direction.

"Could we at least try it?" I asked, finally.

"You really want us to dismantle the pen every night, rebuild it in our room, and then reverse the whole process in the morning?"

"I'll do it."

"Lucien"—Oliver was rubbing his brow in that *dealing with me* way he sometimes had—"if this doesn't work..."

"Then at least I won't have spent a fortnight sleeping on the floor?"

"So you're saying either we do what you want or you move permanently into the study." Oliver had upgraded from brow-rubbing to glaring.

"You said we had to do it your way or send Spud back to the pound."

"This isn't *Lady and the Tramp*. It's a perfectly reasonable dog's home. And, anyway, it's not *my* way; it's *the* way."

I wasn't quite in a glaring-back space, but I definitely hit incredulity hard. "Oh my God, can you hear yourself?"

"What's that supposed to mean?"

"I literally found a dog expert from one of the dog expert books *you got* who says there is, in fact, more than one way to do this, just like there's more than one way to do lots of things, and you won't even try because...because..." I threw the ball with such frustrated distraction that it hit the doorframe and bounced back into the study, much to Spud's confusion. "Because you think things are only good if they...if they *suck*. And...and..." I didn't like being angry with Oliver. I wasn't *used* to being angry with Oliver. "I'm going for a nap."

And then I left the room with grace and dignity. Without, at any point, accidentally stepping on any of Spud's squeaky toys.

Angry naps are both the best and the worst kind of nap. Like probably, from a mature, grown-up, has-a-dog perspective, they're not the best way to process your emotions. But also having feelings is exhausting. And I *had* spent two nights in a row on the floor. I sausage-rolled myself in the duvet, drifted into resentful unconsciousness, and stayed there until Oliver woke me a respectful angry nap length later.

"Lucien," he said. "I'm sorry."

"And?" I replied, only slightly pettily.

"And you may have a point."

"May?"

"I've had a look at the"—he did the *puppy giving paw* gesture—"book, and it's possible I succumbed to a certain amount of confirmation bias."

I blinked at him from within the safety of my duvet wrap. "So we can try the thing?"

"We can try the thing."

"I really will move the pen."

He sat down on the edge of the bed. "You don't have to. It'll be easier with both of us."

"Okay," I said.

"Okay," he agreed.

I had that difficult end-of-an-argument feeling that wasn't quite catharsis, because there hadn't been enough of a blowup, and wasn't quite triumph, even though I'd technically got my own way. It was a sort of low-key not-as-nice-as-it-should-have-been sense of resolution where you were glad it was over but far too aware that it had happened. It didn't help that Oliver still had a slightly tragic look in his eyes.

"Lucien," he said after a while. "Did you…did you mean it?"

"About the dog?"

"About my thinking things are, and I quote, 'only good if they suck.'"

"No," I said and then immediately undid that by adding, "well, not exactly. It's just..." There was no easy way to sum this up. Because people were messy and life was messy and you couldn't actually explain what a person was like in a sentence or a sound bite. "Like, most of the time you're unbelievably kind and compassionate and everything, but sometimes you...I don't know, sort of forget?" Privately, I was pretty sure those *sometimes* were when he was dealing with things he knew his father would have had Very Strong Opinions about and didn't trust his own expertise enough to overrule him. But that was an argument-starting observation, not an argument-ending one.

On account of being a far better, far less defensive person than me, Oliver seemed to be genuinely thinking about what I'd said. "I like to think compassion isn't the sort of thing one just forgets about."

I tried to shrug, but my shoulders were too tightly wrapped in duvet. On the one hand, really nice of him to self-reflect. On the other hand, really annoying of him to...self-reflect. "Not *forget* forget. You just get so caught up in wanting to do the right thing that you sometimes lose sight of who it's meant to be right *for*."

He kept on self-reflecting, like a git.

"Come on," I said, half pleadingly. "You know you don't have to be perfect all the time."

That earned a small smile. "I do, in fact, accept that—though it's taken a lot of therapy to get there."

"And me," I added. "I've been helpful."

"Of course you have. But, as you pointed out yourself several years ago, it isn't the job of a romantic relationship to fix my mental health issues."

"Yeah, but"—at this point, I couldn't tell if I was being play-insecure or real-insecure—"let's not sell me short here."

Slowly, Oliver unwrapped me from my sausage roll. It wasn't

a particularly dignified process because I'd put myself in a bad-mood bundle, which meant I was lying on both edges of the duvet. Eventually, though, I was de-cocooned, and Oliver settled over me with that blend of tenderness and purpose that always reduced me to mush. Sexy mush. Doable mush. "I would never," he whispered. "Don't tell her, but I like you more than my therapist."

It had been, like, *days*. And as much as I'd missed sleeping comfortably, it was far from the *only* thing I'd missed. "Oh...oh good."

"For a start, you don't charge me by the hour."

"Maybe if I did you'd listen to me more."

Okay, so there were times to be pissy. Many times, at least if you were me. But one of those times was absolutely not just as you and your boyfriend were navigating the transition from argument to makeup sex. Thankfully, Oliver was either more mature or hornier than I was. "I deserved that," he admitted. "And I promise I'll do better in future. In fact"—his voice slipped into something more comfortable—"I might start now."

"I'm not sure I like where this is going."

He nuzzled against the side of my neck. "That's a lie, isn't it?"

"Well, obviously. But you listen to me just fine in bed."

"That doesn't mean I don't like hearing you."

I made an embarrassing whinging noise that was half into-itness and half self-consciousness. "You know I'm bad at the sex words and the 'Do me here' and 'Put that there' and 'Oh yeah baby.' And also, don't we have a dog we're responsible for?"

"You should know two things," said Oliver, very seriously. "The first is that I shall under no circumstances ever ask you to say, 'Oh yeah baby.' And the second is Spud's last bowel movement was eighteen minutes ago."

I stared up at him. "Why do I need to know that? Like, the second that. When you threaten me with dirty talk, which I may or may not be into"—I was into it—"that's not the kind of dirty I'm looking for."

Oliver blushed slightly. "I just meant, he's asleep, so we won't be interrupted."

"Then you could have told me the sleeping bit, and left out the canine scat subplot."

"I didn't want you to be concerned about his needs while we were"—Responsible Dog Owner Oliver left the room, to be replaced by Much More Interesting Oliver—"while I'm demonstrating my listening skills."

I gave a kind of squawk. "How selfless do you think I am?"

"More than you pretend to be," said Oliver, catching my wrists and pressing them firmly into the pillow.

"Well then, how easy to ignore were you planning to make this?"

"I was intending to make it very difficult."

"I don't know"—I reared up slightly and nipped at his chin—"I'm pretty easily distracted."

Oliver pushed me back down. Effortlessly because I wasn't exactly trying to resist. "I think I'll manage to hold your attention."

And he did.

He really, really did.

I'll be honest, moving the pen was a bit of a faff. But Oliver, either still glowing with post-bang satisfaction or just being his normal, annoyingly nice self, didn't say a fucking word. Spud, though, found the whole process at least a little disorientating. After all, we'd spent the last few days teaching him that this was a super-special safe space just for him, and now we were tearing it apart to put it somewhere completely different. But by the time we'd got absolutely everything—all his special blankets and all his favourite toys—upstairs and hidden some extra-special treats, his natural puppyish curiosity at being allowed into a new part of the house took over and he was happily snuffling around, exploring and looking for noms.

"Now, this isn't going to be forever." Oliver was sitting on the edge of the bed in his pyjamas, calmly explaining the situation to an attentive but oblivious Spud. "And you're still not allowed on the bed."

Spud wagged his tail. "Ruff."

"Good boy."

"Ruff," agreed Spud.

I face-planted onto the other side of the bed. The angry nap had been all well and good, but something something sleep quality something something REM.

"Now off to bed with you," Oliver concluded. "Your bed, that is."

"I'm in bed," I protested, sleepily. "I couldn't be more in bed."

"There you go. Who's a good boy?"

"Me, I'm a very good boy. I helped move the dog pen and everything."

There was a gentle creak from the bedsprings as Oliver settled beside me. "While I'm enjoying the experience of being in a comedy skit circa 1978, you are aware I'm talking to Spud?"

"Yes," I said in the pillow. "I had definitely realised that. I was just making a funny joke and am not at all exhausted."

"I'm flattered."

"Not from the sex." My protests were, if anything, getting sleepier. "Okay, a bit from the sex. But, also, like life. Stuff. Arghhh."

I was dimly aware I was moving but not quite conscious enough to work out why until Oliver had rolled me gently off the pillow and into his arms. "I know that the CRAPP situation is, well, a crap situation."

I gave a bleary laugh. “Yes. Very situation. Much crap. Wow.”

“But whatever happens, we’ll get through it together.”

Through my increasing fatigue, I mustered a feeble “Yay” and prepared to pass out. Except something was nagging at me. A left-the-oven-on sort of feeling. Or, at least, what I assumed would be a left-the-oven-on sort of feeling if I used the oven with anything approaching regularity.

“I did switch the oven off, didn’t I?” I asked.

“From the state of the roasted vegetables”—Oliver’s breath gusted across my cheek—“I’m not sure you turned it on.”

“No, no, there was smoke and everything.”

“Ah, so they were smoked vegetables.”

“Yes,” I mumbled. “It was a subtle Mediterranean flavour you didn’t appreciate.”

“Either way, everything was fine when I went to turn the lights off.”

“Okay, good.” The nagging feeling continued. “And was the front door shut?”

“Lucien, what’s going on?”

“I don’t know. Something’s…different.”

“This might be a bit of a wild guess,” said Oliver. “But is what’s different that you’re not on the floor in the study?”

Only partially with it as I was, that did make sense. “That’ll be it.” The thoughts stumbled through my brain like drunk students trying to get home at three in the morning. Then another thought stumbled straight through my brain, down my brain stem, and out my mouth. “We’re really doing this, aren’t we?”

Oliver ran his fingertips gently across my back. “Yes, yes we are.”

“All of it. Like the dog and, like…everything.”

“Yes.”

That’s nice, said my increasingly addled brain. *That’s extremely nice*. “Is Spud all right?”

Oliver kissed the back of my neck. "He's fast asleep."

"Oh," I said.

"As should you be."

And then, before I really knew what was happening, I was.

PART TWO

AUTUMN/WINTER

CHAPTER 10

"SO ALEX," I SAID, FROM my face meat into his face meat on account of the fact that, for the first time in quite a long while, we were in the same room. "What's a pirate's favourite cheese?"

Alex perked up, much like Spud did when he was offered a treat. "Ah. I know this one. You'd think it'd be *arrr*, but his first love has always been the sea."

Even by the standards of Alex Twaddle, this made no sense. "What? Are you having a stroke?"

"Don't think so. Face seems okay." He smiled. Then raised both arms. "Arms check out. Am I slurring?"

"No, I was using 'Are you having a stroke?' idiomatically to mean 'I have no idea what you're talking about.'"

"Oh." He lowered his arms. "Then I'm not having a stroke. Or rather, I suppose I am having a stroke in the figurative sense. Sorry, I think I've rather lost track of the metaphor."

"Why," I asked, knowing, as always, I should not, "would a pirate's favourite cheese be the sea?"

"Well, that's what it was last time."

I cast my mind back over the three hundred and seventy jokes I'd told Alex over the last few years and finally remembered myself in a minibus on the way to Alex's own fucking wedding. "Hang on, that was a pirate's favourite letter of the alphabet."

"Same principle applies, surely?"

"*No*," I told him. "Because there isn't a principle. They're unrelated jokes."

Alex was looking perplexed. Which I admit was his usual state. "So what *is* a pirate's favourite cheese?"

"*Yarrrr*lsberg."

"Not Seasberg?"

"*No*."

With a level of persistence substantially more dogged than my actual dog, he asked, "Why not?"

"Because there's no such cheese as Seasberg."

"There's no such cheese as Yarrrrlsberg either."

My brain was doing the mental equivalent of grabbing me by the arm and yelling, *Leave him, Luc, he's not worth it*, but like a football fan about to get arrested for being drunk and disorderly, I carried on anyway. "Yes, there is."

"What sort is it?"

There were a whole lot of skills I didn't have. Cooking, for example. Or DIY. Or speaking more than three words of French, even though it was my mother's native language. Or, apparently, describing cheese. "It's...I think it's one of the ones with holes in? It might be a bit rubbery?"

Alex got that concerned expression he used when he was trying to gaslight me into thinking the real world was the one he lived in, rather than the one I remembered having inhabited before he started talking. "Pretty sure that's Emmental."

"I think there might be more than one type of cheese with holes in it."

With fatal comprehension, Alex nodded. "And pirates like that sort of cheese?"

"Pirates," I told him very, very slowly, "like the syllable *yarrrr*."

"I suppose they do," agreed Alex, grinning. "Although in my experience, not as much as they like the syllable *sea*."

Had I just...lost? Had I, in fact, lost every time for the past eight years?

Fuck.

"See you at the meeting," I said.

"Don't you mean, yarrrr me at the meeting?" Then Alex's eyes widened. "Wait a moment. What meeting?"

"The meeting you organised?"

"Doesn't narrow it down, old boy. I organise two, maybe even three meetings a month."

I sighed. "The meeting you organised for today, where we meet the new earl and, if we're lucky, don't all lose our jobs. The meeting that took a solid six weeks to arrange because the man we're meant to be meeting *with* was, and I quote, 'not feeling it.'"

"Oh, that meeting."

I nodded and went through to what we were charitably calling our open-plan hot-desking area. In reality, it was Barbara Clench's former office, and it was open plan because it contained exactly one desk, and it was hot-desking because it contained exactly one desk. One desk that currently contained Rhys Jones Bowen.

"Hello, Luc," he said, glancing up. "You know what'd be lovely right about now? A cup of tea."

"Well hinted," I told him. "Would you like a cup of tea?"

"That'd be smashing."

"I'll have one too." That was Barbara Clench, lurking in the corner like, well, like a woman whose office had been transformed into a hot-desking area in which she no longer had space to hot-desk. "As you're making."

So I turned round and went straight back out of the office. Since working from home had become a thing, we'd downsized CRAPP HQ, which meant the bottom floor of the building was now being let to a start-up called ERECTUS, who, as far as I could tell, were building an app they couldn't describe to disrupt an industry they couldn't identify.

Technically the kitchen and toilets were a shared space, although in practice ERECTUS had felt fully entitled to slap their messaging over everything, which meant I was left making tea under a big poster declaring itself, or possibly the organisation it represented, to be **The Next Step in Digital Evolution**.

It could have been worse. It could have been sepsis.

I was just plonking teabags into mugs, several of which carried now-discarded ERECTUS slogans, and trying to decide whether I wanted to drink out of *Innovate, Iterate, Indiscriminate* or *The Future of Tomorrow, Yesterday*, when an explosive va-va-vooming made me look out the window.

What a twat, I thought, as an ecologically ruinous vintage motorbike roared past. Followed by *I wonder where that twat's going* as it stopped a little way up our road underneath the reddening leaves of an oak tree.

The amount of time I'd been at CRAPP, I should really have known better than to ask the second question. Because the rider, who was sixty-five if he was a day and had apparently decided to prioritise preserving his ash-grey mohawk over wearing a helmet, was heading straight for our front door.

An optimistic part of me that had yet to wither in the cold light of experience hoped he was here for ERECTUS. A hope that was fleetingly buoyed up when the door was answered by Horse, of Horse and Todd, ERECTUS's cofounders and, as far as I could tell, only employees. Then Horse said, "No," a single syllable he somehow managed to utter in an annoying way. Followed by "Bug people are upstairs." Which meant that this was the new Earl of Spitalhamstead, and, if I didn't move quickly, the first person he met at CRAPP would be Alex.

I moved quickly.

I did not move quickly enough.

"—sorry, old bean," Alex was saying. "Can't slot you in right now. Got rather an important visitor coming."

"Alex," I near-yelled, over the shoulder of the man who was almost certainly the very important visitor. "I think this might, in fact, be the very important visitor."

Alex scrutinised the very important visitor sceptically. I found this particularly galling because Alex never looked at things sceptically. I'd once told him they took the word *gullible* out of the dictionary, and not only had he checked, but he'd spent the rest of the day scouring bookshops for an updated edition. "Seems unlikely, Luc," he told me. "Chap seems like a fearful oik."

"Pride myself on it," said the very important visitor, in the voice of someone trying terribly hard not to sound terribly posh.

"See?" Alex gave me a triumphant nod. "Oiked by his own petard."

Right now, I could try and explain the situation to Alex or I could ignore him. And ignoring him was definitely the path of least resistance. To be fair, compared with explaining things to Alex, tunnelling through a brick wall using only my tongue would have been the path of least resistance. "This way," I said to the very important visitor, hoping to steer him into the meeting room which was also the hot-desking area which was also Barbara Clench's former office.

"What are you doing?" cried Alex. "You can't just let anyone in off the street. What will the earl think?"

"He'll think you're a prick," said the earl.

Alex drew back, genuinely affronted. "I'll thank you not to put words in the mouth of a peer of the realm."

Whether it was a mercy or an absolute kick in the balls that Rhys Jones Bowen chose this moment to come out and check on us, I couldn't say.

"Hello," he said. "What's going on out here then?"

"I'm pretty sure," I replied at full stop-Alex-getting-a-word-in-edgeways speed, "that this is the new Earl of Spitalhamstead."

Rhys Jones Bowen's eyes widened. "Ooh. You look very cool for an earl."

"Thanks," said the earl, sticking his hand out. "Saint."

"That's very kind of you." Rhys Jones Bowen took the hand and shook it warmly. "But I'm just a friendly sort of person."

"Name," said the Earl of Spitalhamstead, who apparently went by Saint and was allergic to sentences.

Rhys Jones Bowen made a misplaced sound of comprehension. "Ahhhh. Rhys Jones Bowen. What's yours?"

"Saint," said Saint.

"Look"—Alex returned to the conversation like an unnecessary 90s reboot—"an earl you may or may not be—"

"He's a fucking earl," I growled.

"—but my friend here has asked you a perfectly civil question, and you're just saying the word *saint* over and over again like you're my uncle Archibald after that unfortunate incident with the croquet mallet."

"My name," repeated the earl with, honestly, less frustration than I would have shown in his place, "is Saint."

"Ah hah!" exclaimed Alex. "So you *are* an imposter. The Earl of Spitalhamstead is certainly not named Saint. You may consult *Burke's* if you need to."

"My name," repeated the Earl, now with about the same amount of frustration I would have shown in his place, "is Hilary Topwith St. John Edmonton Bloom de Lancy, fourteenth Earl of Spitalhamstead. I go by Saint."

"Whatever for?" asked Alex.

"Because of men like my father and my grandfather and my great-grandfather and you."

Having failed to get the *We need to make this man like us* memo, despite having personally sent it, Alex bristled. "I'll have you know, I knew your father, and he was a damn fine chap."

"He was a parasite," said Saint bitterly. "Like all the rest of them."

I'd been doing this job long enough that I didn't have to try very hard to resist asking who the rest of them were and why he—having just inherited a fortune, a peerage, and a dung beetle charity—wasn't one of them.

"Who—" began Rhys Jones Bowen.

I clapped my hands. "Let's get to the meeting."

At exactly ten o'clock, Dr. Fairclough walked through the door of the meeting room/hot-desking area/Barbara Clench's old office. At exactly one minute past ten we were all sitting down while Alex started trying to load Dr. Fairclough's PowerPoint. Eight minutes later, while Alex was still trying to load the PowerPoint, Dr. Fairclough said, "Perhaps we can do without visual aids for now."

"Nearly there." Alex switched on the projector to show the room his desktop wallpaper, which was apparently the Twaddle coat of arms: argent, on two bars wavy azure, two fish rampant gardant. "Just trying to find the file. I knew it was important, so I moved it this morning for safekeeping."

"Thank you for joining us," Dr. Fairclough continued, addressing herself almost exclusively to the earl, who was eating a Jaffa Cake with an expression of epic unimpressedness. "I'm Dr. Fairclough, head of the Coleoptera Research and Protection Project, and I wanted to take this time to outline for you some of the vital work we do here at the Coleoptera Research and Protection Project and how it contributes to the ecological and agricultural stability of the British Isles."

Behind her, Alex had finally found something to show us. Unfortunately, what he'd found was a selfie he'd taken in Mustique with Miffy, his heiress It-girl wife.

Dr. Fairclough glanced briefly over her shoulder, then back at the earl. "Geotrupidae…" she began, and my heart sank. No successful fundraising pitch ever began with the word *Geotrupidae*. "… are an integral part of—"

"I'm going to stop you there," said Saint.

"I'd rather you didn't," returned Dr. Fairclough.

He finished his Jaffa Cake, swung back his chair, and thunked his boots on the table. "I just don't want to waste your time. Truth is, bugs were the old man's thing, not mine."

"Bugs," said Dr. Fairclough, "as you call them, are everybody's thing, for reasons I am about to explain in some detail."

My heart stopped sinking, but only because it had hit the bottom of the Mariana Trench. Pitches that began with the word *Geotrupidae* had a marginally higher success rate than pitches that included the phrase *I am about to explain in some detail*.

"Look"—Saint gave the kind of dismissive hand wave that only the terminally overprivileged could give—"I appreciate everything you're trying to do, but you're not going to convince me that beetles are more important than schools, hospitals, or a cure for cancer."

I bit my tongue incredibly hard. Because once somebody played the *schools, hospitals, and cures for cancer* card, it was *very* hard to get them back onto the importance of dung beetles without ever so slightly implying that they were up their own arse. The thing is, ten seconds' thought would tell you that CRAPP's annual operating budget, translated into school, hospital, and cure-for-cancer money, would buy you half a classroom, one clinic bed, or a tenth of a drug trial that would almost certainly go nowhere. But it was funny how few people reacted well to being told that their grand plans to solve the world's problems were glorified vanity projects. And although it was unfair of me to judge, I had a feeling that Saint was an absolute sucker for a glorified vanity project.

If only we had one to sell him.

"*Cancer*," said Dr. Fairclough, "is an umbrella term describing a set of distinct but related conditions that are highly unlikely to be responsive to a single treatment."

I somehow succeeded in not slamming my face flat onto the table in front of me. "What she means," I tried, "is that cancer already attracts a lot of research funding, and if you want your money to make a real difference, smaller charities like ours can do proportionally more with the same resources."

"I understand what you're saying." Saint was nodding in that indulgent but unyielding way I saw a lot in this job. And not normally from people who wound up as donors. "But, cards on the table, I'm finding it very hard to get excited about insects who eat shit."

He had me there. CRAPP's whole funding model relied heavily on people who were the exact right combination of environmentally conscious and charmingly eccentric.

"Excitement," I tried, very much aware it was a desperation gambit, "isn't *strictly* required to patronise a charity."

Saint nodded again. It was a slow, deliberate nod that said *I hear you* but was lying about it. "I've got a profile," he said. "A platform and property. I know I could be a real advocate for the right movement, but right now, there's a whole lot tied up in"—he made that dismissive, encompassing gesture again—"*this*."

For the first time since Saint had walked through the door, Alex found a space of sympathy with him. "Oh now, when you put it like that, it *is* a bit of a sticky wicket, isn't it? Fellow can't have all of a fellow's cash tied up in one investment. Why, only the other day I was saying to Miffy, 'Miffy,' I was saying, 'do we really need *two* houses in the Maldives? What if something comes up and we wind up short on readies?'"

"See," said Saint, whose antiestablishment credentials were only slightly dented by his taking Alex's spare-villa probs as completely normal, "he gets it. And you're all going to have to get it because at the end of the day, it's my decision."

"Of course," I said and was honestly thankful that Saint cut me off before I could get to a *but* with no follow-up.

"I'm a fair man," Saint concluded, demonstrating that fairest of all fair instincts, a strong desire to tell people how fair he was. "I'll give you a year to wrap things up, find new jobs, all the rest of it. It's a tough economy, and I wouldn't want to be an arsehole."

"Jolly considerate of you." That was Alex, who had apparently forgiven Saint for his oikishness now he was demonstrating an appropriate level of entitlement and arrogance. "Still, bit rough on the old man's legacy, don'tcha think? I mean, Hilary did love his beetles."

"Fuck his legacy. You know what he told me when I said I was dropping out of Oxford to take my band on the road?"

"What?" I asked with instincts honed over several years of being professionally required to pay attention to rich people's bullshit.

"He said, 'That's not the sort of thing de Lancys do.'" Saint frowned into the past with the intensity of a man who'd been carrying a grudge for forty years. "Financed it myself in the end. Had to sell my Bentley."

Alex looked horrified. "Oh, I *say*."

I was ninety-nine percent sure this was fucked no matter what happened, but my job was all about living in the one percent. "That was really wrong of him," I tried, "but if you're doing this just to get back at your dead father, then—I don't know, is that the kind of person you want to be?"

Saint got up from the table with a slow forcefulness that you really had to be a sixty-something-year-old independently wealthy anarchist to pull off. "Yeah," he said. And walked out.

We stared at the remaining Jaffa Cakes for, I don't know, a while.

"Well," said Rhys Jones Bowen at last, "that could have gone better."

CHAPTER 11

ON SATURDAY, I SCHLUMPED DOWNSTAIRS in my schlumping boxers, only to discover that Oliver was up, dressed and ready, with Spud wriggling in his harness.

"Shit," I said. "Is it Big Walk Day already?"

Oliver glanced up with a playful smirk. "No, I'm just introducing our puppy to the leather scene."

"Hey. Spud is far too young for that, even in dog years."

"Ruff," said Spud. Oliver, being Oliver, had been getting Spud used to the harness for the best part of a week, which unfortunately meant he was so comfortable that he thought nothing of zooming around the study, knocking over the wastepaper basket as he went.

"Sorry." I ran a hand through my even-more-chaotic-than-usual hair. "I just...with everything...I forgot."

"Lucien, it's fine." Oliver gazed at me with that horrible, endlessly understanding sincerity that I knew I'd never take for granted because that would involve believing I deserved it. "If you're not feeling up to it, we can go another time."

"What?" I cried. "No. He's worked super hard for this. He's communicating his poo needs, he's started sleeping downstairs, he's had all his injections, and he was a really good boy during the injections..."

"He was a better boy than you were."

"I was concerned. Those were big needles. He's a small dog."

Oliver gently extricated Spud from the wastepaper basket. "As intelligent as he may be, I don't think Spud is especially motivated by long-term incentives."

"But you've put his harness on. We've spent all week teaching him that means something good, and now you're going to dash his little canine hopes."

"True," Oliver conceded. "I'd rather Spud's hopes remained undashed, at least while he's at such a tender age. I can take him by myself if that's easier."

"I don't want to let you down," I plaintived. "Either of you."

"It's Saturday—you're entitled to a day off, and my emotional well-being is not tied to whether you sit out one of the many walks that now lie in our future."

"But it's Spud's first proper walk. With, like, a park and a real risk of seeing rabbits and other dogs and things. I can't miss that. That'd be like missing his first birthday or his first word."

"If Spud has a first word, we'll have bigger problems than whether you miss it or not."

Spud had finally decided I was more interesting than the carpet and trotted over to say hello. "I suppose," I mused, as I bent to ruffle his ears, "he's had his first word, and it's *ruff*."

"Ruff," agreed Spud.

"I think"—Oliver fished out the lead and clipped it deftly to the harness—"that's technically a vocalisation."

"I think *you're* technically a vocalisation," I told him. Very maturely.

He lifted a brow. "Have you been talking to Colin again?"

"He bugs me when Spud's pooing."

"I still think he's just testing your boundaries."

"He's not testing my boundaries," I protested. "He's being a little shit."

"He's a child."

"Yeah, and some children are shits. That's, like, a basic child fact."

I didn't like to think Oliver looked sanctimonious, but he was beginning to look sanctimonious. "If you think of him as a shit, he'll live down to your expectations."

Internally, I would die on the hill of Next Door's Kid's little-shit status. But it wasn't an argument I wanted to have with my partner on a Saturday morning in my schlumping pants on what was supposed to be Big Walk Day. So I just said "I guess" and then "Give me a second" and went upstairs to change.

One pair of slightly less schlumpy pants, a pair of actual trousers, and a marginally better T-shirt later, Oliver, Spud, and I were on our way to the park.

"Morning, Mr. Blackwood," called Next Door's Kid cheerily.

"Good morning, Colin," Oliver called back, turning briefly to wave and then turning back just in time to miss the look of pure, satanic evil that Next Door's Kid shot me a moment later.

One of the things that had sold us on the house when we were first looking at it was that we were within a street-and-a-half's distance of a very pretty park. At the time we hadn't quite articulated to ourselves what we might want a very pretty park *for*, other than that it seemed like a good thing to have access to. I think we'd vaguely assumed it would be nice to go for walks in. Possibly dog-related walks in, although that was slightly before we'd had the whole *Is a dog a thing that is an* us *thing?* conversation and the increasingly uncoded *Is a dog actually a trial run for something more bipedal?* conversation. Of course, in practice we'd never gone for an actual walk in it because as soon as you live in a place, you start blithely ignoring everything that made you want to live in that place to begin with.

So, it felt pretty vindicating to finally be taking our puppy to the park that we'd each secretly dreamed we'd one day take a puppy to. It was one of those crisp autumn mornings, with a pale blue sky and ducks pissing about on the lake, and Spud was skipping around ecstatically like he'd never been out of doors in his life. Which, now I thought about it, he mostly hadn't, unless you counted short training walks and being taken outside to make an entry in the Defecation Chronicle. Of course, that did mean from his perspective we'd essentially taken him into a massive massive toilet. In fact, from Spud's perspective, the whole world was a massive massive toilet.

And, honestly, I could relate.

"Are you all right?" asked Oliver.

"Yeah," I said. "I'm just thinking how from Spud's perspective, the world's a massive massive toilet."

"Lucien, I don't even know where to begin with that."

"How about telling me how extremely charming and quirky I am."

"Truly"—Oliver cast his gaze dreamily upwards—"I don't know how I lived so many years without realising that the one thing I needed to complete me was a man who would tell me that, from our dog's perspective, the whole world is a massive massive toilet."

"Okay," I said. "But it is. And you do."

He adjusted his grip on Spud's lead and took my hand. "You're right. I do."

"And it is."

"And," he admitted reluctantly, "it is."

"Ruff," said Spud, affirming the toiletness of the cosmos. Like, verbally. He didn't demonstrate. Though, of course, my sexy barrister boyfriend had a pocketful of poo bags anyway.

As we strolled along, Spud frolicking joyfully in his massive massive toilet, I tried to enjoy the moment and not think too much about how Next Door's Kid was a sociopathic master manipulator or how a punk earl was about to destroy my livelihood or how that one guy—that one highly attractive guy jogging towards us right now—was definitely checking Oliver out.

I mean, I didn't blame him because Oliver was a smokeshow and a bag of chips, especially when he was all relaxed and wearing one of his well-fitted cream jumpers. Okay, also when he was not at all relaxed and wearing a suit because he had to stop an innocent person going to prison or something. And also all the other times. Anyway, point was, someone was checking out my boyfriend, and it was extremely cool because my boyfriend wasn't checking him out back.

Which meant, after all these years, I'd won at gay.

Oliver gave me a curious look, probably because he'd caught me smiling, and while he saw me smiling more than most people, it was never going to be my usual state. "You seem happy."

Even I knew it was slightly unclassy to boast to your boyfriend that he was so into you he didn't realise how hot other people found him. So I kind of flailed. "Oh, I just…remembered something."

"What sort of something?"

"It was back when we were doing that whole dating-but-not-dating-but-dating business."

"Ah yes." Oliver smiled. "A time in our lives when we were both behaving extremely sensibly."

"For verisimilitude," I reminded him.

He nodded. "Naturally."

"Right. Well, as part of my extremely sensible and verisimilitudinous behaviour back then, I…" Actually, maybe I should have just told him about Attractive Jogging Guy. Fuck. "I mean, you were just very casually being the best thing that had ever happened to me, and I couldn't imagine ever being, like, worth it—"

"Lucien," he said, in this faintly chiding way that I found oddly romantic because it meant he truly couldn't imagine thinking as little of me as I used to think of myself.

"Anyway, as well as all the other shit you were pointlessly good at, you turned out to be amazing with Judy's dogs."

"Ruff," said Spud.

"Not you," I explained. "Different dogs."

"Mruff."

"And"—I turned back to my boyfriend—"in that moment I built this whole scenario in my head about how you were going to get a dog with three legs and you'd be walking your dog with three legs in some park and then some guy would come up to you in the park you were in with your dog with three legs and he'd be all, 'Wow, it's really nice of you to be looking after a three-legged dog,' and you'd be like, 'Yes, I'm just kind of amazing like that.'"

Even in my head, this had sounded pretty bad. It was way worse in my actual mouth. I was sort of hoping Oliver would do the merciful thing and let me drop it. But he seemed far too amused. "And what do I do," he asked, "after I tell a complete stranger how amazing I am?"

"Obviously," I went on helplessly, "he'd be all, 'I find that very sexy, let's bang,' and you'd bail on me and get with Three-Leg-Dog-Park-Kindness-Is-Sexy Guy and you'd have this great life while I was found dead under a pile of empty pizza boxes."

Somehow Oliver contrived to look meltingly affectionate while also making it clear I was talking absolute bollocks. "I can see why this was making you so happy," he said. "You always did love pizza."

"It's not about the pizza." Two seconds ago, I'd been desperate to talk about literally anything else. But I'd come this far. I was seeing the weird three-legged dog pizza death story to the end, no matter what it cost. "It's about how, you know, we're here and it's years later and stuff. So now *we're* in the park with *our* three-legged dog, and Kindness-Is-Sexy Guy can't have you...because...because me."

Oliver gazed at me for a long moment, then looked down at

Spud and said, very seriously, "Don't worry. I won't let Daddy Lucien cut your leg off."

"He's metaphorically three-legged." I pouted.

"Thank you," said Oliver. "This is a very romantic way of pretending you weren't checking that jogger out earlier."

"What? No. Our eyes met as we were mutually checking *you* out."

"It's okay to look at other men, Lucien. I'm not threatened. After all, we have a metaphorically three-legged dog together."

"Ruff," said Spud, apparently happy with his metaphorically three-legged status.

There was no way to keep debating this without sounding mega defensive. But I kept debating it anyway. "No, no. Hang on. I agree with you that neither of us should be threatened because dog, five years, etcetera. And I agree looking isn't cheating, but I genuinely wasn't looking. He just—"

"Slipped and fell on your eyeballs?"

"He wanted you. He totally wanted to do you, right there and then. He wanted to have dirty hot sex with you in this, um, nice family park."

"Morning," said Oliver to a passing dog walker, who was politely pretending she hadn't heard the dirty hot sex talk. "Anyway," he went on, as we wandered down the lake, "I'm very flattered, but I don't think I'm the sort of man joggers check out in parks."

"Oh my God. Which part of the three-legged dog story were you not listening to? You're totally the sort of man joggers check out in parks. Have you seen yourself lately? You're all wholesome and handsome, and clearly up for fucking someone into the mattress."

"Morning," said Oliver to an elderly man and his grandchildren. And then, to me, "I think you're operating from a position of bias."

I mean, I was. But I was also right. On the other hand, this had strayed from reminding Oliver how special he was to me to an argument about whether strangers wanted to do him or not. "Doesn't mean I'm wrong," I insisted, only slightly smugly.

Oliver paused for a moment, allowing Spud to tangle us together in the lead. He leaned in and kissed me in a Saturday-morning-in-public-appropriate way. "I love you."

Taken by surprise, I accidentally blushed. "Oh fuck off."

He laughed and we stood there with Spud gambolling around us, and for a moment I was just filled with this terrifying sense of absolutely-perfect-ness because we were here in our park with our dog on our lazy morning walk, and it was everything I'd never dreamed of because I'd never believed I'd be able to have it and—

"Fuck," I said. "I'm going to lose my job."

CHAPTER 12

WE BOTH KNEW, OF COURSE, what the deal was, CRAPP-wise. We'd known for ages that it was, at the very least, at risk. But saying it out loud, baldly, plainly, and in those exact words—*I'm going to lose my job*—had sort of helped. I mean, I was still an absolute mess but at least I was now an absolute mess who'd articulated a small part of his messiness. Plus it meant Oliver went straight into supportive-and-comforting mode.

He smoothed my brow with his un-dog-occupied hand. "Not for at least a year."

"Yeah, but—but—it's *my job*."

"I know."

"I don't even *like* my job."

He—or rather, the mix of his arm and Spud's lead—gave me a little squeeze. "I don't think that's anywhere near as true as it used to be, and I don't think it used to be particularly true at all."

"What am I going to do?" The part of my brain that absolutely refused to admit my life could be in a good place was going into overdrive. "Find some *other* tiny quirky charity that nobody cares about in need of a fundraiser?"

From the way Oliver was looking at me, I could tell I'd failed some pretty basic parts of rhetorical question construction. "Well," he said. "You *could* do that. It sounds like that might actually be quite a straightforward thing to do, in fact."

"I know, but—"

"Which doesn't mean," he added, "that it isn't scary. Because change is always scary, and I do realise that as somebody who works in a job with a uniform that hasn't been updated since the mid-seventeenth century, I'm not really one to lecture people on embracing newness. But we'll manage, Lucien. We have each other and Spud and a nice house that we can comfortably afford even on one income and—"

"You think we might have to drop down to one income?" My inner drama llama was latching on to whatever it could, and it was taking me along with it.

"I think if we did, it wouldn't be the end of the world. You're already working from home most days, and Spud needs somebody to look after him."

I frowned. "You're saying I should be a house husband?"

"I'm saying we have options. I'm not expecting you to have dinner waiting for me every night when I get home or saying you should be waking me up with French toast every morning." He gave a frown of his own. "Especially not after how it went last time. All I mean is that there comes a point where you can stop running because you're there. And we're—I don't want to presume—but you are very much my *there*, and I hope I'm yours, and everything we do together now is just...it's whatever we make it."

This was very...nice and stuff. Except my brain was still only about sixty percent trained to accept nice and stuff. "Are you seriously telling me that back when we met, you looked at me and the shithole of my life and thought, 'That's someone I want to try and make a home with'?"

"Well"—Oliver stepped delicately over Spud's lead before he pulled us into the lake—"no. I mostly thought, 'There's someone who's far too cool and interesting for me.'"

"Oh I see," I protested, mostly jokingly. "But you don't think that anymore. Now you know how shit and boring I am."

"Yes." Oliver nodded gravely. "I've stayed with you all these years because of how shit and boring you are. Morning," he added to a young woman with pink hair and a dachshund. "Obviously," he went on, "I've never stopped thinking you're cool and interesting. You've just also been good for my self-esteem."

"That does sound like me," I said, because I knew there came a point where my refusal to admit I had positive qualities stopped being cute and started being fucking annoying.

"Besides"—he gently removed a ladybird from my shoulder and deposited it on a nearby leaf—"irrespective of our mutual incapacity to accept that we live up to the standards set by the other, isn't making a home together what we're doing? And have been doing for actually quite a long time now."

I looked at my feet. Which meant I was also looking at Spud, which helped in some ways. "Okay, but if I don't have to make French toast or learn to cook or remember to pick up my coffee cups—"

"I *would* like it if you remembered to pick up your coffee cups," Oliver pointed out, "whether you stay working or not."

"If I don't have to do any of that"—I broke off because Oliver was giving me a stern look—"any of that except the coffee cup thing, then all I'll be doing is looking after a dog. My whole life will be looking after a dog. I'll get…I don't know, whatever the dog-related not-a-Muppet-on-a-boat version of cabin fever is. And then I'll have no choice but to start an Instagram dedicated to my dog. This is *exactly* how people start Instagrams dedicated to their dogs. I'll have been out of work for two weeks and Spud will be all dyed weird colours and dressed in tiny outfits I've bought off Etsy and our whole downstairs will be full of props I've been using for my Dogstagram tableaux and—"

"You *might*," Oliver suggested, "be overthinking this."

"I'm not overthinking this," I yelled. "These are incredibly obvious consequences of me losing my job because of an anarchist peer and having nothing left to care about except a dog."

We'd come to a pretty bench overlooking the lake, and with a suspicious casualness, Oliver sat down. "You wouldn't be left with nothing to care about except Spud."

"And you," I added, loyally. Then my brain caught up with my ears as I realised he'd been using his *leading* tone, not his *playfully chiding* tone. "Oh. You mean…"

He smiled reassuringly. "It *was* always the plan."

"It was, but…" I sat down next to him. At my feet, Spud gazed up at us with the unquestioning faith and adoration you only saw in dogs and children and other people who didn't know any better.

"But what?"

I thought about it for a moment. "Actually," I admitted, "I have no *but*. I was just *butting* out of habit. This was the plan. This is the plan. The plan is this."

"Even so. The plan—as this and as present as it may be—doesn't have to be binding if you don't feel ready."

For a while I distracted myself, fuddling with Spud's ears. Then I glanced up, at all the many and varied families playing happily in the sunlight. And I noticed something, something unexpected. "You've met me," I pointed out. "Have I *ever* felt ready? For anything?"

"No," conceded Oliver. And then, he got this *look* in his eye. A look that said he'd noticed the same thing I'd just noticed. Which was that I wasn't having my usual freak-out. "But am I right in thinking you're using that in the positive sense?"

At my feet, Spud was *ruffing* impatiently. He'd signed up for walkies, not for sitties. And definitely not for sit-while-Daddy-Luc-and-Daddy-Oliver-have-an-intense-conversationies. "I guess so? I mean, I wasn't exactly feeling ready for this one either."

"Mruff," said this one.

"And he seems all right, doesn't he?" I gestured at exhibit D. *D* for *dog*. "He doesn't seem totally fucked up for life or anything?"

Oliver sighed very slightly. "Lucien, your faith in your capacity to totally fuck things up for life sometimes borders on the hubristic."

"Thanks, I've worked really hard on it."

"Spud is a perfectly well-adjusted normal happy puppy. We are, in fact, a good team."

He was right. Our dog was fine. We were fine. Everything was fine. "And you think we're a good enough team to, y'know..."

"Play doubles badminton?"

"Oliver."

"Scam our friends at bridge?"

"No. You know."

"I do know," said Oliver, archly. "But, as with so many things, if you're going to do it, you should probably be able to say it."

There he was, being right again. Like a dick. "Fine. Kids. The kid thing. Do you think we're a good enough team to do the kid thing? Do you want to do the kid thing with me?"

It would be a lie to say it was the happiest I'd ever seen Oliver look, because one of the weird things about being a decent way into a stable and functioning relationship was that if you were doing it right, you made each other happy a fair amount. But he looked at least as happy as he did when I picked my socks up without prompting, which was pretty fucking happy. "Yes, Lucien. I do."

And, on one level, that wasn't news. We'd had the hypothetical version of this conversation about a million times. Okay twice. But, either way, this was different. Because we had a dog now. And that made it real. That made everything real. "Okay," I said. "Great. Cool." And, then, cool and great as all this was, there was also realness to deal with. "Um. How do we actually, like, *get* a kid? Actually?"

Oliver twitched up a sardonic eyebrow. "Well, you see, when a mummy and daddy love each other very much but also lack the material and social capital to support their family—"

"Very funny," I told him. "Yes, yes, everything is part of a complex system and blah blah ethics. But since we're doing this—and we are doing this—how do we…do this?"

"Lucien," said Oliver, laughing in a bemused way, "two of your closest friends adopted a child comparatively recently."

"Yeah, but I wasn't paying attention."

"Of course you—" He broke off. "Spud, no."

Obediently, Spud stopped trying to eat the—on second thoughts, I probably didn't want to know what he'd been trying to eat; I just quietly pretended it was a fallen leaf—and bounced back to accept a treat from Oliver's hand.

"Good boy," he concluded.

Spud stared at me.

"You've just had a treat. You don't get double treats just because there's two of us."

"Arrooou," said Spud, visibly disappointed.

He was then immediately distracted by a duck. It must be nice to be a dog.

"In any case," Oliver went on, "we have several options, none of them without their challenges."

"Okay," I said, trying not to be too proud of myself for not immediately giving up at the mention of challenges.

"So there's adoption like James and James, and although you say you weren't paying attention, you have seen roughly what that looks like."

"You mean, kind of like a wet goblin?"

"The process, Lucien. There's a lot of paperwork and it takes a long time, and my understanding is that while adoption rates are down, the greatest need isn't for people who want a new baby; it's for people who are willing to take a child over the age of three."

"Would that be so bad?"

"Not necessarily. Although by that stage a child's personality is taking a more concrete shape, and any trauma they've experienced is much more likely to cause significant problems."

I pressed a hand to my heart. "Wow, what a beautiful experience this is going to be for us."

"I know you're being sarcastic, but it's incredibly important to have realistic expectations. After all, it's not just our life it's about."

"God, the James Royce-Royces made it seem so easy."

He cast me a sharp look. "You really weren't paying attention, were you? It took them years and quite a lot of money."

"So"—I winced—"option two, then?"

"There's surrogacy."

"Like ask Bridge?"

"No," Oliver replied, "we definitely shouldn't ask Bridget."

"She'd probably say yes."

"Which is why we shouldn't ask her. Leaving aside that she only gave birth a couple of months ago, it would be extremely emotionally complicated, and could hurt all of us very badly. It's not like asking Priya if we could borrow her truck."

"Priya would never let us borrow her truck."

"You're right, that was a poor analogy. My point is, being a surrogate means doing something arduous and intimate for nine months and, at the end of it, giving away a baby to whom you may well have developed an emotional connection. And, of course, for some people it's the right choice, but it's a very big choice and you need to be very careful who you ask to make it."

That was *beyond* fair. Because yes, Bridge was, you know, a human being with agency and a grown-ass woman who could make her own choices. But when somebody would do literally anything for you, you had to be really careful with your anythings. "When you put it like that," I said, "it seems a weird thing to ask a stranger for as well."

Oliver gave a tiny shrug. "That's a little more complicated, and I try to avoid second-guessing the motivations of people I don't know. But if the idea makes you uncomfortable, we probably shouldn't pursue it."

I felt almost as relieved as I had when we'd decided not to get married. "Okay, so what's option three?"

From the look on Oliver's face, I already knew the answer. "There is no option three."

"So it's a complicated, difficult adoption or nothing?"

From the very slightly *different* look on Oliver's face, I knew there was something else. But I also knew it wasn't necessarily the something else I was hoping for. "Now that you mention it..." he began.

"What?" It came out snappier than I meant, but this had been a frighteningly grown-up talk about some heavy topics, and I was starting to wish I could go back to making three-legged dog jokes again.

"Well, I think it might be worth pointing out that when you look into adoption, a lot of the institutions involved will provide information about adoption *and fostering*."

I didn't know what magic it was that let Oliver remind me how little I understood without making me feel like an ignorant prick. But he managed it. "I'm going to have to ask you what the difference is, aren't I?"

"They overlap," Oliver began, which was often his way of starting this kind of explanation, since it let me feel better about having got the overlapping things mixed up. "Especially if you're talking about older children. But broadly the difference is that adoption is permanent, and the child legally becomes your child for all intents and purposes. Fostering can be long term, but you're only looking after the child, and legally speaking, your obligations to them end at the point they return to their family, turn eighteen, or get adopted by somebody else."

I could always tell when Oliver had been thinking about something, and he'd clearly been thinking about this. Even he wouldn't have had that much information just off the top of his head. "I'm going to go out on a limb," I said carefully, "and guess that you want us to foster."

Oliver gave a surprisingly hesitant nod. "I know it's not what people first think of when they think about..."

"Kids?" I suggested.

"Exactly. But there *is* an unequivocal need for foster families. It's a very overlooked part of the system. Because of, well, because of how people who want to expand their family by nontraditional routes tend to be looking for babies rather than older children or teenagers."

This was shaping up to be the most Oliver thing ever. At least, I hoped it was shaping up to be the most Oliver thing ever because the alternative was that Oliver thought that it was the most Luc thing ever, and that might have gone to some awkward places. "Just to check, you want to do this because, like, ethics and shit. Not because you think having a kid we get to give back at some point will be safer with my commitment issues?"

"Absolutely not." Oliver sounded reassuringly firm. "I'd like to do this, but it won't be a trial run or a soft option. It'll be hard, but I think it'll also be rewarding."

It was a beautiful day and I was in a beautiful park with my amazing boyfriend and my adorable dog, and so I allowed myself, in this highly specific and controlled environment, to be performatively crap. Just for a moment. "You know I *hate* hard-but-rewarding."

Oliver gave me a not-the-time look.

"Okay, okay, I'm probably fine with hard-but-rewarding, actually. But I have a relentlessly negative self-image to keep up, and you're making it really difficult right now."

To my relief, Oliver laughed at that. "Duly noted. Although for what it's worth, I really think we'd be good foster parents. I think it's the right step for us."

I'd not looked into things the way Oliver had looked into things. I'd not read the books or watched the videos or done the courses. But I trusted him. And I loved him. And I wanted this. "Yeah," I said. "Yeah, I think so too."

CHAPTER 13

WE'D LOOKED AT SOME LITERATURE (Oliver always had Literature) that evening, and it had turned out that fostering, while not as long and complicated a process as adopting or surrogacy, was still a pretty long and complicated process. Over the next couple of days, we'd talked about it some more, then talked about it some more some more, because it wasn't a decision to be uncertain about, and then filled out some application forms, and now we were… waiting, I guess.

Waiting, looking after our dog, and going back to work. Before work exploded forever.

"Okay," I said to Alex over Zoom, a good couple of weeks into the waiting process. I was wearing trousers this time because I do *sometimes* learn from my mistakes. "What cheese do you use to lure a bear out of a cave?"

Alex, once more dressed as somebody from a historical era mostly notable for its extraordinarily tight trousers, made an intense, thinking face. "I suppose it depends on the bear. What you'd probably want to do is find a chap who has a bear hound, maybe round up a few fellows who are handy with a rifle, and just wait for it to come out on its own. Unless it's in the winter, of course; then you can catch the blighter napping."

Note to self: Don't try to tell Alex a joke about something a posh person is likely to have actually done. Like bear hunting. Or polo. Or throwing poor people in rivers for fun. "Okay, but suppose that in this scenario, you're not aiming to kill the bear—"

"Bit of a rum hunting party if you aren't."

"Let's assume you're with Greenpeace."

"Bunch of interfering stick-in-the-muds if you ask me."

I hadn't been asking him especially. "Okay, but let's say that in this imaginary, purely-for-the-joke situation, you're not trying to kill the bear. You're just trying to get it to come out of its cave. Using cheese."

Alex thought again. "Well, it takes rather a lot of bait to lure a bear anywhere, and you'd probably need to leave it around for some time, and that'd be a deuced waste of good cheese. But"—he raised a finger in a misguided gesture of confidence—"assuming we're also ignoring that for joke purposes, I suppose you'd want something strong-smelling. Maybe a Camembert?"

Why did he always do this to me? Why did I *let* him do this to me? Did I just hate myself even more than I thought? "Umm," I said. "Yes. Sort of."

"Sort of? Is it supposed to be more a gouda or a Port Salut? Humboldt Fog?"

"No, I mean Camembert is the right answer, but you need to *say* it properly."

"Camembert?" said Alex in a surprisingly good French accent.

"No, more like"—this was going to end badly. It was going to end incredibly badly—"*Cam-on-bear!*"

Alex looked genuinely appalled. "Luc! Your French master must have been ghastly. How do you talk to people on the Riviera?"

"Slowly and loudly," I replied, then followed it up at once with, "But no, it's the *joke*. It's… It's *Cam-on-bear*. Because it sounds like *come on, b—*"

"Did I miss anything important?" asked Barbara Clench,

logging in from what looked like the front porch of a cottage with climbing roses around the door.

"Absolutely not," I replied at the same time as Alex said, "Luc's going bear hunting."

"No," said Barbara Clench, witheringly. "He isn't."

"He was looking for tips about bait."

"No," said Barbara Clench, witheringly. "He wasn't."

Alex looked borderline affronted. "He was asking what kind of cheese was best to get a bear out of a cave."

"*Cam-on-bear*," Barbara Clench said. "Now, are we here to discuss bear cheese or have a meeting?"

"Have a meeting," replied Dr. Fairclough, who had logged on at exactly 10:00 and zero seconds. As usual.

"Shouldn't we wait for Rhys?" I didn't especially want to, but I thought we should at least reject the idea formally.

Dr. Fairclough blinked once. "No. Now, I suggest we commence. Given our circumstances, these proceedings should be rather short. We will continue with our existing commitments as normal, and, in the event that a new patron is not forthcoming, we will go our separate ways a year from now."

It was a bit of a downer—okay, check that, quite a *lot* of a downer—to have the boss being quite so calm about the end of all our jobs, her own career, and, given the way she talked about the importance of dung beetles, all life as we knew it. Then again, that was Dr. Fairclough for you. Being calm about things was basically her whole deal.

"C.R.A.P.P. will begin implementing redundancy consultation immediately," added Barbara Clench. "Any of you—any of us—who feel we may need support in seeking new work shouldn't hesitate to ask for it."

"What sort of support?" I asked, partly because I might need it, partly because I didn't have a lot of faith in the kind of support I was going to get from an organisation that would hire Alex, Rhys Jones Bowen, or, for that matter, me.

"Interview practice," she said. Normally, I resented Barbara Clench doing her job, but today I could tell she resented it as much as I did, and that took a lot of the fun out of it. "CV tips. References, obviously. I know it isn't a lot, Luc, but we really are doing what we can."

I'd normally have had a witty comeback. Okay, a snappy comeback. Okay, a pissy comeback. But right then I was just too sad and defeated.

"Arroou?" said Spud at my feet. And I nodded.

"I know," I told Barbara. "I'm just—this is really *it*, isn't it?"

Dr. Fairclough nodded. "Definitionally."

"Pour one out, I guess?"

A look of flummoxation settled onto Alex's face, displacing its previous look of bafflement. "One what?"

Fuck me, I think I was actually going to miss this. "A drink, I think?"

"Really, Luc," replied Alex with a tone of admonishment. "This isn't a time to be celebrating. We're losing our jobs."

"I didn't mean in a celebrating way," I tried to explain. "Pour one out is—"

Explaining idioms to Alex never went well for me, so it was actually kind of a relief when Rhys Jones Bowen appeared on-screen. He was wearing a T-shirt with a photorealistic picture of a much-more-shredded-than-the-real-Rhys-Jones-Bowen chest and abs printed on it. "Hello," he said cheerily. "What did I miss?"

"Luc was asking about bear hunting and celebrating us all losing our jobs," Alex informed him, pouting indignantly.

"I was doing neither of those things," I said, then, to forestall an argument, followed up with, "Technical issues?"

For a moment the assembled CRAPPers tried to figure out who

I was saying *technical issues* to, but Rhys eventually concluded I meant him and, over a slightly laggy connection, said, "Oh. No actually, everything worked like a dream this time. But you see, the thing is, I was eating a chocolate mousse. Then as I leaned over to adjust my camera to a more flattering angle, I spilled the blooming thing all down my front."

That explained maybe half of the current situation, but I needn't have worried because nobody at CRAPP ever stopped a good anecdote before it had gone on way, way too long.

"And," he continued, "I didn't think it would be very professional to come to a meeting with chocolate mousse all down my front, so I went to get changed, but the thing is, it's the day before wash day so I spent ages trying to find something and wouldn't you know it the best I could do was this." He indicated the fake-naked-chest T-shirt. "And I'll be honest, I was a bit concerned it *might* create something of the wrong impression—"

"You think?" I said.

"I did think. But then I remembered that time you showed us all your hedgehog underpants and I decided, 'Well, it can't be much worse than that,' so here I am."

I guess the advantage of CRAPP closing in a year was that it put a strict time limit on how long I was going to have to live with my hedgehog boxers being a regular element of workplace banter.

"Barbara was just explaining," I tried in a vain effort to distract people from the topic of my underwear, "the things that CRAPP will be able to do to support us through redundancy."

Rhys Jones Bowen looked shocked. "Redundancy?"

"You *do* remember that we're losing our funding at the end of the year?" I reminded him.

"I know we *might*," replied Rhys Jones Bowen. "But I'm buggered if I'm letting this place shut down without a fight."

That had...genuinely not occurred to me.

"We might be able to find alternative sources of income," observed Dr. Fairclough, "but the most probable outcome is that they will not be sufficient to compensate for the loss of the trust, and thus our operations will in all likelihood become untenable."

"Well then, let's keep the trust," said Rhys, as if it was the easiest, most obvious thing in the world. "My mum always says, 'You're not beat until they're shoving sawdust up your bum,' and that's how I've always lived my life and how I always will."

In so many ways, he was making sense. In so many ways, he was saying what I'd not quite let myself want to hear. In other ways he was talking about sawdust in bums. "Until they're doing *what*?"

"Shoving sawdust up your bum," Rhys Jones Bowen repeated. "I think it means, you know, until you're dead."

"Do they shove sawdust up dead people's bums?" I asked, even though I was certain I didn't want to hear the answer.

"I think it's an embalming thing," Rhys told me with the airy confidence that had allowed him to bring a different date to every company event I'd ever seen him at. "You know, they pickle you and stuff sawdust up your bum."

It was fucked up that I was going to miss this. "I *really* don't think that's how embalming works."

Rhys Jones Bowen folded his arms in the manner of a man about to die on a very silly hill. "I didn't realise you were such an expert in the field, Luc."

"I'm not claiming expertise. I just don't feel sawdust-up-the-bum is generally a part of funeral preparation."

"We've got a mummy in the Lancaster house," Alex piped up. "Uncle Pongo brought him back from a dig somewhere, just before that nasty business with the shotgun. *He's* full of sawdust."

"Uncle Pongo?" asked Rhys Jones Bowen.

"The mummy."

"Yes"—I joined Rhys on the silly hill, with roughly similar prospects of survival—"but did it go up his bum?"

Alex wrinkled his nose thoughtfully. "Couldn't say for sure. But"—he raised a finger—"interesting story about Uncle Pongo and the shotgun."

"Could we perhaps," suggested Barbara Clench, whose status as office killjoy was *incredibly* useful in that moment, "stop talking about shotguns, bums, and sawdust in any combination?"

"We're not talking about shotguns, bums, and sawdust," retorted Rhys Jones Bowen. "We're talking about my mum and how she'd never take something like this lying down and how we shouldn't either."

I couldn't quite believe that Rhys Jones Bowen was being the voice of, not reason exactly, because the reasonable thing would've been to put the chairs on the tables, turn the lights out, and quietly update our CVs. But the voice of…something. The voice of standing up for ourselves. Of not being total pushovers. Of actually caring.

Except that wasn't true. I could completely believe it. Getting passionate and enthusiastic about something noble but doomed was a completely Rhys thing to do. And, while shooting that down was a very me thing to do, it didn't have to be.

"Okay," I tried, "let's say we don't give up. What do we do instead?"

"Ah," said Rhys Jones Bowen, confidently. "I'm glad you asked me that because…"

I waited.

We all waited.

"Well, the way I see it…"

We carried on waiting.

"You're the fundraiser, Luc," he finished. "My area of expertise is social media management and data protection." For a moment he went silent, consulting his expertise in social media management and data protection. "I suppose we could try to start a hashtag. Something like #theearlofspitalhamsteadistryingtotakeawayfundingfromourdungbeetlecharityandthatsreallynoton."

Barbara Clench, sipping tea on her idyllic cottage porch, looked far less flinty than usual. "I suppose it couldn't hurt. And maybe we *should* try to be less fatalistic. Dr. Fairclough"—she gazed earnestly out of the screen—"what do you think?"

"I think anybody who fails to recognise the importance of coleoptera is an irredeemable narcissist and not worth trying to engage with." That was Dr. Fairclough's answer to everything in one way or another. Like a lot of extremely clever people, she assumed that not agreeing with her immediately was a personality flaw.

"Is it at all possible," I suggested in my best Fairclough-whispering tone, "that the earl's current failure to appreciate the vital significance of the more than five thousand global and more than sixty local species of dung beetle might be corrected if we adopt the right strategy?"

Dr. Fairclough fixed me, or rather her camera, with a steely—or perhaps chitinous—stare. "Elaborate."

"Well..." I was thinking aloud now, but between them, Rhys Jones Bowen and Dr. Fairclough had switched on the part of my brain that, loath as I was to admit it, both enjoyed and was good at my job. "The read I get from Saint—"

"Please don't call him that," interrupted Alex. "The only thing worse than an oik is a titled oik, and the only thing worse than a titled oik is encouraging a titled oik in his oikishness."

I held up one finger. "Okay. Yes. But also, more importantly. No. I think encouraging his oikishness is *exactly* what we want to be doing."

Alex folded his arms and actually huffed. "I'd rather be made redundant."

To my unexpected relief, Rhys Jones Bowen chimed in. "Well, I bloody well wouldn't. If Luc has a secret plan to save CRAPP, then I'm all for hearing it."

"It's not really a secret plan—" I began.

"Really?" Alex unfolded his arms again and leaned forward in curiosity. "Who've you told?"

"Nobody, but—"

Rhys Jones Bowen was frowning. "Seems pretty secret to me then. Can't get much more secret than not telling anybody. Practically what 'secret' *means*."

"Although I will say," added Alex, "that it's rather shabby of you to have been keeping things to yourself all this time while we're all fretting about losing our jobs."

There we were again. This was the CRAPP I knew and loved. "There isn't a plan."

"Then why did you say there was?" demanded Alex. "Won't do, old boy, won't do, getting a fellow's hopes up and—"

"I'm evolving a plan," I said, "right now."

Barbara Clench smiled. "How are you at expectorating?"

"Especially good." And then before the less-in-command-of-their-faculties brigade could ask what that had to do with anything, I barged straight into my main point. "*Anyway*, my read on the new Earl of Spitalhamstead is that he's less a man of strong conviction than a man of strong attitude. It really seems like he just wants to cut us off to stick it to his dad, and so all we have to do is convince him that he wants to"—how best to put this—"remake us in his image."

I mentally counted down until Alex interjected. "I will *not* be remade in the image—"

"Of an oik," I finished for him. "I know, I know. But here's the thing. We don't actually have to change very much at all. It might not seem like it, but the great advantage of being a tiny insignificant charity that deals with something most people"—I anticipated Dr. Fairclough's objection before she could make it—"*quite wrongly* neither know nor care about is that they basically leave us alone. We're the philanthropic equivalent of that streaming service subscription you never quite get around to cancelling."

Alex looked puzzled.

"To that shooting club you keep paying membership fees for?"

Alex stopped looking puzzled. "Ah, you mean, a chap barely ever thinks of us, but there's just enough of interest on the calendar that he doesn't want to drop out?"

"Exactly."

"You know," he mused, "I really should go back to the South Riding Gin and Pellets Club more often."

Barbara Clench was eyeing some part of the screen—probably my part of the screen—with a calculating look. "Suppose we did go in this direction. What do you think we'd actually need to *do*?"

That, of course, was the $64,000 question. Probably more like the $753,000 question, adjusted for inflation. "I *think* what we'd need to do is for me to have a talk with him like I would with any other donor. You know, butter him up and all that. And then I'd need to sell him on something. Probably something big and shiny and superficially antiestablishment."

"Not sure I like the idea of being antiestablishment," warned Alex. "Pretty sure the establishment got that way for a reason."

"I *did* say *superficially*."

This didn't reassure him. "Still, slippery slope."

Dr. Fairclough, though, seemed interested. I felt, over the years, that she'd come to rely on me as a kind of interpreter, helping her get her point across to anybody who wasn't either an insect or an academic. She might almost even have trusted me. "Do you have specifics?" she asked.

I didn't. But I was pretty good at bullshitting specifics on the fly. "Well, most of what we do is so under the radar that the earl won't care at all. Which means if we want to do something big, we probably need to can the Beetle Drive."

This led, predictably, to a chorus of no's from the team.

"Best day of the year is the Beetle Drive," protested Rhys Jones Bowen.

"Certainly our best day financially," added Barbara Clench.

"And it's *tradition*," said Alex, as if this was the only thing that really mattered.

I nodded. "All true. And I love the Beetle Drive as much as anybody." Hell, it was basically my and Oliver's anniversary. "But the whole event *screams* 'late Earl of Spitalhamstead.' It's formal, it's got a slightly twee name—"

"Now hang *on*." Alex was getting indignant again. "What's wrong with *Beetle Drive*? Who doesn't have fond memories of wandering down to the beetle drive on a summer's morning to help raise money for the church roof and—"

"In the twenty-first century?" I said, "Most people. And more importantly, the one person we need to convince we're worth giving tons of money to. A man who probably has a *Fuck the System* bumper sticker on his Porsche doesn't connect with church fundraisers and family-friendly party games. He wants something—and I use this term knowing full well how dated it actually is—*rock 'n' roll*."

From the look in her eyes, I couldn't tell if Barbara Clench thought I was having a moment of brilliance or a complete break from reality. "What would be a more rock 'n' roll alternative to the Beetle Drive?" she asked.

"Well," I stalled, "the Beetle Drive is quite a sedate evening in a nice venue with a sit-down dinner and non-threatening entertainment, so I suppose the more rock 'n' roll alternative would be…sort of the opposite of that?"

Barbara Clench raised an eyebrow. "So a high-energy,

overcrowded day in a terrible venue with no food and threatening entertainment?"

"Yes?" I wince-replied.

"You mean, something in a field with a lot people and very loud noises?" suggested Rhys Jones Bowen.

I nodded.

"Like the Battle of the Somme?" piped up Alex.

"Hopefully not *too* much like that," I told him. "I don't think 'Come sit in mud and let us shell you' will be a great pitch, even for the earl."

Alex frowned. "Pity. After all, beetles *do* have shells."

"Carapaces," Dr. Fairclough corrected him, sounding mortally offended.

Rhys Jones Bowen had a worryingly contemplative look. "Ooh, now that takes me back to my festivaling days. We used to say that was like the Somme."

"Can we please drop the So—" I stopped. "Hang on, run that by me again."

"Beetles," Alex repeated, "have shells, so maybe we could do something—"

"Not you. Rhys."

Rhys Jones Bowen had muted himself and was having a conversation with somebody off-screen. "What was that, Luc? Me? Oh. Right. The Somme. Yeah, like when I used to go festivaling, that was all mud and tents and loud noises, but it was a laugh, wasn't it?"

And then, like Michael Caine at the end of *The Italian Job*, I had an idea. "*That*," I said, sort of as its own sentence. "We're going to do that."

"A festival?" asked Rhys Jones Bowen.

"Yes."

"About the Great War?" asked Alex.

"No."

“Then what—”

“We’re going to pitch the earl a music festival. It’s going to be big. It’s going to be in a muddy field. It’s going to be alternative and edgy in exactly the kind of way that rich people will spend money on, and it’s going to be called”—the word slid into my brain like an unwelcome DM. A word so absurd it was perfect and so-so-wrong-it’s-right that it might, in fact, have been just plain right—“CRAPPstonbury.”

CHAPTER 14

"HI, LUC," SAID BRIDGE, HUGGING me one-armed because the other arm was full of baby. "You smell…rural. That's not a new cologne, is it?"

I gingerly toed off my shoes before stepping onto the immaculate new carpet of the immaculate new hallway of the immaculate new house that Bridge shared with her immaculate if slightly less new family. "No, it's manure."

"Oh, thank God. I thought you were having a midlife crisis."

"Hey, I am too young for this to be midlife."

She wrinkled her nose. "I suppose it depends on when you die."

A little voice at the back of my brain asked me, as it had a few times since those fucking posters, if it was sepsis. "Not until I'm old."

"And you don't think you're halfway to old yet?"

"I…" My mouth flapped on its own for a moment. Oliver would have been able to say something clever and mathematical in this situation about how being halfway towards a thing wasn't the same as being halfway towards a different thing that you wanted to happen at the end of the first thing. I wasn't. Able to say that. "I'm not having a midlife crisis. Anyway, what kind of midlife crisis comes in the shape of a manure-themed cologne?"

"I don't know." Bridge backed off down the corridor and

reversed into the living room. "But if anyone was going to have the kind of midlife crisis that comes in the shape of a manure-themed cologne, it would be you."

"Thanks," I said. "How are you doing? I mean, all of you. With the extra one."

Bridge sat down in a well-sat-in chair. "Tom and I are fine. And so is Extra Welles-Ballantyne."

"Sorry. How is *Autumn*?"

Glancing down at the blanket-wrapped bundle of human who was sleeping angelically against her boob area, Bridge cooed. "She's the most wonderful baby in the world, *whatever* James says."

Ever since Autumn had joined what Bridge still insisted on referring to as our urban family, the WhatsApp group (currently called For He's a Poly Good Fellow) had developed something of a...dynamic. The dynamic being that Bridge would mention that Autumn had done a baby thing, like smiling at her or making a cute gurgling noise, and James Royce-Royce would immediately respond by sharing an anecdote in which Baby J had done the same thing better, and at an earlier stage of development. And, if I hadn't smelled faintly of manure, I'm sure I'd have handled this complex interpersonal situation with tact and finesse.

"Yeah." I nodded. "He's being a dick. I think he's about two texts away from Priya snapping and telling him that his baby, like everybody's baby, is completely normal and uninteresting, and that anything Baby J achieves in life will be because his parents were two affluent upper-middle-class white men."

"That sounds really specific."

"She's already sent me three drafts."

"Awwwww." Bridge could look heart-warmed about the strangest things. "I didn't know she cared."

I was about to point out that she didn't. But actually, yelling at other people on your behalf was very much Priya's love language. "Yeah, yeah, we all care about you. Don't rub it on our faces."

"You care about meeeee," she sang out, making a rubbing gesture with her spare hand.

"Oh, fuck off. Look, do you want anything? Like, tea or vitamins, or...spare nappies or something?"

"Do you realise," said Bridge, "you ask that every time you see me? And it's still weird. No, I don't want any vitamins or spare nappies. I think what I mostly want is to know why you smell of manure."

Taking off my coat, I ambled through to Bridge's kitchen and put the kettle on, then ambled back so I could continue the conversation below a yell. "I was in a field with Judy and a man who rents out toilets."

"What were you doing in a field with Judy and a man who rents out toilets?"

"Having a wild threesome."

Bridge looked disappointed. Or at least as disappointed as it was possible to look if you knew what I was like. "Isn't Judy your mother's best friend?"

The cringe started at the top of my large intestine and worked its way up through my chest and onto my face. Who would have thought that my policy of responding to every comment with the most obvious sex joke could go so wrong? "Oh yeah," I said. "I really didn't think that one through."

"Do you ever?"

I thought it through. "No."

"So why were you actually in a field with Judy and a man who rents out toilets?"

"Well, Judy's lending me the field because she's my mum's best friend. And the man who rents out toilets is going to rent me some toilets to put in the field. Because"—oh God, the more I tried to explain, the worse this sounded—"I'm organising a really cool, extremely rock 'n' roll music festival in the field. To, like, save my job and shit."

Bridge was nodding as if this made complete sense. To be fair, I *had* already told her about the whole losing-my-job thing, and while organising a rock festival wasn't the most obvious plan to save yourself from unemployment, my *last* save-my-job-strategy had been to pretend I was dating a hot barrister, so this probably felt normal by comparison.

"Only, the thing is," I continued, "I don't know how to do… most of the stuff you have to do to organise a really cool, extremely rock 'n' roll music festival. But after about a week and a half of digging, I *did* find some people who'd rent me some toilets. So I did that."

"But you haven't got any, say, bands or anything?"

"No."

"Or catering or influencers or sponsorship?"

"No."

"But you do have toilets?"

"Yes."

"So"—it was Bridge's kindest voice—"it's currently more of a toilet festival?"

"Yes."

Bridge was giving me a gently reassuring look.

"I've fucked this up, haven't I?"

"No!" Bridge got a surprising amount of conviction into one syllable.

I gave her my best give-it-to-me-straight look. "I've organised a toilet festival."

"Toilets are important. I'm sure you'll get all the other things later."

"Oh right." Somewhere in the kitchen, the kettle had probably finished boiling. "Massively successful, very cool, extremely rock 'n' roll music festivals throw themselves together all the time."

Baby Autumn started stirring in her sleep, and Bridge gently bounced her. "Raising money is what you *do*. Besides, you know all sorts of people who can help you out with this kind of thing."

"Not very cool, extremely rock 'n' roll people."

Unlulled by the bouncing, Autumn awoke and started making distinctly hungry baby noises, so Bridge hoicked up her top and let her latch on to a nipple. "First of all," she said, "I'm offended. Because *I'm* very cool and extremely rock 'n' roll."

I was about to suggest that she might not be quite the kind of very cool and extremely rock 'n' roll I was after, but she looked so perilously close to serious I didn't dare.

"Second of all, aren't your parents both very cool and extremely rock 'n' roll?"

They were. Of course they were. And my brain had been dancing around that thought for days while also politely pretending it wasn't. "They are, but...my dad is a malignant narcissist who wouldn't piss on me if I was on fire unless he thought it'd make his dick look bigger, and my mum's been out of the business for years."

"Still, she must know people."

This was going to places I didn't like. Asking Mum for things was fine when it was, for example, "Can you look after the dog this Wednesday?" or "Can you ask Judy to lend me a field to hold a music-slash-toilet festival in?" but I drew the line at "Can I exploit the past you have an ambivalent relationship with and which you comprehensively left behind as a combined consequence of your having me and my dad treating you like total shit?"

So I said, "Not an option."

"Okay but...does it have to be a full-on music festival music festival?"

"Which part of 'very cool, extremely rock 'n' roll' are you not getting?"

Bridge nodded slightly more indulgently than I really liked my friends to nod. "Lots of things can be cool. And lots of things can be rock 'n' roll too."

She was right. She just might have been the wrong *sort* of right. "Remember this whole thing has an audience of one, and that one is a sixty-something punk with a peerage."

"Because the counterculture of the 1970s had everything to do with music, and nothing to do with art, literature, or anything else."

"Are you trying to get me to start some kind of movement?"

Baby Autumn was still happily feeding, and Bridge settled her more comfortably—or at least as comfortably as you could settle a tiny human who was attached to your nipple by their mouth. "As long as you *look* like you *might* be starting a movement, isn't that all you need to do?"

"Okay, but doesn't this just mean that as well as sourcing music from nowhere, I also now need to source art, literature, and whatever else from nowhere *as well*?"

Bridge was giving me an *I honestly can't believe you sometimes* look. "Because obviously you don't know anybody who works in publishing or the art world, or have any friends who are professional caterers, or have any experience in raising money for things."

"I can't just...ask my mates to bail me out."

"You can, Luc. That's pretty much what mates are for."

I squirmed. "But that's..."

"Probably going to be a lot more fun than that time you asked us all round to clean your flat."

I squirmed deeper. "I'm being crap again, aren't I?"

"Nooo!" Bridge got even more emotion into the syllable by stretching it out. "You've just had a lot on your mind, that's all."

Wasn't that the truth? I slumped onto the sofa, any thought of tea abandoned. Which meant I was now someone who went to their friends' houses, complained about my problems, and wasted their electricity. "So much," I agreed. "Between this and the fostering."

I'd *also* mentioned this in the group chat. Or rather Oliver had mentioned it because I'd known if I mentioned it, Priya wouldn't have been able to resist reminding me how absurd it was for me to put myself forward as the kind of person who could provide a stable home to a troubled teenager.

"Oh yes," said Bridge. "How's that going?"

"Well," I told her. "We've got a home visit later today."

Bridge gave me an *I have faith in you but have also met you* look. "How *much* later?"

I looked at my phone. "Fuck."

"Bye."

I bolted.

CHAPTER 15

"FUCK," I SAID AS I opened the door. Then I repeated "Fuck" as I yanked off my shoes in the hall and threw in a "Fuck, fuck, fuck" for good measure as I made my way to the front room. "I'm sorry I'm late," I called out. "Traffic was murder. The social worker isn't here yet, are th—"

"She is," said a woman I assumed was the social worker, who was sitting beside Oliver on the sofa. She seemed...about as reassuring as somebody who was here to nitpick all your flaws could look. Younger than I'd expected, with a warm smile and a trace of a Nigerian accent.

"Hi!" I definitely actually did exclaim, sticking my hand out like I was doing the world's weirdest martial art. "I'm Luc. And sorry about the—the *fucks*—and the smelling of manure. I don't normally smell of manure. Or say *fuck* quite that much."

She took my hand and shook it. "Hi, Luc. I'm Esther." Then, when my arm barely moved, she added, "Please relax. Just a bit. I'm sure everybody has manure days."

"I really don't!" I kept exclaiming unrelaxedly. "I very rarely go near manure at all. Not to, like, a neurotic extent. I'm fine with manure. As in fine, like a normal person. Not, like, someone with a fetish or anything."

There was a silence. Not a long silence but a noticeable silence.

"Lucien is very keen to make a good impression," Oliver explained. "Which I admit might be hard to tell from the look of him."

"And the smell," I added.

"And the smell," Oliver agreed.

Esther nodded a gentle, used-to-working-with-weirdoes nod. "I understand. It can be a bit worrying having somebody come into your house, look at all your things, and ask you a lot of questions. But remember this really is just a chat."

A chat that would probably end with her writing a report about what a fuckup I was.

"I'm not here to judge you," she went on. "Or any one-off manure-related incidents that you may or may not have been involved in."

"Oh good," I said, trying very hard to believe her.

For some reason best known to himself, Oliver—who had never in his life patted his knees—patted his knees and stood up. "Shall we do the tour first?" he asked, with a compensating-for-my-manure-covered-boyfriend brightness. "It's not the biggest house, so it shouldn't take long."

"That sounds good." Esther, sans knee pat, got up to join him. "I mostly need to see the basics. Sitting room"—she made a slightly exaggerated show of looking around—"check. I'll want to look at the kitchen, see the spare room, your room, any bathrooms, and, you know, make sure you don't have a cellar full of dead bodies or anything."

"Ahahahaha," I said and immediately hated myself. "No. We don't. Do we, Oliver?"

Oliver did an incredible job of pretending I was behaving reasonably. "I think I'd have noticed. Also I'm pretty sure I'd have been disbarred."

With an insightfulness that I felt boded extremely badly for me, Esther glanced at Oliver. "Oh, so you're a lawyer."

"Barrister," he clarified.

"I bet if I said, 'Great, mine's a cappuccino,' you'd have heard it before?" She flashed him a disarming smile that would have disarmed anybody who wasn't already a paranoid ball of nerves and self-loathing.

"Just once or twice," Oliver lied.

She turned back to me cheerfully. "So that means you'd be the primary caregiver?"

Fuck. Fuck fuck fuck. "I suppose," I managed, realising half a second too late that a primary caregiver should probably at least be comfortable *saying* that they were a primary caregiver.

"We both work full-time," added Oliver, "but Lucien mostly works from home. He looks after Spud as well."

"Ruff," said Spud, who'd been sitting angelically by Oliver's feet this whole time.

I silently sent him good-boy vibes as we led Esther into the hall and then showed her up to the spare room. It was a good-size space—at least, I hoped it was a good-size space—with a single bed and a little desk. We'd mostly used it for guests, and so it looked quite bare just then, which I pencilled in under my lateness, my swearing, my being covered in manure, and my inability to say what my role in the family would be on the list of things I'd somehow convinced myself she'd use against us.

"We wanted to give the child an opportunity to personalise it," Oliver was saying. And, when he put it like that, it seemed marginally more likely that Esther would go back to the office and write "bedroom adequate" and not "couple expects kid to sleep in white box."

"Yes," I contributed helpfully.

"Lucien and I sleep down the hall. We have an en suite, so the main bathroom will be entirely free."

Esther nodded and smiled and seemed to be making some notes but didn't say anything immediately.

Which I told myself was fine. Didn't mean anything. Wasn't a sign of doom.

We showed her our room, which I'd scrupulously tidied of pants and sex toys that morning, and the bathroom, before looping back downstairs to tick off the kitchen and my study.

"The pen is for Spud," Oliver remarked. And because it was Oliver doing the remarking, not me, there was no implication of *in case you think this is where we intend to keep our foster child.*

"Is he new?" asked Esther.

Which was exactly the kind of question that the material we'd read—the material Oliver had read—told us we should have expected.

"Um," I said, having apparently forgotten the most basic facts about my own life.

Oliver put a reassuring hand on my arm. "A few months, but he's settled in very well. The pen's probably not strictly necessary anymore, but it means he has a familiar space."

"And he's comfortable with strangers?"

Spud gave a cheery "Ruff" of confirmation, which Oliver capitalised on with an opportunistic "As you can see."

Esther made another note. Which probably didn't read *The hot one is a bit too smug*, but only probably.

Having run out of house, we returned to the sitting room, where I stood frozen by an uplighter and Oliver offered Esther a cup of tea.

"That'd be great," she said, "two sugars."

"I'll get it!" I reverted to exclaiming.

I didn't want to look like I was running away, but I'd long since learned you can't always get what you want.

Safely in the kitchen, I took a moment to splash water on my face, which helped slightly with the stress but not with the manure. Then I had a not-that-minor-actually freak-out over which mugs to use. Because, on the surface, it seemed a pretty straightforward choice. When Oliver and I had moved in together and consolidated our kitchens, he'd provided things like a whisk, frying pans that weren't covered in a thin laminate of bacon grease and crockery that actually matched. I'd provided an absinthe spoon, a Breville sandwich toaster with its nonstick coating flaking off, and a collection of mugs that I'd mostly stolen or been given by people with more irony than compassion.

This meant I could go with some nice Le Creuset stoneware mugs in assorted tasteful colours. Or I could give the social worker who was going to decide if Oliver and I were the right sort of people to raise a vulnerable teenager the *Unicorns Are Just Horny Ponies* mug Priya had got me for my twenty-eighth birthday, the *There It Goes, My Last Flying Fuck* mug Priya had got me for my twenty-ninth birthday, the *Cold, Smooth, and Tasty (Like Your Mum)* mug Priya had got me for my thirtieth birthday, and the *Any Text or Photo* mug she'd got me as a moving-in present.

Again, the choice should have been obvious. Except, if I took the nice stoneware mugs out, there was a very real chance Esther would think I was trying to trick her. Because I was clearly not the kind of person who owned nice stoneware mugs, and then she'd probably wonder what else I was lying about. Or she'd start to think that maybe I'd murdered the real Luc O'Donnell and Oliver Blackwood, who were the kind of people who owned nice stoneware mugs, and stuffed them under the floorboards. Whereas if I gave her *Massive Twat* (Priya again, this time just to annoy me), she'd realise what an authentic, down-to-earth person with nothing to hide I was.

Or she'd think I was a misogynist with no sense of boundaries.

Oh.

It was that one, wasn't it?

I went back out with a tray of nice stoneware mugs.

"Everything all right, Lucien?" asked Oliver, since I'd taken about six hours to make three cups of tea.

"Absolutely!" I exclaimed.

"I was just asking Oliver," said Esther, politely ignoring my weird, weird behaviour and taking one of the mugs, "why you decided on fostering."

My mind went blank. "Pardon?"

"I was just asking why you decided on fostering."

"Well," I began. And did not continue until the not-continuing became nonviable. "It just seemed... We sort of felt... We're at a place in our life..."

"Adoption didn't feel like it was right for us," Oliver translated. "Not where we are now, especially not when there's a national shortage of foster carers."

I nodded like a dog on a dashboard.

Esther sipped her tea and leaned forwards. Once again her body language was extremely open, and once again my lizard brain decided this would be a great time to run up the walls and lick its eyeballs. "So"—her tone was effortlessly understanding—"one of the things we need to talk about is where the two of you are coming from, um, family-wise."

Shit shit shit. I was fucked fucked fucked.

"It's not intended to be intrusive or intimidating," she went on, even though I was profoundly intimidated and at least a little bit intruded upon. "But it'll really help me to build a good picture of you both."

With the easy grace of, well, himself, Oliver started the ball rolling. "I'm afraid there's not much to tell, at least where I'm concerned. I had quite a normal upbringing. I was always quite driven, and my parents were strict but fair."

I tried to not actively stare at Oliver. It wasn't that I'd expected him to say, *My parents were arseholes who treated me and my brother like shit, only they did it in such a middle-class way that it took me nearly thirty years to notice*. But it was a little bit uncomfortable hearing him give Esther the exact same line he'd given me on our first date.

"Obviously," I tried, "no one's childhood is perfect."

Probably Oliver didn't want to lay into his dead dad in front of a random social worker, but I hoped he'd feel encouraged to, like, not lie for him?

"That's true," Oliver conceded. "My father..."

He paused, frowning, and I took his hand. Because, distracted as I'd been with my own bullshit, I'd kind of lost sight of how tough this was going to be for him.

"My father," he repeated, "was a complicated man. He...he died a few years ago, and I suppose... I suppose it meant I had to do some thinking."

"What kind of thinking?" asked Esther.

Another pause. "About myself," Oliver offered, a little uncertain.

I squeezed his hand.

"About my values," he went on. "The lessons he'd taught me and whether I was right to learn them." His frown deepened. "Sorry, that's all a bit vague and melancholy. I am actually seeing a therapist."

I'd say this for Esther, she had a fantastic it's-okay-really smile. Even my lizard brain was starting to come down off the ceiling. "No, no," she said. "I asked, and everything helps." And perhaps she could tell that Oliver needed a break, because she turned to me. "How about you, Luc?"

My ability to put Oliver's needs above my own anxieties evaporated rapidly. "Me?"

"Yes."

"Oh. You know. Basically like him. Only not. Normal, I mean. Very normal."

A sharp little light crept into Esther's eyes. Sharp but not unkind.

"Normally when things are normal, people don't say they're normal quite that often."

"I meeeean," I replied, drawing the middle of *mean* out as long as I could in the vague hope that it would buy me some time. "Everybody's got. You know. Circumstances and that. Ordinary normal ordinary circumstances."

I was surprised and mildly reassured when Esther nodded. "Yes. They do. What were yours?"

"Well."

"Yes?"

"Well." I left it there. "Well." I left it there again. Unfortunately, nobody wanted to pick it up or do anything with it. So at last I had to unleave it there and run as quickly as I could into: "Wellactuallymyparentsweresortofeightiesrocklegends."

To my very mild irritation, Esther never stopped looking patient and gentle. If Oliver hadn't been gay as a rainbow butt plug and my boyfriend who I wanted to keep, I'd have said the two of them should date. "Sorry," she said, "I'm not sure I got that."

"My parents," I repeated, my mouth going dry and my tongue feeling way too big all of a sudden, "were, you know, um. Eighties rock legends?"

Esther just nodded. "Mm-hmm?"

"My mum's sort of Odile O'Donnell. Not sort of. Actually. Just. She is. She's Odile O'Donnell. I don't know if you remember *Welcome Ghosts*—you're probably not old enough, *I'm* not really old enough but, yeah, that's her. And my dad's Jon Fleming, one of the original judges on *The Whole Package*, won a Grammy for *Pendulum of the World*, made the final of *Strictly* last year."

Esther was still nodding.

I was still dying. "He walked out when I was really young, and then a little while ago he thought he had prostate cancer so he was all like, 'Son, I totally want you back in my life,' and then he found out he didn't have prostate cancer, so he was all, 'Actually, you know what, forget it.' So that...sucked."

"It sounds like it would."

"Yeah," I said, spiralling into the whirlpool of Esther's unreadable niceness. "It made me feel really shit and worthless at the time. But I had Oliver. And my mum is great. Like the best. Like my favourite person apart from Oliver. And Spud. I mean, Spud's a dog. But, like, he's part of the family, and I don't want him to feel devalued."

"Ruff." Spud wagged his tail, valuedly.

"It's good you had that," said Esther.

"Spud?"

"Your mother."

"Oh yeah. Sorry. That makes more sense. Anyway, she raised me in a really normal, healthy way in a tiny village near Epsom with a weird old lady who's had about ten million husbands and still has about ten million spaniels."

"Mm-hmm," said Esther again.

My words were swirling in the air like flies around a bin you really, really needed to take outside. "Okay. Now I'm saying that, it's sounding a bit less normal than I might maybe have billed it. But it was all like loving and shit. And I could have come out a lot worse."

"It seems like you've been through a lot." Esther's tone was so nonjudgemental that, in the end, it proved fatal.

"Kind of." And, before I could stop myself, I careened on like my disclosure car had hit a patch of reassurance ice. "About a decade ago, the then love of my life sold me out to one of the shittier tabloids for an annoyingly small amount of money, and it basically destroyed my ability to trust anybody for pretty much all of my twenties, but then I got better and I even went to his wedding to show him I didn't care, and I *do* still kind of hate him but in this empowered chill way now."

"Ruff," said Spud, laying his chin on my knee supportively.

I needed to stop saying things. I urgently needed to stop saying things. Preferably ten minutes ago. "So," I said carefully. "Yeah."

Esther finished making notes on my trash fire of a life. "Anything else I should know?"

My whole body tried to sink into the sofa cushions. I had fucked this. I had fucked this so badly. Oliver was looking at me, not with anger or disappointment, but in a way that clearly said, *You have fucked this. You have fucked this so badly*. And that also said, *But if that's what we're doing, we're doing it together*.

"When Lucien and I first got together," he said, completely deadpan, "we were only pretending to date because he needed an appropriate boyfriend to prevent homophobic press coverage affecting his work, and I'd been secretly into him for a long time and thought it was the only chance I'd ever get. Then three years ago, we ran out on our own wedding. We've never been happier."

I squeezed Oliver's hand so tightly it was probably sending Esther red flags. Well, redder flags than the very red, very flaggy flags I'd already flagged. At this point, though, I'd made a choice, and, from the way he was squeezing back, it seemed Oliver was making the same choice right along with me. That it was better to get rejected for who we were than accepted for who we weren't. Because this right here—this messy improbable beautiful shit show—was me and Oliver, and I loved me and Oliver and I wouldn't change that for anything.

"She said *what*?" I asked Oliver. I say *asked*. Honestly I was mostly exclaiming again.

It was two days later and we were in Oliver's study, where he'd taken the follow-up call from Ester, while I'd been hiding in the bedroom, like the extremely mature and grounded person I am.

"She said," he repeated, "it went well."

"She said *what*?" I also repeated.

Oliver raised an eyebrow. "Sorry, my mistake. What she actually said was that you were a hot mess and the last person in the universe who should be around children."

"I mean, that *would* be more likely."

"Demonstrably not true since it's not, in fact, what happened. What happened was, it went *well*."

"It didn't feel like it went well."

"Apparently it's very normal to be nervous—"

"But is it normal to dump your entire personal history and all your childhood trauma and, thinking about it, your adult trauma on a complete stranger who's good at nodding?"

"I think," said Oliver carefully, "*normal* might not be an applicable word in this context."

"Um." I stared at him. "Thanks?"

"I just mean that everything you said—we said—was pertinent information that Esther needed to know in order to make an assessment. But I suspect she's used to it taking more work to get people there."

"She threw me off guard by being nice and understanding."

"Yes, that was dastardly of her." He rose from his extremely ergonomic chair and rested his hands lightly on my hips. "Lucien, for the last time. It went well. Yes, we were nervous, but Esther said that we'd clearly been through our options. And that, while having a new dog was a slight concern—"

"Hey, what's wrong with Spud?"

"As I said: that he's new. That's not a personal insult against Spud. It's the reality of fostering with pets."

"Okay"—I prodded Oliver in the chest—"because if she comes for Spud, I don't care how nice and understanding she is. We will be enemies forever."

"She specifically noted that Spud was clearly well behaved and unlikely to cause problems."

"Good. Right. Good. But also, on a more general level, I'm still dealing with a whole lot of *what* here."

"I mean, I could go into more detail if you like. But the gist is, and stop me if you've heard this one, *it went well.*"

Why was it that repetition only made things easier to believe when those things were bad? "Was she in, like, a completely different room from me? Did you bribe her while I was making tea? Did she accidentally get our file mixed up with somebody else's?" There were, as far as I could tell, no other possible explanations.

"Respectively." Oliver, who had, over the years, developed his own ways of reassuring me, began counting on his fingers. "Only for a few minutes. No. And if she did, it was another gay couple with a dog called Spud and our exact personal histories."

"Oh." I tried to let this information sink in. "Well, in that case we should find out who they are because we'd probably get on."

Oliver gave me a look that was about sixty percent loving and forty percent the exasperated kind of loving. "Lucien."

"Okay. Okay. It's just…I'm finding it hard to believe that she looked at me and was all, like, 'That's the one, the guy whose rock star father walked out on him and then showed up twenty years later with fake cancer—he'll be a good role model.'"

For some reason, Oliver didn't seem to find this idea as ludicrous as I did. "We discussed that."

"What, you discussed what an emotional wreck I am?"

"No, Lucien. We discussed the fact that, in her experience, people with very sheltered backgrounds can sometimes find it harder to empathise with the difficulties looked-after children experience. Whereas people who've been through hard times themselves are often better able to relate."

"It's true," I said. "If we get a kid who's stressed out because they had to watch their absentee father dance a rumba to 'Blackbird on the Wire' with Dianne Buswell, I'll be all over it."

"I feel obliged to point out that you didn't *have* to watch that."

"I still can't fucking believe Craig gave him an eight."

Oliver sighed with infinite patience. "What really matters here, according to Esther, is that we're able to provide a strong, stable homelife. And she believes we can."

"We can?"

"We can," he said firmly. Then unfirmed. "Well, pending an enhanced DBS check."

I looked blank.

"They need to look at court records and make sure we've never been investigated for anything...disqualifying."

"Like what?"

He gave me a use-your-imagination look.

"Oh." Then my brain caught up with my ears. "Hang on, did you say *investigated*? So even if it turned out we didn't do anything, they'd still hold it against us."

Oliver nodded.

"What about, you know, innocent until proven guilty?"

"That's for criminal courts. The question here isn't 'Should you be allowed to go free,' it's 'Should you be given privileged access to a vulnerable child.' There's a good reason it has a different standard of evidence."

That *probably* made sense, although I was mostly just relying on my usual strategy of trusting that Oliver knew what he was talking about.

"It's genuinely a formality in our case," he added.

Only marginally reassured, I rested my cheek on his shoulder. "This is some real grown-up shit, isn't it?"

"Despite how it may sometimes feel"—Oliver's fingers

continued to card soothingly through my hair—"we are, in fact, real grown-ups."

Reflexively, I flinched. "I think I might be kind of scared."

"So am I." Oliver kiss-nuzzled my cheek. "But we'll get through it. We always do."

CHAPTER 16

AS IT TURNED OUT, GETTING an enhanced DBS check took less time and effort than getting a rich elderly punk wannabe to agree to a meeting to discuss your plans to save a minor environmental charity he didn't give a shit about. In the end, the enhanced DBS took the two to four weeks the website said it would and came out basically fine. Finding a place and a time acceptable to the Earl of Spitalhamstead had taken over a month, and probably wouldn't.

The last time I'd been to the Half Moon, I'd been seeing my arsehole dad, in the brief window when he thought he had prostate cancer and I thought he had redeeming features. So I guess it was kind of fitting that I was sitting there now, waiting to pitch a slightly different flavour of arsehole a dung beetle–themed music festival with a whimsically improbable name. To say I wasn't in the mood was to grossly underestimate how vast the distance between me and the mood was right then. I wasn't in the mood. I wasn't near the mood. I couldn't see the mood from where I was. If I typed the mood into Google Maps, it would zoom out so far you could see national borders.

Part of it was that this was always the worst stage in any project. The point where you'd done enough genuine work to prove that the thing you wanted to do was a thing you could actually do. And you now had to put that genuine work in front of some arrogant prick with way too much money so they could spend ten seconds looking at the genuine work you'd done and decide whether the thing you could actually do was, in their judgement, worth doing.

And part of it was just that Saint was a colossal wanker.

And part of it was that, while my job involved a lot of pandering to colossal wankers, this particular colossal wanker had even more power over me than the colossal wankers I usually had to get money out of.

I sighed into my pint of Two Tribes Dream Factory, marginally relieved that I was no longer having to order Monkey's Butthole or Zombie Squirrel Returns. Since I'd been here with my dad, the place seemed to have pivoted back towards music venue and away from hipster-focused craft ale emporium. Which was one of those take 'em where you find 'em victories and would hopefully convince Saint I was down with whatever he thought counted as the kids.

Eventually I heard the roar of Saint's motorcycle, and a few minutes later, he swaggered in, peeling off his gloves with an air of superiority. He half nodded at me, then went straight past me to the bar and, like I remembered my dad doing years ago, just *pointed* at what he wanted. Then, enbeveraged, he swaggered back to the table and sat down opposite me.

"What're you drinking?" I asked, because I thought he'd look down on something as bourgeois as *hello*.

He gave me a smug smile. "Lucky Saint."

"Cute."

Saint's eyes narrowed and he gave me a look that was more challenging than disapproving. "That's a funny way to talk to your patron."

"I didn't think you'd be into hierarchies." Privately, I suspected he was *extremely* into hierarchies, but he'd probably have reacted badly if I'd said *I'm gambling on you not being willing to admit what a hypocrite you are.*

He laughed. "True that. True that. So what am I here for? You said you had a pitch for me."

"That's right." I let it hang there for a while. I was *hoping* I was whetting his curiosity, but I might just have been pissing him off.

"You going to tell me what it is?"

I took a sip of my beer. "Well, we discussed things in the office, and we can all see why you don't want to carry on with your father's legacy."

"Even the posh arsehole?" asked the posh arsehole.

"Even him. But we got to thinking, 'Why *should* this be your father's legacy? Why shouldn't it be yours?'"

Saint didn't look impressed. "Because," he said, "and I really want to make this clear, I couldn't possibly give less of a shit about beetles."

Yeah. I'd been afraid of that. Fortunately, I'd also planned for it. I leaned back, trying my best to look cool and rebellious. And given that I'd once nearly been fired for being a sexually deviant party boy, looking cool and rebellious was actually something I was pretty good at. "Do you want to hear a secret?" I asked.

There was a twenty to thirty percent chance he'd just say no. He was contrarian enough, at least. But I'd played the odds well. "Go on then."

"*Nobody* gives a shit about charities."

"My dad did."

I had no idea if that was true or not, but it didn't matter. I could work with it regardless. "Your dad cared about being a charming eccentric. He cared about guys like Alex saying things like, 'Oh, what? Hilary? Fearfully decent chap; dashed fond of beetles, you know, isn't that queer?' It was about the look of the thing. That's all."

"And you want me to be the same?"

"Not remotely. I want you to"—how to put this, because the

real answer was *I don't want you to be the same; I'm just willing to bet you are*—"think about the message you could send if you remade your dad's pet project in your own image."

He was tempted. I could tell he was tempted. "And what do you know about my image?"

"Nothing," I said. Which wasn't at all true. By now, I'd done a *lot* of research on Hilary Topwith St. John Edmonton Bloom de Lancy. I didn't just know how he dressed, how he talked, and what bike he rode. I knew he'd lived on three different communes, only two of which seemed to have been run by actual cults. I knew he'd spent most of the '80s and '90s touring with a band called Rancid Sputum and that he'd been trying to get it back together as recently as 2016. And I knew what his former bandmates said about him. I didn't want to say he was an open book, but you could figure out a lot from the Wikipedia summary. "That's the thing," I went on. "It doesn't matter. *You'd* be the one in control. As long as we're able to keep our core mission of researching and protecting coleoptera, you can do what you like with the rest."

I was beginning to feel like a cut-rate Mephistopheles who really liked dung beetles because Saint was giving me a wary but tempted look. Unfortunately, I'd failed to account for the lazy rich bastard factor. "That sounds like a lot of work."

"It wouldn't have to be," I course-corrected. "You could just"—I groped for a Saintism—"lay down your vision and then we'd make it happen. Or we put ideas together for you. And you could..." I extended my hand and did up a thumbs-up / thumbs-down gesture like a Roman emperor.

"Go on then," said Saint.

"Go on then what?" I asked. I knew what he meant. But I needed him to think he'd gotcha-ed me.

"Ideas."

Okay, this was it. I had to get this right, if not for myself, then for the—now I thought about it—minority of my coworkers who actually needed jobs. "Well, for example," I offered, incredibly casually, "I'm working on a whole new fundraising initiative. Because I think you're right..." I let that hang for a moment. Everyone liked to be told they were right, even if the thing you were telling them they were right about was completely disconnected from anything they were actually saying. "Our focus has been too narrow. I mean, the tweed-jackets-and-smoking-rooms model of philanthropy went out with fucking Live Aid."

"Damn straight," declared Saint, no longer pretending not to be interested. "You know Rancid Sputum would have been right there if Geldof hadn't been such a cock."

"Such a cock," I echoed affirmingly.

For a moment, Saint just brooded on the cockishness of Bob Geldof. Then he fixed me with this intense stare. "So what you're saying is we're going to do Live Aid. But not shit."

This had gone so much better than I thought it would that it was at risk of circling round into going badly. "In many ways," I said. "Yes."

He was nodding. Oh fuck, he was really in.

And I had some expectations to manage. "It might need to be"—don't say *smaller*, don't say *less ambitious*, don't say *worse and more insect-focused*—"less *mainstream*."

"Yah. Obviously. Sputum doesn't do mainstream."

The problem of pitching an ecological fundraiser headlined by a band named Rancid Sputum was a problem for future Luc to deal with. Future Luc wasn't going to like me very much. I leaned in conspiratorially. "I think in terms of positioning, and attracting the right crowd—"

Saint was nodding again.

"—this needs to feel sort of grassrootsy. You know, authentic music, indie artists, more a down-and-dirty festival vibe than a slick, corporate concert vibe." Because we literally could not afford a slick, corporate concert vibe. "Kind of more CRAPPstonbury than Beetle Aid."

I didn't know if it said encouraging things or terrible thing that Saint was the first person not to find the name completely laughable. "Okay," he said. "I'm picking up what you're putting down. But what makes you think you're qualified to do this?"

There was, in fact, a pretty simple answer to that. As unsexy as it was, organising a music festival was a whole lot like organising anything else. It didn't actually matter how boring or otherwise you were; it mattered if you knew how to book venues, stay on the phone to caterers, and send passive-aggressive follow-up emails to people who needed to be passive-aggressively followed up with. "It's fundraising," I told him. "It's literally my job."

Saint leant back. Shit, I was losing him. "And I can tell you're passionate about your work. But Luc. This is not your job. This is rock 'n' roll. It's not a fête or a bake sale for a church roof."

If I lost this fucker at the last second, I was going to...to probably go home and sit on the sofa and be sad at my dog. I summoned all the rock and/or roll I'd inherited from both my parents and tried to blast them through my eyes at the new Earl of Spunkwhistle. "I can do this, Saint."

"I'm sorry. I don't think you can." He paused regretfully. "Sorry to crush your dreams, but I'm a man who knows his own mind, and this lady's not for turning. It's a hard no."

Well, that was pretty unequivocal. "I appreciate your honesty."

"If it's any consolation, I respect you now."

None whatsoever. "Thanks."

I'd hoped he would at least have the good grace to fuck off and leave me with my respect and crushed dreams. But, to my horror, he went to the bar, casually ordered another pint, and came back to sit with me. "This is a nice venue," he remarked, looking around.

"Maybe if I get the boys back together, we'll think about doing a gig here."

"I'm sure they'd love that," said the robot who had subbed in for me while I dealt with my failure.

"Surprised you knew about it. This doesn't seem like a"—he was clearly looking for a polite way to express how little he thought of my job—"middle-management-fundraiser-for-a-shit-beetle-charity kind of place."

I wasn't sure if he meant charity for shit-beetles or a charity for beetles that is itself shit. But, at this point, I guess it didn't matter. "Thanks. My dad brought me once."

"Your dad has good taste."

I shrugged. "He played here in the seventies."

And by some miracle of narcissism, Saint was looking interested again. "Who with?"

Shit. I honestly, *honestly* had not been meaning to play this card. I *hated* playing this card. I didn't even think of it as a card, more as an old receipt I'd stuck in my pocket absent-mindedly and then accidentally washed with my jeans and kept finding bits of every time I went for my keys. But it was too late now. "Rights of Man."

"He used to play with Jon Fleming's band?"

"He, um, he *is* Jon Fleming."

And to my incredible, unbelievable relief, Saint nodded, took a sip of his pint, and then said, "Fucking sellout."

What with all professional hope being dead, I saw no reason to carry on being professional. "Oh thank God. For a horrible moment I thought I was going to have to pretend I liked him."

"Jon Fleming"—Saint was going into full pontification mode—"was a legend. But then he got old and he got scared and he pissed it all away for a reality TV deal. And why?"

I didn't think he was actually asking.

"Because he didn't trust the music, that's why. Rights of Man will go down in history as one of the all-time rock greats, but Fleming? He's shat all over it because he wants his name in the *Radio Times*. It's like Ringo Starr becoming the voice of Thomas the Tank Engine, if Ringo Starr was John Lennon and the Beatles weren't completely fucking overrated."

I nodded and made *mm-hmm* noises. I had a great line in *mm-hmm* noises. They were really useful for implying that I agreed with at least some of a donor's weird bullshit opinions without committing to any given one of them.

"With Sputum," Saint said, turning the conversation back to him, "there was none of that. We stayed true, right till the last."

I wondered how aware he was that, of the four original members of Rancid Sputum, he was the only one still living the punk rock dream. Rik Jism, lead guitar, had gone back to his original name of Richard Smoddle and now worked for Deloitte. MagiMix, bass guitar, was teaching in a primary school in Droitwich Spa. As for the drummer, Gary the Cosmic Fuckstone, he'd set up a well-respected raw foods blog and died from a bad mushroom in 2019.

"No money telling us what to do." Saint was still in full flow. "No corporate sponsors. No censorships. No record labels. No pandering to Middle England just for radio spots. Hundred percent underground. Hundred percent real."

"Mm-hmm," I said again. "Yeah."

Gradually, Saint percolated out of nostalgia for the glory days of Rancid Sputum. "Hey." He looked at me closely enough that I felt uncomfortable, which, honestly, didn't have to be that closely. "If you're Jon Fleming's kid, that means you're Odile O'Donnell's kid as well, right?"

I really wanted to keep Mum out of this, but there was no point lying about it. "Yeah."

He was getting a glint in his eye. Nothing good ever came from old men with glints in their eyes. "Now *she*," he proclaimed, "is true. Rock. And. Roll."

"Mm-hmm." I was really, really, *really* hoping that this wasn't going to descend into an OAP creeping on my mum.

"Did her thing. Made her point. Fucked off. Class fucking act."

"Mm-hmm," I said, with the *hmm* getting rather higher pitched than the *mm*.

There was a long pause, during which I went from being glad Saint had stopped talking about my mum to wishing he'd at least talk about something. "Maybe I was wrong about you," he decided finally.

"Mm— What?"

"Maybe you *are* the right man to pull off CRAPPstonbury."

At this point I had no idea what was happening. I was pretty sure I'd either won or lost or Saint was just trying to get into my mum's pants. So, in desperation, I threw up devil horns and said, "Fuck yeah."

"Fuck yeah," agreed Saint. "Fuck the man. Fuck the system."

I opened my mouth. Closed it again. And finally went with, "Mm-hmm."

He downed his pint with a worrying first-of-many energy. Then he looked me right in the eyes and said, "Let's go fuck shit up, Luc Fleming."

I did not want to "go fuck shit up" with Saint. I could, in fact, think of few things I wanted to do *less* than "go fuck shit up" with Saint. But Saint was the kind of man who believed he had a will of iron when what he actually had was a lifetime of getting his own way. Which meant he was the kind of man who would bully people he had power over into doing things they didn't want to do, and still feel like he was being an antiestablishment rebel.

So I went and fucked shit up with Saint. Because the alternative was to admit that I'd rather lie on a sofa with a puppy than spit off a bridge onto a policeman, and that would probably—scratch that, *definitely*—have made him declare me insufficiently rock 'n' roll to be in charge of a beetle-themed music festival. That had been my idea in the first place. And that he hadn't even known he wanted until I'd suggested it to him.

God, rich people sucked.

Fucking shit up with Saint wasn't the worst night of my life. In my twenties I'd spent a whole lot of nights doing awful things I hated with awful people I also hated. It was up there, though. We almost got arrested twice, and almost got killed, now I think about it, literally every time we got on the motorbike. Because he made me ride pillion and insisted that motorcycle helmets were, and I quote, "For fascists."

The following morning, I peeled myself out of bed feeling worse than I had in a long, long time and stumbled downstairs determined to not let the pissing Earl of pissing Spital pissing Hamstead stop me giving my wonderful dog his morning walk.

I was intercepted by Oliver, who was, of course, already up, dressed, breakfasted, and on his way out the door. Or at least he'd usually be on the way out the door. This time he was waiting for me wearing his concerned-yet-compassionate face. "Lucien," he said at once, "you should probably know that you're in the papers again."

I buried my face in my hands. "Fuck. Is it bad?"

The six seconds it took Oliver to respond didn't fill me with confidence. Neither did the fact that when it came, his answer was, "Yes and no?"

My face remained steadfastly enhandenated. "Oh God, it's going to be all 'Wild Child Luc Is at It Again,' isn't it? 'O'Donnell Falls off the Wagon, *Strictly* Star Son Saucy Shenanigans Shame.'"

"That last one was actually rather good."

"Yeah, I missed my calling."

Oliver was looking…actually how was he looking? Not *grave.* I almost wanted to say *awkward.* Except why would he be looking awkward? "The good news," he said, "is that there's nowhere near as much *wild child* framing as you might be worried about."

"What's the bad news?"

He unlocked his phone and held it in front of me.

I read the headline.

"'Past It Party Boy Paints Town Dead'?" I snatched the phone from his hand and started scrolling. "'Aging D-list no-lebrity Luc O'Donnell spotted in tragic attempt to recapture his glory days.' Those utter bastards."

"It does seem a little premature."

"*And* they deliberately picked the most unflattering pictures."

Oliver gave a little cough. "They've *always* picked the most unflattering pictures."

"Yeah, but it used to be unflattering in a sexy, self-destructive way. Now it's…it's…" I pointed at a picture of me yawning as Saint attempted to bum a cigarette off a young woman who was clearly vaping. "*This.* I look like I'm trying to suck off a water buffalo and the water buffalo isn't even interested."

"I think," said Oliver, in mild bemusement, "you just look like you're yawning."

"What time was that even taken? It was, like, half nine. Why was I yawning at half nine?"

"Because you'd been forced to go drinking with a profoundly tedious man."

"Are you sure? Are you sure it's not because I'm an aging D-list no-lebrity who needs to be in bed with cocoa by eight o'clock or else he's grumpy the next morning?"

To my profound unamusement, Oliver was beginning to look profoundly amused. "You know, you *do* sometimes rather enjoy going to bed with cocoa. And you usually *are* grumpy in the mornings."

"Well yeah, because cocoa is great and mornings are the worst, but..."

Oliver placed his hands on my shoulders and looked me in the eye reassuringly. "They're just pictures. Everybody has bad pictures."

They did. And while I was pretty self-centred a lot of the time, I'd never really had the energy for full-on vanity. "And they're not going to... This isn't going to get in the way of fostering, is it?"

"A newspaper article that says you're too grown-up and sensible to be partying all night?" Shifting his hands from my shoulders to my waist, Oliver drew me in for a kiss. "I don't think that will be a problem, no. This"—he gently retrieved his phone—"means less than nothing. Truly."

"Ruff," agreed Spud, who had finished his breakfast and now wanted to know why his daddies were standing around looking at a funny shiny rectangle instead of taking him walkies like they were meant to.

And you know what? They were right. They were *both* right.

Aging Party Boy Luc had come out for one night to get a dickhead peer onside. The press had been mean about him, like they always, always were. And that was it. There in our hall with my boyfriend and our dog and our passed DBS checks and our about-to-be-foster-parents-ness, absolutely nothing else mattered. Nothing else could possibly matter. Nothing could get in the way of—

Spud started sniffing the floor and walking in a circle.

"Okay," I said, pulling somewhat reluctantly out of Oliver's embrace, "this one definitely needs to go walkies. Have a good day in court."

Oliver kissed me once more for luck. "Have a good day at home."

And all at once I was overwhelmed by the thought, the strange but not unwelcome thought, that I would. That even with Saint, even with my job on the line, even with the tabloids saying mean things about my age, life choices, and body, I was going to have a *good day*.

I was going to have a whole lot of good days.

For a good long time to come.

PART THREE

WINTER/SPRING

CHAPTER 17

PREPARATIONS FOR CRAPPSTONBURY HAD TO go on hiatus over the holidays as we pivoted briefly towards our seasonal Adopt a Beetle programme. Normally this wouldn't have been required because, most years, we sold about six of them, and three of those were Dr. Fairclough shopping for Christmas presents. Unfortunately—or, I suppose, fortunately—this year Rhys Jones Bowen had gone viral.

I'd mostly lost track of his career as an influencer because following his OnlyFans account had wound up doing weird things to my algorithm, but he'd come into my office one morning to tell me that he'd "done a Tick Tock" and that it had "got pretty popular, actually," and suddenly we had an awkward shortage of adoptable beetles.

The TikTok that Rhys Jones Bowen had done turned out to be a series of short music videos in which he performed CRAPP-themed parodies of various seasonal favourites including "Ding Dung Merrily on High," "Fairy Tale of Poo York," and "All I Want for Christmas Is to Adopt a Dung Beetle Through the Coleoptera Research and Protection Project's Adopt a Dung Beetle Scheme." Like a lot of things that get popular on the internet, I honestly couldn't tell if the videos were amazing or terrible, but what I thought spectacularly did not matter. People loved them enough that we wound up with one thousand seven hundred and thirty-three personalised Beetle Adoption Packages to lovingly source, assemble, and detail.

The whole project had been overwhelming and fiddly and, since each adoption had been retailing at £4.99 since 1993, it probably didn't make back in donations what it theoretically cost us in worker-hours. Then again, *worker* was always a slightly tenuous way to describe CRAPP employees, so in a lot of ways it was the most productive we'd been in months. Dr. Fairclough had been resistant to the whole project because she felt naming insects was needlessly anthropomorphic, but she *had* been able to provide us with well over a thousand unique images of beetles from her personal files. Barbara Clench, for her part, had turned out to be exactly the woman you wanted running things when the job involved doing more or less the same thing with slight variations one thousand seven hundred and thirty-three times as efficiently as possible. And Alex, somehow, turned out to be an absolute genius for naming dung beetles.

"That's a Colin," he'd say, and it would absolutely be a Colin. "Esmerelda. Monty. Godolfin."

Sitting on the office floor making adoption certificates and drinking cocoa with the cold and dark safely outside the windows, I spent most of December feeling weirdly upbeat, weirdly positive, and weirdly not especially bothered by how fucking doomed we all were.

Then January rolled round, the cold and dark stopped being a novelty, Oliver and I got notice we'd been approved for an emergency placement, I remembered that I was still the barely adequate thread by which all our jobs were hanging, and things very much reverted to the status quo, doomed-wise.

"Did you hear," I asked Alex over Zoom, a few days after New Year's, "about the cheese factory that exploded?" And then, before he could go off about safety standards in the dairy industry, I went straight through to the punch line. "All that was left was de Brie."

"No," he replied with sincere concern. "I hadn't. That's terri—" Then he stopped and seemed to realise something. In a perfect world, that something would have been *Luc is telling me a joke*. Hell, not even a perfect world. Just a mildly less annoying world. That I did not live in. "Hold on a moment," Alex went on. "Might not have heard you right. Did you say all that was left was *debris* or all that was left was *the Brie*?"

"Yes," I replied, wondering if this might finally be my moment.

Alex blinked. "Which?"

It was not my moment. "Both?"

"No, no." Alex was looking into the middle distance like he was trying to remember something extremely complicated. "You definitely only said one of them."

"But I *meant* both."

"Well"—Alex turned his attention back to the camera, his expression a mix of betrayed and suspicious—"that seems wilfully obtuse."

Less late than I'd been expecting, Rhys Jones Bowen logged on, interrupting the discussion of my wilful obtuseness. "Sorry I'm a bit delayed. The cat was interfering with the wireless. Anyway, what have folks been up to?"

"Telling jokes on company time," replied Barbara Clench.

"Really, Barbara?" Rhys Jones Bowen stroked his beard in confusion. "That doesn't sound like you."

"She means me," I clarified.

"But," added Alex, "he hadn't got around to the joke bit yet because he was just telling us about this terrible explosion at a cheese factory. There was only Brie left."

Rhys Jones Bowen shook his head solemnly. "Shocking, that is, really shocking. And you know the worst thing about it?"

"I suppose it depends on what the other cheeses were," mused Alex. "Be criminal if they lost a supply of Stilton."

That didn't seem to be the direction Rhys Jones Bowen was going. "The *worst* thing is that the bosses will have known about it. There'll have been people on the factory floor telling them for years. 'That's an accident waiting to happen,' they'll have been saying. 'It's not right to make people work in these conditions.' They'd have pursued industrial action, I'd imagine, except of course the cheese industry is famously anti-union."

"So we're all on the same page," I tried, forlornly, "this whole situation is fictional."

Rhys Jones Bowen gazed out of the screen knowingly. "I'm sure that's what they *told* you, Luc. That's what they always say when these kinds of issues come up. 'Oh, you're just scaremongering. We've had professional risk assessments done, and there's nothing to worry about.' But it's not them who have to pick up the pieces, is it? It's not the CFO who has to tell little Timmy that Mummy isn't coming home from work today because she was killed by a catastrophic buildup of pressure in the curdling vats."

Too late, I made a token attempt at damage control. "Should we—"

"Not that they care," Rhys was continuing. "You know why the Brie survived, don't you? Because that's what they serve at their shareholders' meetings. So of *course* that would be safe. It's the regular cheese for the working people they'll have been cutting corners on."

Alex stiffened, which looked particularly formal since he was still, several months in, wearing full historical costume. "Steady on, this is sounding dangerously like pinko talk."

"How about"—Barbara Clench called us quietly back to order—"we set aside the controversial cheese tragedy and focus on C.R.A.P.P. business."

"Fuck, God, yes *please*," I blurted in desperate support. "I want to kick off the New Year by giving you a quick recap on where things stand with CRAPPstonbury."

"Over budget already?" asked Barbara Clench. With how our relationship had evolved over the years, I couldn't quite tell if that was playful banter or a serious complaint. Possibly it was both.

"Hey, the field was free," I told her, and got an approving nod in return. "And I managed to keep the toilets under a grand."

Barbara Clench looked unconvinced. "I still feel they should have been cheaper."

"Maybe," I conceded, "but look at it this way. If we're going to skimp on *anything*, it probably shouldn't be the thing that stops the whole event being awash with human faeces."

Even Barbara Clench couldn't quite find an argument for rolling the dice on that one. "Fair point. What about catering?"

"I've reached out to some local businesses, so that might actually not cost us anything. Plus"—I nodded towards Rhys Jones Bowen—"is Bronwyn still doing the pop-up?"

"She is," Rhys confirmed. "She's got very into street food lately, and she thinks that'll go down well with a festival crowd." He paused for a moment, then waved a finger in the universal gesture of just-remembered-something. "Oh, but there might be a bit of a problem with the choir."

The Skenfrith Male Voice Choir had become something of a fixture at CRAPP events since their debut at the Beetle Drive five years ago. I'd originally not planned to book them for CRAPPstonbury on the grounds that Saint would probably think they were too conventional, but I'd come to the conclusion that if I built the whole event to please Saint, it would completely bomb, we'd make no money, and we'd all lose our jobs anyway.

So Skenfrith were in. Or at least they should have been.

"What's the issue?" I asked.

Rhys Jones Bowen looked grave. "Politics."

"What sort of politics?"

"Well," Rhys began. And it was not a good *well*. It was the kind of *well* that inevitably came before a long, detailed story about a large number of people you'd never met and couldn't keep track of. "You know how Uncle Alan used to be managing director?"

The *used to be* was telling me pretty much everything I needed to know. Still I said "yes" and waited for the rest of the narrative.

"He'd been doing the job for years—and very well, too, if I'm any judge—but then Bill Thomas, who'd been after the position since '97, over the holidays, he managed to stir up enough discontent amongst the regulars to force a vote of no confidence."

"What did Uncle Alan do?" I asked and, to my horror, realised I was actually interested.

"Well, he didn't take it lying down. He rounded up his supporters and he said if that's the way you're going to be, then you'll be forcing me to go independent. So now there's *two* Skenfrith Male Voice Choirs, and they're both expecting a place at our next fundraiser."

"We probably have room for two male voice choirs if it comes to it," I suggested. "Actually, it might help because we're a bit short on acts."

Rhys Jones Bowen shook his head. "I don't know, Luc. There's bad blood there—the last thing you want is for your festival to be caught in the middle of a male voice choir feud."

I was about to ask how bad it could be, but...we were talking about a group of middle-aged British men with a hobby they took seriously. It could be very bad indeed. "What if we just booked Uncle Alan?"

"That would look like nepotism," Rhys warned me. "We might open ourselves to legal action."

"Is that likely?" I asked, guessing the answer well in advance.

"Probably." Rhys Jones Bowen gave an apologetic nod. "That

Bill Thomas is a litigious bastard. He once sued the local pub for running out of crisps."

Once again, some weird part of my brain wanted to know the rest of the story, but it was technically a workday and I technically had a festival to organise. "From a wider perspective," I segued, "do any of us know anybody who might get the word out? Because right now our headline acts are a Rancid Sputum reunion that might not happen, some guys who do Ed Sheeran covers that I once nearly booked for a wedding that didn't happen, and one or both of the two male voice choirs from Skenfrith."

Silence answered. It answered at some length.

"Okay." I tried to sound cheery. "We'll work some things out. I'll make some more phone calls. Alex, maybe ask if Miffy can—I don't know—mention us on Instagram or something? Get photographed in front of a conspicuously placed CRAPP logo? Endorse dung beetles?"

Alex gave me an enthusiastic but painfully clueless salute. "Shall do, Captain. You can rely on me *implicitly*."

I gave him a sceptical look. "Rely on you to do *what*?"

"Oh, you know"—he gave an affable hand wave—"whatever it was you were talking about just now."

That was very much as I'd expected. "Cool," I said. "Good to know you've got my back. Now"—around my ankles, Spud started yapping his somebody-at-the-door yap. I glanced down at the clock on my screen. "Fuck," I said unprofessionally aloud, "they're early."

"Who's early?" asked Barbara Clench.

I hadn't discussed the fostering thing much with the CRAPP crowd. It hadn't seemed important, what with the whole we're-probably-losing-our-jobs backdrop it was happening against. Unfortunately, that meant none of my coworkers really knew how to react when I said, "The, um, the people who are delivering my child?"

CHAPTER 18

OLIVER AND I WERE BOTH painfully aware how bad an impression it would make to leave Esther and Jasmine—we knew the kid's name from our rigorous pre-fostering briefings—waiting on the doorstep while we got our shit together, so we hustled Spud into his pen, gave each other silent *This is it* looks, and then dashed to the front door and threw it open wearing our warmest, most welcoming faces.

But it wasn't Esther who greeted us. It was a man in a black polo shirt, short-sleeved despite the January weather, wanting to know if we were Luc O'Donnell and Oliver Blackwood.

"We are," Oliver told him.

There was a van behind him—also black—and at a nod from Black Polo Shirt Guy Number One, some other Black Polo Shirt Guys opened the doors at the back and hauled out a young girl. She was pale with that kind of dishwater-blond hair, and she was… *scrawny* sounded mean. But there was a definite feral-cat vibe about her, like she was simultaneously hungry and wanted to kill you. Although the wanting-to-kill-you thing might have been at least a little bit to do with the handcuffs.

"Excuse me," I said, "what the actual fuck?"

"Hmm?" replied Black Polo Shirt Guy as if he neither knew nor cared which specific fuck I was questioning the actuality of.

Oliver translated. "Why was she restrained?"

"She got violent."

"There are three of you," Oliver pointed out, "and she's fourteen."

Black Polo Shirt Guy shrugged. "We've got a zero-tolerance policy."

Two large men escorted the violent fourteen-year-old to our door and uncuffed her. Then they dropped her possessions beside her in a black bin liner, and she glared up at them with what I felt was pretty justified resentment.

Oliver half stooped towards her. "Hello, Jasmine," he said in a tone I'd never quite heard him use before. Which was a little bit jarring because I thought I knew all of the Olivers.

"Jaz," she replied.

"Hello, Jaz," Oliver corrected himself. "I'm Oliver, this is Lucien—"

"Luc," I said.

"We'll be looking after you," he went on, while I signed for Jaz like she was a Parcelforce delivery.

Jaz looked less impressed than I had ever seen anybody look about anything. And I'd gone to see the *Maleficent* movie with Priya.

Undaunted in the face of our new foster child's visible contempt, Oliver kept robustly to the script. "If you've got all your things, maybe you'd like us to show you to your room?"

She barely even shrugged.

Before taking her inside, Oliver turned his attention to Black Polo Shirt Guy. "I'll be making a complaint," he told him.

"You do you, mate," Black Polo Shirt Guy replied with the kind of apathy you had to really, really work at.

Then he and his co-polo-shirtists slouched back into their van, leaving me and Oliver officially in loco parentis. And, unofficially, completely out of our depth.

"Come on," I said, hoping a less formal approach would fail less hard with our guest…child…oh fuck.

To my relief, Jaz grabbed her bin liner and followed us inside. Once the front door was closed, it was safe to let Spud out, so I went through to the study and opened up his pen. For which I got no gratitude whatsoever because there was a new human in the building and Spud apparently didn't care about all the nights I'd spent sleeping on the floor with him.

"Ruff," he declared, bounding into the hall and sniffing at Jaz's knees, because Oliver had painstakingly trained him not to jump on people. "Ruff."

Jaz looked down. "Hey."

"That's Spud," I told her. "Spud, this is Jaz."

"Ruff," said Spud.

"Can I help you with your bag?" Oliver suggested.

That didn't get a reply, but I saw Jaz's grip tighten slightly on her bin liner.

"Are you hungry?" he tried.

Jaz shook her head.

"Would you like a drink?" *I* tried. And then, petrified I'd given the impression I was trying to ply her with alcohol: "Like water or Coke or something. Coke like the drink. Not like the stuff you put up your nose."

She shook her head again.

Oliver gave her his best and gentlest smile, which was a smile that made *me* feel safer and more loved than anything else in the world, but which seemed to wash over Jaz like a fart over a rock. "You probably want to get settled in. We'll show you your room."

We took Jaz upstairs and showed her the featureless magnolia cube we'd accidentally prepared for her to sleep in.

"You can decorate it however you'd like," Oliver told her, while I cringed at his side. "And there should be plenty of space for your things. If there isn't, we can always invest in some storage solutions."

Jaz had no strong reaction to that whatsoever. To be fair, I wasn't that interested in storage solutions at that age either. Or, for that matter, my current age. Which was probably why Oliver had a study you could find things in and I didn't. Letting her bin liner flop down on the floor like she could not possibly have given fewer shits about its contents, Jaz sat on the bed, staring at the walls as if she was in prison.

Still undeterred, Oliver pressed on. "Lucien and I will both be working from home today. He'll be downstairs, I'll be upstairs, so if you need either of us, that's where to look. The bathroom is just along the corridor, and there's spare bedding in the ottoman in the hall."

Jaz looked like she was barely paying attention.

"Lucien and I will probably be breaking for lunch around one"—Oliver's undeterred valour continued valiantly undeterred—"but if you want anything before then, do let us know. Or if you're comfortable, we're more than happy for you to look after yourself, if that's what you prefer. The kitchen's downstairs and, well, I'm sure you can find it."

"Sure," replied Jaz in a tone that said *I know you want me to say something, and this is something*.

"We'll leave you to get settled in," Oliver concluded, with studied cheerfulness. Then, as we slipped out the door, he stopped with his hand on the handle and added, "Open or shut?"

Jaz gave another of those not-even-a-shrugs.

Oliver left the door hanging ajar and we retreated downstairs. Behind us, we heard the decisive *click* of Jaz pulling it all the way closed.

And then we went and hid in the kitchen like grown-ups.

"Fuck," I said as quietly as I could manage, because while I wasn't too concerned about Jaz hearing me swear, I didn't especially want her to realise quite how incredibly uncool and unconfident I was. "Are we going to be shit at this?"

Oliver reached across the kitchen table and took my hand. Then he said, very clearly, very calmly, and with far greater conviction than I could possibly imagine having, given how things had gone so far, "No."

"Um, are you sure?"

"Yes."

I cowered in my seat. "Why?"

"Well firstly," he said, in a level tone that I hoped was aimed at reassuring me, not himself, "because 'not shit at this' is a fairly low standard to set for ourselves. And secondly, because we're intelligent, well-intentioned, caring people who will do everything we can to make this work."

"Is that enough, though?" I asked. "Because it kind of seems like she hates us."

"I'm sure she doesn't hate us." He sounded like he meant it. Okay, he sounded about ninety percent like he meant it. Maybe eighty.

"She's said six words since she stepped through the door. And two of those were to Spud."

A slightly distant smile played across Oliver's lips. "I don't want to lean too hard into stereotypes, but I think that might just be because she's a teenager."

"You think?" I was kind of having a weird moment where I couldn't tell if I wanted Oliver to be the rock beneath my wings or my partner in panic. He was clearly steering hard into *rock*, which was comforting on one level. But on another, sneakier level, it made me worried in a way I couldn't quite put my finger on. "I mean, I wasn't expecting her to skip over the threshold in a gingham dress and do a musical number about how she has a home at last. I was just… I suppose I don't know what I was expecting."

"Remember, they brought her to us in handcuffs with her belongings in a bin liner," said Oliver with a voice I recognised from when he talked about his more difficult clients. "It's understandable that she has issues trusting authority."

"Okay." I tried not to squeak. "I *understand* that. I'm understanding it. I'm accepting its understandability. What the fuck do we do about it?"

Oliver's face was getting barristerer by the second. "Well." He put his hands over mine like he was telling me it was sepsis after all. "I think we do have to accept that we might not be able to do anything."

"Oh wow." This time I did squeak. "What fantastic foster parents we're going to be."

He'd gone full rock. Given how I was reacting, that, too, was probably understandable. "That's not what I'm saying. But, in my job, something you have to get used to is that there are some people who can't be helped. It's still important to do your best for them, but sometimes it fails, and you can't blame yourself."

"Jaz isn't a job, Oliver. She's a person."

"All of my clients are people," he replied, a little sharply. "And I assure you I never lose sight of that. What's important here is to recognise that we have a very clear role in Jasmine's life."

"God, you make it sound so fulfilling."

"This isn't about us, Lucien. This is about Jasmine and what she needs."

I stood up in a flail, even though it meant shaking off Oliver's hand. "That's the whole problem. I don't know what she needs. She's just sitting in a bare room looking hostile with bits of sad."

"You do know what she needs," Oliver said firmly. "We've received guidance on this. She needs stability and a warm, welcoming environment, and I honestly think we can provide that. Give her time to settle in, and everything will be fine."

I didn't feel very fine. Or like fineness was on the horizon. But if anything was going to wreck our chances of long-time fineitude with Jaz, it was me freaking the fuck out in the kitchen when she could walk in at any second.

So I swallowed my furball of fear and uncertainty and raw selfish insecurity and said, "Yeah. I guess you're right."

We barely saw Jaz at all that day. Oliver felt it was very important that she have her own space—I tried not to compare that too directly to what he'd said about Spud—so we stayed out of her room and just called from the corridor at lunchtime to see if she wanted anything. From her silence, we assumed that she didn't.

Although I was still feeling a little bit shaken up about the whole there-is-an-actual-human-with-complex-needs-depending-on-us-to-fulfil-those-needs thing, it was competing for headspace with the whole I-need-to-organise-a-very-cool-and-appropriately-alternative-music-festival-or-I'll-lose-my-job thing, and because apparently today was one of my pretending-to-be-a-professional days, the job thing won out.

So I sent the obligatory follow-up emails and the enquiry emails and the follow-up phone calls that had to come after the enquiry emails, and by five I'd at least got confirmation from the three mediocre wedding bands I'd been trying to book. Admittedly, in two out of three cases, the confirmation had confirmed that they didn't want to play my festival for shit-beetles, but Harvest Moon had been willing to do it. Although apparently they'd changed their name to Stardew now.

"Well," I said, putting a half a tick next to *book bands* in my mental list of things that needed doing, "that's nearly a win, isn't it, Spud?"

Spud said...Spud said nothing. Because Spud wasn't there.

"Spud?"

We'd left the pen door open because Spud was pretty well socialised by now, but on days I was home, he usually stayed in the study anyway for pack animal reasons. I got up from my desk and started searching.

"Spud?"

The patio doors were closed, and I couldn't see him in the garden, but I went out anyway just in case he'd developed some previously unknown doggy superpower and slipped through the keyhole or something.

"Spud!" I called out loudly enough that I was probably causing a minor nuisance to the neighbours.

An unwelcome face appeared over the fence into Next Door's Garden. "Lost your dog?"

"No," I lied unconvincingly.

"Yes, you have," replied Next Door's Kid with mocking triumph. "You're such a dickhead that your dog ran away, and you're too much of a dickhead to admit it."

I tried very, very hard to be the adult in the room. But I wasn't actually in a room and didn't feel much like an adult. "Up yours," I replied, extremely adultly.

"Up my what?"

I suddenly remembered that I was talking to a child and therefore couldn't explain either what I expected him to put things up or what I expected him to put up it. "Your...yours," I finished. It wasn't my finest hour.

"My yours?"

"Yes." I turned around to go back into the house.

"You going to call me a bum-face again?" asked Next Door's Kid as I walked maturely away.

I ignored him.

"Bum-face," he yelled, and then laughed his Gatling gun laugh.

Inside, I locked the doors carefully behind me and continued the search. Assuming the doggy-superpower scenario was off the table—which, let's be clear, it should have been from the start—Spud had to be in the house somewhere.

I started on the ground floor, hoping he'd not found a way to get into the fridge or something, which, again, seemed unlikely, assuming ordinary dog parameters. When that failed, I went upstairs, calling for him as I went.

Finally I heard a muffled "Ruff."

"Spud?" I stood mid-corridor and called out again.

"Ruff." The sound was coming from Jaz's room.

I approached cautiously and knocked on the door. "Jaz?"

No answer.

"Is Spud in there with you?"

"Ruff." That was Spud again, unless Jaz had a really good line in dog impressions.

From a certain point of view, I could have left it there. The missing pet mystery was solved, so I could, in fact, have just gone back to work. On the other hand, for all I knew, Spud was trapped alone in a sparsely decorated room. Although if he was, that meant we'd progressed from a missing pet mystery to a missing child mystery, which wasn't strictly an upgrade.

"Can I come in?" I asked.

Still no answer.

"Okay, I actually don't even know if you're there, so I'm going to come in unless you tell me not to."

I gave Jaz a count of five and then, when she said nothing, I eased the door open.

She was, in fact, there. She was lying on the bed, with her back propped up against the wall. I noticed that she was barefoot and that her toenails were painted a bright electric blue. Mostly, though, I noticed that she had my fucking dog on her lap.

I mean technically he was *our* dog. Mine and Oliver's. And even more technically he was all three of our dog, mine, Oliver's, and Jaz's on account of how she was in fact part of the family for as long as she needed to stay with us.

But less technically, she'd been here five minutes, and my fucking dog was lounging across her legs like they were the most comfortable place in the world.

"You okay?" I asked both of them, trying to sound friendly instead of horribly betrayed.

"Ruff," said Spud.

Jaz didn't say anything.

"Is he going to be..." I tried, then I went to, "It's just, we've got this quite strict training thing."

And for the first time since she'd arrived, Jaz said a whole sentence. "I can look after a fucking dog."

It would have been hypocritical of me to say *Language*, but also I felt I should probably say *Language*. I didn't, though, because as well as being a hypocrite, I was also a coward. "Okay," I said instead. "Let me know if you need anything." And I beat a hasty retreat downstairs.

My Spudless workday ended well enough, dog-treachery aside, and I didn't really begrudge Jaz the company. It was probably nice for her to hang out with somebody she could not-talk with.

Oliver made us a Tuscan bean stew for dinner on the basis that it would keep warm and have flexible serving portions, so Jaz could choose whether to join us or not. I wasn't especially surprised when she chose *not*, and I just about heard Oliver's voice from upstairs as he told her that she was welcome to change her mind anytime and that the leftovers would be in the fridge if she was hungry later.

"It's fine," Oliver reassured me when he came back down.

Once again, I did my best to be the fineness I wanted to see in the world. It lasted for as long it took me to tear off a chunk of focaccia and dip it into the balsamic-vinegar-and-olive-oil drizzle that Oliver had set out in a dish for us. "Is it? She hasn't eaten all day or left her room, and she's still hardly said anything to either of us. And what she has said had *fucks* in it."

Oliver frowned. "We should probably make sure we teach her to moderate her language."

"Great," I said with extremely fake enthusiasm. "How?"

"Set positive examples and clear boundaries."

"Great," I said with equally fake enthusiasm. "How?"

"By being explicit about what we require from her and responding consistently. The advantage of human beings relative to dogs is that you can actually explain things to them."

It wasn't the perfect time for it, but I tried to lighten the tone. "You've met my work colleagues. Explaining things to human beings is way harder than you make it sound."

"Young people are malleable," Oliver said, setting down his fork. "They rise or fall to your expectations. We just need to make sure ours are appropriate, bearing in mind that she's probably extremely traumatised."

I was just doing my best *Yeah, I guess you've got a point* nod when a voice came from the kitchen door.

"I'm not traumatised."

We both looked around to see Jaz in the doorway, bright blue toenails standing out sharply against the dark-grey dining room carpet.

"Would you like some dinner?" Oliver offered. "It's Tuscan bean stew."

She crossed the kitchen floor with quick, short steps and grabbed what was left of the focaccia. "I'm not *fucking* traumatised."

And before we could reply, or demonstrate our compassion, or set clear boundaries, she was gone.

OLIVER INSISTED THAT WE FOLLOW her. Which I didn't think was a great idea, but then my record when it came to evaluating idea-greatness was pretty damn spotty. I mean, my main contribution to the fostering process so far had been showing up late to our first home visit and being mildly resentful our foster kid got on with our dog.

We stopped outside Jaz's door, and Oliver knocked politely.

There was no answer.

He knocked again. "Jasmine?"

"Ruff." Once again, not Jaz.

"Jasmine," Oliver continued, "I understand that this is difficult for you and you're upset—"

Finally, she spoke. "Fuck off."

"Ruff."

"You stay out of this," I told Spud.

Oliver gave me a don't-anthropomorphise-our-pet-in-serious-conversations look. Which was a weirdly specific look to have, but he nailed it first time. "Jasmine," he repeated, "I understand you're in a difficult situation, but I'm going to ask you to kindly moderate your language while you're staying with us."

"Fuck off," was Jaz's predictable reply.

Oliver took a deep breath. "Once again," he said, "I understand that you're upset, but this is making me feel quite disrespected. I'm going to give you some space now, but when you're feeling ready, I would very much like it if you apologised."

Jaz didn't even dignify that with a *fuck off*.

We crept back downstairs. Normally, I'd have said something glib about how Oliver looked as bad as I felt, and that was true in a way, except it was less *as bad* than *as blank*. Because, honestly, neither of us really knew how to react.

"She'll come around," Oliver said with a confidence that I'd have called unearned in anyone else and was getting a bit fifty-fifty on, even with Oliver.

"Will she?"

"Clear boundaries," Oliver repeated as if it was some kind of mystical incantation, "and consistency."

That made sense, but it made sense in a kind of *well duh* way that, if I were Oliver, I'd probably have had a fancy technical name for. Like, obviously I wasn't about to cheerlead for unclear boundaries and inconsistency; I just wasn't sure this was the best boundary-drawing strategy we could possibly be using. The problem was, I couldn't really think of a better one. I almost envied Spud. He could draw clear boundaries by pissing on lampposts, and right then that had an appealing simplicity to it.

Either way, neither of us wanted to go from feuding with Jaz to feuding with each other, so we sort of let it drop there and did our best to have a nice evening. Which, and this will sound shit unless you've lived it, meant crashed out on the sofa together, with Oliver working on his laptop and me quietly watching one of the few reality shows my dad hadn't been in yet.

Come bedtime, we slunk upstairs, calling out a good night to Jaz as we went. We'd discussed whether to enforce a formal lights-out time for her and concluded that we probably should, except in that exact moment it didn't feel like the right approach. Besides, Oliver had read some research on how teenage brains are all weird with melatonin or something, so she could be expected to keep unusual hours.

Lying curled up in the dark, a terrible thought struck me.

"Oliver," I whispered.

"Yes?"

"You know how...like...you know how a big part of why we had to be strict about Spud sleeping up here is because otherwise we'd never..."

Oliver rolled over to face me. "Are you asking if we can have sex with a child in the house?"

I made a sort of *mm-hmm* noise.

"As in right now, or as in would it be inappropriate in general?"

Much as I would have loved to be the horny little fuck bunny the newspapers apparently thought I was too old to still be, I'd mostly meant in general. "The second one."

"Then no, it wouldn't be inappropriate."

I wriggled, partly from discomfort but partly because wriggling in bed next to Oliver was just nice. "Doesn't it feel icky, though?"

In the dark, I couldn't see the expression on Oliver's face, but I also totally could. "Lucien, how do you think straight couples with more than one child get that way?"

"I don't know. Judicious use of holidays? Sleepovers? Artificial insemination?"

"Parenting involves sacrifices. It doesn't involve *that many* sacrifices or nobody would do it. We should restrict ourselves to our bedroom, but otherwise I can't see there being any issues."

That was a satisfying-ish answer for about three minutes. Then I found myself somewhat fatally asking, "But what if it's, like, *loud*?"

"I have faith in your self-control."

"I bloody well don't."

"Then"—Oliver bit me wickedly on the collarbone—"I shall buy you a ball gag."

Okay, that had escalated quickly. "I wonder why they don't put that in the parenting manuals."

"Oh, they do. It's usually in the chapter after clear boundaries and expectations."

I pulled a face which I was quite glad Oliver couldn't see. "You're just exploiting the fact that you've read books and I haven't."

"There *is* a simple solution to that," Oliver pointed out.

"But that would involve reading," I said with what I hoped was a playful whine. "I hate reading."

"You read that book about dogs."

"Only to prove you wrong."

I could feel Oliver's smile next to me. "I think that tells us some very important things about your personality. Now, we should probably go to sleep. It's a school night."

I'd got so used to *school night* being used as a general term for *night where you have to get up at a sensible time in the morning* that it took me a second to realise he meant it literally. Jaz would be starting her new school tomorrow, and, as primary caregiver, I had some care to primarily give. In this case, dropping her off, attending a meeting with something called a virtual school, and picking her up again at the end of the day.

"Oliver," I whispered again as I felt myself drifting off.

"Yes?"

"Do I need to know what Pupil Premium Plus is?"

He gave me the gentlest of squeezes and kissed me on the back of the head. "I'm afraid so."

The following morning, I discovered to my cost that dressing like a grown-up and dressing like an adult were two different things, and I'd spent most of my life doing the second one. I was pretty sure my skintight fuck-me jeans and my skintight fuck-me T-shirts—crap,

I had a lot of skintight fuck-me clothes—weren't the kind of thing you wore to take your foster kid to school. At the other end of the scale, I had suits I wore to meet our richer, more arseholey donors, but, at a West London comprehensive, those were going to scream *tryhard wanker*. And people would probably scream *tryhard wanker* directly at me. Or, I don't know, whatever the youngs were yelling at the olds these days. *Rizzless skibidi* or something. In the end, I pulled out the most appropriate bits of the smart-casualish ensembles I used with mid-level donors. So, sensibly cut jeans, with no obvious rips, and a shirt that didn't show my nipples.

Downstairs, Oliver was already mid-bircher. He hadn't put a jar out for me, but that was less from a lack of thought than from having thought enough to know that even with an early start, I'd avoid the bircher out of the fear I'd die from a health overdose.

"You can probably give Jasmine a little longer if you think she needs it," he said. "At her age, sleep cycles can be complicated."

"She prefers Jaz," I reminded him.

"I'm sure she does. But we're not here to be her friends, we're here to be her foster parents, and I think it's useful to remind ourselves of that."

This was another one of those situations where I saw his point, wasn't sure I agreed, but hadn't done enough research to disagree effectively. I was actually nervous enough that I didn't feel like breakfast, but I knew if I didn't have something, I'd wind up in a very important meeting with my stomach making weird noises and my brain constantly jabbing me with examples of things I could be eating.

I was just in the process of making myself a couple of slices of toast from the thick white bread that Oliver bought under sufferance and didn't eat, and which I let go mouldy three times out of five, when I noticed a bowl in the drying rack. I *never* put things in the drying rack. I'd sometimes put them in the dishwasher if I was feeling extraordinarily virtuous.

I pointed the renegade bowl out to Oliver, who didn't seem surprised.

"I assume Jasmine got up in the night and had some stew," he said. "Which I think is a good sign."

"It's a good sign that she's 'Be Our Guesting' us?"

Oliver gave me a quizzical look.

"Refusing to come to shared mealtimes and then feeding herself at midnight, possibly with the help of an animated candlestick."

"It's a good sign that she already feels comfortable treating the kitchen as her own."

That was way glass-half-fuller than I was personally capable of, but that was probably the morning talking. And the fact I had to go to school. In my thirties.

I whacked two slices of bread in the toaster. And then, when they came up far too pale, whacked them immediately down again.

"You know," Oliver told me, "you *could* just turn the dial up."

"Then they get burned."

"Don't they get burned this way as well?"

I slammed the *cancel* button, and two perfectly browned slices of toast popped up. "Not if I'm quick."

"And you couldn't be just as quick on a higher setting because..."

I gave Oliver a playfully grumpy look. "I've got a system and the system works."

"I think those are, at best, each half true."

Before I could defend my extremely sensible toast preparation scheme, we heard rapid footsteps coming downstairs and Jaz, wearing most of a school uniform, appeared in the kitchen, grabbed a slice of bread from the same packet I'd made my toast from, rolled it up, and started eating it butterless.

"Good morning," said Oliver.

I followed up with a, "Hey, Jaz."

"Ruff," said Spud, who had just appeared in the kitchen, attracted by the combination of new human and food.

"We got you a tie," said Oliver while I was measuring out Spud's breakfast. "I'll fetch it for you once I'm done."

Another barely-a-shrug from Jaz. "All right."

"We'll need to sort you out a blazer as well," he continued. "The tie only really comes in one size, but we didn't want to get you a blazer that didn't fit."

Spud was happily working his way through his meal, and Jaz had largely finished hers. They were both equally silent.

"Lucien can take you in on Saturday perhaps," Oliver pressed on. "Or after school one day this week."

"Sure."

Once Spud had finished his meal and we'd attended to his morning doggy needs—and those needs had been duly recorded in the Secret Diary of Spud's Arse Aged Zero and Three Quarters, which we were mostly keeping out of habit these days—Oliver set out to catch the train and I set out to do my first-ever school run.

Or at least I tried to.

"I can walk," Jaz told me, tying her new official school tie resentfully around her neck.

"It's your first day."

"I've had a lot of first days."

"And I need to be there for a meeting anyway."

She made an infinitesimally tiny gesture which eloquently told me that she didn't give a shit what I needed to be there for.

"Look." It was time for me to put my foot down. Which I could do because I was an adult and she wasn't and this was my job and holy fucking piss balls I hated it. "I'm driving you. That's... that's it."

"Whatever."

There was no more argument. Which I suppose...score one for

clear boundaries maybe? Then again it didn't seem like she'd ever cared one way or the other. And so ten minutes later—after a certain amount of faffing around getting Spud into his pen because apparently having a new person in the house had made him excitable and he was giving intense I-will-bolt-out-the-door-and-get-run-over-if-I-have-a-chance energy—we were in the car and I was backing us carefully out of the driveway.

In some ways, I'd been dreading the drive as much as the meeting. Because, while I had learned how to car shortly after we'd moved to Havering, in practice driving had remained very much Oliver's domain. It fed slightly into his control freak tendencies but, since I liked to fall asleep even on short journeys, it was probably safest all round.

Half into the road, I stalled. Which I suspected wouldn't do much for my image as a forceful authority figure, or a reliable caregiver, or as remotely competent.

"Sorry." I probably shouldn't have said that. After a bit of fiddling, I restarted the engine, backed us approximately two inches further, then stalled again. "Shit." I *definitely* shouldn't have said that. "I mean...sugar."

Jaz gave me a look of such withering contempt that I regretted every single decision that had brought me to that point. Individually. In chronological order.

Attempt number three saw me getting us neatly out of the drive, into the road, and then stopping dead at an awkward angle across two lanes. "Fu...pity's sake."

Then, just when I thought things couldn't get more humiliating, Jaz said, "Do you want me to drive?"

"Do you know how?" It was the wrong answer for six different reasons.

"Do you?"

"Yes." It was my protesting-too-much tone. Everybody could

pick up on my protesting-too-much tone, even people who were technically children. "I've just... I'm a bit out of practice."

To my relief—and it said a lot about how low my bar for relief was right then—Jaz was so fundamentally uninterested in me that she didn't even want to revel in my misery and embarrassment. She just turned and stared out of the window.

After a couple of deep breaths and a moment to remind myself that I could do this, that I was a grown-up, and that I did, in fact, more or less know how cars worked, I drove us away.

Jaz's new school wasn't that far from our house, so the trip was only about ten minutes, but ten minutes became an unbelievably long time when you were in a car with a teenage girl who had known you for a day, seen ample evidence you were shit at pretty much all life stuff, and saw no reason to say words in your presence.

After about three of the ten impending minutes, I was finding the whole vibe so unbearable that I heard myself say, "Sorry we upset you last night," just to break the silence.

To my surprise, it actually worked. A bit. "I'm not traumatised." Jaz didn't even look away from the window.

"I mean..." This probably wasn't the right way to go. It probably wasn't setting clear expectations or anything. "Everybody is a bit, aren't they?"

At the very least, I'd got her attention. She whipped around and glared at me. "Oh right, because that's what he meant, wasn't it? 'She's extremely traumatised but only in the exact same way everybody else is because shit is hard for everyone and I'm not making any assumptions about her mum or her life or anything.'"

Oliver would have wanted me to pick her up on saying *shit*, but while my parenting instincts weren't stellar, now seemed like a terrible time to do that. "No," I admitted, "he probably didn't mean that."

"Just because I'm *looked after*." She said the words with a mix of disgust and sarcasm I recognised better than I liked to admit.

"You *did* get delivered to us in handcuffs," I pointed out.

Her face said that this wasn't a big deal, but her thumb traced unconsciously at a line around her wrist.

"How did that... What went on there?" I asked.

"Like they said, I got violent."

This was going to places I was not at all qualified to go, which, thinking about it, was a huge fucking problem because going there was kind of my job now. "Violent how?"

"Spat at one of them."

"That...doesn't seem like a good reason to handcuff you."

She shrugged.

Apparently, the conversation had come to a natural stopping point. I permitted myself a cautious whisper of optimism that she at least hadn't spat on me yet.

CHAPTER 20

WE ARRIVED PRETTY QUICKLY AT St. Jude's Church of England Academy, and I parked us, very inexpertly, in a dull grey car park down a dull grey road behind some actually fairly nice but still pretty dull redbrick houses. It wasn't my first visit. I'd been with Oliver as part of the endless round of pre-Jaz meetings when we were scouting schools, but I still got a kind of itch in my stomach just looking at the place. There was just something about school buildings that made me feel fifteen and in trouble, even though I definitely wasn't one of those things and was only sometimes the other.

The sign between the car park and the entrance to the school proper very firmly instructed all visitors to report to reception, so to reception we reported. Or at least I reported. Jaz trailed behind me looking like she'd rather be anywhere else, or perhaps with any*one* else. With the possible exception of Oliver.

The receptionist was a friendly-looking woman in perhaps her mid-forties with her hair in a bob and her glasses halfway down her nose.

"Can I help you?" she asked.

"Luc O'Donnell and Jasmine Johnson. We have a meeting about her..." Fuck. Fuck fuck fuck. "Her personal plan thing?"

The receptionist looked at her computer screen helpfully.

"Personal Education Plan? You'll be meeting with Miss Collins and a representative from the virtual school at nine fifteen."

"And my mum," said Jaz.

The receptionist looked at her quizzically. "Pardon?"

"He'll be meeting with Mum. She'll be coming too."

The receptionist looked back at the screen. "Oh yes. I was just talking about staff. There'll be a social worker there as well."

At the mention of a social worker, Jasmine scowled, but the receptionist ignored it and so did I.

"If you'd like to take a seat."

There were low, not especially comfortable chairs by one wall, the kind that one hundred percent of waiting rooms and reception areas seemed to have, as if they were all handed out centrally from some giant not-especially-comfortable-chair warehouse. Nearby, a neat white table had a few copies of the school newsletter laid out for people who wanted something to read but didn't have phones.

I *did* have a phone. But the irrational voice at the back of my brain said that the newsletters were there as a test. A Good Parent Test to see if I was Taking an Interest or not. They weren't, obviously. They were probably just the cheapest reading matter the school had to hand and could be sure was appropriate for children. I picked up a copy anyway and leafed through examples of year seven artwork, poems written by year eights, details of the year nine geography trip to the Lower Lea Valley, and a bunch of other things that I should have been paying attention to and having opinions about but could only really respond to with a silent *Well, that seems nice*.

I was just *well-that-seems-nice*-ing my way through the diary dates and the notice congratulating something called "Sparx Maths Champions" when I heard a cheerful "Hi, Luc, hi, Jaz" and looked up to see Esther making her way past me to sign in at reception.

I said hi to Esther in return and, beside me, Jaz murmured

something under her breath that could just about have been mistaken for a greeting from a long distance in a bad light.

"Getting to be a bit of an old hand at this, aren't you?" said Esther to Jaz with what I read as genuine sympathy but which I strongly suspected Jaz read differently.

"S'pose," Jaz muttered. She was still staring at her phone—a cheap pay-as-you-go job that it was presumably my and Oliver's responsibility to keep topped up and, for that matter, monitor her use of.

Esther gave me a typically bright look. "Miss Collins should be ready for us soon. Don't worry, Luc, I've met her before and she doesn't bite."

I gave what I hoped was a good-humoured smile. "Oh good."

"And you'll soon get used to how everything works," she added.

Unusually, this actually prompted Jaz to make an audible response. "There'll be a *lot* of meetings."

"How many?" I asked, trying not to sound like I hated the idea more than I did in fact hate the idea.

"Every time I change schools." She was counting on her fingers now. "Then a couple of months after changing schools, then a few months after that, then special extra ones every time I"—she moved her fingers from counting duty to air-quotes duty—"'display challenging behaviour.'"

I probably shouldn't have been asking but I did. "How often do you display 'challenging behaviour'?"

"Quite a lot."

"I don't suppose you'd consider...not? I mean, it'd save us both a lot of meetings."

Jaz looked at me like I was the world's least skibidi person.

Esther just laughed in a way I found reassuringly professional. "That *is* pretty much the size of it. But"—she gave me a look that I found uncomfortably understanding—"has 'Just don't' ever worked for you?"

"No," I admitted. "Then again, I'll go a very long way to get out of a meeting."

Jaz was still ignoring us, so we just had time to lapse back into another awkward silence before the receptionist put down her phone and told us that Miss Collins was ready for us.

Esther, who had clearly worked with this school before, led me and Jasmine the short distance up the corridor to the deputy headmistress's office, which, it seemed, was also the office of the school's designated teacher for looked-after and previously-looked-after children. Presumably because they were in fact the same person.

I'd expected Miss Collins to look the way I remembered teachers looking when I was Jaz's age, which was to say ancient, withered, and extremely unradical. When she turned out to be slightly younger than me, and probably less withered as well, I felt kind of personally attacked. Sitting beside her was a man of similar insultingly-my-agedness, who was not only wearing a grey cardigan but also seemed to be made entirely out of them.

"Mr. O'Donnell?" Miss Collins didn't give me a hand to shake, but she indicated a chair for me to sit in. One of three currently unoccupied. "Jasmine? Do take a seat. Mr. O'Donnell, I don't think you've met Mr. Lorimer. He's Jasmine's liaison with the virtual school."

"Hi, Jaz," said Mr. Lorimer in a voice like an overworked vicar.

Jaz grunted something that might have been *hi* in return.

With all the introductions, I hadn't quite got around to taking a seat yet, but Esther had taken hers comfortably enough and I followed suit. Jasmine stayed resolutely standing.

"You can sit down," Miss Collins told her. "You're part of this meeting too."

Jaz looked at the chair like it was booby-trapped. "Where'll Mum sit?"

Mr. Lorimer looked at Jaz with forlorn, slightly wet eyes, which might just have been the only eyes he had. "We're not expecting her, I'm afraid."

"She'll be here," Jaz insisted.

"None of us have heard from her," explained Esther, gently. "We'll find her a seat if she shows up, but it's unlikely—"

"She'll *be here*," Jaz insisted again. "She knows about this. She's been told."

The briefing Oliver and I had been given about Jaz's homelife had been highly detailed in some ways, infuriatingly vague in others. We knew that her mother was a single parent, that she had some kind of highly nonspecific mental health condition, and that Jaz had been put in the system for *severe neglect* rather than *abuse*. But a combination of confidentiality rules and the telephone game of institutions talking to institutions had left us otherwise in the dark. We'd been told rather more about the kinds of behaviours we could expect, although we'd also been warned that the thing we should expect the most was *the unexpected*.

"We could give her five minutes?" I suggested. The meeting was already due to start, but I was used to operating on CRAPP time and delays were well baked into my regular working practice.

Miss Collins looked disapproving. "I don't think that would be appropriate. We have a lot to get through. Normally we'd want to start by looking at what's been going well and what our challenges have been so far, but since Jasmine—"

"Jaz," Jaz and I said simultaneously, and Jaz gave me a look of what I could only describe as grudging solidarity.

"Since Jaz is new to the school and I believe"—Miss Collins looked to me for confirmation—"new to your family as well, we should look instead at how things went at your previous school."

This second *your* was directed at Jaz, which I appreciated because it would have felt ick as fuck if this whole thing had been us talking about her as if she wasn't in the room. Jaz, though, seemed to appreciate it a lot less. She slouched against the chair she was reserving for her mother and said nothing.

Esther leaned over to her and said, very quietly, "This is your space. You can say anything you need to say."

Jaz, as ever, wasn't in much of a mood to say anything.

"Perhaps," prompted Mr. Lorimer, "you could tell us something about your goals relating to attendance?"

We'd also been informed that Jaz's attendance at her previous school had been dog shit. Obviously it hadn't been put in those exact words. Nor did Jaz herself seem inclined to put it into those words. Or indeed any words.

"In your last term at Bellefield," Miss Collins added, "you seem to have been going to far below eighty percent of your classes."

"Eighty percent doesn't sound too bad," I said.

Except it was clearly the wrong thing to say because Miss Collins gave me a stern whose-side-are-you-on look that made me feel like I'd been caught passing notes in class. "It's a day off a week," she pointed out. "And I said *far below*."

"I was ill," Jaz muttered.

Mr. Lorimer leaned forwards earnestly. "Remember that this is a fresh start. Previous challenges only matter insofar as we can learn from them."

"Guess I'll *learn* not to be ill then," replied Jaz with a level of contempt I didn't think I'd heard her use even with Oliver.

"I seem to remember," Esther prodded, "the fighting was also something you wanted to improve on."

Jaz scowled. "I want people to stay out my face, yeah. You can write that down as one of your little targets if you like. 'People should stay out of Jaz's face.'"

"Okay." Mr. Lorimer nodded encouragingly. "But maybe we could phrase that in a more helpful way."

"'Jasmine would like,'" said Jaz, her voice dripping with so much sarcasm that it probably constituted a slip hazard, "'to build more productive relationships with her peers.'"

The three other adults in the room made three other sets of notes. I shifted uncomfortably in my chair. "Unless I'm missing something, I don't think she actually *meant* that."

Jaz shot me a look that was almost conspiratorial. "It's quicker this way."

"I know this seems a bit tickboxy and corporate," Esther said soothingly. "But having clear goals really does help."

Set boundaries. Have high expectations. Oliver would have been so much better at this than I was. I stayed mostly quiet while the rest of the room went through the frankly bewildering business of trying to set SMART targets for a child's happiness. Having done a lot of this kind of stuff in Barbara Clench's mandatory team-building meetings, it felt wrong to me to see it applied to something that mattered, rather than to the number of staples we were using. But I also kind of couldn't look away. It was like a car crash, except a bunch of experts kept explaining very sincerely that if the crash went on long enough, the cars would actually come out of it better off.

After that there was the well-meaning conversation around what the school could do to support Jaz in achieving her specific, measurable, achievable, realistic, time-constrained goals that we were all, it seemed, now agreeing to accept. And once again I tried incredibly hard not to feel useless because I didn't even know what sorts of things we should've been asking the school for. Someone brought up biweekly meetings with a pastoral support coordinator, and that sounded like a good thing? But maybe it was a bad thing or a thing that wouldn't help or a thing that had been tried already or a thing that would make Jaz feel judged and overwatched.

I glanced over at her, hoping for some kind of clue about her, y'know, needs, but she seemed as in the dark as I was. Or perhaps she'd just given up on anything working. When I did catch her eye,

I mostly got can-you-believe-this-shit looks from her that I tried really hard not to mirror. Tried really hard and, ultimately, failed.

Because, like, could you believe this shit?

When we were done and we'd all agreed that we knew what our roles were and what we were accountable for and that we'd been appropriately pupil-centric and receptive, we set a follow-up meeting for half term.

"It would probably be best," said Miss Collins, "if Jaz started formally on Monday, rather than coming in halfway through a school day. If you'd like to stay a little while"—she was looking at Jaz now—"we could get somebody to show you around, so things are a bit less confusing next week."

To my utter unsurprise, Jaz gave one of her patented barely-shrugs.

A few short minutes later, an earnest-looking sixth former was getting ready to give us the tour. But *us* turned into *just Jaz* when Esther touched me on the shoulder and said, "Luc, have you got a moment?"

Since Jaz was clearly going to be fine without me—and probably substantially happier—I had no excuse for telling our social worker I *didn't* have a moment. "Sure," I replied. And then, because it felt like the responsible thing to do, I added to Jaz, "You going to be okay?"

I didn't expect an answer. I didn't get one.

Meanwhile, Esther ducked into a free classroom and I ducked after her.

"So," she said. It was pretty much a sentence by itself.

I winced. "Did I fuck that up horribly?"

"No." From her tone it was a very *literal* no. The no of "You didn't fuck up *horribly*," not the no of "You didn't fuck up *at all*."

I was still wincing. "Yay?"

"You have the right instincts," she told me. "You're *supposed* to be on Jaz's side, and more importantly she's supposed to *feel* like you're on her side. It's just…"

"Just?" I was asking a lot of one-word questions today.

"Don't forget your job is to look out for her best interests. Not to make her like you."

I let out a burst of nervous laughter. "Oh, don't worry, I'm pretty sure there's no danger of her liking me."

"You know"—Esther had folded her arms and was giving me a too-insightful-for-comfort look—"I don't think you actually believe that. I think you know you're a likable person, and I think you know how to be charming when you have to be. And those are good qualities. You're still allowed to be a human being here, Luc."

"Oh good." I sounded flatter than I'd meant to.

"Just remember to be a parent as well."

The part of me that still felt like it was fifteen and in trouble was laughing unhelpfully at that. "I…I don't suppose you've got any tips?"

Esther sat casually on a desk in a way I thought she probably would have done when she was at school too. "Mostly, keep doing what you're doing."

I felt like there was a *but* coming. Which is why I said, "I feel like there's a *but* coming."

"*But*"—Esther let it hang there a moment—"don't undermine the other people who are part of this. We don't know each other that well, but the impression I get is that you're not the sort of guy who usually goes in for Personal Plans and Goal-Setting and Student-Centred Learning Approaches."

There comes a point when you're wincing so much that it's the gaps between winces that actually feel like gestures. This wasn't one of those gaps. "Was I eye-rolling really hard?"

Esther did the *lil' bit* sign, the one where you hold your fingers like two millimetres apart and make an embarrassed face.

"I guess I just...I don't feel like you can boil a human being down to a few action points and notes for improvement."

"Oh right." Sometimes Esther could really give Jaz a run for her money on the sarcasm front. "Now you've pointed that out, I'll rethink my entire approach to my profession. We *know* that, Luc. Even Doug"—she caught my blank expression—"Doug Lorimer knows that. But it really does help to have—"

"High expectations and clear boundaries?" I echoed Oliver from half a city away.

"Basically, yeah. And look, if it's any consolation, thinking your kid is so unique and special that the rules that work for everybody else, however imperfectly, aren't good enough for her is a *very* parent mindset. Just...if you could shade it down like ten percent."

I nodded. I was weirdly tempted to give her one of Jaz's almost-shrugs. "I'll try."

"That's all any of us can do."

Oliver kind of kept saying that as well. But for some reason—maybe because Esther was an authority figure, not my boyfriend—it was more reassuring. And, fuck me, I needed the reassurance.

THE DRIVE HOME WAS ALMOST a perfect mirror image of the drive out. A mirror image in the sense that we'd turned around and were going in the opposite direction. Not in the metaphor sense where either of us had done a 180 on our attitudes.

After Esther's little chat, I did wonder if I should try to do some damage control on the whole Personal Education Plan thing. Like try to convince Jaz that I didn't think it was bullshit. Except while I understood rationally that the people who did this kind of thing for a living probably knew what they were about, I still didn't think I could be enthusiastic about SMART goal-setting in a way that wouldn't come across as incredibly fake and insincere.

So instead I went with a nice neutral, "You hungry?"

She didn't answer.

"Okay, let's try it a different way. *I'm* hungry, so I'm going to stop for something to eat, and I can't leave you in a car because that would be illegal."

From the look she gave me, she felt that was very much a *me* problem. Fortunately, it wasn't quite enough of a *me* problem that she'd actually refuse to get out. So when I stopped outside a place that called itself the Cosy Café and went in to investigate their all-day breakfast and pie 'n' mash offerings, I had a bitter teenager shadowing me.

The small café I'd stopped at was one of those places with a menu as long as your arm covering everything from a full English breakfast to a homemade curry, so I stood there for a moment looking at my options while Jaz stood beside me radiating misery.

"You want anything?" I tried.

Jaz made a noise that I *thought* translated as "I'm fine" but could have been anything.

I tried again. "If I got you some chips, would you eat them?"

The movement of her head was *just* close enough to a nod that I thought it was probably worth ordering the chips on spec. I got her a tea as well because Oliver had looked up some research on adolescents and caffeine, and apparently we shouldn't have been feeding her coffee. And because I didn't want to be all rules-for-thee-and-not-for-me, I got a tea for myself as well.

Once I'd paid at the counter, we sat down and waited for our food, not quite looking at each other until Jaz, in her best don't-give-a-fuck-voice, said, "You forgot your receipt."

It felt a bit out of nowhere, but at least she was talking. "I'd just lose it. Anyway, I'm not really a reconciling-my-bank-statements kind of guy."

For no reason I could understand, a look of puzzlement settled over Jaz's brow. "How you going to get the money back?"

Between Oliver talking law and ethics, and my colleagues talking nonsense, I had a lot of experience with having no fucking clue what people were on about. This felt closer to the Oliver end of the spectrum. "Get my money back for what?"

She waved her hand over the table and looked at me like I knew nothing about how the world worked. "This. It's an expense, isn't it?"

"Not that much of an expense. I think it was like fifteen quid?" Shit, I was bad with money.

Every word out of my mouth seemed to bring me a rung lower in her estimation, and I hadn't been that high up to begin with. "It's an expense," she said. "Like as in, you can expense it. Get your money back off the agency. Or the government or something. I don't know how it works. You should, though."

I probably should have. "Honestly," I told her, putting my hands up in a too-defensive-for-talking-to-children gesture, "that's exactly the sort of detail I tend to screw up."

The puzzlement on Jaz's brow only deepened. "So what'd you bring me for?"

"I told you, it'd be illegal to leave you in the car."

I'd been joking, but she didn't seem to quite get it. "You could've took me home first. Got a takeaway or something."

"I guess I thought stopping at a café would be…nice?"

"Nice?" Coming from Jaz, the word sounded almost foreign.

"Well, I *am* meant to be looking after you."

And *that* got a laugh. I wasn't sure why. Or at least I wasn't sure why until she said, "Oh yeah. That's right. I'm a looked-after child, aren't I. Sooo looked after."

A friendly-looking waiter set down a plate of chips in front of Jaz and a full English in front of me.

A thought struck me. "Y'know, Oliver's vegan so if you did want to eat something with meat in it, now would be a good chance. I can still order you a bacon sandwich or something."

Staring me dead in the eye, Jaz reached down, grabbed one of my two sausages between thumb and forefinger, picked it up, and took a bite out of it.

"Hey, I said I could order you something."

She set the remaining half sausage down on top of her chips. "I'm good."

"I don't care if you're *good*, that's my fuc—flipping sausage you've just stolen."

"You know"—Jaz glared at me contemptuously—"I *have* heard the word *fuck* before."

"Not from me you haven't."

All the scorn in the world was channelling itself through Jaz's eyes and into my soul.

"Not *intentionally.*"

For some reason the scorn continued.

So with trademark Luc O'Donnell maturity, I reached across the table and stole one of her chips.

"Hey!" The amount of outrage she managed to pack into one syllable with such a small larynx was genuinely impressive.

"Don't like it, do you?"

"You've got your own."

"And I'd have got you your own sausages if you'd asked," I replied, feeling *almost* like a real grown-up. Well, as much like a real grown-up as I could feel when I was two steps away from getting into a food fight with a teenager. "Anyway, technically this is all my own because I paid for it and we've established I'm not going to be able to claim the money back."

I'd meant it as lighthearted, but Jaz went silent at once and started staring intensely into her tea.

"Sorry." I was probably apologising too much. It probably wasn't parental to be apologising this much. In the hope of salvaging what I'd almost thought was a positive interaction, I pivoted to, "Do people really claim it back off tax or something every time they take you somewhere?"

Jaz nodded. "I cost a lot of money."

That was, I supposed, strictly true. "Well yeah. But that's kind of what having a kid is like, isn't it?"

"Your own kid," Jaz half agreed. "But I'm not. I'm just some poor little looked-after girl. Who wants to pay for that?"

I knew from my many, many terrible life choices how awful it could feel to be pitied. And I was whatever-the-opposite-of-oblivious-is enough to know that anybody who called themselves a *poor little something* on no account wanted to be thought of as a poor little anything. But Jesus fucking Christ, she was an actual child.

Unfortunately, my stunned silence had given Jaz's brain ample space to answer for me. "This is the bit where you tell me how different you are and how much better it'll be this time."

I really wanted to. Because I really thought we were and I really hoped it would. But it also felt like a huge trap. So I said, "Would you believe me?"

Jaz glared. "Would *you?*"

We didn't really say much after that. We just sat in silence while Jaz ate her chips. And the rest of my sausage. And half my bacon.

"The actions," Oliver was saying into the phone, "of your employees were unacceptable."

Jaz was in her room. Spud was in her room with her. I was on the sofa watching *Taskmaster* with the sound off and the subtitles on. At the other end of the phone, somebody in an office was saying something evasive that I was very, very glad Oliver was dealing with instead of me.

"Contrary to what you may believe, 'We have a zero-tolerance policy' isn't a blanket excuse for you to do whatever you like."

Oliver stood stock still while the, I'm sure, extremely underpaid and underappreciated person at the other end of the line trotted out the next bit of whatever script they were working from.

"My tone is not combative."

Okay, maybe they weren't working *precisely* from a script.

"Your working practices contravene the recommendations of the Children's Commissioner, the UN Committee Against Torture, *and* the UN Convention on the Rights of the Child."

A pause. Quite a short one.

"No, I'm simply stating the facts of the situation."

Another pause.

"I'm aware of that."

And another.

"I'm aware of that also."

A final, extremely long pause.

"I understand. Thank you for your time." He hung up and sat down next to me. "Well, that could have gone better."

"Not interested?" I asked, pausing *Taskmaster* at just the right moment to catch Greg Davies with his mouth hanging open like an overheated Irish wolfhound.

"Oh no, they were absolutely *delighted* to have me calling them up to say that they needed to make massive changes to their working practice. There's nothing that large institutions love more than change."

I laid my head against his shoulder in a way that, in our private love language, said *I'm here for you*, even though to an outsider it might have looked more like *I'm extremely sleepy*. "So what now?"

To my...not surprise, really, but deep sadness, this was one of the few situations where Oliver didn't have an answer. I didn't like Oliver not having an answer. I didn't like Oliver not having an answer almost as much as Oliver didn't like Oliver not having an answer. "Human rights law is more Jennifer's area than mine, and Jennifer's a little distracted at the moment, what with...what with everything."

He had a point. Jennifer and Peter had a whole lot of everything going on right about then. "So are we just going to drop it?"

"They delivered a child to us *in handcuffs*," Oliver replied. "Dropping it shouldn't be an option."

The *shouldn't be* hung there like one of my socks on the back of a chair. It was, now I thought about it, the first time I'd really seen Oliver run up against something he couldn't solve. That we couldn't solve between us.

"Unfortunately," he went on, "we might have no alternative. There's already campaigns about this. MPs have brought it up in Parliament. We could *possibly* sue the security company, try to force a test case. Only…"

"Only I can't imagine that being remotely what Jaz wants?" I said.

Oliver nodded and let himself slump against me so we made a sort of mismatched A shape on the sofa. "Probably I shouldn't even have taken it this far."

I took his hand and squeezed it. "No. No, you should have. What they did was fucked, and when something's fucked, you can't just sit around and not say, 'That's fucked.' You have to stand up and, and…"

"And say, 'That's fucked'?"

"Yeah."

Oliver squeezed my hand back. "Still, I'm not sure Jasmine would appreciate it."

That felt like an understatement. "I don't think it's about being appreciated, though, is it?"

"No. No, I suppose not." Beside me, Oliver shifted through tense into restless into active in the space of three heartbeats. He stood up, unnecessarily decisively. "I think I *will* email Jennifer. It can't hurt and she might value the distraction."

"If you think it's best," I said, not quite wanting to go full *Don't get your hopes up*.

"Besides," he added, "I've been meaning to chase her up about that dinner party."

Oliver was still looking deeply dissatisfied. "If it helps," I said, "I think it's kind of hot that you tried."

"To organise a dinner party? Lucien, I know you're easily pleased but—"

"To help. To make things right."

He gave me a weak, slightly self-recriminating smile. "I'm not sure I did either of those things. I think I just wasted a lot of people's time."

Leaning forward, I beckoned him towards me, and when he came over, I took him by the fingertips and drew him down into my lap. I let my forehead rest against his so our eyes blurred together, Oliver's this perfect silvery horizon. "One of the many, many annoying things that you've taught me is that standing up for what you believe in is *never* a waste of time."

"I've taught you that?"

I gave an exaggerated shrug. "I mean, it was you, Disney movies, or motivational posters. But either way, it's true."

He laughed. And then when he was done laughing, he kissed me.

CHAPTER 22

BANGBANGBANGBANGBANG.

"Ruffruffruffruffruff."

"Lucien, can you possibly get that? I'm in the middle of braising tofu."

Bangbang.

"Ruffruffarooou."

I'd had worse starts to my weekend. But not, admittedly, recently.

Bangbangbang.

Making my way apprehensively into the hall, I wondered who the hell was hammering on our door so aggressively at such a boring time on a Saturday evening.

After I opened the door and the noise abruptly stopped, I still wondered who the hell had been hammering on our door at such a boring time on a Saturday evening because it took me a few seconds to recognise the angry woman in the denim utility jacket and satin athleisure trousers glaring at me from the doorstep.

It was Next Door's Kid's Mum.

"Do you have any idea," she began. It wasn't a promising beginning. "What that…that chavvy termagant you've brought into our community did to my son?"

I didn't. I probably should have. I probably should also have not been hoping it had been something painful and humiliating. "Whatever it was," I said in my best conciliatory voice, "I'm sure"—*he deserved it*—"it won't happen again."

"She threw him in a wheelie bin."

Doing my best conciliatory voice had drained so much of my energy that I was completely unable to maintain my best conciliatory face or say the best conciliatory words. "Oh, thank fuck," I said.

Next Door's Kid's Mum stared at me like I'd just made a joke about the queen dying on the day of her official state funeral. "*Excuse* me?"

"Well, I was worried it was something serious."

"She *threw him*," Next Door's Kid's Mum repeated with a note of rage so finely tuned it could shatter wineglasses, "in a *wheelie bin*."

I felt a totally inappropriate and annoyingly hard-to-suppress urge to giggle. "Which is bad," I conceded at once, "but it's also a bit…I mean…it's a bit Dennis the Menace, isn't it?"

"A bit *what*?"

Next Door's Kid's Mum was at least my age, so it wasn't an obscurity-of-reference issue. It was an acceptability-of-reference issue. "I just… It's more of a *youthful hijinks* kind of vibe than a"—I saw the look on her face and decided against finishing that sentence—"okay, it's still bad. And we'll still talk to her about it."

"He could have been *killed*."

I just about stopped myself saying, *Could he, though?* And for that matter from adding, *He could have got sepsis*. And to my immense relief, while I was stopping myself saying things, Oliver appeared behind me.

"Hello, Jacqueline."

"Oliver." Next Door's Kid's Mum inclined her head a fraction of an inch. "Your *guest*—"

"Foster child," corrected Oliver.

"Threw *my son* into a *wheelie bin*."

Oliver nodded once with barristerial gravitas and said, "Is Colin okay?" Thinking about it, I should probably have opened with that too.

Next Door's Kid's Mum didn't look mollified exactly. But she gave an impression that moll could be an option in the future. "He'll recover."

"Well, that's the most important thing." Oliver sounded like he actually meant it and, worse, he probably did. "And you can be assured I'll be having words with Jasmine about her behaviour and she'll be suitably punished."

Glad as I was that Oliver was handling this, he was definitely Handling This. And it hadn't passed me by that he was doing the bad kind of *I* statements. The kind that you used when you should really be doing *we* statements.

"If this happens again..." Next Door's Kid's Mum warned.

And I was disproportionately proud of myself for not replying with *If this happens again what?*

"It won't," replied Oliver for both of us. And he said it with such certainty and such finality that Next Door's Kid's Mum actually took it as a valid answer.

She straightened her jacket and gave him another nod. An I'm-glad-we-understand-each-other nod. "Thank you, Oliver."

"Not at all. Thank you for bringing this to our attention."

And then she was gone, and Oliver was halfway up the stairs before I could remind him that Next Door's Kid was the living incarnation of the devil's arsecrack and had almost certainly deserved whatever happened to him. Or, for that matter, ask whether this was perhaps the kind of parenting decision that we should maybe talk about.

"Jasmine," Oliver was already saying through Jaz's door.

There was the predictable no reply.

"Jasmine, you can come out or I can come in."

There was still no reply, but we both heard a shuffling from inside and then the door edged open and Jaz edged around it. "What?"

"We've just been speaking to Jacqueline from next door," Oliver said, in his best firm-but-fair voice, "and she told us that you'd thrown Colin into a wheelie bin. Is that true?"

Jaz said nothing.

"Is that true?" Oliver repeated.

Jaz folded her arms.

Oliver looked down at Jaz with the kind of compassion I really doubted she'd appreciate. "You're not helping yourself. This is your opportunity to give your side of the story."

My brain couldn't quite help hearing that as *You may harm your defence if you fail to mention when questioned something you later rely on in court*. I suspected that Jaz's brain was similar.

"He had it coming," said Jaz at last. And with a tremendous effort of will, I didn't say, *See?*

Oliver gave an understanding nod, which only went down well if you thought he actually understood. "However you might have been provoked, we don't solve our problems with violence."

"*You* don't," Jaz replied, suddenly sounding almost passionate. "I'm *traumatised*, remember?"

Taking a deep, centring breath, Oliver got as far as "Jasmine, that's—" before Jaz cut him off with "My shitty headcase mum didn't bring me up right, so I have *inappropriate strategies*. I *lash out* and make *bad decisions*."

I knew Oliver wasn't immune to sarcasm. But he seemed to have developed a hell of a resistance to it where Jaz was concerned. "And what's important," he said fatally, "is that we help you change that."

With an exasperated "Fuck off," Jaz turned around and vanished into her room, slamming the door behind her.

"Jasmine?" Oliver called after her.

I put my hand on his arm and whispered, "We need to give her space, remember?" but he seemed to feel the giving-people-space rule was currently less important than the letting-people-know-they've-done-a-bad-thing rule.

"Jasmine," he went on, "you will need to apologise to Jacqueline and Richard."

Silence.

"You can do it in person, or you can write them a letter."

Silence.

"Jasmine, you need to make a decision on this."

"Fuck off."

Oliver stood very still, his hand resting on the doorknob. "I'm going to come into your room now, because I'm going to need you to speak to me face to face."

I wasn't sure why he waited after that. Like he thought he was going to get an *Okay, that seems reasonable, thank you for informing me in advance* or something. Funnily enough, he didn't get one.

He opened the door, and we went into Jaz's room to find her lying on her bed radiating surliness and staring fixedly at her phone. "Jasmine," Oliver said, "which is it going to be?"

Jaz didn't even acknowledge our presence. Through the open door, Spud nosed his way in and hopped up beside her.

"Jasmine," repeated Oliver. I got that he felt that using her full name helped maintain boundaries, but I thought he might have been overdoing it just the scoochiest of scooches. "I'm asking you a question. I want an answer."

With a sense of timing I almost envied, Jaz let that hang for a moment, then just said, "No."

"Pardon?" asked Oliver, incredulous.

"No. I'm not apologising."

"I'm not giving you a choice."

Jaz said nothing.

"You can take it as read that you're *already* grounded," Oliver went on, "but if you continue with this attitude, things will only get worse for you."

Jaz's eyes flicked up from her screen. "How?"

"For a start, you can hand over your phone."

Jaz didn't hand over anything.

"I mean it."

Somehow, the fact that Oliver *meant it* didn't make Jaz any more inclined to do what she was told.

Which was probably why Oliver reached over and plucked the phone out of her hand. Which was probably why she lost her shit so completely.

She sat bolt upright, her face even paler than usual. "That's fucking mine."

"Yes, and you'll have it back when you've apologis—"

"That's fucking stealing."

"I assure you it's no—"

"Give it back."

"When you've—"

"What if my mum calls?"

"If your mother calls," replied Oliver, "we will need to inform social services because she isn't supposed to have unsupervised contact with you."

"You fucking little—" She lunged for Oliver, and he stepped back sharply, tucking the phone into his pocket, well out of reach. Unless she wanted to try putting him in a wheelie bin, and I didn't fancy her chances.

"Give it back," she screamed. "It's *mine*. You've no *right*."

Oliver was projecting icy calm. Except I knew he only projected icy calm when he felt neither calm nor icy. "I have the right," he said coldly, "and the responsibility. You know what you have to do, and I have faith that you know how to do it."

Words had failed Jaz, and she was now glaring at Oliver like she believed she could give him brain cancer with her eyes and that he'd deserve it if she did.

Oliver had withdrawn tactically to the doorway. "Lucien and I will be downstairs once you've made your decision."

I wasn't keen on suddenly being included in the *and I*. Because this had very much been an Oliver moment. And while the Oliveryness of the moment had led to some good outcomes, like Next Door's Kid's Mum going away relatively quickly, it also seemed to have some...some...disadvantages. He was probably right that we couldn't let our foster kid get away with throwing other kids in wheelie bins, but I couldn't help wondering if there was some magical middle ground between "get away with" and "immediately write a formal apology about."

Either way, we were kind of committed now. And, since he'd said we'd be downstairs, that put us back at the kitchen table, talking in low voices, trying not to admit that neither of us knew what we were doing. Something Oliver was a lot better at than I was.

Fucking miserable didn't even begin to describe it.

"You know," I began, fully aware that this wasn't really the time and wasn't going to be helpful, but with a pressing need to be heard that had been building all evening without my quite noticing, "Next Door's Kid actually is an absolute piece of shit."

From his sharp intake of breath, I sensed Oliver didn't like the direction I was going in but was doing his best to go with me anyway. "Suppose we stipulate for a moment that Colin is indeed an extremely unpleasant child," he said in his best lawyerese. "Does that mean that Jasmine was correct to throw him into a wheelie bin?"

"Okay"—I put up one finger—"I know that the right answer

here is 'No, it doesn't,' but I really think you might be underestimating quite how much of an absolute piece of shit that kid can be."

"I might," Oliver conceded. "But that's rather the heart of the issue. In *reality* there's no level of piece-of-shit-ness that makes it acceptable to throw a child into a wheelie bin."

Stressed-out-inadvisable-levity Luc took over my body for a few seconds. "I mean, it sets one hell of a clear boundary."

"If an adult had done it"—Oliver's eyes were their warmest kind of stern—"it would be clear child abuse."

That was the problem with being a parent: Things kept getting all serious on you. It was hard to be inadvisably levitous when clear child abuse was on the table. "Okay, yes. It was wrong. We all agree it was wrong." *Funny as hell, though.* "But I'm sure Jaz knows it was wrong too."

"She might. Or she might think that kind of behaviour is acceptable if somebody is"—I could spot Oliver's *using my words against me* tells a mile away—"enough of a piece of shit. If she knows it was wrong, our job is to help her to act on that knowledge. If she doesn't, it's our job to teach her. Either way, she needs to understand that we won't turn a blind eye to her acting out."

"And you think grounding her, taking her phone away, and making her write an apology letter, all at the same time, will help with that?" I really hoped I was keeping the what-are-you-on tone out of my voice, but hope isn't the same as expectation.

"You'd rather we spent the rest of our lives living next door to people who harboured a deep resentment against us?"

Honestly, I thought that ship might have already sailed. "You realise Next Door's Kid's Mum—"

"Jacqueline," Oliver reminded me.

"You realise she called Jaz a 'chavvy termagant'?"

In Oliver's eyes, I could see the war between his desire to have a positive relationship with the Next Door's Kid's Family and his need to call out classist language. “That was wrong of her, but I suspect she was very angry.”

“What even *is* a termagant?” I asked.

“A harsh-tempered or overbearing woman.”

I tried not to think in terms of points, or to see our family and next door as competing teams. But I gave points to our team. “So she was being sexist as well.”

“Using gendered terminology, certainly. But as I say, she was probably angry. Her son *had* just been thrown in a wheelie bin.”

Screw it. I was done being dispassionate. I was all in on Team O’Donnell-Blackwood-Johnson. “Says her,” I rebutted, super eloquently. “You never even got Jaz to tell us her version.”

“She didn’t deny it.”

I leaned back on the kitchen chair. “Oh, great lawyering. Is that what you say in court? ‘My client didn’t deny it the one time they got asked, so you should lock them up, Your Honour.’”

With, honestly, more calm than I might have deserved in that exact moment, Oliver raised an eyebrow. “I think I’d make a slightly better case than that. But in general, if one of my clients answered any question I can easily think of with the words ‘He had it coming,’ I would revise my expectation of winning that case downwards. Precipitously.”

“Okay but, like, you know you got really intense in there, don’t you?”

From the way Oliver looked at me, he did not, in fact, know he had got really intense in there. “It was a difficult situation that I dealt with as best I was able.”

And that finally got us to the heart of the problem. “Right,” I tried, wanting to be decisive for once, rather than nervously *okay-butting* my way through the whole conversation. “Only the thing is, was this really a *you* thing? Like, shouldn’t it have been more of an *us* thing?”

Oliver nodded, but I didn't think it was a good kind of nod. "It should, but you apparently didn't want to back me up."

Whoa whoa whoa whoa whoa. That really wasn't where I'd been going with this. "How could I back you up when I had no idea what you were planning to do?"

From the way he was looking at me, Oliver literally could not comprehend what my problem was. "It should have been obvious. Jasmine had done something wrong, so we needed to—"

"I swear if you say 'Set boundaries,' I'm going to throw a banana at you."

Oliver's lips tightened just fractionally. "We needed to discipline her. We needed to do it in a compassionate way, which we did—"

"Did we?"

"Yes."

I put my head in my hands. I really didn't like getting into putting-my-head-in-my-hands-level arguments. Especially not with my actual life partner. "Oliver," I pleaded, "can you just sort of...can you listen to yourself here, because you're sounding a bit..." I was *this close* to saying *Like your dad*, but we were in too small a space for me to be throwing grenades. So I said, "Fifties patriarch."

"Ah yes." Oliver's fine line in weaponised sarcasm zinged into the room. "Because fifties patriarchs were renowned for their hands-on, child-centric approach to parenting."

"Is making a kid write a longhand apology letter and then confiscating their phone when they don't like the idea really a 'hands-on, child-centric approach'?"

"Ye—"

"And don't just say *yes* like you're this..." I didn't have words. Oliver always had words and I never did, which was what made this so difficult. "Like you're the one who gets to decide. You know what a rhetorical question is. You know the reason I said 'Is it?' is because I think 'It's not,' and you can't gaslight me into thinking you've got a monopoly on right answers here."

My brilliant, beautiful, barrister boyfriend took so many things so seriously and held himself to such high standards. Accusing him of gaslighting me wasn't just a jab; it was a knife in the ribs. "Lucien, I—"

And for once he had nothing. Which I thought meant *maybe* I'd…I'd what. Won? This wasn't a winners-and-losers thing. This was a shitty little argument about something shitty that our foster daughter had done to next door's shitty child, probably because he'd done something shitty.

"I—" he repeated.

And before he could finish the sentence, or even make another attempt at starting it, Jaz appeared in the kitchen door holding a neatly folded piece of paper that she must have ripped out of one of her schoolbooks.

"Here," she said. "Now can I have my phone? Please."

Oliver rose and took the letter. Then, because he was no fool, he actually read it to make sure it didn't say "Screw you, sucker," and when he was satisfied that it actually was the thing he'd asked for, he drew Jaz's phone from his breast pocket and handed it back to her. "There," he said. "That wasn't so difficult, was it?"

Jaz said nothing. She just turned and slipped away upstairs.

Oliver passed me the note, and I skimmed it out of curiosity. Jaz's handwriting was…well, it was better than mine, but that wasn't saying much. The letter itself said:

> *Dear neighbours. I am very sorry for my behaviour. I have emotional difficulties and do not always ~~practice~~ practise good coping strategies. I am trying to be better. Apologies. Jasmine.*

Having been with her in her first school meeting, I read the whole thing in that flat, going-along-with-it monotone I'd heard when she was setting her goals for the coming term. I didn't think she meant a word of it. At least not in a healthy way. I was beginning to suspect that *I don't practise good coping strategies* was her *I'm a fuckup who eats pizza in my pants*.

Oliver, though, seemed pleased. Worse, he seemed vindicated.

"You see," he told me. "All we needed to do was be firm and set clear boundaries."

I should have been glad he was right. Because we *were* both on the same team. All three of us were on the same team—Team O'Donnell-Blackwood-Johnson—and if Oliver acting like the dad from a mid-century sitcom actually worked for us, then more power to him.

Then we heard a familiar paws-and-feet combo coming downstairs.

And a click and a vanishing *ruff* and the bang of the door slamming as Jaz and Spud disappeared into the night.

CHAPTER 23

I WAS HONESTLY A BIT surprised that Oliver didn't object to me going after Jaz. It was probably unfair, but I'd half expected him to be all, *She's just doing it for attention* or *She'll be back in her own time* or *Something something or she'll never learn*. But as it turned out, he didn't want our fourteen-year-old foster daughter wandering the streets of Havering after dark any more than I did and, since one of us had to stay home in case she came back, we sort of agreed without directly saying so that it was probably best if I was the one who went after her and Oliver was the one who... stayed out of her face.

I wasn't quite sure where Jaz would go, but she'd taken Spud with her rather than, say, a backpack full of clothes and twenty quid in cash or two silver candlesticks, so it seemed like the park was a decent bet. It was closed at night, but the fence was low and Jaz didn't strike me as the kind of person who'd worry a huge amount about official opening hours. Pinning, if I was honest, way too much hope on my ability to think myself into the mindset of an angry teenager, I dashed off in that direction.

A very, very short way into the dash I began wishing I'd stopped to grab my coat, because it was January and it was after sunset and I was fucking freezing.

I caught sight of a familiar figure with a familiar dog at its heels about half a street ahead of me, and I quickened my pace to try and catch up. As I'd predicted—and I tried not to be too smug about predicting it—she scrambled over the gate into the park and waited a moment while Spud followed her through the railings.

Shit, this was going to be so bad for his training.

Since I was more than a foot taller than Jaz,, getting over the fence should have been way, way easier for me than it was for her. But she was young and agile, and I was maybe two-thirds of one of those things. Plus I was wearing impractically tight jeans. So while she and Spud were happily vanishing into the gloom of the park, I was getting my balls snagged on an iron spike and once again wishing I'd made different calls about several of my recent choices.

It was at times like these I was really glad I wasn't Oliver, because he'd have known real statistics about how many different ways a young girl, or, for that matter, a skinny dude with the muscle tone of a house cat, could get totally murdered to pieces in a situation like this. Without those statistics, I just did my best to freak myself out with guesses.

About halfway across the park, my naturally longer stride started making a difference. Enough of a difference that I had to ask some difficult questions about whether Jaz actually wanted to be caught up with (probably not), if she realised I was me and not some random murderer (hopefully so), and what I was going to say when I finally got to her (no fucking clue).

I tried to solve all three problems by yelling,, "Jaz, it's me, Luc," but she either ignored me or didn't hear.

At last, she came to the lake and sat down on a little bench looking over the water. Which solved the what-if-she-gets-away problem but didn't do much for the how-do-I-deal-with-this problem. Then again I *was* in loco parentis, so it's not like going up to her was actually inappropriate. It was just awkward. And they really should warn you about that more. You hear so much about how parenting is challenging and stressful and expensive. And very little about how you spend most of it faintly embarrassed.

As I got closer to the bench, Spud looked around at me and started yapping in a way I thought coded as *Hello, Daddy Luc* and not *Get away from my human, you weird stranger*. And that, finally, got Jaz's attention. She pulled out an earphone and looked up at me. Even in the dark, I could see her doing the is-this-person-a-threat calculation and, to my relief, coming down on the side of "no."

"You should probably come home," I told her. But when I saw the look of revulsion that crossed her face at hearing home used to describe the place she was staying with me and Oliver, I corrected to, "Back to the house, I mean."

"Or what?"

"I mean, it's pretty cold."

Spud made a rumbling noise and curled tighter onto Jaz's lap, as if demonstrating his utility as a coldness-reducer.

Hoping she wouldn't find it too intrusive, I sat down on the opposite end of the bench. There was enough of a gap between us that she couldn't really complain. After all, it was a public park and so we had the same right to be there. Which was technically no right at all, on account of how closed it was.

Very pointedly, Jaz put her earphone back in.

Hoping that the softly softly approach would work better than the storm-upstairs-and-demand-she-write-apology-letters approach, I just let her sit for a while with Spud on her lap. In the winter-evening silence, I could just about hear the tinny music coming from her headphones, which probably meant it was unhealthily loud, which probably meant I had a parental obligation to tell her to turn it down for the good of her hearing. Only right now, parental responsibilities weren't what I was thinking about, because the music was strangely, naggingly familiar. And there aren't many things in the world more distracting than a song you recognise played just quietly enough that you can't recognise it.

"Is that…is that *Welcome Ghosts*?" I asked.

Jaz pulled her earphone out again, which made the music loud enough that I didn't need her to answer anymore. "What?"

"Are you listening to *Welcome Ghosts*?"

She gave me one of her expected-by-now not-shrugs.

"Isn't that a bit retro for you?"

Turning her head about an eighth of a degree, she said, "I can't afford new music. Because I'm *disadvantaged*."

"That doesn't make sense. New music isn't more expensive than old music."

"Then I was born in the wrong decade."

That also didn't make sense, but it was the kind of not-sense-making thing that people actually said and actually meant, so I let it slide and carried on staring out at the lake.

I hadn't been intending to use silence as a weapon—it was more that I really didn't know what to say—but eventually she offered, "My mum likes it."

I didn't know much about Jaz's mum, but since all I knew about her dad was that he wasn't in the picture, that probably put her mum squarely in *Welcome Ghosts'* target demographic. "That's cool," I mumbled, more as filler than as a way of describing the specific coolness of any specific thing. Then, fully aware I was about to come across as deeply tryhard and awful, added, "My mum, um, sort of wrote it."

Jaz looked at me like she couldn't imagine a universe where anything I'd said made sense. Which wasn't that different from the way she usually looked at me and was slightly more positive than the way she usually looked at Oliver. "You what?"

"My mum's Odile O'Donnell. I'm Luc O'Donnell. My dad is… Like, my mum wouldn't want me to say he's the guy the album is *about*, because, y'know, it's *hers*, not *his*, but...she wrote it after my dad left."

Sometimes, in either a good moment or a bad moment, depending on how you thought about it, I was beginning to kid myself that I could read Jaz, if not well, then at least not-completely-terribly. And right now, I was reading conflict. As if she wanted to be interested but couldn't because this whole conversation, from her perspective, was obviously a trap. So she made a kind of noncommittal noise and started paying really close attention to scratching Spud behind the ears.

I let things simmer for a moment, partly because I was out of ideas again and partly because my phone had just buzzed. I looked down to see a text from Oliver: Are you all right? Where are you both?

I didn't want Jaz to think I was blanking her, but she was from a generation who lived their whole lives on three screens at once so I figured I could at least reply without her feeling emotionally abandoned. I sent back: In park everything fine give us a bit and then slipped the phone back into my pocket.

"What happened?" I asked the lake in the hope that Jaz would hear it. She tensed, and it took me a heartbeat or two to realise that since we'd just been talking about her mum, she'd probably thought I was asking about her homelife, so I clarified quickly, "With Next Door's—with Colin, I mean."

"Put him in a bin."

In her defence, it was a completely truthful answer. "I got that much. *Why?*"

At some point over the course of her short life, Jaz had perfected the art of looking apathetic and defensive all at once. "'I lashed out inappropriately,'" she recited, "'because I need to develop more effective strategies for managing my emotions.'"

There were a lot of ways I could have responded to that. And the one I picked was probably a lot less mature than it could have been. "Oh cut it out, I'm trying to ask you a question here."

"I have *emotional trauma*," Jaz continued. "Because of my *bad parents*. Which is why I have to come and live with you and Oliver so you can *save me*."

Fleetingly, I considered trying to claw my way back to a properly adult tone. Then I decided I couldn't be fucked. "Do you *actually* think that's what I want to hear, or are you just being a—"

"A *what*?" demanded Jaz, in a tone that echoed Next Door's Kid more than either of us should have been comfortable with.

"A…nnoying?" I tried.

"Fuck off, Luc O'Donnell."

Okay, I needed to parent that. I needed to be all stern and all *Now, Jasmine, that isn't the kind of language we use in this household*, but the words stuck in my throat. "Jaz," I tried instead, "please don't. I'm being serious. I know Colin is a prick. I just want to know what he did that made you shove him into a bin."

"He didn't make me," Jaz insisted. "'I am responsible for my own behaviour. Nobody controls my actions except me.'"

"Okay, this whole bit"—I waved my hand at her—"officially stopped being cute three sarcastic buzzwords ago."

In the dark, Jaz glared at me. But at least she'd stopped spouting institution-speak.

"I want to know," I repeated, "what Next Door's Kid did."

"Why?"

Well fuck. I thought kids grew out of the *why* stage around three. Then again I suppose it didn't count when it was a reasonable question. "Honestly? This is probably awful parenting, but mostly because I don't like him and I'm hoping you'll say something that reinforces my opinions."

Jaz went back to focusing on Spud.

"Don't get me wrong, you're still totally grounded or whatever."

At the other end of the bench, Jaz's desire not to engage lost a brief battle with her desire to remind me how bad a job I was doing. "'Grounded or whatever'? You really suck at this."

"Believe me, I know."

"Like, I don't respect you *at all.*"

That was incredibly fair. I wasn't an easy person to respect. "Tell you what, how about we stick a pin in that and you just answer my fu—flipping question."

I wasn't anywhere near confident enough to say that my strategy had worked or that I'd got through to her or that I'd worn her down, but Jaz did seem, for the moment, to have run out of ways to be hostile. So instead she looked down at the little bundle of fur in her lap and said, "He took Spud's ball."

The phrase "That little fucker" slipped out before I could remember to be parental, but I very smoothly glossed over it by saying "Go on" immediately afterwards in my best calm-and-listening voice.

"It went over the fence," she explained. She didn't explain *how* it had gone over the fence, and it occurred to me that she maybe didn't like to admit that she'd been doing something as wholesome and well adjusted as playing fetch. "And I told him to give it back, and he said he wouldn't, and I said he would or I'd make him."

I was really, really, *really* trying not to savour this. Okay, I was mostly, mostly, *mostly* trying not to savour this.

"Then he said, 'How?' and then he pulled out his phone to take a picture of me or something, so I grabbed it and took it around the front and chucked it in the bin, and then when he went around to get it, I tipped him in and shut the lid."

I really, really, *really* tried not to laugh. Okay, I vaguely, vaguely, *vaguely* tried not to laugh. "That," I said in a tone so forcedly solemn that it was basically parody, "was very wrong of you."

"I know," replied Jaz, seeming a bit confused about where I was going with this.

"Which is why you're grounded and had to apologise and everything," I added, hoping that if I reinforced the punishment bit, it would matter less that I was also reinforcing the throwing-Next-Door's-Kid-in-a-bin bit.

"I know," Jaz repeated.

I let out a long breath, not quite able to keep the elephant out of the room. "But he *did* have it coming."

Jaz looked blank.

"All that shi—stuff about, like, controlling your emotions and appropriate responses and…and everything. That's all, like, that's all really important and true and you absolutely shouldn't do this again. But, like…"

"Like what?" asked Jaz. It was the least porcupinish I'd ever seen her, possibly because I was doing such a bad job at this that she didn't know how to react. Sort of the parenting equivalent of that time that one guy beat a really awesome computer at Go by playing so incompetently it didn't know how to counter him.

I tried to arrange my thoughts into something resembling a coherent life lesson. "I guess just… You're not… The thing is, wanting to slam Colin into a wheelie bin doesn't make you a bad person. And it doesn't mean you're damaged or whatever. Everybody who knows what Colin is like wants to throw him in a wheelie bin."

"They just don't have the balls to do it?" Jaz suggested, half smiling.

Fuck. "No. No, that makes it sound cool. Which it"—*lie, Luc, lie like your foster placement depends on it*—"absolutely wasn't. But it also wasn't… I dunno. Look, sometimes these things happen, and we mess up, or we…we react weirdly or pretend we can speak French or something. And that doesn't have to mean anything super deep if we don't want it to."

Jaz gazed at me with adolescent contempt. Then she let her attention drift back to Spud, and then, as if she was talking to the park or the sky instead of to me, she said, "I reckon he's tired."

And without another word, we went home.

CHAPTER 24

JAZ SETTLED IN OVER THE following week. Unfortunately, what she settled into was an unshakeable belief that Oliver was an arsehole and I was a loser. Which, all in all, made for a few tense days on Team O'Donnell-Blackwood-Johnson. Next Door's Kid's Mum and Next Door's Kid's Dad had at least accepted Jaz's apology letter at face value—more than face value in some ways because Oliver had explained a bit of the context to them and, being nice middle-class people, they'd bent over backwards to explain how Extremely Sympathetic they were about Jasmine's Special Circumstances. Although they made sure to explain it in a way that also made clear that if Jasmine's Special Circumstances so much as mildly inconvenienced them or their son again, they'd be calling out a SWAT team.

Still, apology duly written and duly accepted, Oliver seemed to consider the matter closed, which I actually found a bit upsetting because as far as I was concerned, the matter was sort of ajar. Because it was becoming increasingly clear that me and Oliver had quite different parenting styles, and I would have quite liked to have a sensible, mature conversation about our different parenting styles. Except it was incredibly hard to find the time to have a sensible, mature conversation about our different parenting styles because we were both too busy parenting. It was sort of like we were in a boat, and we were both bailing water out of the boat, which meant the boat was sinking, but also neither of us were steering and we were probably overdue an iceberg.

So I did what I usually did in scary, complex, icebergy situations—I pretended it wasn't happening. Which was pretty easy because my job, for however long it lasted, was an endless source of displacement activity.

"What do you call cheese that doesn't belong to you?" I asked Alex.

Alex didn't think about this one for as long as he usually did. "Casei, I suppose."

I looked blankly into my camera. "What?"

"Well, 'That doesn't belong to you' is sort of a relationship descriptor, so I suppose that implies you're looking for the genitive, although in that case the grammar's all mixed up. You'd more be describing the not-belonging-to-you-ness of the cheese. If you were just saying 'cheese that isn't yours' or something like that, it'd take the nominative, whether it belonged to you or not."

This was very much the wrong conversation to be having on a Friday. Or any day. "I was going to say, 'Nat-cho cheese.'"

Alex blinked. "Pardon."

"Nat-cho cheese. *Nat*, like *not*. Then *cho*, like…now I come to think of it, like a slightly culturally appropriative way of saying *your* but also together like the word *nacho*. Like the food."

It looked as though Alex understood. Which scared me. "Excellent example, Luc. So yes, in *nacho cheese*, it's actually the *nacho* that would take the genitive while *cheese* would take the nominative. Although I suppose thinking about it, that might also depend on whether nacho cheese is cheese *of* a nacho or cheese *for* a nacho."

My phone rang, and I had never in my life been so glad to be distracted from something I was already using as a distraction. "Hang on," I told Alex, "I've got to get this."

Slipping my headphones off, I answered the phone.

"Mr. O'Donnell?" I was pretty proud of myself for recognising Miss Collins's voice. "Please don't worry too much, but I wanted to bring this up early. Jasmine's teachers are telling me that she hasn't done any homework this week."

Fuck. We'd fucked it up again. "Sorry," I said reflexively. Then added, "We'll get on that right away."

"Otherwise," Miss Collins continued, "she's made a very positive start."

I should have felt good about that but, selfishly, I didn't. It was like she was saying that everything was fine, apart from the bit that Oliver and I were most responsible for. "Thanks," I said anyway. "That's good to hear."

The nanosecond Miss Collins had gone, I was texting Oliver. Jaz hasn't done any homework we suck as parents.

The reply took a while to come through because Oliver's day involved some pretty big chunks of can't-look-at-a-phone time. When it finally came, it was: We don't suck as parents. Which was reassuring. Except it was swiftly followed up with: We should however be a little more proactive in our monitoring.

We don't want to be helicopter parents, I replied. It was the gentlest way I could think of to broach the whole we-are-coming-at-this-in-extremely-different-ways issue.

Oliver three-dotsed me for quite a while, suggesting he was composing his thoughts. Thoughts that finally landed on my screen as: It isn't helicopter parenting for us to make sure she's doing her schoolwork. It's doing her a disservice not to.

He was right about that. I just wasn't quite sure Oliver's style of monitoring would be well received. Your right, I sent back—followed by *your followed by *you're because fuck predictive text. Then I added, I'll talk to her when she gets home.

If you want to wait, we can do it together was the reply. And I tried really hard not to read mistrust into it, or to take *We can do it together* to mean *I can do it my way and you can watch*.

But I didn't want to get into that right then, especially not by text. So I sent back a casual Its cool followed by No sense dragging it out.

That got nothing back for a while. Then, just as I was turning my attention begrudgingly back to work, I got an Okay and then about eighty seconds later a Let me know if you change your mind and then, two minutes after that, By the way, Brian and Amanda can't make next weekend, Jennifer and Peter can't make the weekend after, and Bridget and Tom are busy for the rest of the month so we might have to postpone dinner until February.

Ah yes. Because as well as looking after a homework-averse teenager, we were also trying—and had been trying since before Christmas—to host a dinner party with the friends we hadn't seen in what had started as months and was now becoming months and months. Post-pandemic, when we were all really excited we could see each other again, we'd started a regular dinner party thing which had swiftly become an irregular dinner party thing which had then become an ad hoc dinner party thing and had finally become a *Hey, remember when we used to have dinner parties?* thing. Were going to run into valentines at this rate, I sent back.

It's all couples, Oliver replied, so maybe we should steer into it. Either way I'll keep you posted.

I sent a quick okay and he went quiet after that. But just as I was slipping my phone back into my impractically tight jeans, it buzzed again. Looking down, I saw a picture of a whale.

Moby Dick? I asked.

A little obvious, I admit.

I love you I sent back in a moment of intense dick-related sentimentality.

Because I felt weirdly reassured that, even after five years,

Oliver was still sending me dick pics. The fact he was still managing to source new dicks to send me was a very Oliver-specific reminder that whatever arguments we had, whatever the differences might be between us, deep down we were solid. That we were, in our own silly, idiosyncratic way, as inexplicably enduring as a classic knob joke.

If she hadn't been grounded, I probably wouldn't still have been driving Jaz to and from school. Fourteen was young, but it wasn't needs-constant-handholding young. Hell, it was only two years off from is-it-really-okay-that-you-can-join-the-army young or maybe-we-should-think-about-letting-you-vote young.

But she was currently being *punished*, and since in practice she lived in her room anyway, about the only part of her punishment that actually felt punish-y was the part where she had to get picked up from school by some wanker in a secondhand EV.

Even then, I never met her at the gates because I remembered my own school days well enough to know that she'd have had the shit bullied out of her if I had.

"Good day?" I asked as she threw her bag carelessly onto the back seat and herself carelessly onto the front.

Not-a-shrug.

"I got a call this afternoon," I continued, as if it was this super-casual thing that I'd just happened to remember, instead of the start of a conversation I'd been rehearsing for more than two hours.

Oh really, that's interesting. Who was the call from and what was it concerning? is what a completely different child might have said to a completely different parent in a completely different situation. I got nothing.

"Apparently you haven't done any homework yet?" I didn't like to pat myself on the back, but I was proud of *yet*. Like I was saying,

I'm sure you'll get around to it, and don't forget that Oliver and I, your supportive foster parents, are with you every step of the way!

Even with the *yet*, she still said nothing.

"Is there…is there a reason for that?"

Perhaps I'd just got foster-parent Stockholm syndrome, but I took her continued silence here as an actual win. Only a few days ago, I was pretty sure, she'd have assumed I was attacking her and said something self-destructive about how it was because she was a fuckup who couldn't be trusted.

Then again, maybe I was just projecting.

"I don't want to push," I went on.

That got a reaction. She stared at me with a don't-shit-on-my-head-and-call-it-a-beret expression. "Yes, you do."

"I…" Figuring I couldn't sink much lower in her estimation, I chose honesty. "I don't *want* to. I just sort of *have* to."

"Or what?"

"Or they'll take you away."

And that, it turned out, was *too* honest. She kicked hard into the footwell. "You don't get to say that."

"Sorry, I just—"

"I *was* taken away. I *am* taken away. *This* is away. *You're* away."

It wouldn't be completely true to say I'd never thought of it like that. I'd thought of it like that quite a lot. Or at least I'd thought of all the pieces of it, just never quite in the right order. I mean, I'd known Jaz wasn't super stoked to be with us, but it never quite occurred to me that the way she felt about being placed with me and Oliver was the exact same way we felt about having her placed somewhere else. That somewhere out in the world there was a Team Johnson that had to be broken up so that Team O'Donnell-Blackwood-Johnson could be a thing.

Oliver would probably have pointed out that I was using

imprecise language. That it was more accurate to say that Team Johnson had broken down of its own accord and that Team O'Donnell-Blackwood had come along to pick up the pieces and form Team O'Donnell-Blackwood-Johnson in the aftermath. But I'd have bet CRAPP's entire annual operating budget on that not being how it felt to Jaz.

"Is it..." I was super aware that there were approximately eight million wrong things I could say in this situation and somewhere between zero and no right things. So I focused on the homework issue like a giant coward. "Are you finding the work too difficult?"

"Fuck off."

"I'd offer to help out, but honestly, I kind of suck at most things."

From the way she looked at me, it was the first thing I'd said all day that she'd believed. "It's not too difficult."

"Then is it..." Of the eight million wrong things to say, I couldn't even think of one. "I don't know, are you just being a dick?"

Probably I shouldn't have given myself points for the fact that Jaz at least hadn't *expected* that one. "What?"

"Sorry. Bad phrasing. It's just...either there's a reason you're not doing homework or there isn't, and if there is we can help but if there isn't then, like..."

"Then I'm just being a dick." She looked sullen. And possibly like she was internalising *is a dick* and adding it to *is traumatised* and *makes bad choices* on her roster of self-definition.

"No!" I insisted very fervently. "Not, you know. Not actually. I mean sort of actually but only in the same way that... Look, can we pretend we had this conversation without the being-a-dick framing because I don't think it's helping."

Jaz buried her face in her hands. "How did I get stuck with you?"

"Spat on a security contractor?"

"If I spat on you, do you think they'd send me to somebody who isn't shit?"

"Do *you*?" I gave her a meaningful look. Then realised that I was meant to be meaningfully looking at the road, oversteered, and very nearly swerved into oncoming traffic.

"We're going to die," Jaz said calmly. "I'm going to die in a car crash because the socials decided my mum was too fucked in the brain to look after me and gave me to a guy who can't drive."

"I can drive," I insisted in the face of all the evidence.

"Prove it."

Fortunately, while I had a great many self-destructive impulses, the desire to show off behind the wheel wasn't one of them. So instead, I tried, "I'm sorry about your mum."

"Don't talk about my mum."

I kept my eyes squarely on the road. "Right. Sorry."

"You know nothing about her."

"Gotcha."

"Or me."

"Right."

"Are you just agreeing with everything I say now?"

It hadn't been a deliberate strategy, but it seemed to be working. "Looks like."

"You suck."

"Yup."

"Odile O'Donnell is a shitty musician."

"Hey!" I de-road-eyed for a tenth of a second, then got control of myself. "I'll lay off your mum but you lay off mine, okay?"

I could *feel* Jaz rolling her eyes. "Whatever."

"No. Seriously. My mum is off limits."

"What'll you do? Ground me?"

I screeched the car to a halt half up the kerb. I'd failed two driving tests on parking and this was nowhere near my best work. "Jasmine," I said. "I'm being *really* serious here. My mum gave up everything to look after me when my dad left, and no matter how angry you are with me, you do *not* under any circumstances bring her into it. Do you understand me?"

Jaz stared at me. She didn't look scared exactly. But she did look uncertain. "Whate—okay."

"We good?"

Her expression melted into abject disdain. "Right up until you said 'we good.'"

"It's a phrase. It's an ordinary phrase that ordinary people use."

Neither getting nor really expecting any kind of reply from Jaz, I pulled us back into the road and finished the extremely short drive back to the house. As I was completing my second, only mildly more effective attempt at parking, she said, "It's online."

"What?" I wasn't trying to be sharp. I'd just completely lost track of what was going on.

"Homework. Mostly online. Don't have a computer."

I didn't like to assume my foster child was lying to me, but the alternative was that the way people did homework had changed so radically since my own childhood that I felt about a million years old, and in some ways that was worse. "Is that normal?"

Jaz nodded.

"How did you do homework at your old school?"

"Lorimer got them to buy me a laptop. They kept it."

That seemed to check out. "Well, we have computers in the house, so I think this is a pretty solvable problem."

From the way Jaz was looking at me, it didn't seem like she had any faith in my problem-solving abilities.

An hour of failing to set up a new user account for Jaz on my desktop later, I came to the conclusion that she was probably right.

Still, she did start on some homework, which I took as a good sign, and that meant Oliver couldn't really tell me I was Doing It Wrong when he came home from work and I filled him in on how things had gone.

Not that I thought he *would*. Not that he ever normally *did*. It was just a fear I sometimes had because of my own issues. Because, y'know, I have bad coping strategies.

"Apparently her old school got her a laptop," I explained to Oliver while he crushed garlic and I pretended to chop carrots. "But she had to leave it behind."

Oliver moved on to sautéing onions. "That's understanda—hold on a second, when you say 'got her,' they didn't buy it with her Pupil Premium Plus money, did they?"

I shrugged. "No idea. Sorry, I'm still a bit vague on the details."

Removing the sautéing onions from the heat, Oliver gave me his this-is-important look. Maybe I'd been jumping the gun on the whole wouldn't-tell-me-I'd-been-doing-it-wrong thing. He turned off the hob and strode purposefully into my study, where Jaz was sitting with Spud on her lap and making disgusted expressions at a virtual learning environment.

"Jaz?" said Oliver in a voice I still thought was more suitable for talking to pets, even if he'd managed to resist calling her Jasmine. "I need to ask you some questions about the laptop you were given by your previous school."

Jaz spun around in my chair with a face like incredibly defensive thunder. "What? I told Luc. They've got it. I've not."

"I'm sure that's—"

"I'm not fucking lying."

"I didn't say you—"

"Look"—she pointed at the screen—"I'm doing my fucking homework, all right? You don't need to be up my arse all the time."

I couldn't help looking where she pointed. "What the hell does 'label the plan, front, and side elevation' mean?"

Jaz's shoulders dropped. "I don't know. I think they did it when I wasn't here."

It hadn't been planned, but my interruption provided just enough of a distraction that Oliver could get a full sentence out. "Jaz, did they buy the laptop with Pupil Premium Plus money?"

She glared at him like she wanted him to die slowly from something that also gave him diarrhoea. "Yeah."

"You're sure?"

"No. Because I'm a stupid looked-after girl who doesn't know anything."

Oliver gazed compassionately at her the way he gazed compassionately at me when I was shitting on myself. Unfortunately, it was still the wrong gaze for the wrong audience. "Jasmine, you're not stupid and I think you know a great many things. Now if you'll excuse me I have to go and send some emails."

Which left me and Jaz alone with very little idea what the fuck was going on, either with Oliver or with Jaz's geometry homework.

"What's even the point?" she demanded, clicking random parts of the screen and seeming unsatisfied with the outcome.

"Oliver knows what he's doing," I told her, partly from a protective instinct and partly because he almost always did.

"Not him. This." She pointed at a digital mix of blocks and graph paper. "When will I *ever* need this?"

Somewhere, buried deep in the national curriculum, there was probably a topic I could look at and say with absolute honesty that I used in my day-to-day life. Off the top of my head, I couldn't say what it *was* but I could definitely say what it *wasn't*. And it wasn't labelling the plan, front, and side elevations of meaningless sets of cubes. "Well," I tried, "maybe you'll...you could want to be an engineer one day?"

She looked from me to the blocks and then back to me. "This is what engineers do, is it?"

"I mean, not literally this. Not exactly literally this. But it probably develops, I don't know, spatial awareness?"

Whether Jaz was feeling more scorn in that moment for me or for her maths homework was honestly a toss-up. "Spatial awareness?"

"School is important?" I tried, wishing the question mark wasn't quite so audible.

With a sigh to break the world, Jaz turned back to her incomprehensible geometry and I, having satisfied myself that yes, she found my company less appealing than schoolwork, went back into the kitchen to finish chopping.

I was just about done with the carrots by the time Oliver came back. The butter in the sautéing pan had gone all yellow and clumpy, and needed remelting, but there were worse problems out there than clumpy butter and, from the expression on Oliver's face, he was dealing with at least one of them.

"What was all that about?" I asked in the most nonconfrontational way I could manage. Which wasn't *that* nonconfrontational on account of *What was all that about?* being kind of an inherently confrontational sentence.

"It appears that Bellefield stole from our foster child."

"Bellefield?"

"Jasmine's old school."

This was still making limited sense at best. "It's not stealing to ask somebody to give school property back when they leave."

"Jasmine's Pupil Premium payments aren't school property. The money is assigned to her, personally. The school gets to spend it, but whatever it spends it on is *hers*."

The sense that this was making had got slightly less limited, but only slightly. "Hang on, we can just make the school buy her stuff?"

"It's not as *Daily Mail* headline as it sounds. It's not as though the government is handing out free money to buy PlayStations for transgender immigrants. But schools get a certain amount of discretionary funding per capita for LACs"—I interrupted him with my look of incomprehension—"looked-after children, and that money is meant to be spent directly on the children in question. Operative word *meant*."

I moved on to slicing mushrooms. "Is it even worth trying to get it back? Like, she's fine with my desktop, and we could probably buy her a laptop anyway."

It hadn't been my intent to give Oliver an ethical question to analyse, but I guess, from his point of view, it was practically a perk. "I suppose," he said, "you could argue that we can afford to buy a replacement, whereas the school is probably quite short on IT equipment. But it's a matter of principle. This is technically theft."

"Technically," I admitted. And I was doing the *technically* voice.

"Which in the eyes of the law is in fact the same as *actually*."

That was true.

"Also, and I'm trying not to overvalue this as a factor because it really shouldn't form part of my considerations, but not only did they technically steal—they technically stole *from our foster daughter*."

This right here was the difference between me and Oliver. He'd have a thought like that and follow it up with *But I mustn't let it sway my objectivity*. I heard it and went immediately to *Let's fuck those fuckers all the way up*. "Good point. They've messed with Team O'Donnell-Blackwood-Johnson."

Oliver gave me a slight smile. "I notice you've put your own name first."

"Well, when *you* name the team you can call it Team Blackwood-O'Donnell-Johnson."

"I was thinking of Blackwood-Johnson-O'Donnell."

This was like when everybody had kept putting me in the *kill* spot. Best strategy was to change the subject. "So how are we going to get Jaz's laptop back?"

"I've sent them an email reminding them of her rights. I'll give them a day or so to respond and then..."

"Then?" I asked.

Oliver had a slightly wicked gleam in his eye. "Well, I suppose I'll need to start asking around. See if anybody knows a good lawyer."

God, it was embarrassing how hot it was when Oliver got all *I will use my barrister superpowers to stand up for the rights of the people I care for*. If Jaz hadn't been home, I'd have pushed him against the fridge and done things that might have invalidated the warranty. As it was, I was forced to restrict myself to a soupy smile, a kiss on the cheek, and the kind of mushy, heart-warmed feeling I didn't like to acknowledge having.

Of course, chances were Jaz wouldn't give a fuck if Oliver got the laptop back or not. And, even if she did, she wouldn't admit it. But that wasn't the point. This was the Oliver I knew and the Oliver I loved, and I was so glad and, honestly, so fucking relieved—that he was trying to be that Oliver for Jaz as well as for me. Even if she couldn't, or wouldn't, see it.

For the first time in a while—perhaps even since that time he'd tried to raise a formal complaint about the handcuffs—I felt like we were on the same page. Like we really did have a chance of being Team O'Donnell-Blackwood-Johnson or Johnson-Blackwood-O'Donnell or whatever.

Like we were a family.

CHAPTER 25

ONCE OLIVER DECIDED TO MAKE something happen, you could be really sure that thing would happen. Which was great in the bedroom and also great when it came to getting laptop-related justice for our foster daughter.

In practice, though, retrieving the computer that Bellefield had bought for itself with Jaz's money became a bit of a mission. It turned out Jaz had moved around a whole lot, and so her last school had been in Kent. Which meant that one of us had to make an annoying late-in-the-day drive into the arse end of nowhere. And since Oliver was the more confident driver and had been the one sending the *I think you'll find* emails and casually dropping that he was a legal professional, it made more sense for him to be the one who went up nowhere's arse and for me to be the one who stayed home giving primary care.

Last year, when we'd first started discussing the whole fostering thing, I'd been fucking terrified at the thought of being primary anything. But while I wouldn't go so far as to say I was nailing it, or even Blu Tacking it, I was kind of getting used to it. At least as it applied to a relatively self-sufficient teenager who hadn't needed much in the way of nappy changing or spoon-feeding. Who, if I'm being honest, hadn't needed much in the way of me being around her at all if she could possibly help it on account of me being old and crap.

Of course, so far my primary caregiving had also involved Oliver doing all the cooking because subjecting Jaz to my attempts at food would probably constitute child abuse. But with him somewhere the wrong side of Maidstone, that wasn't an option. Which meant either we starved, I braved the kitchen, or I gave up and got pizza.

Jaz had just disappeared into the study with a couple of slices of American Hot when Oliver rang.

"Hi," I said, very chill and with it. "Just doing the washing up after making dinner."

Normally a pointed silence didn't work over the phone, but Oliver and I had been together so long that we *made* it work.

"Just doing the washing up after ordering dinner," I corrected.

Oliver continued to be pointedly silent.

"Just putting the bits of paper towel I was eating my pizza off into the bin after completely failing to provide food in a responsible way."

"I hope you and Jasmine are having a wonderful time," Oliver said at last, more amused than sarcastic but still a bit sarcastic.

Much as I loved Oliver, since he was both vegan and a proper grown-up, I *had* kind of missed eating pizza off a disposable crockery substitute in a room not designed for eating in. "We are," I said, "or at least I am. She's got history homework."

"And you're—"

"*Yes*, I'm sure she's doing it. I mean, not right now—she's eating pizza. But I went and checked before the pizza got here, and she's writing a thing about the history of British democracy."

"And you've—"

Oliver's concern for Jaz's education was touching. His concern that I wouldn't share that concern was unflattering. Warranted but unflattering. "Yes, I've checked if she needs help. I said 'Do you need a hand?' and she said, 'What do you know about the Magna Carta and the emergence of Parliament?' and I said 'Nothing' and she sort of stared at me like I was a total dickhead."

For a moment Oliver was silent again. Then he said, "Which one?"

"Which dick or which head?"

"Which Magna Carta?"

I half sat on our kitchen table, because I was a bit too restless to just use one of the chairs, but this conversation was getting complicated enough that I wanted at least a little bit of arse support. "How many are there?"

"Several. The first was in 1215, but there were multiple other versions of it throughout the thirteenth century."

"See, this is why you should handle the homework stuff," I told him.

There was a different flavour of silence. A slightly uncomfortable one. "Yes well. Unfortunately she takes my offers of assistance even more poorly than she does yours."

She did. I was very aware she did. But neither of us really knew what to do about it because while *I* looked at Oliver's slightly stuffy attempts to give Jaz pointers on maths or English or French—or, now I thought about it, on literally any school subject because he was infuriatingly competent like that—and saw a charming man making a sincere, if awkward, attempt to be helpful, she saw an arsehole trying to control her, make her feel bad, or control her *by* making her feel bad.

All of which made this feel like a good time to change the subject. And for reasons I can't really explain to myself, I decided it was a good time to change the subject in an oldey-timey forties gangster accent. "So," I said, "dids ya gets tha goods?"

There was a microscopic pause in which I *think* I heard Oliver deciding not to laugh in case it encouraged me. "Please never do that again."

"I regretted it immediately. Did you get Jaz's laptop?"

Oliver sighed.

"Is that a no?"

"It's a yes, but I don't feel good about it."

I made a sympathetic sound. "Were they wankers?"

"They were..." He broke off with another sigh. "There's a saying that you should never underestimate how hard it will be to get somebody to understand something if their job depends on them not understanding it. They were like that, only rather than 'job' it was, well, 'access to quite an expensive laptop.'"

I felt a sordid mix of guilty and excited that we'd just got a free thing. "Is it very expensive then?"

"By the standards of a barrister and the son of a successful recording artist? No. By the standards of a British state school? Yes."

I felt even more sordid. "Oh."

"Quite. Essentially, they tried very hard to pretend that they didn't know that anything they bought with Jasmine's Pupil Premium Plus money was Jasmine's property, and I had to remind them rather more tenaciously than I would have liked that they did know and, more importantly, so did I."

"So they *were* wankers?" I asked.

"I think this is one of those situations where wank is very much in the eye of the beholder."

"That's a bad place for wank to be."

"Isn't it just? But, no, they weren't being wankers. They were trying to retain resources for their own students at the expense of a former student. And I can't entirely blame them."

"I can," I said cheerfully. "They stole our kid's laptop. To give to other kids who aren't our kid. Fuck 'em."

"Lucien, I've spent the last three hours arguing with some very tired, very underpaid educational professionals. This is sadly not a *fuck 'em* situation."

Oh God. It didn't feel fair that Oliver could feel so bad about doing a fundamentally good thing. But that was who he was. While everybody else was celebrating a win, he'd always be there empathising with the people he'd beaten. If I didn't love him so much, I'd have found it spectacularly annoying. As it was, I just wanted to make him feel better. "Still," I tried. "It was a point of principle. You really like points of principle."

"I *try to be principled*. You're making it sound like I have some kind of ethics fetish."

"You basically do."

"*You* have an ethics fetish. I just have ethics."

I thought about that. "Okay. Fair. And I guess you're right. It does feel a bit...grubby, doesn't it?"

"Yes."

I squirmed and levered myself out another slice of pizza. "I mean, we could give the laptop back?"

"No," Oliver said very firmly. "It's rightfully Jasmine's property. She gets to decide what to do with it."

I agreed. I probably agreed too quickly because, despite all the complex feels, the likes-free-stuff part of my brain took over with uncomfortable speed. "You going to be home soon?" I asked.

"A bit under an hour, I think—I'm at a service station on the M20."

Naively, I'd assumed he'd just be calling from the car, but of course Oliver would never use a mobile phone while driving, not even hands-free. *It still constitutes a distraction*, he'd say, looking all noble and shit, *and has been shown to contribute to accidents*. So I let him go, and we said our goodbyes and our I love yous and our goodbyes again. Then he texted me a picture of the front cover of a children's book about a pig, and it took me about twenty minutes of Googling before I could send back Dick King Smith, right?

He didn't reply for an hour, of course, because if he wouldn't talk on a hands-free kit while driving, he *certainly* wouldn't text while driving. And when I did get back a Well deduced it was timed to coincide exactly with the door swinging open and Oliver coming home, laptop under his arm, the recyclable carton from his service station dinner in hand.

He presented the laptop to Jaz without ceremony, and she took it much the same way. She managed a *thanks*, but it was the thanks of somebody who suspected that not saying *thanks* would be a whole conversation that she couldn't be fucked to have.

Still, she *did* say it. And while it wasn't likely she and Oliver would become best friends overnight, it felt like a tiny pebble on the scales of her maybe thinking he wasn't always a complete dick who only existed to make life difficult for her personally.

As we discovered two days later, it was a very tiny pebble.

"I *can't* go," Jaz was yelling at Oliver on Sunday. "I'm *grounded*. You can't say I'm *grounded*, then make me *go places*."

Oliver didn't pinch the bridge of his nose, but he gave strong pinching-the-bridge-of-his-nose energy. "I think you'll find I can."

"Don't think of it as being dragged out to visit your boring foster carers' boring family," I suggested in my best helpful voice. "Think of it as a rare chance to meet a reclusive famous person."

Jaz fell heavily back onto her bed, and Spud jumped onto her chest. "I like *one* Odile song. I'm not a fan. And I have to do homework. You've been on at me for a week to do more homework."

"And you've made excellent progress," Oliver positively reinforced, "but today you're coming to visit Luc's mother. She's asked to meet you."

A deep, aggressive shudder started at the crown of Jaz's head and ended at her now-bright-purple toenails. "I'm not a zoo animal."

"Well no," I agreed. "Because zoo animals don't get taken out of the zoo to visit the keepers' mums."

"I'm staying home to look after Spud," Jaz declared.

"Spud will survive an evening on his own," replied Oliver firmly. "He's well past the stage where he struggles with separation."

Still flat on her back, Jaz angled her head into an optimal glaring position. "How do you know? You asked him?"

Oliver—my poor, sweet, sometimes extremely unable-to-read-a-room Oliver—couldn't quite resist responding to that with, "Effectively, yes. He's *my* dog, Jaz—I actually know him quite well."

"Our dog," I corrected.

"Mruff," added Spud, I thought a little ambiguously.

"*You* want me to stay home, don't you?" Jaz asked Spud, and Spud *ruffed* , much *less* ambiguously, and licked her face.

"In my profession," said Oliver archly, "we call that 'leading the witness.'"

It wasn't a joke Jaz appreciated.

"Come on," I said. "Spud'll be okay, and Mum and Judy are actually pretty cool people."

"Oh well, if *you* think they're cool," Jaz replied so laconically I thought her heart had stopped.

Time for an alternative strategy. "Okay, how about this: Oliver and I aren't going without you. So either you get your shoes on and come with us, or we just *stand here*. Like this." I folded my arms and gave her a look that I'd been designing for maximum teenager-annoyance factor.

I was pleased to see Oliver doing the same. He also folded his arms and looked down at Jaz with an *I'm not angry, I'm just concerned* expression that I could never have equalled in a million years.

She ruffled Spud's fur and pretended to ignore us.

We kept it up.

She kept up ruffling.

I was just beginning to worry that we'd picked the wrong teenager to get into a battle of wills with, but six ruffles later,

Spud did us a solid by bouncing off onto the floor, at which point Jaz sat up and said, "Fine," in a tone that suggested it was anything but.

We said goodbye to Spud, who definitely seemed like he'd miss Jaz more than me or Oliver, and got into the car with all the enthusiasm of two middle-aged gays and a teenager who hated them. Oliver, reverting to his role as natural driver, took us off in the direction of Pucklethroop-on-the-Wold.

"Your mum a lesbian then?" asked Jaz conversationally when we were far enough onto the motorway that talking to us became marginally less boring than ignoring us.

I twisted in the passenger seat so hard and so fast that I hurt my neck. "Sorry, what?"

"Well, she lives with another woman. Anyway, isn't it genetic?"

"That's complicated," said Oliver at once. Nobody could deliver an authoritative *That's complicated* quite like Oliver.

"Which?" asked Jaz.

"Both," I replied. "Mum and Judy are sort of…they're sort of really good friends?"

"So she *is* a lesbian."

"No, I mean *really,* really good friends." I realised that wasn't helping. "I mean, it's not a euphemism."

From what I could see with my head still at a weird angle, Jaz was looking incredibly blank.

"It's like…" I grasped for language she might understand. "It's like they have a queerplatonic relationship, except they're both straight."

I'd thought it was a bit of a long shot, but Jaz came from an unprecedentedly queer-literate generation, so she just said, "Ohhhh," and then, "why didn't you say that in the first place?"

Conversation was mercifully light after that, partly because Oliver had put on the first season of *In the Dark*, one of the few true crime podcasts he was okay with, and even Jaz wasn't quite willing to talk over an in-depth analysis of a historic child abduction.

When we pulled up on Old Post Office Road, Mum and Judy and Judy's many, many dogs were already waiting for us. And I suddenly, and retroactively, agreed with Jaz that she should have stayed home because this was going to be *unbearable*.

"Luc, mon caneton!" Mum rushed down to the car to embrace me in a full-on French kiss-on-both-cheeks kind of way. "And Oliver, and you must be Yasmine."

"Jasmine," corrected Oliver.

"Jaz," corrected me.

"Yeah," said Jaz.

"Hullo," called Judy from the doorway. "Would come down and press the flesh and so forth but thing is, can't actually be buggered."

Mum turned to look at her heteroplatonic life partner accusingly. "Judy, you could be buggered to come all the way to the door. Why not be buggered to come a few steps further and make our guests feel welcome?"

"What can I say, I'm feeling a very specific level of buggery today, and no amount of buggering about is going to make a buggering bit of difference."

"Can you *please*," I begged, "stop saying *bugger* and *bugger* variants. Jaz is going to think you're incredibly weird."

"I am sure Jas does not mind." Mum pronounced Jaz's name with a soft *J* at the front and an *S* at the end in a way that made it sound officially twelve percent cooler. "Do you, Jas?"

"I'm fine," Jaz murmured. It was the kind of *I'm fine* that could mean anything from *I am actually fine* to *I am six seconds away from a total fucking meltdown*.

This had, however, played right into Mum's hands. "You see. She is fine. She says she is fine. Judy can bugger all that she wants."

"Good to know," said Judy. "Now come on, let's get inside. As my ex-husband used to say, it's cold enough out here to freeze the tits off a cardboard nun."

I was this close to demanding to know who the hell this husband had been and what exact context he'd said that in, but since it *was* probably cold enough to freeze the tits off a cardboard nun, I didn't want to be hanging around outside any longer than was absolutely necessary.

Once we were inside, we settled down in the living room, where Jaz pointedly said hello to every member of the household with more than two legs. I think she'd probably meant it as an insult, but if that'd been the plan, she'd picked a terrible strategy, at least where Judy was concerned.

"Beautiful girls, aren't they?" she said. It wasn't really a question. "That one's Eugenie. She's soppy and dull as a post but an absolute love deep down."

Jaz whispered a soft "Hey, Eugenie" to the dog but otherwise ignored everybody.

"So." Mum clapped her hands, all business all of a sudden. "Who is hungry?"

"Oh no," I tried, "we forgot you were cooking and we've just had our dinner."

Oliver gave me *behave* face. "Lucien is teasing, Odile. I assume you've made the special curry again?"

"Of course I have." Mum looked maliciously overjoyed. "I know how important it is to you both."

"We've been looking forward to it all week," said Oliver. The worst of it was he wasn't even really lying. Well, he was lying about the *we* part. But Oliver had developed a masochistic fondness for Mum's special curry. I think it made him feel like part of the family.

Still, I glared at him. "Oliver. We've been together for five years. You can stop pretending to like Mum's special curry. It's shit, and we all know it's shit."

Jaz looked up from the dogs. "How come he gets to talk like that and I don't get to talk like that?"

"You *do* get to talk like that," I reminded her. "You tell me I'm shit all the time."

Oliver's mouth drew into a thin little line. "Or equivalently, *neither* of you get to talk like that and we should all be polite and grateful to Odile for hosting us this evening."

"Do not worry, Oliver," Mum told him. "I know he loves my special curry really."

"I really don't."

"Then *why*," asked Mum with a pedantic triumph more appropriate to somebody about a tenth of her age, "do you *always* come over on special curry night?"

I was low-key aware that Jaz had been silent through all of this, but I tried not to second-guess what that meant. "Tradition. And intense self-loathing."

"Well, whatever you may think, I am going to carry on making the special curry exactly the way I have always made it, although if anybody wishes to assist me in the kitchen, they will be most welcome."

I passed. As did Oliver. It had taken him a couple of years, but he'd eventually managed to overcome his good-guest instincts and leave Mum to commit her gastronomic crimes alone. Which worked out better for all of us.

Jaz, though, did not pass. Which confused the fuck out of me. While she cooked a fair bit at home, it was only ever for herself and usually at two in the morning, having refused to eat dinner with us. So when she (and the dogs, who, like Spud, had found a new favourite, the fickle bastards) followed Mum out into the kitchen, I wasn't sure how I was meant to react. Whatever passed for my parental instincts were telling me that this was a *Give her space* moment, not a *Keep an eye on her* moment. And, for once, I trusted them. Especially because I'd learned the hard way that *Keep an eye on her* moments often turned into *Make her feel backed into a corner* moments.

"So," Judy said brightly. "How's married life treating you?"

"We're not married," Oliver pointed out.

Judy waved a dismissive hand. "Pish posh. Civilly partnered life. Same thing."

"Much as it always was," said Oliver, "only now if one of us dies, the other one will actually have rights."

"Very much my experience," Judy agreed. "Last thing you want is for one of you to be found decapitated on a yacht in the Azores with ninety pounds of cocaine and a defrocked bishop and the other one not be able to do a damned thing about it."

Oliver and I gave each other weary, knowing looks. "This is where we say, 'Yes, but that isn't likely to happen,'" I tried, "and you tell us it actually happened to one of your husbands, isn't it?"

"Don't be silly." Judy looked almost affronted.

Still in visiting-the-in-laws mode, Oliver went full contrition mode. "I'm sorry, Judy, we shouldn't have presumed."

"We *weren't* married," Judy went on. "That's sort of the point of the story. Made it very tricky with the authorities."

"But the Azores-cocaine-bishop-decapitation thing..." I prompted.

"Back in '74. Don't remember much of it. Bit of a wild time, if I'm honest."

I was about seventy percent certain that about seventy percent of Judy's stories were made up on the spot, but if my maths was right, that made me four hundred and ninety percent certain that at least some of them were true. "Well." I gave a could-be-worse kind of a shrug. "We've successfully dodged that bullet."

Judy gave a nostalgic sigh. "Apparently so. If only poor Terry had."

"I thought you said he was decapitated," said Oliver with barristerial attention to detail. "Not shot."

"Well yes, but they found his head eventually and—"

Tragically, and by *tragically* I mean *thankfully*, we never found out what had happened with Terry's head, because we were interrupted by a scream from the kitchen.

CHAPTER 26

I SAY A SCREAM. IT had been two screams. Both, as far as I could tell, of frustration rather than fear or pain or even really anger.

"Tell this girl," Mum said when Oliver and I burst into the kitchen to get our parent on, "that she is the worst sous chef I have ever had. No, wait, that *anybody* has ever had."

"Jaz," I said as deadpan as I could manage, "you're the worst sous—"

"Tell this old lady," Jaz replied, more to Mum than to me, "that she's a fucking shitty cook."

"Language," said Oliver at roughly the same time that I said, "I think she already knows."

"Shitty!" Mum sounded way more indignant than she had any right to feel, given that the shittiness of her cooking was a matter of extremely detailed public record. "Does this look shitty to you?"

She pointed at the carnage of vegetable matter strewn across her work surfaces. Unlike Oliver, I wasn't an expert in the British legal system, but I had a feeling that evidence-wise, Mum's case for slander was on a pretty shaky footing.

"Is that rhubarb?" I asked.

"Judy had a lot from her garden," Mum explained, "and it's really the same as celery."

"And grapefruit?"

"Very healthy. A lot of vitamin C."

"And turnips?"

Mum gave a Gallic shrug, which was, in its own way, just as expressive as one of Jaz's. "Well, Oliver is vegan. I need to bulk it out with something."

"I'm not eating a rhubarb, grapefruit, and turnip curry," Jaz told me. And, honestly, I didn't blame her.

Oliver, on the other hand, blamed her at least a little bit. "Jasmine, we are guests in Odile's house."

"Yeah, but that don't mean she can fucking poison us."

I made a doomed effort to play peacemaker. "If it helps, she's not killed me yet, and now that she's stopped putting meat in everything, we're not even likely to get salmonella."

"Luc." Mum gave me a look of mostly play disapproval. "Do not talk about your mother as if she is not in the room."

"*You're* talking about my mother as if she is not in the room," I pointed out. "And you *are* my mother."

Mum folded her arms and looked haughty, smearing cinnamon up her sleeves as she did so. "Your mother can talk about herself however she wants. It's her right as a reclusive eccentric older French lady."

Of the many adjectives Mum had just applied to herself, I thought maybe half actually applied. "You're doing this deliberately, aren't you?"

With another scream, this time of "Why are you all so fucking weird," Jaz retreated from the kitchen, looking like she couldn't imagine anyone who could possibly be having a worse experience than the one she was having right at that moment.

"You know," said Mum as the last of the dogs vanished into the hall in Jaz's wake, "I think I like her very much."

Despite this, Oliver still seemed to feel the need to say, "I'm sorry she was so aggressive."

Mum made a *bof* gesture. “I’m not a fool, Oliver. I know that this is a very silly situation and that the special curry is something of an acquired taste.”

“It’s not an acquired taste, Mum,” I corrected. “It’s often literally inedible.”

That left Mum profoundly unimpressed. “I’m sure it is, with that attitude.”

“Either way”—Oliver circled back to his point with typical tenacity—“she didn’t respond appropriately. I’ll go and ask her to apologise.”

More than anything I wanted to say, *Please don’t*, but I didn’t quite have the courage.

Which meant I was super glad when Mum said, “Please don’t.”

“She was very rude,” Oliver reminded us all.

Mum shrugged again. “So was I. You’ve been having the sex with my son—”

“Mum, you could have put that *any other way*.”

“—for a very long time. Surely you’ve worked out that we’re quite a rude family.”

“I am *not*,” I protested. “I’m polite as balls when I’m around other people.”

Oliver gave me a look.

“When I’m at work,” I corrected.

Oliver continued to give me a look.

“When I’m at some bits of my work.”

Looks persisted and, indeed, spread.

“Sometimes,” I said very firmly, “I have to go and be polite to rich arseholes who I need to give us money, and when I’m doing that specific professional task I am, in my own estimation, *as polite as balls*.”

“The politeness or otherwise of the O’Donnells aside,” replied Oliver, refusing to be distracted, “Jasmine needs to learn to control her emotions, and she won't if we keep ignoring this sort of behaviour."

I tried a thing. It was a bit of a desperate thing in some ways, but it felt like it *might* make sense under the Oliverian parenting paradigm. "Okay, but look at it this way—Mum is basically Jaz's foster grandmother, and grandparents letting their grandkids get away with murder is a time-honoured tradition."

"In some families, perhaps." There was an edge to Oliver's voice I didn't love as much as I could have. I might almost go so far as to say I didn't like it. Didn't like it at all. "But my grandparents never—"

As the only person in the room who had successfully parented for more than eight minutes at a stretch, Mum stepped in with infuriating effortlessness. "Now Jas has gone"—she deployed a sly and intensely weaponised smile—"it means I am in need of a kitchen helper."

The part of Oliver that believed people Jaz's age should respect people Odile's age was pitched into sudden conflict with the part of Oliver that believed people his age should respect people Odile's age. The better of those two very similar parts won. "Of course, Odile," he said. And then, once he'd rolled up his sleeves and grabbed a kitchen knife, he added as gently as he was able, "Are you absolutely sure about the rhubarb?"

One of Mum's many superpowers was never being sure about anything while also being absolutely certain about everything. "It's traditional."

"I really don't think it is," I said ill-advisedly.

"Of course it is. That is why when the cockneys want a curry they say, 'I am going for a rhubarb.'"

They say you wind up marrying your parents, but I was pretty sure I'd wound up working with mine, because this was the exact kind of conversation I had every day in the office. "I think that's 'a ruby.'"

Mum looked at me like I'd completely lost it. "Don't be silly, Luc. You can't put rubies in curry."

Of all the things I could possibly have said in that moment, "Obviously they're not literal rubies" was far from the worst. But that didn't make it good.

"Well no," Mum conceded. And then with a twist of parental genius I hoped I could one day emulate, she pivoted to, "It's probably a metaphor for rhubarb."

With no further comment, Mum dumped a whole fennel in front of Oliver, who dutifully sliced it.

Unable to watch while my mum forced my boyfriend to be her kitchen accomplice, I slunk back into the living room, where I found Judy alone. Well, alone save for Michael of Kent, who had decided to stop following Jaz around and go sit with her mistress.

"Too many cooks, eh?" Judy observed.

"I think Mum might be too many cooks all by herself."

Judy nodded sagely. "She has a fierce will, your mother."

"A fierce will which she uses exclusively to force people to eat terrible curries?"

"There are far worse things to use a fierce will for."

This was one of those unanswerable Judy statements you just had to nod at and move past, so I nodded and moved past it. "Any idea where Jaz is?"

Judy looked blissfully unconcerned. "Probably upstairs. I wouldn't worry. Young things like that can mostly look after themselves in my experience."

"In your experience?" I asked, only slightly terrified of the answer.

"I was young once, too, you know. She must be, what, fourteen?"

"That's right."

"Good age, fourteen. Young enough that the world still has wonder in it, old enough that you can actually go looking."

I squirmed slightly. "Yeah, I think these days going looking for wonder in the world is just a recipe for getting online groomed."

"Well, you know best," said Judy with the air of a woman who firmly believed I did not, in fact, know best.

Still committed to Operation Give Jaz Her Space, and pretty sure that someone would have noticed if she'd climbed out of a window or otherwise vanished into the wilds of Surrey, I perched on the arm of the sofa.

After I'd spent half an hour navigating small talk with Judy, Mum emerged from the kitchen and announced, with misplaced pride, that the special curry was ready.

Oliver followed her through with five bowls on a tray. "Where's Jasmine?" was his first comment and only question.

"Upstairs I guess?" The *I guess* had been a bad choice. Oliver didn't see much room for guessing at the best of times, but especially not where Jaz was concerned.

He set the tray down on the coffee table. "If you'll excuse me, Odile, I'll go and get her."

It would be fine. Probably it would be fine. Going-and-getting-Jaz duty fairly often got handled by whoever happened to be closest, and I *was* sitting down and Oliver *was* standing up, and saying *Are you sure you won't make a complete arse of this?* wouldn't demonstrate the commitment to trustful coparenting that Oliver and I had agreed on. Y'know, back before we'd tried to coparent. All of which meant there was no valid objection I could make to Oliver being the one who went to retrieve Jaz and me being the one who stayed behind eating spiced rhubarb and turnip.

"How is the special curry, mon caneton?" asked Mum cheerfully.

"It's terrible, Mum. You know it's terrible. I know it's terrible. Even Oliver knows it's terrible. In fact, I sometimes think you deliberately make it more and more terrible every time just to see how long it'll take him to admit it."

"And I sometimes think you are a very ungrateful son."

Judy was tucking into her bowl with genuine gusto. Then again, Judy was practically made of gusto. "Tiny note"—she jabbed a finger at the bowl—"needs more turnip."

"Does anything," I protested, "ever *really* need more turnip?"

But I didn't get an answer, because there was shouting again.

After leaving Mum and Judy to debate the optimal turnip-to-grapefruit level for a curry, I dashed upstairs to see what had happened with the going-and getting-Jaz mission. As I got closer, I began to catch one side of a very repetitive conversation, which seemed to be going:

"Fuck off."

Then.

"No. Fuck off."

Then.

"Fuck *off*."

Finally, I could hear Oliver. "Odile is serving dinner. You're being rude."

"Just give me it back."

I had no idea what the *it* Oliver wasn't giving back was. I did, however, take some small comfort from the fact he didn't reply, "Give it back *to me*," which his mother certainly would have. His actual reply, "It isn't yours," was at least an inarguable fact. Which made it harder for Jaz to argue. Harder but not impossible.

"Everything okay?" I asked, poking my head around the door into my mum's bedroom.

At first I was so focused on my boyfriend arguing with our foster kid that I didn't have much attention to spare for anything else, but as I progressed from head-poking to whole-self poking, I was sort of kicked in the face by a boot made of feels.

It's not that I'd never been in my mum's bedroom before. I'd spent all the bits of childhood I could remember in this house, and there'd been nights I was ill or couldn't sleep or just liked the idea of a bigger bed. But I hadn't properly been in there as an adult. As somebody who could see my mum as, on some level at least, a human being with her own shit going on. And I hadn't been prepared for how different that would be.

For a moment or two, I wasn't able to...do or...think much. Mostly I just stood there, looking around. Really looking for the first time. At the discs on the wall—a few gold from before my dad, one platinum from *Welcome Ghosts*—at the pictures on the sideboard, all from her younger days. All with the light and the crowds and the music. All, and wasn't this a headfuck and a half, from when she was younger than me. Like, way younger than me. Like, before-I-met-Oliver younger than me.

And that was when I realised: This wasn't my mum's room at all. It was Odile's. It was where Odile O'Donnell had gone so that Luc O'Donnell could have something that almost looked like a normal life.

Then I also realised that this was the place Jaz had gone without asking. And that the thing she was demanding Oliver give back to her was my fucking mum's fucking guitar.

"Excuse me," I said, "the *fuck*?"

The look in Oliver's eyes was giving me 10/10 for sentiment and 2/10 for execution.

Jaz glared up at me with a bitterness she normally reserved for Oliver. Which felt two different kinds of bad. Then a third kind of bad that came from feeling guilty about one of the first two kinds of bad. "I was just having a go," she muttered.

I glared back, distantly aware I wasn't handling this well but having no idea how to make myself handle it better. "You don't just 'have a go' with my mum's stuff."

Jaz didn't even look at me, and it felt incredibly pointed that she didn't even look at me. "All right sorry."

"Don't 'all right sorry' me," I snapped. "I know what 'all right sorry' means."

"Jasmine," said Oliver, levelly. "We're not—"

But he didn't get to finish the thought because with a final, somehow ever more expressive "Fuck," Jaz left my mum's room and stormed downstairs.

Oliver and I followed her, Oliver first laying my mum's guitar gently down on the bed. When we caught up with her by the front door, it was clear that Jaz'd been planning to leave the house entirely but had been intercepted by Mum and Judy.

"Where are you going, chérie?" Mum was asking.

Jaz answered with the all-purpose shrug.

"Wherever it is," Judy added, "lot of perverts around this time of night. Take a dog. Maybe also a gun."

It was probably my imagination, but I swear I saw Jaz perk up at the suggestion.

"Judy," said Oliver in his best grown-up-in-the-room voice. "Please don't try to arm our foster daughter."

"Also," I said, still way closer to authoritarian mode than I was comfortable being, "you're not going anywhere."

Jaz's hand was on the door.

"Has something happened?" asked Mum. It wasn't really a question. Or rather it was, but the question wasn't *if* something had happened; it was *what*.

"We found Jasmine in your bedroom," Oliver explained.

"With your guitar," I added. For some reason, this was the bit that was most offending me.

Mum looked at Jaz in a way I remembered her looking at me so many, many times down the years. It was a look that said, *You fucked up, we both know you fucked up, but we're also all the other person has, so I'm going to love you anyway no matter what.* "Is that true, Jas?"

Jaz looked down. "Yeah," she said. And then, completely without provocation, she added a sincere-sounding, "Sorry."

I was almost hurt. She never apologised to me or Oliver that quickly. At least not if she meant it.

"You know," Mum added, "if you had asked, I would have said it was okay."

Jaz mumbled another apology.

"Was she any good?" she asked me and Oliver, and then, when neither of us had anything resembling an answer, she asked Jaz, "Are you any good?"

Even by Jaz's standards, her response was noncommittal. A sort of slow twitch and a half shake of the head and a barely audible sound that somebody who was extremely dedicated to charitably interpreting teenage noises might understand as "dunno."

"Well then," announced Mum as if that solved everything and we no longer had any problems to discuss whatsoever, "the special curry is waiting. Come, everybody."

"Hang on," I said, "you can't just *come everybody* this under the rug. She was...she was in your room. With your stuff. It was—" I was going to have a really hard time saying what it was without using emotion words, and I hated using emotion words. "It was... intrusive. And personal...and that's...like, that's *your* space and—"

"Yes," said Mum, looking at me almost sternly now and nodding in a this-nod-has-a-double-meaning kind of way. "It is *my* space. Not yours. And this is my house, and when I say something is over, it is over."

"But—"

"Ah." Mum raised a finger. "Over."

Jaz was still looking kind of on edge, and I was still *feeling* kind of on edge, and that was especially shitty because I didn't want to be in my thirties and feeling shitty because things weren't cool between me and a fourteen-year-old.

"You must forgive Luc," Mum said to Jaz. "He is very protective of his old maman."

Jaz didn't seem particularly forgiving, but she was visibly less tense than she had been, which hopefully meant she'd be a lot less likely to straight up bolt. Because that would have been twice in under a week, and twice regardless of timeframe seemed like a bad number of times for us to trigger a teenager's fight-or-flight reflex.

"Alors." Mum was still talking to Jaz. "Do you want to run out into the night, or do you want to come into the front room and eat the special curry?"

I raised a hand. "If that's a general question, I'll take running into the night, please."

CHAPTER 27

TURNED OUT, IT WASN'T A general question. So we trooped back into the front room to eat rapidly congealing special curry. It had gone tepid while we were looking for Jaz, but that hadn't so much harmed the flavour as moved it sideways into a realm of parallel horribleness. And, for a good five minutes, dealing with the grim reality of a turnip, rhubarb, and grapefruit curry was enough to keep us all distracted from the lingering awkwardness of my recent fuckups.

Eventually, though, tension started creeping back into the room. And I wished I could have chased it back out again, but I had no idea how. Like was this a "What have you been up to at school, Jaz?" type of situation? Or was it a "Have you gone back to *Drag Race* yet, Mum?" type of situation? Or even the moment for "So Oliver, lawyering, eh?" Except I kept thinking about all the ways all of them could go wrong and, in the end, said none of them.

"Anyway, Luc," asked Mum conversationally, "how is everything with this…this SHITstock you are working on?"

"CRAPPstonbury," I corrected her. "And…you know, okay."

Judy glanced up from a forkful of flabby yet over-spiced rhubarb. "Is this the toilet festival?"

"It is not," I said for the too-manyth time, "a toilet festival."

"Really? You seemed to be asking that fellow for an awful lot of toilets."

"Festivals *need* a lot of toilets." I was sick of explaining this. "People have to stop acting like it's weird to book toilets for a festival."

To my at best partial relief, Mum was on my side. "It's true. Toilets at festivals are very important. When I played Reading in '82, things got so bad that your father pissed in a bucket and tipped it all over Lemmy from Motörhead." She looked that mix of melancholy, wistful, and resentful she always did when she spoke about Dad. "Still, the Enid were good that year."

Jaz continued poking at the special curry, which she'd eaten a whole lot more of than I'd expected. "Toilets were bad when I went too," she said.

"Aren't you a little young for festivals?" asked Oliver.

We were getting back to normal, which in this case meant that Jaz had way more hostility for Oliver than for anybody else. "Not if they don't check IDs properly."

"If it isn't a toilet festival"—Judy still seemed to be puzzling the whole situation out—"how are the non-toilet aspects going?"

"Ironically," I said, "they're going a bit toilet. It's amazing how few international megastars want to play a charity gig for dung beetles where they'd have to be billed below a rich arsehole's vanity band."

Mum looked unbothered. "Really, aren't most bands rich arseholes' vanity bands?"

"Some of them are probably poor arseholes' vanity bands," Judy pointed out. "In my experience, the wealth of the arsehole makes very little difference."

Taking the opportunity to set down his spoon, Oliver glanced at the rest of the adults. "Could we maybe say *arsehole* just slightly less in front of Jasmine?"

Walking up to the open goal and kicking the ball straight through it, Jaz looked Oliver square in the eye and said, "Don't be an arsehole."

"Jas." Mum somehow managed to sound nonjudgemental without doing that thing I sometimes did where I gave away that I was secretly amused. "That is a very bad thing to call Oliver. He is not being an arsehole. He is only being a prude. When you get to my age, you learn that they are very different, and arseholes are far worse."

Jaz gave a half nod, then, by some weird miracle, said, "Sorry" again.

While Oliver and I were both adjusting to the shock, Jaz took another bite of special curry, then put her spoon firmly down and pushed the bowl away. "You…you do know this is shit, right?"

Oliver froze. I…I didn't. I was pretty sure I knew how this was going to go.

"Of course I do," Mum replied. "I do not have the Alzheimer's."

Most people, when confronted with Mum's completely blasé attitude towards pretty much any criticism, gave up. Jaz, somehow, didn't. "Have you tried making it *not* shit?"

Mum shook her head. "Non."

The expression Jaz was directing at Mum in that moment could only be described as *affectionate hatred*. "Why?"

"Ah, well, you see I am terrified that people will reject me, so I try to push them away by forcing them to have unpleasant experiences."

I couldn't quite tell if that was truer than Mum would have readily admitted, or a pointed comment about Jaz, or a pointed comment about me.

"No, seriously," Jaz pressed, "what's the deal? This is weird. Like, it's not normal. It's weird."

Mum continued to look utterly unbothered. "I am a star of the rock 'n' roll. We are not meant to be normal."

Jaz carried on stabbing Mum with her eyes. "That's not an answer."

"I got to fifty," said Mum laconically, "and I realised I was a terrible cook. So I decided I had to either learn or steer into it. I steered into it."

I was used to Mum by now. And so was Oliver. Jaz was not. "That's—that doesn't make *sense.*"

"Makes sense to me," replied Mum, giving Jaz a taste of her own medicine, shrug-wise.

Jaz looked like she was about to yell for the third time that evening. Instead, she just turned to me and asked accusingly, "Is she always like this?"

"Pretty much."

She almost, almost, looked sympathetic. "No wonder you're like that."

"Honestly, some days I'm amazed I survived."

Mum and Oliver were both giving me cut-it-out looks. Mum's seemed playful. Oliver's didn't.

"Excuse me," Mum fauxtested, "I think you will find I was one of the all-time *great* mothers. I am up there at the top of the list with Clytemnestra."

To which Jaz asked, "Who?" and Oliver asked, "Are you *sure* that's the one you mean?" and I didn't ask anything because my lack of knowledge of Greek mythology was matched only by my lack of caring about my lack of knowledge of Greek mythology.

Since Mum had no interest in expanding on her self-comparison to a long-dead and probably fictional woman who, knowing my mum, had probably done some really serious murders, that led to the teeniest of lulls in the conversation. Which gave Mum exactly enough time to ask Jaz, "So why *were* you playing on my guitar?"

I hadn't known Jaz that long, but I'd already had a lot of practice spotting her there's-more-to-this-than-I-want-to-talk-about signs. She'd look away, then give a one-word answer she'd chosen with expert precision to avoid arguments with people she thought looked down on her.

"Bored," she said.

"That is understandable," agreed Mum. "It must be extremely boring visiting your foster father's weird, not-normal maman."

The use of the phrase *foster father* got a noticeable wince from Jaz.

And then my mum got to her feet with a speed and a decisiveness that made her look more like the woman who had played the Reading Festival in 1982 than I'd seen in a long time. "Come, come," she said, "let us do something less boring."

I'd expected Jaz to keep up her mask of studied apathy until either she or Oliver and I were dead. But she was watching Mum now with something that still didn't feel like *interest* but looked quite a lot like caution. "What?" she asked.

"I am going to teach you to play the guitar."

Jaz's face set. "I can already play the guitar."

Mum had a way, sometimes, of telling you she was through with your shit without telling you she was through with your shit. She was, in the nicest and most comforting way possible, through with Jaz's shit. "Please remember, I am a legend of the rock 'n' roll who has been in hiding in a tiny village in Surrey for longer than you have been alive. This is not an offer most little girls get."

Little girl had been calculated. I was sure of it. Because Jaz went at once to "I'm not a little girl" without objecting to anything else Mum had been saying.

"Jasmine," said Mum, deploying the full-official-name bomb with surgical precision, "come and play the fucking guitar with me."

And, while Oliver and I looked on in stunned silence, Jaz kinda ...did?

"Goodbye, Odile," Oliver said as we were leaving. "And thank you for a lovely evening."

I went with a less formal "Bye, Mum," and Jaz followed with an even less formal sound that might have been a good night.

We piled into the car, and Oliver took us out into the not-especially-wild Surrey night. "I actually thought," he said, "that went rather well."

Jaz didn't have any comment, and right then neither did I. It wasn't that I disagreed. More that I didn't want to jinx it.

"And it was very generous of Odile," added Oliver, "to lend you a guitar to practise on."

Jaz was clinging on to Mum's spare-spare-spare guitar like she was afraid somebody would...now I thought about it, like she was afraid somebody would do exactly what they'd been doing her whole life. Decide they'd get to keep it even though it had been given to her. Stick it in a black bin liner and then put her in handcuffs. Just generally be a prick to her about it.

"Seems like a nice one," I added, trying to sound upbeat.

"Said she nicked it," Jaz offered.

Unlike me, Oliver was really good at keeping his eyes on the road, but his jaw tensed. "I'm sure she didn't."

He'd met Mum. He'd heard her stories, and some of my dad's stories, and a lot of Judy's stories. I didn't for one second believe he was *actually* sure she didn't. He was just making a parenting call. And I, perhaps because I was tired and perhaps because I was still high on the evening not having been a total disaster, decided to make a different one. "Oh, I'm sure she did. Mum had a pretty intense youth."

Oliver flicked me a look out of the corner of his eye that said, *Please, Lucien.*

"To be clear," I said, "stealing is still bad. It's just like..." Fuck, I'd started this with good being-honest-to-our-foster-kid intentions, and now I was going down a rabbit hole into a train wreck. "It's just like that bit in *Love Actually*, you know?"

"What?" Jaz sounded genuinely confused. "She's going to make creepy videos of some girl she's obsessed with?"

I'd assumed she'd just not have heard of the movie, but they did put it on TV every Christmas. "No, I mean—"

"Trish says that's stalking. She says that guy should be locked up for being a weirdo and a perv."

Oliver said, "Trish might be overstating slightly, but she has a reasonable case" at the same time that I said—I thought more importantly—"Who's Trish?"

"Girl from school," said Jaz, noncommittally.

"Friend?" I asked.

I took Jaz's total silence as a yes.

"If you'd like to have her over for dinner one evening," said Oliver, "she'd be more than welcome."

"I'm not fucking six."

I half turned in my seat again. "You know that adults have people over for dinner too. Oliver wasn't saying we'd get jelly and Party Rings."

"Oh, that reminds me," put in Oliver, recalled to another of our adulting duties. "Jennifer and Peter can't do first week of February."

"We *might* have to just accept that not everybody can make it," I told him. "Priya's already told me she's busy—and I quote—'any weekend where you're throwing the kind of party that has canapés.'"

With a perverse teenage will—the kind that felt the only thing worse than having to talk to adults was having adults talk to each other about things you weren't interested in—Jaz said, "Brian."

"What?" I asked, and Oliver asked, "Pardon?"

"Bloke she nicked it off."

I didn't think my mum knew any Brians. "Really?"

"Yeah. Said she nicked it off him at uni."

I also didn't think Mum had ever been to university. "When was this?"

"'Oh seven,'" Jaz quoted directly. "Apparently, he'd taken a really long break for work, then gone back to finish his degree. Then there'd been a party to celebrate, and she'd nicked one of his guitars because she figured he wouldn't need it anymore if he was going to be an astrophysicist."

Okay, *that* was making more sense. "When you say 'a really long break for work,'" I tried, "do you mean 'he spent thirty-three years as lead guitarist of Queen'?"

I was still twisted around enough to see Jaz shrug.

"I *think*," Oliver said gently, "before we got distracted, you were about to explain to Jaz that even if Odile stole her guitar, stealing is wrong in general." He paused a moment. "Also, for some reason, you were doing it through the medium of *Love Actually*."

I tried to spool my brain back to the state it had been in three minutes ago and, at best, partially succeeded. "Oh, right. I mean it's like that bit where Bill Nighy is all, 'Don't buy drugs. Become a pop star, and they give you them for free.'"

Oliver groaned. "I *really* don't think that was supposed to be good advice."

"No, right, but I mean, like, some things are okay when you're a rock star and not when you're a normal person."

Jaz didn't seem to like that. "Not sure that's fair."

"It isn't," Oliver agreed. "Although I suppose you could argue that it's indicative of a certain systemic hypocrisy at a societal level, so it's probably to some extent realistic."

"Is that just a fancy way of saying life isn't fair?" asked Jaz, who'd honestly decoded that quicker than I had.

"And that therefore if you do want to get away with stealing," Oliver continued, "you should make sure to become rich and successful *first*." Then, remembering himself, he added, "Although you shouldn't be stealing even *if* you'd get away with it."

"Because it's wrong," I added, probably too helpfully. After a few minutes of silence, I craned around again to see Jaz cradling the guitar. "So"—I attempted to sound super casual—"you think you'll go back for lessons?"

I should have known better than to ask a direct question. Jaz, like always, interpreted it as a trap and clutched the guitar to her chest. It wasn't until I'd turned back around and let her feel I was barely paying attention that she said, "She's going to make me eat more of that shitty curry, isn't she?"

I flipped down the sunshade to look at her in the little vanity mirror. It saved my neck and saved her from direct eye contact. "Hard to tell. She mostly only makes it for people she likes."

Jaz visibly relaxed. "Oh good."

"Then again, I think she likes you."

CHAPTER 28

HAVING JAZ BE PART OF our life, Oliver and I both agreed, was a wonder, a joy, a blessing, and a privilege.

But sweet holy mother of absolute fuck were we glad when she finally told us she was spending the evening with a friend.

"She'll be okay, right?" I asked Oliver, when it was too late to change anything, even if she wasn't.

"She'll be fine," Oliver reassured me. "I've double-checked with Trish's mother, and they really are going to her house to"—he searched for the right words for a moment—"I think just *generally hang out*."

"Cool."

"Of course now I think about it, Trish's mother *did* sound rather a lot like Jasmine doing an old-woman voice."

"Shit." My heart actually, honestly-to-God, not-a-metaphor skipped a beat. "Should we… Oh, you're taking the piss."

"Of *course* I'm taking the piss." Oliver put the last mug into the dishwasher and set it to an ecologically friendly cycle. "She's having a normal evening with a friend, like teenagers do. It's good. It's a positive development."

I looked down at Spud. "Hear that, boy? It's just you, me, and Daddy Oliver this evening."

Spud looked legitimately crushed. "Arooou?"

"Okay, don't be like that."

"Aroooou."

"Oliver!"—I turned to my boyfriend—"Spud's being a dick."

"He's not being a dick." Oliver dropped into a half crouch, and Spud scampered over to him. "You're not being a dick, are you, boy?"

"Ruff."

"Traitor."

Oliver stood back up and led Spud out of the kitchen. "He just misses Jasmine. Which is another good sign. It means she's settling in well. Now come on, we should be going."

We should. We should definitely have been going. This would be our first meal out in ages. I grabbed my coat and went to stand by the door like an overexcitable puppy.

Oliver, substantially less overexcitable and nowhere near as puppyish, attached Spud securely to his lead. "Do you have the bags?" he asked without looking up.

I said "Yes" instinctively, then "No" honestly. Then I went back to the kitchen, retrieved a couple of the other sort of doggie bags, came back and said, "Okay, actually yes. But Spud isn't going to want to poo in the pub, is he?"

"I'm sure he'll wait until he's outside. And he *probably* won't need to go at all. But if he does, we'll be very glad we brought the bags."

Our first date had been at an extremely swanky high-end restaurant. It had also been part of a wider plan to rehabilitate my public image, save my job, and generally stop my life from being ruined. Well, given where I was in those days, from being *more* ruined. Somehow, though, this trip to a decently reviewed local pub with our rescue dog that we were slipping into the two-to-three-hour window when our foster daughter was out the house seemed way, way higher stakes.

"He'll be okay, right?"

Oliver gave me an indulgent smile. "Spud will be okay. Jasmine will be okay. They'll both be okay. Neither of them are going to poo anywhere they shouldn't or bite any strangers. Now come on, I know we don't have a booking to be late for, but it's a popular place and it does fill up."

So we set off. The pub we'd picked was only a short walk from our house because while Spud *could* go in the car, he didn't much like it, and all three of us felt like we could do with the exercise. Of course, we'd also picked it because it was dog-friendly, but that had narrowed our options down far less than I'd expected. Whether from a gradual cultural shift or the sudden need to accommodate a bajillion lockdown puppies, half the venues in London seemed to have gone puppy-positive.

This particular venue advertised its puppy-positivity with a sign reading "Dogs with well-behaved owners welcome," which I tried to find annoying but secretly found cute.

Other than that, it was just a very nice, very straightforward English pub, with one of those white-paint-black-beams facades that I wanted to call Tudor, but mostly because that was the only historical period I actually knew.

"There are...a *lot* of people here," I said, a bit nervously, as we were shown to our table. "And a lot of dogs."

"Ruff," agreed Spud, less nervously.

"He's ready for it," replied Oliver, looking down at our contribution to the general doggishness.

For a moment or two, Oliver and I busied ourselves with the menus, and I felt briefly guilty. "Sorry, they seem a bit low on vegan options."

Oliver gave me a think-nothing-of-it smile. "That's to be expected. They do doggy ice cream, which will please Spud, and a vegetable chilli, which I'm sure is lovely."

"Are you?" I asked. "Or are you just being nice?"

Oliver reached across the table and took my hand. "What matters is that we're here together. Just you, me, and Spud."

"Ruff," said Spud. And there was an answering "Ruff" from another table. Followed by another "Ruff" and then two yaps and a growl.

I peeked suspiciously over to where the other noises had come from. There was a corgi lurking nearby, and whereas every other dog in the place looked deeply chill, it looked twitchy, stressed, and about to take its twitchy stressedness out on anybody who got near it.

But as Oliver had said, this wasn't about having a wide range of vegan options, or not being exposed to yappy animals, it was about being together, so I ignored the corgi, smiled back at my boyfriend, and just said, "Yeah."

"It's been a while," he added.

And I said "Yeah" again.

"And also"—he sounded uncharacteristically hesitant—"and also *a lot*."

In many ways, it was a massive relief to hear him admit it. "So much a lot. Like looking back—"

"Ruffruffruff *yap* ruff," interjected the evil corgi.

"Looking back," I continued, "getting a dog to see if we were ready for a kid was kind of lowballing it."

Oliver laughed, and I was glad he was laughing again because I'd been missing it. "Just a little," he agreed.

"Do you think it's too late to start training Jaz with one of those clicker things?"

"I don't think she'd respond well to it." Unfortunately, while I'd been going for wryly amusing, Oliver ran very quickly out of both wryness and amusement. "Then again, I don't think I know *what* she'd respond well to."

There was...not bitterness exactly, but there was an edge to

Oliver's voice that I really hoped wouldn't last the whole evening. "You do," I told him. "At least, you do as well as I do."

"That's very kind of you, but it's simply not the case."

The boyfriend-instinct in me wanted to disagree because the alternative was to tacitly say, *You're right, you flat-out don't get our foster daughter*. But while I'd never have put it that harshly, there was, perhaps, the tiniest smidgen of truth in the idea that he and Jaz didn't quite fit perfectly into each other's worldviews. So I went with the safely neutral, "We never expected this to be easy."

"No," Oliver agreed, and then pulled his phone out. Which I thought was weirdly rude of him until I realised that this was an order-on-the-app place. "Do you know what you want, by the way?"

I'd barely thought about it, but fortunately this was a pretty typical pub, menu-wise, and being a filthy carnivore, I could just go straight for the burger option.

Oliver tapped our choices into his phone and scanned his card, and then I once again had his utterly undivided attention. Which I'd missed almost as much as making him laugh.

"Yapyaprrrrrufffyap."

Mostly undivided attention.

"Rationally," Oliver said slowly, and I could see him glancing at the evil corgi out the corner of his eye, "I understand that it isn't my job to make her like me. I just think"—he gave my hand a little squeeze and his lips narrowed—"I don't think I'd accounted for how bad it would feel when she didn't."

"Yap," said the evil corgi. "Ruff. Ruff. Rrrrufff. *Yap*."

"Also," Oliver went on, letting the next table's dog distract him from what I was beginning to realise was a genuinely hard topic for him, "I'm immensely glad that we trained Spud better than that."

"Ruff," said Spud.

"Daddy Oliver is right," I told him. "You are the *goodest boy*, aren't you?"

To my relief, Spud had no sense of irony, so he *didn't* respond to this by making the exact kind of scene I was congratulating him for not making. Instead, he just thumped his tail on the ground and looked happy.

"At the risk of sounding unbelievably *Daily Mail*," Oliver went on, "I find it very hard not to think you shouldn't be allowed a dog if you're going to let it carry on like that. If nothing else, it's very unfair on the dog."

A waiter passed by the evil corgi's table, and it snapped at her. Not so close that she was in any real danger, but close enough that it made her jump.

"It's pretty unfair on the rest of us too," I said. "Then again, it might just be corgis in general. Have you ever met a corgi that wasn't a massive dick?"

Oliver gave me a playfully superior look. "I like to think anything can be its best self, given the opportunity. Even a corgi."

"Are you telling me that corgi"—I jerked my head towards its arse, which was currently sticking out from under the table, probably because the rest of the corgi was doing something evil beneath it—"is misunderstood? Does it have a tragic backstory?"

"Yes, its tragic backstory is that it was bred to run around on a farm, herding animals, and it was bought by two Londoners who thought it would look good on TikTok and demonstrably did not train around its natural instinct to nip at animals and control the space it's in."

"Ruff," said Spud, supportively.

I plonked a depressed elbow on the table. "Well, now I just feel bad. It's no fun being mean about a dog that's secretly yearning for the wide-open fields of...of...wherever there are wide-open fields."

"I'm sorry." I'd been mostly messing around, but Oliver looked genuinely chastened. "I didn't mean to rain on your snark parade."

"Oh, come on. You know my snark parade's all-weather."

His smile had taken on a slightly strained edge. "All the same, this is our one evening to ourselves and I'm…I'm not being a very good companion."

"Oliver"—I squeezed his fingers tightly—"you're companioning fine. And Jaz will come round."

"What if she doesn't?" he asked. "She could be with us until she's eighteen. That's a long time to live with someone who resents you."

"She doesn't resent you." I paused. "Okay, she probably does."

"Reassuring. Thank you, Lucien."

"No, I mean, like, only the really general sense that she probably resents everything because she's fourteen and she's been treated like shit."

"And I'm trying to help her."

"Yeah. And you can and you will. It's just…" I tried to think of the most Oliver-friendly way to put it. "It's just going to be a bit of a learning process."

Oliver was gazing at me with some messy mix of hope and not-quite-getting-it. "You think she'll eventually learn that I'm not her enemy?"

That wasn't a million percent what I'd been going for. But I didn't think it was going to be helpful for either Oliver or Jaz—or, for that matter, our date night—if I tried to make Oliver think about things the same way I did. Especially because the way I thought about things was usually crap and frequently wrong. "I think," I said slowly, "if we can find a way to show her…" I trailed away, out of ideas and out of options.

"That I"—Oliver had an eyebrow in its most sardonic position—"like the corgi, am misunderstood."

"No, well. Not exactly. Well. She just needs to see…like…the good person that you are. That I, and everybody else who's ever met you, know you are."

"When you first met me, you thought I was a dick."

"And now I'm completely in love with you," I cried, triumphantly. "So you see, it works."

He laughed again, one of his softer laughs, his *I'm only now admitting how vulnerable I've been* laugh. "Thank you, Lucien. You always know exactly the right thing to say."

"No, I don't. I say the wrong thing all the time."

"And yet somehow it works for you. For me. For us."

The waiter the dog had snapped at appeared briefly by our table, setting down my burger and Oliver's chilli. He glanced up at her and gave a reflexive yet utterly sincere "Thank you, that looks lovely" before turning back to me.

Glad of the interruption, I looked down at my burger. "Okay, there's a slim chance we need to get out more because this very ordinary pub burger is looking a-fucking-mazing right now."

"I am glad to be doing something together," Oliver agreed. "Although I suppose from a certain perspective, the fact that your burger is looking a-fucking-mazing suggests we should carry on exactly as we are. Clearly it means we appreciate things more."

"But I *hate* appreciating things," I play-complained. "Is this what being a grown-up is like? You never get any quality time with your partner and all your friends are constantly busy so suddenly a meal in a dog-friendly pub in Romford is the highlight of your month?"

Oliver gave me a strangely contented smile. "It seems so. Which is"—he paused for just a moment—"scary if you let it be, but from another perspective, perhaps rather wonderful?"

Fuck, I hoped he was right. "Fuck, I hope you're right."

And Oliver laughed again. Louder this time, loudly enough that it set off the misunderstood corgi. "Frankly, so do I."

"Hang on," I protested, "I just did the *everything will be okay* routine for you. It's your turn to do it for me."

"I'm afraid, my dear Lucien, that we are in uncharted territory for the both of us. But everything *is* going to be okay. It's like you said about Jasmine—"

"Oh my God. You're supposed to be helping, not using my words against me."

"I'm using your words *for* you."

"That's even worse."

"All I'm saying"—he set his fork down beside his bowl of chilli, took my hand up again, and kissed my fingers gently in that maybe-cheesy-but-not-cheesy-to-me way he had—"is that it, and by *it*, I mean everything—being alive, being a grown-up, life in general—is a learning experience."

I tried to scowl through my schmoop. "This is the bit where I'm supposed to relish an opportunity for growth, isn't it?"

"How about, for now, you work on relishing your cheeseburger?"

"But what do I do *after* I've relished the cheeseburger?"

"That's a post-cheeseburger problem."

I took a bite. "Okay, yeah. The live-in-the-cheeseburger-moment plan is really working for me."

"You see?" Oliver was smiling his most reassuring smile. "Being a grown-up isn't so bad."

"Mrrfgh," I contributed.

"Mruff," Spud contributed.

"We'll make more time for each other moving forward. And once things settle down, we'll see our friends more often as well."

"Will we, though?" I asked, looking up reluctantly from my burger. "Right now we can't even organise a dinner party."

Oliver gave an almost missable flinch. "It's true things have been a little difficult. But that's only because we have Jasmine, and Bridge has Autumn, and everybody has new responsibilities that we need to work around. Once we're all together, it'll be just like old times."

"You really think?" I asked.

"I really think."

And I believed him. Mainly because I really, really *wanted* to believe him.

But what I think I missed, looking back, was that he really, really wanted to believe him too.

"THE PROBLEM, YOU LONG SAXON prick," Bronwyn was saying through Zoom into my computer and through that into my ears, "is that *he's* impossible to work with."

"I am *not* impossible to work with," James Royce-Royce replied and then, because he was taking this call with Baby J on his knee, he added, "Daddy's not impossible to work with, *is he*?"

James Royce-Royce's habit of asking Baby J to back up his every statement had been annoying even *before* Baby J had got old enough to actually do it. "No?" said Baby J, not sounding super confident, if I was honest.

"He has no experience in site-specific catering."

"Excuse me"—James Royce-Royce tried to restrain Baby J from doing something potentially destructive to his computer—"I've made a sausage plait for the queen."

Bronwyn gesticulated at the screen. "*See*. I've had to deal with this all week."

"See," mirrored James Royce-Royce, "she has no respect for my experience."

"You don't want respect," Bronwyn said over any intermediarying I might have been planning, "you want obedience."

"Okay," I tried at last, "perhaps we can all accept that both of you bring valuable and unique—"

"What *she* brings," James Royce-Royce interrupted, "is seven different ways to make a mess with jackfruit."

"Oh, get your head out your arse, arsehead."

James Royce-Royce clapped his hands over Baby J's ears. "*Language.* You see the kind of *unprofessionalism*—"

"Oh, because it's the height of professional to bring a toddler to a work meeting, isn't it?"

"He's *very precocious.*"

"Please." I don't think I actually screamed. I might have actually screamed. "I know you're both doing me a massive favour here"—James Royce-Royce and Bronwyn opened their mouths—"and if *either* of you says that you're doing me a favour but the other person is lucky to have the exposure, I will...well, I won't do anything on account of the whole doing-me-a-massive-favour thing, but you'll have been really predictable and I hope you'll feel bad about it."

Baby J said "Arsehead" happily into the silence.

And then my phone started ringing. I glanced down at my desk in the fervent hope that it would be somebody so important that I could cut this meeting short.

Then I realised that by fervently hoping that, I had massively jinxed myself. Because I *did* have to cut the meeting short. Because it was St. Jude's Academy.

"Sorry." I didn't even bother to hide my apprehension. "You both make really good points, but I have to get this. It's Jaz's school."

I de-headphoned and wheeled my chair away from the computer. "Hello?"

"Mr. O'Donnell?" It was Miss Collins. She sounded... I was going to go with *studiedly professional.* "I'm afraid you'll need to come and pick up Jasmine."

It was not picking-up-Jasmine time. It was not even close to picking-up-Jasmine time. "Can I ask why?"

There was a moment's silence from the other end of the line, and then Miss Collins said, very calmly, "She's been suspended."

James Royce-Royce and Bronwyn had been very understanding about my need to bail immediately, and not entirely trusting myself to jump straight into the car from a standing start, I took a moment in my study to compose myself and message Oliver.

That took longer than I expected it to, because I wound up typing and deleting the same message six times over, working through different phrasings until I finally said fuck it and went with Jaz has been suspended.

While I was waiting with a nauseous knot in my stomach for him to reply, I also noticed a long chain of messages in the Are the Straights Okay (Dinner Party Remix) group.

CANT DO HTIS WEEKEND BABYSITTER HAS SCROFULA. This was Bridge.

Sorry, did you say scrofula? That was Peter.

I was unsurprised to notice that James Royce-Royce had followed up with We thought Baby J had scrofula once, but then James Royce-Royce had brought him down to earth with It was nappy rash.

Definitely scrofula? Peter again. Like the king's evil scrofula.

DON'T KNOW ABOUT TAHT SHE DFEINITELY SAID SCROFULA

I refuse to believe your babysitter has scrofula. That was Priya.

YOUR NOT EVEN COMING TO THE DINNER PARTY SO YOU SHOULDN@T CARE.

I don't care. I feel like Priya's predictive text probably filled in *I don't care* whenever she let it pick the first three words for her. But your babysitter can't have scrofula.

Maybe it was scurvy? James Royce-Royce had suggested. A lot of people these days aren't eating anything like enough fresh fruit and vegetables.

Do people still even get scrofula? Jennifer. In industrialised countries, I mean. I don't want this to be a conversation about global health inequality.

You do a bit, don't you? Peter.

A series of typing-dots came from Brian, followed by: Scrofula is actually tuberculosis of the throat. It's caused by the same bacteria that causes it in the lungs so it's uncommon in this country because we vaccinate against TB anyway. It still happens sometimes but most of the examples I can find are from the states.

Then he linked a couple of sources. Then he linked some truly disgusting images of an elderly woman with suppurating lesions on her neck.

OKAYN IT MIGHT NOT BE SCROFULA, Bridge admitted. IT MIGHT BE MUMPS.

Hoping to drag things back in a semi-productive direction, I sent: So next weekend then?

Next weekend as in this weekend coming, asked Jennifer, or next weekend the weekend after that?

Figuring the rest of the chat could work that out amongst themselves, I stood up unsteadily and went out to the car. Once I was behind the wheel and making the best attempt I could to psych myself into effective-solving-problems-parent mode, as opposed to parent-who-has-blatantly-fucked-up mode, I checked my phone one last time.

Are the Straights Okay (Dinner Party Remix) had devolved into a conversation about the correct usage of "next weekend" that I found even less appealing than the scrofula discussion, and that probably did not bode well for the vibe if we ever finally got round a dinner table.

Less appealing still, Oliver had texted back. His message had been even shorter than mine. A clear, to the point: What happened?

I guess I'll find out when I get there.

We'll talk about how to handle this when I get home.

And I guess that was fair? Like at least it was a *we* statement. I'll fill you in soon as I can.

Thank you. There was a pause and then a little three-dot moment and then: I love you.

I sent back an I love you to without even stopping to second-guess myself, which I thought really showed how far I'd come. Then I sent a *too which showed how far I hadn't. Then I put my phone away like a responsible driver, pulled out into the road, and immediately stalled.

I definitely did not take that as a sign.

Jaz was waiting at the school gates clutching her bag and looking anywhere but at me. The sky behind her was as grey as the car park, and the wind kept blowing her hair across her face. She seemed to have got bored of pushing it out again.

"What happened?" I asked.

Silence.

I waited for her to get into the car and to my relief she did, but when I got back into the driver's seat, she kept looking out the window at the drab, suburban streets of Havering.

"Miss Collins will tell me if you don't," I pointed out. Honestly, she'd probably already put the details in an email—these things had to have a paper trail because of accountability and shit. "But I'd like to hear your side of it."

After a while Jaz just said, "Challenging behaviour."

I tried to keep my tone…not light—I didn't want to sound like I wasn't taking this seriously—but nonjudgemental. "They wouldn't have sent you home just for being challenging."

"Challenging don't mean challenging. It means *challenging*."

I bit my lip and took in a short breath. "Jaz, don't make me say something really wanky."

"Bit late for that."

"No, I mean really wanky. Like, 'I'm trying to be on your side but you're making it difficult.'"

"Fuck, that *would* be wanky."

"Right? So can you just, like, tell me what happened?"

For a while, Jaz decided that no, telling me what happened was too much of an imposition on account of how I was the living incarnation of crap and so talking to me wouldn't be worth the oxygen atoms she exhaled while doing it.

But eventually she gave up and just said, "Fighting."

I didn't say *Did you win*. Partly because even I have *some* parenting instincts and partly because I'd never really come from a winning-fights-is-good culture. "Who with?"

"Someone."

As nonanswers went, it was almost beautiful. It did technically tell me that it had been an individual, rather than a group of people or, I don't know, a dog or something. But it also made it very clear that she still didn't think I was worth talking to. "This someone have a name?"

Silence.

"What happened to building more productive relationships with your peers and all that?"

A little more silence. Then, "Tried it. Didn't work out."

I let that rest and just drove us a little further, keeping my eyes on the road while also trying to be at least *aware* of Jaz in case she tried to wrench the door open and leap out while we were moving.

And although I wouldn't have called it a strategy, or even a ploy, it did sort of work.

"Trish," she said, so out of nowhere that it took me a moment to piece the context together.

"Your friend Trish?"

Jaz still wasn't looking at me, but I could imagine her look of contempt as clearly as if she'd been jamming it in my face.

"I mean, not now, I guess?" We'd come home the same way we had the first day I'd taken her in, so we were driving past the Cosy Café again. "Do you want some chips?"

Nothing.

"Do you want me to order some chips that you can then eat off my plate?"

Nothing.

So, in the absence of any better ideas, I tried what I'd tried last time. I ordered a plate of chips and a Coke for Jaz and a full English and a coffee for me, and we sat down at a tiny, uncomfortable table, and I waited for her to decide that speaking to me would be less awful than staring at me.

It was, unfortunately, a plan that relied on me having more willpower than a fourteen-year-old. "Seriously," I asked. "What happened with Trish?"

"She got in my face," Jaz said, keeping that face well away from me by staring out the door, "and I'm bad at controlling my emotions, remember?"

"I don't want to hear about your emotions," I said. Then realised that sounded bad and back-pedalled: "I mean, if you want to talk about your emotions, that's fine, but you don't need to keep telling me how bad at controlling them you are."

"It's what people keep telling *me*."

I gave a shrug. "They're your emotions. Do you need other people to tell you about them?"

"Must do," she said, completely deadpan. "Otherwise, why would they keep doing it? 'Specially when they're all on my side and looking out for me."

I did my best not to get angry, which I was finding harder than usual. I reckoned I was normally pretty chill with Jaz's behaviour—too chill by far for Oliver—but when she got all laconic and self-loathing, it started pushing some highly specific buttons. "Can you just tell me what Trish did?"

"It's not about what Trish did," Jaz informed me piously. "I cannot control her actions, but I can control my response to—"

"Jaz, can you please cut it out with the mindfulness talk—you clearly think it's bollocks."

"You're so shit at this."

I clenched my jaw. "Jaz, please. Tell. Me. What. She. Did."

And then, in the middle of a small café in Havering, Jaz replied, "She said I was the reason my mum tried to kill herself."

And I, in an all-time great display of parenting skills, replied, "Fuck, I hope you punched her fucking lights out."

Unblinking, matter-of-fact, Jaz said, "Smacked her head off a table."

Okay, that might have been going a bit far.

For a minute or two we went back to sitting there in silence, with Jaz eating my chips even though she had her own. Then I said, "Look. Ignoring what I said about seventy seconds ago, I obviously don't think beating another girl's head on a table is a good thing."

Jaz put her hands together as if in prayer. "Thank you, wise one, for teaching me right from wrong."

"*But also*," I went on, hoping that I was only fucking this most of the way up, "what she said was, like, properly not okay."

"Is that you showing empathy?" Jaz's voice was ninety-nine percent scorn and one percent...actually the one percent was probably just more scorn, but I was trying to be optimistic.

"It's me saying that… I mean, I'm not you—"

"Well done. They should give you a prize."

I ignored her. I was in a very literal sense the adult in the room. "When we were visiting my mum, and I thought you were messing with her stuff, you know how I kinda lost it?"

"Kinda," Jaz confirmed.

"And I shouldn't have. But I did because, you know—that's my fucking mum, Jaz. I'm not making excuses for me and I'm not making excuses for you, but from when I was eight until when I met Oliver, my mum was basically all I had."

For a moment, the teeniest, tiniest possible moment, I thought I saw something in Jaz's eyes. A begrudging flicker of connection. Then she blinked it away like a bit of dust or a stray eyelash. "You're right," she said. "You're *not* me."

I shrugged. "Don't have to be."

"Still." She sounded almost triumphant. "You're stuck with me now."

Okay, this was going to a button-pressing place again. "We're not stuck with you."

Jaz gave an exhalation that could just about have been called a laugh. "True. You can send me back whenever you want."

"And we don't want. To send you back."

For the tiniest fraction of a second, Jaz looked like she straight-up hated me. "Oh, you fucking saints."

That felt like a good thing to tactically ignore. If nothing else, I honestly didn't think it was on Jaz to be grateful to me and Oliver for—to use the technically and legally correct term—*looking after* her.

But the unfortunate thing about not giving Jaz the reaction she was probably looking for was that we lapsed into another silence and, this time, it didn't break. We finished our meals without saying another word, and then we got back in the car, and I drove us home.

I stalled twice on the way.

Jaz didn't say anything about that either.

"I still feel I should say something," Oliver reiterated, once he'd got home that evening and I'd explained the situation.

"Say what?" I asked. "I don't want to be all don't-you-trust-me, but, like, do you think there's some magic thing that you'll say that I didn't?"

Oliver looked sheepish. He liked to think of himself, I knew, as the sort of person who had a high opinion of others. Which meant that being confronted with the fact that his high opinion of others sometimes, just *sometimes*, came with an implied *but not as good as me, obviously* was a bit of a headfuck for him. "Of course not," he half lied. "It's just—"

"She knows she did a bad thing. She knows we don't like that she did a bad thing. She's been sent home from school because of the bad thing she did. What else is there?"

I got a nasty feeling that Oliver was suppressing a scowl. "It was a *very* bad thing."

"She hit someone. And she was *extremely* provoked."

"From what you've said," Oliver reminded me, "she beat another girl's head on a table. That isn't teenage hijinks. That's a disturbing level of violence."

I propped my hips on the kitchen counter and leaned. "Okay, but what do you want to say about that? 'Hi, Jasmine, I just want to tell you that I'm concerned you might be a danger to yourself and others'?"

"Perhaps we could"—Oliver's mouth seemed to be getting dry—"invite her to see things from Trish's perspective?"

"Trish said it was Jaz's fault her mother tried to kill herself," I pointed out. "What *perspective* could she possibly have to make that okay?"

"The perspective where it led to her head being bounced off of a table?" suggested Oliver, mildly. "I'm not saying we make this about blame. I'm suggesting we take a restorative approach."

I felt my own lips tighten. "Will the restorative approach involve writing any kind of letter?"

"That's not funny."

"How about," I tried, "whatever we decide, we decide on it *later*. The school will want to be involved anyway, and it's probably best for"—I gritted my inner teeth and used the mature parenting name—"Jasmine if we work with them instead of…you know, like…not against them but not with them?"

"Orthogonally from them?" suggested Oliver.

"Yeah, that."

Oliver gave me a *You have made a sound argument and I acknowledge it* nod. "Very well, we'll revisit the matter once we've had a chance to confer with the school."

"We have a meeting on Monday," I told him. Jaz had warned me that there'd be a lot of meetings. I hadn't expected the next one quite this quickly.

"Good." Oliver nodded again. "Just as long as Jasmine understands that this is a punishment, not a holiday."

I gave him a helpless look. And not the sexy kind of helpless or even the romantic kind of helpless. "Oliver, I am absolutely certain that she doesn't think staying with us is a holiday."

"What does that mean?" he asked, a touch sharply.

"It means," I said, "that she just really misses her mum."

"Her mother was neglectful."

That was…strictly true. And considering the space Oliver was in right now, *strictly true* was all he'd listen to. But this wasn't a *strictly true* kind of situation. It was a messy, complex, stabs-you-in-the-heart-fucks-you-in-the-head, family-matters-but-also-hurts-you-but-also-still-matters situation. I could see that; I could see it *so clearly*. And Oliver couldn't. Or wouldn't let himself. Even though deep down, I knew he understood as well as I did.

Which meant I was going to have to remind him.

Which meant I was having to go there.

Not all the way there. But more of the way there than I really wanted.

I swallowed hard, took a deep breath, and said as calmly and not-trying-to-start something-ly as I could possibly manage, "I suppose you don't miss your dad then?"

Oliver stiffened. "That's a completely different situation. I know my parents weren't perfect, but things never got so bad that the state had to intervene."

"No," I admitted, partly out of fear of escalation and partly because he was *technically* correct on that one. "But they got so bad that when David died, you dropped a truth-nuke on his funeral, so… I mean. You *must* understand that it's possible to have complicated feelings about a parent."

I could see Oliver breathing. He wasn't like me when it came to emotions. They didn't scare him in the same way. But he did have very particular ideas about what you should feel and when and about who, and he didn't like deviating from them. "I suppose," he said, very carefully and very slowly, "that you raise a valid point."

"I do," I said, trying not to sound actively triumphant. "I raise as fuck a point that is valid as shit."

"You're also extremely mature."

"Mature *as shit*," I agreed.

Oliver arched an eyebrow.

"Okay, I'll stop it now."

"Please do." Oliver's face had softened, and I privately gave myself exactly one relationship point for us navigating a potentially tense conversation with something almost approaching grace.

"Are you going to be okay?" he continued. "We hadn't planned on Jasmine being home all day."

I nodded. "I'll be fine. Work's going pretty smoothly, so I'll just be at home sending emails and having meetings."

Oliver looked concerned. "You're sure? Because I can probably arrange to work from home as well if it's a problem."

"I'm sure. I've double- and triple-checked my calendar. Unless something goes incredibly wrong, it's plain sailing until the end of the week."

CHAPTER 30

SOMETHING WENT INCREDIBLY WRONG.

The morning was fine. I got up, saw Oliver off to work, and even managed to persuade Jaz that no, just because she was suspended didn't mean she could lie in, because her teachers would be sending her work to do remotely. On the laptop that she now had.

Then around noon I heard an engine.

It wasn't a familiar engine. I'd have recognised Saint's bike anywhere, and this wasn't Saint's bike. But it was definitely Saint's vehicle-of-some-sort. There was just something about the sound of a noisy penis extension of a car roaring to a stop outside a quiet private home on a residential street that had the *aura* of the new Earl of Spitalhamstead.

Since I hadn't been expecting him, I was in my study. Since I was in my study, Jaz was nearer the door than me. And ordinarily that would have been fine because most days getting Jaz to answer the door would have been a mission all of its own. But *today*, maybe because she was bored, maybe because some sixth sense had told her it would make things difficult for me, or maybe because the universe itself had decided it was a good day to piss on Luc O'Donnell, she jumped straight up and went to see who it was.

"Who the fuck are you?" she was asking as I came into the hall.

"Who the fuck are *you*?" Saint asked back.

"Rescue dog," Jaz told him, which led to a distant *Ruff* from Spud, who was still in the kitchen having lunch.

These two meeting was my worlds colliding in the worst possible way. Although right then I couldn't tell if I was worried my foster kid would make me look bad to my boss or my boss would make me look bad to my foster kid. Honestly, it would probably be both. "Saint," I said, "this is Jaz. She's my and Oliver's foster daughter. Jaz, this is Saint, he's—"

"A friend of Luc's," Saint interrupted with a presumption so typical I couldn't even be particularly bothered by it. And then, "Jazz. As in the music?"

"Saint," she said. "As in the people who hang out with God?"

Saint nodded. "Like it."

Okay, this had gone non-disastrously so far. And since I didn't trust either of them to quit while they were ahead, I quit for them. "Great. We've established that both your names also have secondary meanings. Now can we get past the who everybody is question and get to what everybody is doing here? I'll start. It's where I live. Same for her." I tried to make assertive eye contact with Saint, which was hampered by the fact he was wearing mirrored aviators. Because of course he was. "Your turn."

Saint pulled the glasses down and looked at me over the top of them. "We're getting the band back together."

Fuck. I'd left the problem of pitching an ecological fundraiser headlined by a band named Rancid Sputum for future Luc to deal with and, as I'd predicted, future Luc was now incredibly pissed off at past Luc for getting him into this mess. Which meant future Luc—or I suppose present Luc—very nearly just came straight out with *We're fucking not*.

But by some random blessing of the coleoptera gods, Jaz stopped me blowing up my job, my coworkers' jobs, and an environmentally vital beetle charity by asking, "What band?"

"Rancid Sputum," Saint replied at once, as if he expected Jaz to have heard of them despite the fact that they'd broken up before she was born and had never actually put out any albums, had any fans, or played any gig bigger than a pub toilet.

Jaz never looked impressed. And to be honest, nobody ever looked impressed with Saint; he just filled their impressed-ness in with the power of his own privilege. But something about Jaz's truly iconic inability to give anything even resembling a fuck seemed to get through to him. Just a little. "Rancid what?" she asked.

"Sputum." For the first time, I heard an edge in Saint's voice that suggested he might not be totally convinced it was a name destined for rock legendhood.

"Sputum?" Jaz repeated.

"The thing you've got to remember about Sputum..." began Saint. I suspected he'd started getting that thing where you said a word so much it either goes meaningless or becomes nothing but meaning, so he was essentially just saying the word *sputum* over and over again to a disinterested teenager. "What you've got to remember about Sputum," he repeated, "is that we were less about what we were called than what we were about?"

I didn't wish Saint harm, but I was beginning to be oddly curious about whether Jaz could actually make him die of cringe. "You were about what you were about?"

He nodded, confidence flowing back as the part of him that had been flirting with self-awareness remembered that he was, like, really stupendously fucking rich. "That's right. What're you about, kid?"

Jaz gave no visible reaction. "Fourteen."

I half expected him to ruffle her hair, but fortunately for his hand, he didn't. "Nice. C'mon, Luc, we're going."

"Um...so...I kind of have a job to do? And a teenager I'm responsible for?" I really wished I'd been able to sound surer about both of those things.

"Your job's working for me," Saint pointed out, temporarily forgetting he wasn't into hierarchies. "And the kid'll be fine. Leave her a pack of cigarettes and a credit card for emergencies."

Jaz nodded. "Yeah, leave me at home with a pack of cigarettes and a credit card. Esther will love it."

"You don't even smoke," I retorted.

"I'm going to start because you're a bad parent."

"Hey," I protested, stung. "I am a below-average parent at worst. And I'm sorry, Saint, but—"

"Got to be now, Luc," declared Saint.

"Does it, though? Does it really?"

"It's the moment," Saint was still declaring. "I can feel it in my balls."

The spirit of Oliver swept spontaneously over me. "Can you not talk about your balls in front of my foster daughter?"

Saint was visibly unmoved. "What can I say, the Gentlemen have strong opinions. Now, time's wasting. Get in the car. Kid can come if she wants—it'll be an education."

I was pretty sure it wouldn't, in fact, be an education. I was pretty sure that it *would*, in fact, be a complete disaster. But just like the last time Saint had decided to drag me off on one of his awful, selfish, posh-bastard whims, I really didn't think I had much choice. Or if I did, the choice was to go along with what he wanted or accept that he'd pull CRAPP's funding and get me and everybody I worked with fired.

Fuck.

I looked back at Jaz. She'd *probably* be okay on her own. But only probably. And maybe only *okay* in the sense that she, personally, would be perfectly happy. Not in the sense that she'd stay out of trouble. At the very least, I suspected that she'd be off down the park with Spud the moment my back was turned.

Fuck.

"Jaz," I said. "It's looking a whole lot like we're going to need to go and put a punk band back together. You all right with that?"

Jaz looked suspicious. "How long'll it take?"

I had no idea. "I have no idea."

Without further comment, Jaz vanished into the kitchen and returned with half a loaf of white bread and Spud. "Can't leave him if we don't know when we're coming back."

Fantastic. The teenager with trauma-related anger issues was a more responsible dog owner than me. Actually, I was kind of proud of her for it, which *maybe* was a positive parenting sign? "And the bread?"

Jaz looked at me like she couldn't possibly imagine how I could bear to be me. "Might get hungry."

Instead of the bike, Saint had rocked up in a jet-black Cadillac convertible like an edgelord Elvis. Jaz jumped in the back far more enthusiastically than she ever got into the car with me, and Spud jumped in after her. I hung back to lock the door and send Oliver a quick note saying Took jazz and spud to get band with saint will explain later. Which was all I could manage before Saint bullied me into the passenger seat. Which felt like a metaphor for my life right now.

We were halfway along the A13 before I thought to ask where we were actually going.

"Clapham," said Saint, as if it was an explanation.

"Okay." I attempted a conciliatory nod. "Why Clapham exactly?"

"Gary the Cosmic Fuckstone."

Ah. Right. Because we hadn't actually had this conversation yet. "Umm, I'm not sure that'll work."

"It's fine." Saint waved a hand that I was pretty sure he should have been keeping on the wheel. "Me and the Fuckstone, we go way back."

"It's not so much—"

"Like *that*," he added, crossing his fingers.

"It's just," I finished, "he's sort of dead."

The Cadillac screeched to a halt, very nearly getting us rear-ended by the much less obnoxious car behind. "Sorry, what?"

"He's dead. He died in 2019."

Saint didn't look remotely close to believing me. "Bullshit."

Sighing, I pulled out my phone and brought up *Gareth Bennet's Guide to Mindful Eating*. There were pictures that, despite the enormous beard and Alan Titchmarsh wellies, even Saint couldn't deny were definitely of the man he'd known as Gary the Cosmic Fuckstone. The final update was a tasteful memorial postdated, as I'd told him, from 2019. It read, "Gareth's family is sad to report that he passed away on Tuesday as a result of an improperly sorted mushroom foraging. Well-wishers are encouraged to donate to one of the following charities on Gareth's behalf."

"Fuck." Saint looked like he was processing an entirely new concept. I liked to think it was "his own mortality," but I suspected it was just "having to deal with inconvenience." After a moment, he looked at me solemnly and said, "No wonder he wasn't answering my texts."

He pulled out his phone, ignoring the angry honking from behind us, and started scrolling. "The others are fine, though."

"Fine in what way?" I asked, because from what I'd seen of Saint, his definition of *fine* was substantially different from most people's.

He turned the screen to face me. Sure enough, the two most recent replies said: Love to catch up but really busy this month and what part of "never call me again you narcissistic shitbag" did you not understand?

"If I'm honest," I began, "those don't look super *super* promising."

"I know the guys," he said. "They'll be solid."

I let that go. But I made myself a private bet that they would be deeply, deeply unsolid.

I understand this is your job, said the latest in Oliver's long line of texts, but I worry it's setting a bad example for Jasmine.

I looked at Jaz. She seemed, more than anything, bored out of her skull. Which, given that we'd just been on a two-hour drive in an open-topped car in the middle of winter, said something for her resilience. I was feeling like my sinuses had been flushed through with dry ice.

Still, from a certain point of view, I *had* taken Jaz to school. Okay, to a school. Okay, to a road opposite the primary school that Michael "MagiMix" Giffard now worked at.

I think were okay there, I sent back. If anything I think saints boring her straight.

"Are you sure this is the right thing to be doing?" I asked. Again.

"MagiMix'll be out soon," Saint insisted. "And once he sees me, he'll remember what it was like back in the day."

I nodded ambiguously. "I'm sure he will."

Parents began flooding through the school gates, and then children began flooding out. We got some funny looks, but to my relief nobody actually called the cops on us. And Spud handled the whole situation really well, sitting on Jaz's lap, wagging his tail, and only barking at passers-by in a friendly way.

Then nothing.

Fighting very hard to keep my expression non-told-you-soey, I said, "*How* soon exactly?"

Saint waved at the passing crowds. "The kids are all gone. How much can a teacher have to do in an empty school?"

Despite never having worked in education, I strongly suspected the answer to that question was "Quite a lot, actually."

"Spud needs a piss," Jaz remarked to me, Saint, and the world in general. And then, without waiting for permission—which was fair in a way because it wasn't like Spud was going to—she climbed out of Saint's open-topped car without bothering to open the door and lifted Spud after her.

Saint followed her with his eyes for a moment. "Come on. She's got the right idea."

"Taking a dog to piss on a wall?"

"If MagiMix won't come to us, we'll go to him."

Fuck. Fuck fuck fuck. Fuck fuck. We were definitely going to get arrested. For trespassing at a school for five-to-eleven-year-olds. Fuck.

Saint was already striding onto school property, with Jaz watching him over the wall. And from the look on her face, yeah, I definitely didn't have to worry about him being an undue influence on her.

Although I did have to worry about the fact that I was now effectively supervising two children, one of whom was in his sixties and both of whom I really needed to keep eyes on. "Jaz," I called out, "once Spud has finished, you're going to need to come with us."

Jaz dutifully sauntered in the vague direction of the school building, Spud skipping merrily behind her. She was giving *whatever* vibes, but I had a feeling she did in fact want to see how this would play out. Not in a good way, but I'd take what I could get.

By the time I caught up with Saint, he was standing at the reception desk. Behind the desk sat the receptionist: a youngish man wearing a grey jumper and an expression of mild panic.

"Sir," the receptionist was saying, "I don't know who that is, and I'm going to have to ask you not to swear."

"MagiMix," Saint repeated. "Fucking *MagiMix*. He works here." Then he turned to me. "Tell this dickless sellout to get MagiMix."

Desperately wishing Saint had kept me out of this, I tried to smooth things over with the dickless sellout. "We're looking for Michael Giffard."

With the kind of relief that comes from dealing with somebody slightly less awful than the person you've just been dealing with, the receptionist nodded. "He's the deputy head."

"Tell him Saint's here to see him," said Saint.

Deciding that just-going-along-with-it was the better part of valour, the receptionist picked up the phone, dialled an internal number, and waited. After long enough that Saint had begun to get visibly impatient, which, honestly, wasn't that long at all, we heard the click of someone picking up. And then, "Mr. Giffard? Sorry to bother you, there's a Mr. Saint here for you."

"Just Saint."

The receptionist listened to the other end of the phone for a couple of seconds, then put his hand over the receiver. "He says he can't see you today."

"Tell him that's bollocks."

The receptionist's eyes widened. "I will no—hang on, I think he heard you."

"Tell him to come out here." Having realised that the primary school deputy headteacher formerly known as MagiMix could hear him over the phone, Saint had raised his voice into a natural posh-person bellow. "And look me in the eye like a man."

"Girls've got eyes too," Jaz pointed out, but Saint either didn't hear or didn't care.

Setting the handset down, the receptionist looked up at Saint as pleasantly as he could manage. "I think he's on his way."

"See," Saint told me, or possibly the receptionist, or possibly fate itself. "That wasn't hard, was it?"

"Mruff," replied Spud.

Which meant the receptionist noticed him through the

Saint-field for the first time. "I'm afraid you'll need to take the dog outside."

"That's nice of you," Jaz replied at once. "But he's already had a piss, thanks."

Before that conversation could go anywhere worse than it had already gone, a man who I assumed must be MagiMix appeared. He did not, by any stretch of the imagination, look like a MagiMix. He looked like a Mr. Giffard, deputy headteacher of Celvestune Primary School. I mean, yes, he still had a pierced ear, just about visible after decades, but otherwise he was small, slim, balding, and wearing glasses chosen for practicality rather than fashion.

"Saint," he said in clipped, polite tones that implied a way posher background than you'd expect from somebody co-running a state primary. "What are you doing here?"

And yet again, Saint pulled down his shades. "We're getting the band back together."

MagiMix—who, thinking about it, I should probably have been calling Michael or perhaps Mr. Giffard—peered at me and Jaz in a very, very headteacherly way. "Is this *we*?"

"No," said Jaz emphatically.

"Not exactly," I half agreed.

"Ruff," explained Spud.

Saint put his hand between my shoulder blades in a way that felt way more invasive than it probably should have. "My friend Luc here—Luc *Fleming*—"

Mr. Giffard looked profoundly unimpressed. "Am I supposed to know who that is?"

"Odile O'Donnell's son," Saint told him. And the look that flowed, just briefly, over Mr. Giffard's face was equal parts affirming and uncomfortable. Because I hated trading on my mum's name but I always kind of liked it when people remembered her. "My friend here is putting together a music festival. Wants Sputum to headline."

The idea that the son of a rock legend wanted a completely unknown and defunct punk band to headline a new music festival was *already* so sus that I wouldn't have blamed Mr. Giffard for calling bullshit. Add to that the fact that he'd actually *met* Saint, and it seemed very likely that his crapometer would be pinging off the charts.

He gave me a but-most-of-all-you've-let-yourself-down look. "Is that true?"

"I mean," I hedged, "*want* is a strong word. I work for the Coleoptera Research and Protection Project and—"

For the second time in the short conversation, recognition gleamed in Mr. Giffard's eyes. A much more comfortable, much more natural kind of recognition. But also a much less expected one. "Oh, you're with C.R.A.P.P.?"

I consider it a massive tribute to how fucking great I am at my job *actually* that I took this completely in stride. "Yes. I don't recognise you from the donor list, but...have we done outreach work with you?"

"Year six did a project on you last term," he explained. "That Welsh guy who does your social media is amazing at getting kids excited about conservation."

Okay, so being fair, I suppose I had to take that as a massive tribute to how fucking great Rhys was at his job as well. It didn't mean I had to like it. "Yeah, I think it's because he's got the mind of a ten-year-old."

Mr. Giffard took that more seriously than I intended. "It's a good quality to have in some lines of work."

"The beetles," Saint explained with a level of contempt I could accept from Jaz but not from somebody nearly five times her age who owned half a county, "were the old man's thing."

"They were a good thing to have," said Mr. Giffard, not helpfully from the point of view of someone who didn't want Saint made incredibly angry. That someone being me. Then, even less helpfully by those standards, he went on, "At least he cared about something other than himself."

Saint took that about six different kinds of badly. The only question was which he'd act on first. "You never really *got* Sputum, did you, Mix?"

Beside me, Jaz laughed the laugh of someone who found the idea of "getting sputum" as absurd as I did and didn't have a job that relied on her hiding it.

I was beyond relieved that Saint ignored her. I was less relieved that Mr. Giffard didn't ignore him. "First," he said, "it's Michael. Mike to my friends, which you *aren't*." Saint looked like he was about to object to this, but Mr. Giffard didn't give him time. "I have a school to run. I have kids to look after. I'm sorry...Luc, is it?"—he turned briefly to me—"I actually think C.R.A.P.P. does good work, but *this* man f—messes up everything he touches."

At which point Saint shoved the deputy headteacher of Celvestune Primary School in Droitwich Spa full in the chest. "Fuck you, Mix."

"Oi," commentated Jaz from the sidelines, "manage your emotions, Granddad."

"Ruff," agreed Spud.

I tried to deescalate, but *deescalate* wasn't in Saint's vocabulary, so I got as far as "I don't think this is..." before Saint and Mr. Giffard had gone tumbling into a display of year three art and crashed to the ground amidst a cloud of brightly coloured cut-out hands.

"You *fucking* traitor."

"You arrogant manchild."

It was around the "arrogant manchild" stage of the encounter that Saint threw the first punch.

CHAPTER 31

TO MY *UNBELIEVABLE* RELIEF, ONLY Saint got arrested. Because Mr. Giffard explained very kindly that I'd had nothing to do with my patron's behaviour and had, in fact, been trying to smooth things over.

"Don't worry, Luc," Saint had told me as the police were telling him he had the right to remain silent and I was wishing to God he'd exercise it. "All part of the rock 'n' roll lifestyle. Now go get Rik Jism, and we can still make this happen."

I gave a can-do nod. "Sure. But just to be clear, if by some strange million-to-one chance, the guy who called you a 'narcissistic shitbag' *doesn't* want to be part of the big Rancid Sputum reunion?"

"Then"—Saint was giving me it's-not-you-it's-me vibes, which were not vibes you wanted to be getting from the guy in charge of whether you and your entire office would have jobs at the end of the year—"honestly, I might not be feeling the whole festival thing. Like, if you can't make Sputum happen, how're you going to pull together the rest of it?"

I had a number of answers to that, but most of them involved pointing out to Saint that the other acts, caterers, and the like didn't have specific reasons to hate him personally. But I didn't think that would go down well. So I mustered a weary "You can count on me" instead.

As Saint vanished into the distance with his police escort, I realised that I wasn't strictly—and by *strictly*, I mean in any way at all—insured to drive his car.

His car that Jaz was now fiddling with in ways I should probably have been worried about. "What are you—"

"Putting the top up. Not taking another two hours in *that*"—she indicated the very open-topped vehicle—"in *this.*" She indicated the wind, weather, and general miserable vibe of the day.

"And you know how?"

Apparently, that didn't deserve an answer. She just wrangled the roof of Saint's impractical, probably deadly, sixties convertible neatly into place, then jumped in the front with Spud on her lap.

Not sure what else to do, I got in beside her. After all, it wasn't like we could walk home.

Jaz was watching me with even more suspicion than usual. "Is this," she said, "like, your actual job?"

I nodded only a bit sheepishly. "Kind of? It's usually a lot less weird." I thought about it. "Slightly less weird."

"How did you...just how?"

"Honestly," I told her, "I ask myself that question most days."

Most of the time, Jaz had absolutely zero engagement with me, my life, or my work. But most of the time, being engaged didn't make me so obviously uncomfortable.

"And is that guy really going to fire you if you don't get a bunch of old men who hate him to be in his shitty band?"

I nodded. "Pretty much."

"Does he want you to bring the dead one back and all?"

"I think even Saint isn't quite that unreasonable."

Jaz looked out over the pleasant views of Droitwich Spa, Spud snuggling down beside her. "He's a prick, isn't he?"

"Yup."

There was a fatal silence. "He's going to fire you anyway, isn't he?"

"Probably."

There was an even more fatal silence. "And you're still going to do everything he says?"

When you put it like that, it did sound like a pretty rubbish deal. "Looks like. But I spent most of my twenties giving up on everything. So I'm trying something different."

"What? Failure?"

I thought about that. "Yes. Because… Oh, look, you've had all the 'It's better to fail than never try' lectures. Don't make me go there."

She scowled. "You just did."

"That wasn't a lecture; it was a sentence. Now let's go get Rik Jism."

As I grappled with the reality of starting a car that was built in the 1950s, Jaz turned to me with a look of malicious innocence. "What's Jism mean, anyway?"

I scowled. "You know, and I know you know. Otherwise you wouldn't be asking me."

Jaz ruffled Spud's ears. "We don't know what he's talking about, do we?"

Figuring I'd dodged the jism as effectively as I was going to manage, I got us back on the road to London, trying not to think too hard about the fact that I was driving a car that predated the Big Mac, the moon landing, and airbags.

Substantially longer than I would have liked later, I parked us opposite the overpriced London flat Richard Smoddle had presumably not bought with Rancid Sputum money. In terms of "things to get arrested for loitering outside," it was, I suppose, a slight upgrade from Celvestune Primary School and definitely a better bet than Deloitte, which would have put us on the wrong side of some very serious security types.

It took a while for Richard Smoddle to show up, and when he did I wasn't really sure how to approach him. Which was probably why his first reaction to me was "Sorry, not interested" and his second was "Look, there's laws against aggressive begging."

Like Mr. Giffard, the artist previously known as Rik Jism was a skinny white guy in his sixties wearing a suit and tie. Unlike Mr. Giffard, the suit was Savile Row and the tie was—okay, honestly, I don't know much about ties. It looked expensive and probably not made of polyester. When he spoke, though, he had the traces of an Estuary accent, which I hadn't expected after the wall of posh that was Saint and MagiMix, and his eyes were a cold grey that said I was wasting his time. And his oxygen.

"Okay," I tried again, "but the thing is I'm looking for Richard Smoddle."

"I'll let him know if I see him," Richard Smoddle replied, pushing past me.

And so, swallowing the smooshed, stained, slightly smelly remains of my pride, I fell back on, "I'm looking for Rik Jism."

Richard "Rik Jism" Smoddle turned slowly to face me. "How the fuck did you hear that name?"

"Some old bastard," said Jaz.

"I work with Saint," I clarified.

"Fuck me." Richard Smoddle looked like I'd just told him I'd run over his cat and also that I'd sliced it into thin strips, laid it over ciabatta, and served it to him at lunchtime as a prosciutto sandwich. "I thought I told him I never wanted to see him again."

"You probably did," I admitted. "But ask yourself this: Would he have remotely listened?"

Richard Smoddle glowered at me. "You'd better come up."

He let us upstairs into his tiny but eye-wateringly swanky apartment. Then we sat on an uncomfortable sofa in an open-plan kitchen-dining-sitting-living area that seemed as though nobody ever lived, sat, dined, or kitched in it while I explained to Richard Smoddle the farcical sequence of events that meant I now really badly needed him to rejoin Rancid Sputum for one last vomit-stained hoorah.

"So if I can't get you and Magi—and Michael to reform Sputum, just for one day, it's looking like Saint will pull my funding, and not only will I lose my job but so will a bunch of other mostly nice people. Plus, it'll do some very bad things to the UK's soil aeration."

Richard Smoddle stared at me silently. Then he carried on staring at me silently.

Eventually, the silent staring got so intense that I found myself saying, "Um. Well?"

"Just waiting," Richard Smoddle not-really-explained.

He really wanted me to say, *For what?* and this was definitely a give-the-client-what-they're-after situation. "For what?"

"For you to get to the part where this is my problem."

Meeting Mr. Giffard, who for all his half-buried toffery had actually heard of CRAPP, actually cared about what we did, and actually seemed not to be an absolute piece of shit, had lulled me into a false sense of security. "I thought you might, y'know, want to help?"

"He's always like this," Jaz added. "It's not just you."

"Why would I want to help that arrogant fuck Hilary de Lancy?" asked Richard Smoddle.

"Old times' sake?"

It was a long shot. I'd been gambling on all old men on some level wanting to recapture their youths, no matter how shitty. As someone whose old-manhood was less comfortably distant than it once was, and whose youth had been deeply shitty, I should have known better.

"Let me tell you about old times." Richard Smoddle leaned forward, suddenly sounding a whole lot more Rik Jism-y. "Old times was me, MagiMix, and Gary the Cosmic Fuckstone following Saint around like a sack of pricks with us doing whatever the fuck he said and him doing whatever the fuck he wanted. And you know what I learned from that?"

"That it's a bad idea to form major life philosophies based on your interaction with one unpleasant person in the eighties and nineties?" I suggested hopefully.

Jaz hadn't seemed to be paying attention. Mostly she'd been looking around Richard Smoddle's apartment like it was a spaceship. But now, with Spud nestled on her lap, she said, "That if you were going to be a lonely miserable bastard anyway, you'd rather be a rich lonely miserable bastard."

Richard Smoddle did a got-it-in-one finger-snap-point-thing. At Jaz, not at me. "For years, all Saint talked about was fighting the power and fucking the system and how we didn't need anything except the music. Well, guess what?"

I nodded. "It's a lot easier to not need anything except the music when your dad's an earl?"

"Yup. Saint taught me that I needed to look out for myself because no other fucker would. So I'm going to ask you again. Why is *your* job at *your* charity *my* problem?"

I had no good answers. Or rather I had answers that might have been good in other contexts like *The ecosystem is all interconnected and our work really does make a material impact* or my old standby of *Donating to obscure charities will impress your hipster friends*, but there was no way I could pretend that helping me and CRAPP out of a bind was in Richard Smoddle's direct self-interest.

So I opened my mouth, hoping something brilliant would come out. "We can probably swing you free food?"

Back at home, I sat on the sofa with my head in my hands, Oliver concernedly beside me and Jaz in the armchair with Spud, not exactly revelling in my misery because she didn't really *do* revelling, but certainly not in any way brought down by it.

"We're fucked," I was saying, and it was testimony to how seriously Oliver was taking my fuckedness that he didn't bother to call me out for saying *fuck* in front of Jaz. "I had one job and I fucking fucked it."

"Your job," Oliver told me in his most everything-is-all-right-and-you-are-wonderful voice, "was to rebuild, with no notice, bridges that another man had burned a decade ago. You did as well as anybody could have."

"Ruff," agreed Spud, which I double-appreciated on account of Jaz being his favourite human now.

Jaz had no words of consolation for me herself, but I took the fact that she wasn't telling me that *actually no, I was a shit person who had done shit* as her own brand of sympathy.

"Well." I tried to remain stoic and philosophical, which were two things I was, of course, extremely good at remaining. "We planned around this, right?"

Oliver nodded. "We did. We don't need two incomes."

"Three incomes," Jaz reminded us, and I genuinely couldn't tell if she was being bitter or consoling. "You get cash for me, too, remember."

"You see," continued Oliver, still soothing. "It's not even really a financial hit."

Sniffling slightly, I looked over at Spud. "I'm going to make you *so many* tiny outfits. With, like, hats. Adorable hats."

"You're fucking not," Jaz told me on Spud's behalf, and Spud backed her up with a low growl.

"Hey," I protested, "I'm having a bad day. You don't get to be snarky at me when I'm having a bad day."

"You don't really get to be snarky with *anybody*," Oliver added. "Kindness costs nothing."

Jaz considered this. "Yeah, but rudeness don't cost nothing neither and it's more fun."

"Jasmine..." Oliver was just beginning to shift to stern mode when my phone went off.

And, of course, it was Saint.

"Sorry." I sighed. "I'm not unemployed yet, so I should probably take this."

I went into the hall and then through to the study so that Jaz and Oliver wouldn't have to listen to whatever my half of the conversation with Saint was going to sound like. Though probably what it would sound like was me saying *Yes, yes, whatever you want* like a spineless prick.

"Need a ride," Saint said, with no other greeting.

And, while that was annoying, I *did* still have his car. "Where are you?"

"Nick."

"Nick who?"

For a moment the line was quiet. Then, "Was that a joke?"

It had been a long evening. "No?"

"I'm in nick. The nick. The slammer. Chokey. The clink. The big house. The naughty box. Peel's penthouse. Room One No Fun."

I was about to ask him if there was anybody else he could possibly call, but I stopped myself. Because the answer was almost certainly "no." I would've felt sorry for him if not for the tiny, tiny detail that he was ruining my life.

Then a further detail occurred to me. "Hang on, are you still in Droitwich?"

"Course."

That was two hours away. That was a four hour round trip. That was a completely unreasonable thing for anyone to ask anyone. Especially if the first anyone had made the second anyone do that trip once already.

"Okay," I said, too tired to argue. "Text me an address. I'll be there."

In some ways, it almost felt fitting that this sputum glob of a day should have such a rancid fucking ending.

I'd hoped that seeing Saint walking out of a police station would feel a tiny bit satisfying. It would mean that at least his actions had mildly inconvenienced him.

Temporarily.

Though probably not as much as they'd inconvenienced Celvestune Primary School, the arresting officers, the staff at the police station, anybody who'd been unfortunate enough to be put in an adjoining cell, or, for that matter, me.

"Hey." With an infuriatingly matey smile, Saint jumped into the passenger side. I'd sort of assumed he'd be the kind of guy who insisted on driving, but thinking about it, he *was* from a background where chauffeurs were normal. "Thanks for the pickup."

"No problem."

"Fucking pigs," he said to nobody in particular.

I gave a kind of "Yeah" out of principle, but Saint didn't seem to give a shit one way or the other.

"So," he asked, "we on?"

"On?"

"For the reunion." He threw actual horns. "Rancid Sputum together again."

Keeping my eyes firmly on the road, I tried to give a measured response. "Saint"—I kept my voice as calm and level as I could manage—"of the four original members of Rancid Sputum, one is you."

"Right." He nodded as if that was good enough to end the conversation.

"One is dead."

"Drawback," Saint admitted.

"One quit music to become a primary school teacher, and when you went to see him, you punched him in the face and got arrested."

"Part of the life. You get drunk, you get loud, somebody gets his face broken, you play the gig anyway."

"When you're twenty-five and in the Sex Pistols," I agreed. "Not when you're sixty-eight and, I'm going to keep saying this because I really think you need to adjust your expectations around it, the deputy headteacher of a primary school in Droitwich Spa."

"You can take the man out of the metal, Luc," Saint declared, on the basis of no evidence. "You can't take the metal out of the man."

Eyes on the road. Eyes on the road. We were on the M40 now, and if I played it smart, I'd make it home without either one of us strangling the other.

I didn't play it smart. "One," I said, "I'm pretty sure that's meaningless. Two, he didn't agree to do the gig. And neither did Richard."

In my peripheral vision, I caught the look of shock on Saint's face. "Not Jism too. There's no way."

"Please at least call him Rik."

Saint, as ever, wasn't listening. "I'm telling you, Luc, if you knew Jism like I know Jism, you wouldn't swallow it."

I gritted my teeth. "For the last time, Richard Smoddle—much like Michael Giffard—doesn't want to be in Rancid Sputum anymore. He doesn't think there's anything in it for him."

"But what about the music?"

This was beyond exasperating. I'd failed to save my job, and now I was having to save the ego of the man I'd failed to save my job from. "He doesn't *care* about the music, Saint. Also—and there really isn't a nice way to put this, so I'm going to have to stop trying—he fucking hates you."

"Jism?" said Saint, unbelieving.

"Yes. Rik Jism hates you. Properly, actually, seriously thinks-you're-a-terrible-person-style hates you."

"Jism?" said Saint again, as if he was a stuck and mildly pornographic record.

"Yes." My jaw creaked beneath the sheer sustained pressure of my teeth gritting. "Jism."

"That *bastard*."

I made a noncommittally affirming sound. And for a little while we drove on in silence.

"That fucking *sellout*."

I made an even more noncommittally affirming sound, and we drove on in silence just a little more.

"You know his real name's Smoddle?"

I'd used it to his face. Within the last half hour. It was pretty likely that I knew more about Richard Smoddle than Saint ever had. "I do, in fact, know that."

"Jism was my idea," Saint told me. I coloured myself completely unsurprised. "I said to him, 'Rick, people hear *Jism*, they know you're coming for them.'"

I made a sound so noncommittal it wasn't even especially affirming. I just carried on driving. We'd made it through Warwick and were coming up to Northend.

"Well, *fuck him*."

I nodded.

"Fuck them *both*."

I nodded again.

"And fuck this whole reunion festival."

I nodded one last time and then realised this was probably my last chance to save my job. And by chance, I meant a thing's chance in a place where that kind of thing would have a notable lack of chances. "Look, wait a min—"

"Shut it down, Luc. It was a noble effort, but some dreams were never meant to be."

And that was it. Up until right then, I don't think I'd really been letting myself believe that this might not work. Because as I'd painstakingly taught myself over the past five years, I was really good at this kind of thing. The plan had always been to pitch the idea as an ego project, then bring it home on the strength of actually organising a good concert. But I had fatally underestimated the size of Saint's ego. Most people were okay if you just named a library after them—they didn't also expect you to let them write all the books. In hindsight, it had been over the moment Saint had shown up on my doorstep in his fucking terrible mirror shades and demanded we get the band back together.

Although admittedly, maybe telling him directly to his face that his former bandmates hated him might not have been the best call either.

Northend was behind us now, and I tried my best to pull it together because I had the other half of this miserable fucking drive to turn this around..

"What if," I tried, "what if you could, like, show them you could do it alone?"

"I'm not a solo act, Luc. I need..." He groped for the right phrase and, because the actual right phrase was *people who'll do everything I tell them to*, steadfastly refused to find it.

"But think of the platform you could give to young, up-and-coming bands who want to be just like you." Given the circumstances, I was pretty proud of myself for that one. That was some medical-grade bullshit right there.

"Kids today don't have the ambition," Saint said, with the self-assurance of a man who had gone through life assuming that what was true and what was convenient for him were the same thing.

"Right, but—"

"My mind's made up. If they're out, I'm out, and if I'm out, you're out."

It was tempting, so tempting, to just pull the car to the side of the road and ditch him there and then. But that wouldn't have been professional.

Then again, professional had got me precisely fuck all so far.

I slammed on the brakes, letting the car come screeching to a halt in the middle of the road in the middle of the night in the middle of a motorway in the middle of, of—fuck, where even was I? "You know what. That's the way you want it? Fine."

It had sounded less childish in my head.

Saint gaped at me, too surprised to be betrayed and too betrayed to be surprised. "The fuck, Luc?"

I didn't bother answering. I just got out the car and walked away. And Saint, being Saint, came straight after me, leaving the Cadillac right where I'd left it, door hanging open, a traffic jam already building up behind it.

"The fuck, Luc?" he repeated as he trailed after me.

Not wanting an irate peer following me all the way to—to wherever I was going, into a service station it looked like—shouting *The fuck, Luc* every twenty paces, I stopped, turned, and with great dignity and self-possession, replied, "The fuck."

"The *fuck*?"

I almost wanted to see how much of a conversation we could have using only the words *fuck* and *the*, especially because in a weird way this was probably the closest Saint and I had got to understanding each other. But it did eventually reach the point where you needed verbs. "You're firing me, Saint. I don't have to pretend to like you anymore."

He put his hands up in a gesture of ironic disbelief. "Oh right, because *everybody hates Saint*. Because Saint is such a prick, yah?"

I was beginning to suspect that if I got out of this with my career intact, it would only be because Saint's mind couldn't actually encompass the idea of people having an issue with him. "Grow the fuck up, you selfish, self-absorbed, self-deluding, overgrown teenager. You know you're old enough to be my dad, right?"

"Yeah, and you're acting like mine."

I was sure he'd meant that as a burn. "What, trying to run a beetle charity? Yes, it's my *job*. Have you not been paying attention?"

"Man." Saint sounded a level of disappointed he had no right to sound. "I thought you were *cool*."

I actually laughed in his face. "Oh. My. God. Are you trying to peer-pressure me? We aren't peers. You're *a* peer, but that's not the same thing."

"You know I don't believe in hereditary privilege," replied Saint.

It was predictable. So predictable that I could probably have had the whole pointless argument in my head without him even being there. I opened my mouth to reply and then stopped because what was the point? I didn't know much about the music of Rancid Sputum, but I sure as hell knew this song. There were some people—like Saint, like good old Jon Fleming—who were so wrapped up in themselves that even calling them out on it was just feeding their egos. It felt weirdly freeing to finally put that lesson into practice. To tell myself someone wasn't worth the effort and actually believe it.

"Fuck off, Saint." I turned my back on him. "You're boring."

Probably I shouldn't have expected Saint to have more self-respect than to unironically yell "Don't walk away from me" as I walked away from him. But he kept shouting, and I kept walking, my heart beating faster and my feet keeping pace.

Fuck.

The reality was, I'd had nothing to lose. Saint was going to keep throwing his toys out of the pram, and if I kept giving them back to him, all I was going to get for my trouble was a teddy bear in the face.

But also fuck.

This was it.

Even if CRAPPstonbury went ahead, CRAPP wouldn't last past the end of the year. And then what would happen to Alex and Barbara and Rhys and Dr. Fairclough? What would happen to the UK's population of *Trypocopris vernalis* and the soon-to-be unaerated soils of its moorland habitats?

What would happen to *me*?

CHAPTER 32

BANBURY, BY THE WAY. I'D been in Banbury. From a certain perspective, that had been pretty lucky because it meant there was actually a train station and so I could, eventually, at far too much expense and with far too many changes, get back to London, and from there onto a night bus, and from there home.

On the whole, though, I was pretty proud of myself for not going completely to pieces. Not on the way back, and not the day after. The day after I told Saint to fuck off and also that nobody liked him and also that he was boring. I had a little cry on the train, but other than that I was extremely mature and sensible and goal-oriented.

The goals I was orienting in the immediate aftermath of the great Enbanburying were finding a new headliner for my hopeless rock festival, making sure I was home to pick up our Ocado delivery for dinner party supplies, taking Jaz to a meeting about the whole her-being-suspended thing, and then, straight afterwards, taking her to a guitar lesson in Surrey.

Finding a headliner for a music festival with no budget and no audience went about as well as could be expected. The Ocado order went somewhat *better* than expected, which is to say they actually delivered what we ordered instead of random crap we couldn't use which they would persist in calling "necessary substitutions."

In the end, the school meeting wound up being the lowest-stress part of the day. Jaz said all the things that she was supposed to say, and I felt I'd walked a better line between "advocating for her" and "undermining the process." We'd still had to make some adjustments to her Personal Education Plan, and there was talk of the school counsellor getting involved so Jaz and Trish could take part in some nonjudgemental restorative discipline, but, at the end of the day, I thought we got off pretty lightly.

Although she *did* insist we stop at the supermarket on the way to Mum's.

"Not having that fucking curry again," she explained as she swiped a bottle of Thai fish sauce and a packet of chicken breasts through the self-checkout.

"The special curry," I told her, "is a time-honoured tradition of the O'Donnell household."

"It's shit."

"It's a shit *tradition*."

Jaz started bagging. "Starting a new tradition."

The little piece of me that really wanted Jaz to accept she was part of the family melted slightly. Because this was good, right? If she felt she was able to start traditions? O'Donnell-Blackwood-Johnson traditions.

I pulled out my card to pay, and she looked at me with deep suspicion.

"I can get this," she told me. "I've got money."

"You've got pocket money," I replied. "That I give you. To spend on, I don't know"—I tried to think of things teenagers would buy that didn't sound condescending—"stuff for yourself."

"This *is* for myself. I don't want to eat the curry."

"I'm not letting you spend your own money on chicken breasts. Especially not when we're both going to eat them. That's like…that's just fundamentally wrong parenting."

Jaz looked at me like I'd spat in her face. Or—and I didn't *know* but I was beginning to think this closer to the mark—like I'd insulted her mum.

"I just mean," I said very quickly and very carefully, "that I'm here and I've already got my wallet out. It's kind of you to offer, but—and it took me a long time to realise this myself, so I don't blame you for not believing me—it's okay to let other people do stuff for you."

Jaz didn't reply, but she did let me pay. Still, she was silent all the rest of the way to Pucklethroop-on-the-Wold.

When we arrived, Mum opened the door and two of Judy's dogs bounced out to greet us—okay, to greet Jaz—but Mum was pleased to see me.

"Mon caneton." She hugged me. "Chérie." She hugged Jaz. "Why are you holding a packet of chicken?"

"Making dinner," Jaz replied.

Mum looked crestfallen. Crucially, though, and credit to Jaz for playing this one right, the kind of performative crestfallen that didn't actually mean she was in any way hurt or upset. "Oh, but the special curry!"

"It's shit," Jaz told her. "I'm making soup."

"Might be nice for a change," said Judy, who'd crept into the doorway to greet us. "Actually very partial to soup. Reminds me of my old grandfather."

"Fond of it, was he?" I asked warily.

Judy shook her head. "No, but he once threw a tureen full of minestrone at the vicar. Can't remember why now, but still every time I look at a pot of broth, I think of him."

With a look of feigned betrayal, Mum threw her hands in the air. "Fine, fine, reject the special curry, see if I care. Then one day when I am dead you will say to yourself, Luc, you will say to yourself, 'Do you remember the days when Maman used to make for us the special curry?' And you will reply, 'I do, Luc, but now she is dead, and we will never have the special curry again.'"

I was rolling my eyes at this, but Jaz, who was basically an eye roll in jeans and an ill-fitting jumper, seemed to take it incredibly seriously. "I don't have to." Her voice wobbled slightly. "You can make the curry if you want."

"Let." This was Judy. "The girl. Cook."

"I *am* letting the girl cook." Gently shooing us aside, Mum sailed serenely into the house. "I am just also reminding her and my horrible son that one day I will be dead and then they will appreciate me and I will look up at them from the afterlife and I will say, 'Serves you both right.'"

"Down," I corrected her. "Look down at us."

Mum gave a little laugh. "That is sweet of you, mon caneton, but there is a reason they say the devil has the best songs. Now"—she clapped her hands—"while I am still alive, you should both come in."

I sighed. "Leave it out. You'll outlive all of us."

Jaz murmured something under her breath which I could have sworn was *No, she won't*, but I let it go. With two of the dogs—Eugenie and Camilla, now I had a better look—trailing after her, Jaz went into the kitchen, where I was ninety percent certain she couldn't do any more harm than Mum or I would, and I went to settle down in the front room with the rest of the nominal adults.

"Sorry about the curry," I told Mum, even though we both knew I wasn't really. "But Jaz knows what she's doing. She cooks for herself all the time at home."

"Oh really?" Mum seemed at least mildly curious. "What sorts of things?"

"Soups? Stuff with rice, I think. It's mostly while Oliver and I are asleep."

Judy made a sound of nostalgic reverie. "Takes me back. I had a husband once, liked to cook while I was asleep."

"That's nice," I said. "What did he cook?"

"Meth."

I should have seen that one coming. "So"—I steered the conversation firmly away from hard drugs—"how is everybody?"

"Extremely upset about the murders." Mum looked suddenly grave.

Okay. They weren't doing this to me again. Despite the alarming death rate amongst Judy's husbands, this was not going to be a real thing. I kept my tone very normal. "Murders?"

"Oh yes." Mum sounded genuinely upset. "First there was that nice Aisha girl. Then the police lady. Then John, then Matt. We're terrified about who will be next."

"If anything happens to Andrea," Judy confided, "frankly, I don't know what we'll do."

I searched my mental list of shit my mum could be talking about. Fortunately, it was a fairly short list. "*UK Traitors*, season one?"

"I will tell you what." Mum grew conspiratorial. "They are playing, as they say, a blinder. The Faithfuls do not seem to have a clue what is happening."

Judy leaned back in her chair. "Next season," she declared, "you and me, old girl. We'll take 'em all out."

"Please don't," I said. "One parent on reality TV is bad enough."

"Did you see your father on the last *Celebrity Bake Off*?" asked Mum. "His savoury quiche was a disgrace."

It was probably a measure of how far Mum and I had both come that Jon Fleming making a tit of himself on national television felt neither good nor bad. It was just a slightly annoying fact of life, like the weather or Ed Sheeran. "Between *Strictly* and the *Celebrity Big Brother* announcement, I must have missed that one."

"You know, back in the day, your father used to have much

more dignity than this. If he wanted to be on television, he'd just whip his dick out at the Grammys."

I put my head in my hands. "Can we not? I don't think I'm strong enough to talk about my dad's dick right now."

Always sensitive to my moods—even if I did have to express them through the language of dicks—Mum came and sat on the sofa with me. "Is something wrong, mon caneton?"

Being asked was like being pricked with a pin, if instead of a person I was a balloon full of jelly. I flobbered down into a pile of fuck. "Honestly," I told her, "I'm not doing great."

"Non?"

"I always knew CRAPPstonbury was going to be a reach. But the one thing it had going for it was that even if the event sucked goat arse, as long as Saint's band was playing, it would probably be enough that he'd keep funding us."

Mum gave me supportive mum face. "It was a good plan."

"It was an okay plan," I conceded. "But it had a tiny, tiny flaw."

"Which was?" asked Judy, blunt as ever.

"That Saint's a piece of shit who has systematically alienated everybody in his life."

"I know a lot of men like that," said Mum, with a shrug. "People still work with them."

"I'm betting that's because either the music was good or the money was good." I sighed. "Here, the pitch I was making to two old men with quite busy, quite sorted lives was, 'Do you want to play mediocre punk rock with someone you hate for free?'"

Judy nodded. "That does sound like a bit of a tough sell."

"Right?" I nodded with her. "So now all I've got is a festival I've thrown together with a limited plan, hardly any acts, no marketing, and, if I'm lucky, adequate toilet facilities. The whole thing is going to be a colossal waste of everybody's time and energy unless it's either so cool that Saint comes crawling back anyway or so successful we can tell him to shove his money up his arse. Neither of which is going to happen."

"You don't think you can make something that is cool and successful?" asked Mum, her natural sympathy on the brink of war with her natural overconfidence in my abilities.

"I've got a wedding band, a male voice choir with complicated internal politics, and, now I think about it, inappropriately high-end catering."

Judy grinned. "Sounds like a recipe for a hell of an evening, if you ask me."

"Does it sound like a recipe for giving lots and lots of money to an insect-themed charity?" I asked. "Because that's what it really *needs* to be a recipe for."

It took more consideration than I thought should have been necessary before Judy conceded, "No, more a recipe for waking up next morning in a haystack wearing someone else's underthings."

"Well then." Mum had shifted into full *here for you* mode. Which I felt ambivalent about because I was past thirty now, and it seemed wrong to still need my mum to be there for me. Except I really needed my mum to be there for me. "What do you think you will need to make this festival work?"

My whole body made a gesture of surrender, because I had no idea and no idea where an idea would come from. "I don't know? A miracle? Actual rock stars? Something like that episode of *The Vicar of Dibley* where Kylie Minogue shows up and opens their village fête for them?"

"I'm sorry, Luc," said Mum, giving way more time to the suggestion than I'd expected or it had deserved. "Kylie has not liked me since I called her a 'soap opera reject with no staying power' in 1988. Retrospectively, that has not aged well. But in my defence, I was very high."

Much as I loved Kylie, I hadn't actually been banking on

the *Vicar of Dibley* gambit. "Okay. We'll put Kylie on the back burner."

Mum, however, was still not ready to give up, either on me or my objectively doomed rock festival. "Is there really nothing I can do?"

I gave her a smile that aimed for wry and landed on pathetic. "Not unless you want to stage a surprise comeback tour using CRAPPstonbury as your first UK date and debuting a bunch of never-before-heard songs or something."

Mum gave me that Gallic shrug I knew so well. "Okay."

It took a while for my brain to catch up with my ears. "What do you mean *okay*?"

"I mean *okay*. I'll stage a surprise comeback tour using CRAPPstonbury as my first UK date and debuting a bunch of never-before-heard songs or something."

I wasn't, at this stage, at all sure what my face was doing. It didn't really know what expression was appropriate, so it was just kind of trying them on at random to see what fit. "Do you *have* a bunch of never-before-heard songs or something?"

"I suppose it depends," Mum mused, "how many you think is a bunch."

I hesitated. This was feeling simultaneously too much like a dream and way too real. "Um, more than three?"

"Oh." Mum looked entirely chill. As if this wasn't slowly inverting several distinct chunks of my world. "Then yes, I probably do have a bunch."

"But...you gave up music?"

There was that shrug again. I was beginning to feel, Oliver aside, that I lived in a world of shruggers. "I gave up the life. Because I had a bad breakup and a baby and I'd said everything I wanted to say at the time. I never gave up *music*. You can't give up music, not really."

"So, what?" My voice had gone slightly hoarse. "You've been wanting to make a comeback all these years, but you haven't because...because..." I hated having to think this, much less say it. "Because of me?"

Her expression shifted from *whatever you need* to *get over yourself*. "Luc, you're my son. It embarrasses me when you're an idiot."

"I'm sorry. I just—"

"Stop it. I've been happy this whole time. I have a son I love and a friend I love who has dogs I put up with—"

"Steady on, old girl," Judy protested. "Friendship only goes so far, you know. Love me, love my menagerie."

"Shut up, Judy. I'm trying to have an emotional moment here." Mum turned back to me. "When you have lived the way I have lived," she went on, "it stops being about wanting and not wanting. I had a career, and that was good. I had a family, and that was good as well. And for a time my family needed me not to be doing the tours, and so I was happy to not, and now my family may need me to do the tours again, and so I am happy to."

I was having a lot of trouble following this. But maybe that was the problem. Maybe I'd been trying too hard and hanging on too tight just kind of in general. Kind of forever.

"Life is very nice," Mum said, "when you let it be."

"But, but—" I wasn't really sure what I was protesting anymore. It may well have just been the principle of the thing. "What about—what if—"

"Did you just break your *entire* brain?" asked Jaz, coming back through from the kitchen with bowls of soup that smelled and tasted far better than anything any of the rest of us, with the possible exception of Judy, could have made.

"Luc is confused," Mum explained, "because I have offered to kick off my new tour at his festival, and he thinks I am old and have gone past it."

"I don't think you've gone past it," I said at once. "I just thought...I don't know, that you'd put it behind you."

"Well, I have. But lots of things are behind me. I still sometimes turn around and look at them."

Jaz sat down on the arm of the sofa next to Mum, with a familiarity that felt strange to me. At once right and the tiniest bit jealous-making. "So where you going?"

"Going?" asked Mum, now at least joining me in Confusedville.

"On tour."

"I hadn't really thought about it." Mum looked momentarily contemplative. "The usual places, I expect. Unless they also think I am old and have gone past it."

"Mum." I was sounding the teeniest bit exasperated now. "Nobody thinks you've gone past it."

"Bon." Mum clapped her hands. "Then it is decided. I will launch a comeback tour, and it will begin at Luc's festival and it will be called"—she glanced at Judy for inspiration—"what do you think, something that says, 'Here I am, I am now in a different stage of my life to the one I was in before, but that stage is still important and so I have come to share it with you.'"

"Eras?" suggested Judy.

Mum nodded. "Parfait. It will be called the Eras tour."

"I *think* that one's taken," I told her.

Mum's face screwed up in older French lady displeasure. "Surely not."

"Taylor Swift did it."

"Oh well, that is very unfair of her. How many Eras can she have? She's only twenty-two."

"I think she's substantially older than twenty-two," I pointed out.

"No, she's not. She has a song about it."

"That song came out more than a decade ago."

"Nooo," declared Mum, looking suddenly distressed. "That is impossible."

Before Mum could vanish down the where-has-the-time-gone rabbit hole I'd been trying very hard to stay away from since my thirtieth birthday, Jaz brought us back to practicalities. "Are you seriously going to start your big comeback at *his* festival?" She pointed a spoon at me.

"I'm sure Luc knows what he's doing," said Mum with mummian conviction.

"I think we've actually established pretty well that I don't," I replied.

Jaz nodded unsupportively. "That."

And Mum made the loosest, most no-fucks-givenest shrug I'd ever seen, and I'd seen a lot of no-fucks-given shrugs. "Well. Then I'm sure *I* know what *I'm* doing."

In a perfect world where I was a perfect son, my faith in my mother would have been as unshakeable and irrational as her faith in me. But it wasn't a perfect world and I was so far from perfect that if you looked up the word *perfect* in a dictionary, you'd read the definition of the word *perfect* and then think, *On an unrelated note, that Luc guy is a bellend.* "But the festival's in six months. You can't throw a tour together in six months."

Mum just smiled. "Mon caneton," she said, "you are forgetting. I may be old. I may live on a street called after a post office that isn't there in a village with a very silly name, but deep down…deep down I am a motherfucking force of nature." She finished the last of her soup and stood up. "Now, Jas, it is time for your guitar lesson. And after that, I am going to make some calls."

CHAPTER 33

DESPITE HOW IT FELT, GETTING to the point where the government would let us take full responsibility for the well-being of a vulnerable teenager had not, in fact, taken longer than getting ten adults with jobs to agree on a day when they could all be in the same room at the same time. But it had been pretty fucking close.

To say the day of the dinner party had been hectic would be... well, it would be entirely accurate. Because it had been hectic. It had started at the crack of dawn, when Oliver had got up and started removing the arils from a pomegranate. Which I'd have offered to help with, except I didn't know what an aril was or how to remove one. Plus, it looked like one of those sharp-knife jobs, and the last thing any of us wanted was for us to be serving our guests a barley-and-Luc's-finger-blood salad.

Instead, I'd tried to make myself useful in a more furniture-focused way. Our dining table, which was lovely, hadn't really been designed to take eleven, so we'd needed to borrow a spare from the James Royce-Royces. That spare had been living under the stairs since we'd *last* tried to hold this damned party over a month ago, and I got to work shunting the two tables together, then covering them with the natural-look organic linen tablecloths that Oliver had bought from John Lewis's when we'd *first* tried to hold this damned party the previous year.

"No, no, no," he said from the doorway as I was smoothing down the wrinkles on table number one. His fingers were murderer-red from pomegranate. "Table protectors first."

"Doesn't the tablecloth protect the table?"

Sometimes when Oliver was being stressed, me being silly was helpful. Sometimes, though, it was the opposite. And, sometimes, neither of us could tell which. This was definitely the third kind of sometimes. "The tablecloth," said Oliver, with a slightly desperate smile, "makes things look neat and provides limited protection against stains. The table protector prevents heat damage and worse spillages."

"Okay." With the jury out, I gambled on playful. "So that's a table protector to protect the table and the tablecloth to protect the table protector?"

"I'm aware that it's fussy, but it does actually work."

"So do we need something else to protect the tablecloth which protects the table protector which protects the table, or will the tablecloth be all right on their own?"

Oliver's look was sliding from *I am mostly enjoying the joke* to *I really hope you're joking.*

"The things that protect the tablecloth that protects the table arc called..."

"Fuck. Place mats."

The fact that I'd literally forgotten place mats existed put an end to my honestly pretty feeble tableware-based comedy routine. Once I'd grabbed them from the cupboard and laid them out, I followed Oliver into the kitchen.

"Remember," I said very firmly, "this is something we're doing with people we like because we enjoy it. It's not a test we can fail or trap we can fall into. It's just dinner."

He used the back of his wrist to push a lock of hair away from his forehead, leaving a streak of scarlet pomegranate. "Rationally,

I know that. But I haven't done this level of cooking in quite a long time, and it's harder than I remember it being."

"I promise you," I told him as confidently as I could manage, "this will be the best Levantine-themed meze selection thingummy any of us have ever had." I thought for a moment. "Well, except James, probably. But he has a Michelin star, which is basically cheating."

Somehow, that at least half worked. "I know. And you're right. It's just...this took a lot of organising, and I want it to go well."

"And it will go well," I said, in my calmest, most reassuring voice. "These are our friends. They're just going to be happy to see us and each other. We've got this."

Either convinced or making a show of being convinced for my benefit, Oliver nodded and hurried off to do whatever arcane cooking-related activity he needed to be doing next.

While I'd been forgetting place mats and trying to remind Oliver to have a sense of perspective, Jaz had been on Spud duty. She'd done his feeds, and his walks, and by the time I was satisfied that the table was as presentable as I could get it, she'd come home, got Spud comfortable in his pen, washed her hands, and joined Oliver in the kitchen, where she was sautéing onions like a pro. I wasn't quite naïve enough, or for that matter closet-Tory-voting enough, to assume this meant that being suspended had been good for her. But I did hope that maybe now she'd had a chance to settle in, now she was getting guitar lessons off my mum, now Oliver and I had maybe managed to show we were on her side, she was starting to feel at least a little bit at home.

"And you're *sure* I can't help?" I asked, hovering in the doorway and sincerely hoping for a negative response.

If I hadn't already worked out how much the whole dinner party thing was getting to Oliver, I'd have got the message when he replied, "Actually, there's rice soaking over there that needs to be put on," instead of "Oh dear God no."

As it turned out, we were saved from discovering how badly I could fuck up the simple act of putting wet grains in hot water because the doorbell went. And for the less than a minute it took to walk into the hall, I was grateful to whatever cosmic force had saved us from the pan of burning slush I would inevitably produce. Then I actually *opened* the door and I remembered that since it was too early for guests and too late for post, that meant it could only have been bad news.

It was bad news in the shape of Next Door's Kid's Dad. He was wearing beige chinos and a blue polo shirt, holding a cricket ball, and looking furious. "Your guest—"

"Foster daughter," I corrected him.

"Your *foster daughter*"—he put a whole lot of poison into the words—"has just fucking smashed our fucking greenhouse."

I tried not to add *have a greenhouse* to the list of reasons I thought Next Door's Kid's Parents were wankers. Objectively, I knew that greenhouses were perfectly normal things to have and probably some non-wankers had them. But Next Door's Kid's Family had such an aura of wank that it seeped into everything I associated with them.

"When was this?" I asked, trying not to jump immediately to *Are you sure it wasn't your incredibly shitty child.*

Next Door's Kid's Dad narrowed his eyes in a why-are-you-not-agreeing-with-everything-I-say kind of a way. "About an hour ago."

Bollocks. The timeline checked out. About an hour ago, Jaz had been out with Spud, and unless we invented a dog-to-English translator ASAP, he wasn't going to be much use as an alibi. "I'll have a word with her," I tried.

"You said that last time." Next Door's Kid's Dad was raising his voice just slightly in a way that I didn't like but also didn't quite feel I could object to. "And look where that's landed us."

As preoccupied with cooking as Oliver was, his Spidey sense for social disapproval must have started tingling because he appeared, aproned, sweaty, and lightly dusted with cumin, beside me. "Hello, Richard."

Ah yes, I'd forgotten that Next Door's Kid's Dad was an actual Dick. Although not the kind I liked to get pictures of. I mean yes, actually the kind I liked to get pictures of, in that me and Oliver had the whole pictures-of-men-named-Richard joke. But I wouldn't want a picture of him specifically. Because he was a dick.

"Hello, Oliver." Next Door's Kid's Dad gave him a curt nod of recognition that made it way too clear he'd decided Oliver was the mature one in our relationship. "I was just telling your partner that something's happened to our greenhouse."

"He's accusing Jaz of smashing it," I clarified.

With the air of a person handing over a piece of damning evidence, Next Door's Kid's Dad handed Oliver the cricket ball. "Colin saw her throw this through one of the windows."

"Oh, did he?" I said, and Oliver said, "Oh, did he?" but I think we both meant very different things by it.

"Thank you for drawing this to my attention," Oliver continued. "I assure you it will be dealt with."

"Make sure it is." Next Door's Kid's Dad was talking to Oliver, but he made a point of looking at me.

Apparently, there was some kind of adulting rule I didn't understand which made "Make sure it is" a perfectly acceptable way to end a conversation with a neighbour, because Next Door's Kid's Dad left it at that, and Oliver went straight back through to the kitchen, where Jaz had done a way better job than I would have done of not letting anything catch fire.

"We could leave this until after dinner," I stage-whispered to Oliver. "No sense in letting it spoil our afternoon."

But we couldn't. Or at least Oliver couldn't. It wasn't in his nature. "Jasmine, I need to ask you about something."

I could see Jaz going fight-or-flight pretty much instantly, but she managed to keep it together just long enough to say to a panful of onions, "Hang on, these are nearly done."

"I need to talk to you now."

I, I noticed, not *we*.

Jaz conscientiously turned the hob off and pivoted to face him. "What?"

"Richard from next door says you smashed his greenhouse." Oliver was doing his best to sound firm but not angry. I wasn't sure it was helping.

"Didn't."

"He says Colin saw you."

"Lying."

Oliver looked at Jaz, and the way he looked at her made my stomach crawl. When I was in school we'd done *To Kill a Mockingbird*, and there's this bit, right at the end, where Atticus Finch nearly turns his own son in to the cops because he thinks he might have done a murder. And okay, that's probably good ethics and shit because murder is bad, and okay, he's the guy who inspired basically every lawyer to want to be a lawyer. But my takeaway from that book has always been that Atticus Finch was a fucking terrible dad.

I was getting strong Atticus Finch energy from Oliver right now.

"And why would he do that?" he asked.

"Kids do lie," I pointed out. I'd been trying really hard not to say *because he's a piece of shit*, which meant I was way more pleased than I should have been when Jaz answered, "Because he's a piece of shit?"

"Jasmine," Oliver Atticused. "That's not helpful. We're not angry with y—"

"You got nothing to be angry *about*." Jaz was backed right up against the cooker now, and I thought I could see her hands shaking. "'Cause I ain't fucking done nothing."

Oliver, still holding the evidence ball, put his hands up very slowly. "I'm not saying you have."

"You fucking are."

In Oliver's defence, from his perspective he honestly wasn't. In Jaz's defence, from her perspective he totally fucking was.

"Jasmine," said Oliver because he was still stubbornly clinging to the belief that calling her by her full name made him sound authoritative instead of like he just didn't care. "I've asked you before to try to moderate your language."

I opened my mouth to try and say…something. I wasn't sure what exactly. Just something gap-bridging or oil-water pouring, but even if I'd been able to think of the perfect, magic phrase that would make everything better, it wouldn't have mattered. I'd never have got a word in.

"I didn't fucking do nothing." Jaz wasn't exactly screaming, but she was very, very far from having effective strategies for managing her emotions. "What about fucking innocent until proven guilty?"

I was very *slightly* proud of Oliver for not going off on a tangent about burden of proof and how it related to evidentiary standards in the separate spheres of jurisprudence and law enforcement. But, honestly, it might have been better if he had. "I'm just trying to find out what happened."

"Well I don't fucking know, do I?" Jaz was sounding almost panicked now. "I just know it wasn't fucking me, but you don't fucking believe me. Nobody ever fucking believes me."

And Oliver, my poor, sweet, honest Oliver, said, "It's not about believing. It's about the truth."

Because, for him, it was. For a long while after I'd found out what Oliver did for a living, I'd not been able to understand how he could defend somebody if he didn't think they were innocent. But after about the fourteenth time of him explaining it to me, I'd sort of got my head around it. In his line of work, you didn't believe in the person; you believed in the system—as shitty and broken and unfair as it was—and the ideas *behind* the system.

You didn't defend your client because you thought they were a perfect angel who'd done no wrong, or even an imperfect human who'd done some wrong but not the particular wrong in question. You did it because a zealous legal defence was their right, no matter who they were or what they were accused of doing. Even if they were—as the slang apparently went—an experienced crim who rocked up and said, "Let's call the crown to task."

Everything had gone very quiet. Jaz looked up at Oliver, almost pleading, if you could plead in a really angry way. "I didn't. Fucking. Do it."

And because he couldn't not, Oliver came back with, "Language."

With a look that was perilously close to betrayal, Jaz stormed out. I ran after her into the hall but, at least this time, she stayed in the house. I heard her footsteps on the stairs, and the slam of her bedroom door.

When I was sure she hadn't bolted into the wilds of Havering, I went back to the kitchen, where Oliver was standing pale and stock still, the rice he'd put on in my absence boiling over in the background. I looked at him. I looked at him and the greenhouse-murder-weapon he'd been clutching throughout the entire conversation. And I said, "That's not Spud's ball."

CHAPTER 34

I UNDERSTOOD WHY OLIVER'S FIRST instinct, when I pointed out the exonerating ball evidence, was to run to the stove and deal with the rice pan. I *sort of* understood why his second instinct had been to take over sautéing the onions.

But I'd have thought the instinct to apologise to Jaz for not having her back would have occurred to him at *some point*.

"Are you not going to say you're sorry?" I asked.

"To Jasmine?" Oliver was still distracted by the onion pan. "I realise she was upset, but as I said, I wasn't accusing her of anything."

I tapped the cricket ball on the kitchen table distractedly. "Okay, but she clearly *felt* like you were accusing her of something."

Oliver half turned, and I got the strong feeling that Catty Oliver was about to enter the building. "So I should go to her and say, 'I'm sorry you felt like I was accusing you'? That's the kind of thing that ends YouTube careers."

"You could say, 'Sorry I didn't believe you.'"

To his credit, Oliver seemed to consider this one. "I suppose I could, but she responded with hostility, and I'm concerned if we reinforce that, it will just lead to her acting out more and worse in the future."

"Oliver, she's a human being, not a naughty puppy."

He seemed to consider this one too. "Even so, we can't reward her for swearing at authority figures."

I was about to protest that we weren't only supposed to *be* authority figures. That our job had to include making her feel safe and cared for and supported and not just disciplined. But then I heard footsteps on the stairs and clammed up for fear of saying something out of context that would make everything worse.

With hindsight, she came into the kitchen almost uncharacteristically calmly. When she went to work putting together the fillings for the shish barak, I got an I-told-you-so-ish glance from Oliver. I was sure he was taking this as evidence that his firm but fair parenting stance was paying off, but I felt uneasy. Not so uneasy, mind you, that I wasn't almost immediately distracted by the realisation that people who didn't ordinarily live here were about to come into my house. Maybe it was a side effect of sharing the space with Oliver, maybe it was a consequence of hating myself less than I used to, but either way the moment we were officially Expecting Company—and Oliver's dinner was nice enough and high-effort enough that it moved things definitively into the Company zone—even my normally slovenly brain got hyperfixated on every dusty surface, unswept corner, and un-put-away coffee mug.

Which meant when our guests arrived, I was giving the toilet a last-minute scrub.

"Hang on," I yelled downstairs, "with you in a second."

As quickly as I could manage, I flushed the loo, returned the brush to its holder, and pelted downstairs.

"Nice gloves," said Peter when I opened the door with my Marigolds on. "But if this was a sex party, you should have told us in advance."

I tugged ineffectually on one yellow finger. "No, absolutely not. Just a regular no-sex dinner party. Come in."

Jennifer and Peter hung their coats in the hall and followed me through to the dining room, where Oliver met us still slightly rumpled and mid-cook.

"Hi, Oliver"—Jennifer gave a warm, friendly grin—"Luc was just telling us this was a fetish party."

Oliver laughed. It was, I couldn't help noticing, his *good with people* laugh, which was a whole lot less sincere than the *I have utterly failed to pretend I don't find this funny* laugh I usually went for. "Lucien," he said with mock severity, "it was supposed to be a surpr—" An alarm started beeping in the kitchen, and I thought I could smell something just a little bit burny. "One moment, make yourselves comfortable."

"Not sex-comfortable," I added, although honestly, my still only half-off rubber gloves weren't selling it.

"Now I'm kind of offended," said Peter, and I couldn't tell if being so flippant represented a total inability to read the room, or exactly the right ability to read it.

And before I could make a decision, the door went again, and Oliver stuck his head out of the kitchen with a, "Lucien can you—"

I finally got the second glove off and then realised I was now *holding* a pair of Marigolds with no convenient or inconspicuous place to put them down. "On it," I called over my shoulder as I let in the next couple.

"Helloooo," trilled James Royce-Royce, flinging his arms about me in an archetypally Royce-Royceian embrace while behind him James Royce-Royce waved a silent "Hi."

In the dining room, Oliver—well aware that he was come-dine-with-me-ing for a professional—appeared once more in the doorway. "Starters will be ready in a few minutes, and I'm sure the rest of the guests will be arriving soon."

"Except Bridge," I added, "who will almost certainly be late."

Oliver gave me a hopeful look. "You never know, maybe things have gone really smoothly this time."

I pulled out my phone and opened Are the Straights Okay (Dinner Party Remix). "Her last message was twenty minutes ago and it reads, 'babysitter disaster start without us.' Only it's all in block caps and none of it is spelled right."

"Perhaps it won't be as bad as she thinks it is," Oliver replied, with more hope than expectation. "It's usually at least *slightly* less bad than she thinks it is." Something else was beeping. "Back in a second, I have pitas warming."

Before anyone could say anything about pitas or food in general or, indeed, any fucking thing, James Royce-Royce whipped out his phone. "Have I shown you the pictures of Baby J on his tricycle?"

Honestly, I couldn't remember. Also, what did he think we were going to say to that? *Actually, James, we've all seen enough pictures of your fucking infant to last us until we're dead, rotted, and dug up a hundred and forty years later to make way for a new block of flats.* On top of which, I was pretty sure looking at pictures of somebody else's adorable son right now was the last thing Peter and Jennifer wanted. They'd tried another round of IVF at the end of last year, and it had gone about as well as all the rest. But when James Royce-Royce swanned into the dining room and asked the exact same fucking question, they put brave faces on and made *oh isn't he sweet* noises with the best of them.

Although since Brian and Amanda were the next couple to arrive, the best of them was a pretty low bar.

"I thought"—Brian peered over James Royce-Royce's shoulder—"that this party was going to be a baby-free zone."

"Physically," Oliver called through from the kitchen, "but not conceptually, unless you really want me to institute penalties for thought crime."

"I'm game," said Amanda, thumping a bottle of Stroh 80 onto the table. "Anybody who mentions babies does a shot."

Jennifer eyed the bottle. "You know, I think I might actually be up for that."

Looking very close to being the *bad* sort of tense, Oliver appeared in the doorway again. "You are *not* turning this party into a drinking game. Besides, there's a minor in the house."

"Fuck, really?" Brian looked almost personally betrayed.

"I'm fourteen," Jaz yelled from the kitchen.

Brian heaved a sigh of relief. "Thank fuck. That's old enough we can say *fuck*, right?"

"No," insisted Oliver.

"Yes," insisted Jaz.

"Like, I think it's a can-but-probably-shouldn't kind of situation?" I tried. Which I had meant as a compromise but which just seemed to annoy all three of them.

Since everybody who wasn't expected to be Bridge levels of delayed—or, I suppose, in our new normal of most people coming as at least a couple, Bridge-and-Tom levels of delayed—had arrived, Oliver began serving the starters.

"I'm sorry," he said. "We're going to have to start, or everything will be completely ruined."

Jennifer slid into one of the slightly mismatched chairs and laid a napkin on her lap. "If anyone would be okay with that, it's Bridge. I don't think she's eaten a starter since we were in sixth form."

"At uni," I said, "we used to tell her things began an hour earlier than they really did. The problem was she worked it out, so we stopped, but then everybody's sense of time was—"

"So," announced Oliver, accidentally cutting me off, "we're opening tonight with a meze of Levantine-themed dishes."

With Jaz's honestly surly assistance, he started setting out various bowls and plates laden down with the fruits of his (and Jaz's, and to a much, much lesser extent, my) day of labours. The results were, and I say this despite my intense pro-Oliver bias, mixed. The salad had come out well, or as well as a salad *could* come out, which meant it was...fine, but even I could see that the hummus looked grainy and the spices were falling off the za'atar crackers.

Rationally, I'm sure Oliver knew that he wasn't in competition with our friends. And that he definitely wasn't in competition with James Royce-Royce, who, lest we forget, had once made a sausage plait for the queen. But the thing about dinner parties was that they were always at least a bit of a personality test. We hadn't held one for a while, which upped the pressure a lot, but the last one had been at Bridge's, pre-baby, and she'd just made a massive pasta bake, given us all bowls, and told us to dig in. And the one before that had been at Priya's, and, over her girlfriends' protestations, she'd prepared no food at all and insisted we just order takeaway like, as she put it, "normal people."

Then again, Brian and Amanda had done a three-course medieval banquet, and Peter and Jennifer had done something quite similar to what Oliver was attempting. Although I think the big difference there was that Peter and Jennifer are *both* low-key foodies, so neither of them was working with a giant Luc-shaped millstone around their neck.

"This is lovely," said Peter. And he didn't mean to, but he said it in such a kiss-of-death way. When you said *This is lovely* about a wide, mixed spread of food somebody else had made, it meant you wanted to be nice but couldn't actually think of a single specific good thing to say.

James Royce-Royce had been meticulously working his way through the bulgur wheat and pomegranate salad. "Would you like the tiniest bit of professional advice?" he asked, and then without really waiting for a reply went on, "Because you've chosen a recipe with quite a lot of pomegranate, it would have been a good idea to include something to balance out the tartness of the arils. A touch of Greek feta, maybe?"

With incredible composure, especially given how much effort he'd put into getting those arils out in the first place—I think, I still wasn't sure what an aril was—Oliver said, "Thank you, James. That's a good tip."

"These pitas are wonderful," offered Amanda, folding a notably sparse helping of subpar hummus into a little mini-wrap. "I tried making my own once, but I could never get them this warm and even."

Oliver didn't flush, but he did look slightly sheepish. "That's very kind of you, but they're store-bought. I just heated them in the oven."

Some part of me knew I shouldn't say, "And a damn fine job you did too." The trouble was, that part wasn't my mouth.

Fortunately, I was spared having to witness the cringe I'd spread, because our doorbell went and I shot up to get it so fast you'd think my chair had caught fire.

"Sorry we're late." Tom was already taking off his coat. "You remember how our babysitter got scrofula?"

"It wasn't scrofula," yelled Brian from inside.

"No no," said Bridge cheerfully. "Turned out it actually was. He'd been on holiday to a high-risk area."

"So we lined up another one," Tom continued as I led them through to the dining room and everyone got settled, "but she went on one of those Jack the Ripper walking tours."

I leaned back in the chair I'd just reclaimed. "If this ends in a murder..."

"Don't be silly." Bridge dived supportively into the grainy hummus. "She eloped with the tour guide."

Tom nodded. "I'd say it was a shock, but Chel always was a sucker for a girl in a top hat."

"Anyway," Bridge went on, "the next one won an all-expenses-paid trip to Paris and cancelled on us, the one after that broke both legs in a car accident, the next one fell into a cage full of hyenas—"

"My God." James Royce-Royce clapped his hands to his mouth. "How ghastly."

"Oh, she was fine." Unlike his wife, Tom was avoiding the hummus. "Apparently, hyenas only normally attack humans if they feel threatened. But she was really shaken up and didn't want to be babysitting immediately afterwards. Then the *next* one—"

"Hang on"—I raised a finger—"how many babysitters did you go through for this?"

"Fourteen," said Bridge. "Bit of a 'mare really."

From there, things eased into a comfortable fine-ness. The tragic mediocrity of the starters had taken a toll on Oliver, but everybody else was politely ignoring it and throwing themselves into the kind of conversations you had when you'd unwittingly drifted past the stage of being used to group hangs. We'd done a pretty good job—okay, an all right job; okay, a job—of keeping up with everyone on an individual basis, but the dynamics were different when it was all of us, or even a medium-size subset of all of us, and we were kind of rusty.

Once we'd consumed all of the excessively arilly, or possibly insufficiently feta-y salad and disappointing hummus and spice-denuded crackers we could reasonably want, Oliver began to clear the table for the main. "Next"—Oliver was still anxiously stuck in cooking show voiceover mode—"we'll be serving shish barak with pine nut oil and a green salad."

"You know, you don't *have* to do the announcing thing," said Jennifer. "It is *strictly* optional."

"Oh, but it's so much more fun," replied James Royce-Royce. "Really, it's the reason I became a chef in the first place."

James Royce-Royce gave a rare smile. "It's true. He does it at home."

"What?" asked Tom. "For every meal?"

"Meals. Snacks. Cups of tea."

"That's a lie." James Royce-Royce made a gesture of extravagant outrage. "I do not do it for tea." He paused. "Well, unless it's tea and biscuits."

Emerging from the kitchen, Oliver began laying out shallow bowls full of fancy dumplings for the meat eaters, and a tiny rice-and-lentil dish for himself, the name of which I had listened to once and then promptly forgotten.

"Now this," declared James Royce-Royce, "looks *very* special."

And it did. The starters had come out iffy, but the shish barak, as far as I could tell, had worked extremely well. As it should, given Oliver had spent the last week risk-managing all the potential fuckups and making at least one trial batch a night. To be honest, it meant I was kind of sick of shish barak, but, as party sacrifices went, I could live with it.

Peter, having finished his first dumpling and started his second, was nodding enthusiastic agreement. "Really good. I mean really, really good."

"Especially for a man who doesn't eat meat." James Royce-Royce seemed to be experiencing genuine foodie joy. "Without being able to taste as you go, this is excellent."

Finally beginning to relax, Oliver nodded a polite acknowledgment of our friends' praise and said, "Thank you." Looking demurely down, he took a bite of his own meal. He got about two chews in before he paled, set his fork to one side, and spat something into a napkin with far more delicacy than it should have been possible to spit anything into anything.

"Is," I asked, "is everything okay?"

His expression unreadable, Oliver took a knife and began picking through the contents of his lentil-and-rice bowl. Finally, he turned to Jaz and said. "Jasmine, did you put lamb in my mujadara?"

Jaz had a wicked little smile. "Yes," she replied. And then, as Oliver's jaw began to clench and his lips began to get very thin and very tense, she went on, "See how that worked? You asked me. I told you. I may be traumatised, but I'm not a *fucking liar*."

CHAPTER 35

YOU KNOW THAT BIT IN a horror movie where everybody realises that they've been eating human flesh this whole time and there's this silence broken only by the clink of people putting down cutlery and everybody starts avoiding each other's eyes?

This was that, only without the cannibalism.

"Do you have any idea," Oliver began, and knowing what I did about Jaz, *do you have any idea* was quite possibly the worst opening he could possibly have picked, "how wrong"—okay wait, *that* was the worst opening—"what you just did is?"

"No," said Jaz, "because I don't know right from wrong, do I? I'm the girl that gets suspended and puts kids in bins and breaks windows and put meat in lentil stew on account of how my headcase mum fucked me up, remember?"

Jaz's righteous indignation was *slightly* marred by the fact that she had, in fact, done three out of those four things.

"Jasmine." Oliver's voice was calm. "Go to your room. We'll discuss this later."

For a moment I thought Jaz was going to literally laugh in Oliver's face instead of just metaphorically laughing in Oliver's face. "Oh my God, are you sending me to bed without any supper? What *will* I do? You gonna take away my pony next?"

"Jasmine." Why Oliver still believed that repeating Jaz's full name over and over was on the same *planet* as a good idea, I couldn't work out. "Go to your room. And leave your phone."

I'd expected her to fight him on that one, but she'd gone too deep into not giving a shit. She yanked her phone out of her pocket and skidded it across the table at Oliver. "Right. Fine. Whatever."

She made for the door, but Oliver somehow, *somehow*, wasn't finished yet. "Jasmine, please don't just say, 'Right, fine, whatever,' then walk away."

"You told me to go to my room," she said, half turning. "I'm going to my room."

I reached out and rested a hand on Oliver's arm. "Let her go," I said. "Please. We're having dinner."

Perhaps it was the *please* that did it because Oliver never could resist a social nicety. And also because he, like, cared about me and shit. Either way, he said nothing else, and Jaz took the opportunity to slip away as discreetly as she could manage, given the apocalyptically massive scene she'd caused.

"Y'know," said Brian, "if I could be sure my kid would turn out like that, I'd almost be willing to have one."

"When it's your fucking uterus," replied Amanda, "be my guest."

Under my hand, Oliver's arm was trembling slightly. "Jasmine is wonderful in many ways," he said carefully, "but fostering has not been without its challenges."

"How about," I suggested, "we just move on and... What do you want to do about food?"

Oliver was looking down at his contaminated mujadara. "Honestly, I think I'll be fine. I can fix myself something later."

The carnivores in the room went guiltily back to their shish barak. And, for about as long as it took to eat a dumpling, we all sat in awkward silence until Bridge, as much to get the conversation moving as anything else, piped up with, "I don't suppose I can bore people with baby pictures, can I? It's a bit"—she pulled a self-consciously embarrassed face—"new-mum stereotype, but, well, new mum."

James Royce-Royce's phone was already out. "Oh, if that's what we're doing, I also have some fabulous ones of Baby J I don't think I've shown you."

Brian and Amanda shared weary looks. "I suppose," she said after a moment of silent couple telepathy, "it's better than sitting here watching Oliver not eat rice."

"I'm sorry, I'm being inconveniently vegan again." He was trying to make it sound lighthearted, but between being tricked into eating meat and having a public blowup with his foster daughter, we could tell his heart wasn't all that light actually, thank you.

Which was why Amanda felt the need to come back with a "That's not what—" which she was unable to finish before she was drowned out by Bridge and James introducing their baby and toddler photos as if they were a plate of Levantine dumplings.

"And there he is on his tricycle again."

"And there she is rolling over."

"Here's him standing on one foot—you know most children can't do that until four."

"He was holding him up," James Royce-Royce clarified.

"Nothing in the books says you can't be holding him up," protested James Royce-Royce.

Bridge, who had been leaning across the table to show me her own pictures, returned her arse to her seat. "Autumn's just started blowing bubbles. It's sooooo cute."

James Royce-Royce nodded. "That's a five-month development milestone. Although I'm *sure* Baby J started when he was only—"

"James." Bridge seemed to be wincing with her whole body. "Could you maybe…not?"

"Not what?" asked James Royce-Royce, in such sincere innocence I almost felt bad.

"Not," said Bridge hesitantly, "um. Not turn around every time I mention something about Autumn and tell me that Baby J did it better?"

Even James Royce-Royce, drama queen that he was, didn't do the fingertips-to-chest-how-very-dare-you gesture often. He was doing it now. "Well, *pardon me* for being *proud* of my *son.*"

"It's not about being proud of your son," Bridge tried to explain.

"You just kind of take all the oxygen out of the room," added Tom.

James Royce-Royce took an ironically deep breath. "All the *oxygen* out of the room."

"This is new and exciting for us." Bridge sounded slightly plaintive. "But it's hard to be excited when you won't give us a moment to...well. Be excited."

The fingertips-to-chest-how-very-dare-you gesture was rare enough. James Royce-Royce kicked it up a notch to the palms-crossed-faux-mortification pose. "Oh no! There's a space that isn't totally dedicated to celebrating a straight couple's biological child! Whatever shall we do?"

"First," said Tom, way snappier than I'd ever heard him, even when he'd been dumping me, "not fucking straight."

"And of course we want to celebrate Baby J too," added Bridge, who was psychologically incapable of not seeing at least a little bit of the other person's point of view. "But you can be a touch..." To my horror, Bridge was shooting a *help me out* look squarely in my direction. "A touch, you know..."

"Dominatey?" I suggested, trying to throw it out there like a tennis ball and realising only afterwards that it might have been a bit more like a stick of dynamite.

"*Dominatey!*" James Royce-Royce projected.

"Don't want to be a dick, Luc," James Royce-Royce added, "but that's not even a real word."

I shouldn't have got involved, because it inevitably meant teams were going to form, and once teams formed it was all over.

"All Luc means," Bridge said, making the teamification irreversible, "is that I'm not the only one who's noticed and not the only one who's been bothered."

James Royce-Royce fixed me with a look of real betrayal. "Is that true, Luc?"

I did *little bit* fingers.

"Well, of all the—" For a moment, James Royce-Royce looked genuinely betrayed. "I'd expect that from her, but as a gay man, I'd have thought you'd understand."

Aaaand now we were playing the bad gay card. Shit. "Hold on, that is *not* fair."

"Also, once again"—Tom was fully glowering now—"feeling pretty fucking erased over here."

"I just meant," said James Royce-Royce—and if the teams hadn't fucked everything, this would, because nothing good ever came after *I just meant*—"that you should see our perspective. Fostering is different, of course, but we've both had to go through a lot of intrusive poking and prodding and proving we're worthy just to get something that straight"—he just about checked himself—"opposite-sex couples take for granted."

The late-in-the-game change of terminology didn't entirely placate Tom, but he retreated to the quiet kind of angry. Bridge, who hated the thought of making anyone feel bad in any way, was close to welling up with a mix of hurt and sympathy and just general sad.

Then there was Jennifer.

Jennifer was sitting very still, and Peter said, definitely on her behalf, "James, mate, believe me, not all straight people take having kids for granted."

I liked to think that, had I been in James's position, I'd have handled things better, but who was I kidding? I'd have gone completely to pieces. Especially because, teams-wise, things seemed to be lining up into "James and James" and "everybody else." So on the whole, he could probably have said something a lot worse than, "I'm sorry, Peter, but it's simply not the same."

Okay. Maybe not *a lot* worse.

"Ex. Fucking. 'Scuse me," said Jennifer in a voice so slow and so careful you could almost miss the rage and pain in it. "Do you want to talk about getting poked and prodded and made to fill out forms? Do you want to talk about being made to feel *inadequate*?"

"You shouldn't feel inadequate because you're not using your body as an incubator," cut in Amanda.

Which I think she'd intended to be supportive, but it didn't land that way with Jennifer. "Well, I do anyway."

"Well, that's fucked in the head."

Charitably, Amanda meant that it was fucked in the head on a societal level, but, once again, it didn't land that way with Jennifer. "Oh, *sorry*, Amanda," she snapped. "I forgot that feeling sad because I might never have children of my own makes me a bad feminist."

"And what does 'children of my own' mean?" demanded James Royce Royce.

Oliver, who for this whole conversation had just been staring into his bowl of rice, lentils, and malicious lamb, took a measured breath. "I think that these are complex topics, and clearly we're very—"

"Oh, for *fuck's sake*," half bellowed Brian, "can't you have a fucking opinion for once in your fucking life?"

Okay, this was past teams and into an all-against-all knife fight. I got as far as "Hey" before Brian barrelled on.

"We came out here," he said, "to have dinner. Not to have baby shit rammed down our throats."

The softer spoken of the James Royce-Royces raised a pale eyebrow. "Choice of words?"

"You're our *friend*," pleaded Bridge, now properly crying. "You should care about our baby shit because *we* care about it."

"Please"—Amanda stood up in a decisive kind of way—"carry on telling me what I should care about. That's exactly what I want from a dinner party."

Jennifer, having spoken her piece, had gone deadly quiet, but Peter—one arm around her shoulder—still had voice left in him. "It doesn't matter to me what you do or don't care about, but if you could go five minutes without pissing on everybody else's life choices, that would be fab, actually."

"Particularly," added James Royce-Royce, "when those life choices have come at such immense personal cost."

Brian was on his feet as well. "Right, of course. Because we're the ones who are doing it wrong, aren't we? Because we didn't hit thirty and suddenly decide to change our entire personalities overnight."

"Our personalities didn't change overnight," Bridge protested. "It's just...well—it's hard to explain."

Amanda folded her arms. "Yeah, yeah. Brian and I *wouldn't understand*, would we? Because being a parent is so magical and transformative and we're denying ourselves the wonders of life if we don't shackle ourselves with a hungry squealing money sink for the next twenty years."

"I mean, I think they stop squealing *eventually*," I tried, which earned me an *I love you but that didn't help* look from Oliver.

"Well, I'm sorry." James Royce-Royce had joined the standing crowd, and James Royce-Royce was sitting beside him trying desperately to tell him not to through eye movements. "But the real simple truth is that ever since Baby J came into our lives—even though he's not *our own child*"—he glared at Jennifer, who in the interim had also started crying, albeit with barristerial reserve.

"James," she managed, "I really didn't mean—"

"I have never," James Royce-Royce continued, "experienced such *joy* or such *pride* as I have with Baby J. Especially—"

In our immediate circle, nobody could do a face like thunder quite as well as Brian. I think it was the beard, which made him look a bit like a friendlier version of Thor. Well, normally friendlier. "Especially *what*? Especially compared to selfish pricks like me and Amanda who waste our time and energy on crap the rest of you have grown out of?"

"You *do* play a lot of video games," said Tom, whose catty streak I'd almost forgotten in the decade since we dated.

"*Especially*," James Royce-Royce finished, "because Baby J will be under a microscope his whole life because, unless things get radically better in the next twenty years, nobody will ever let him forget that he's the adopted son of two gay men."

"Pretty sure Autumn won't forget she's biracial in a hurry either," replied Tom, who had abandoned anger in favour of withering sarcasm. "But somehow I still manage to avoid treating her like she's the second coming of Jesus, Elvis, and Einstein all at once."

There were some fires that Oliver would always put his hand back into. "I think," he said, "we're clearly all feeling things very strongly right now and—"

But before Brian could tell him to shut up again, we were interrupted by an almighty crash from upstairs.

CHAPTER 36

THE GUESTS STAYED IN THE dining room, presumably still tearing each other apart over things that were mostly the fault of fate, society, or nobody. Oliver and I hurried upstairs to see what had happened this time.

The noise had come from the bathroom, and while normally we'd be extremely cautious about bursting in on anybody—especially Jaz—in that context, the door was ajar and the crash had been loud enough that it sounded like a real emergency.

And for a moment, it looked like one. A proper call-an-ambulance emergency, because the bathroom was spattered red like we were in the intro sequence to an episode of *CSI: Havering*.

But Jaz didn't look hurt. Shocked, yes. Quite wet, yes. But not hurt. Also her hair was clipped back and about two-thirds damp and brightly coloured, so even without the skills of a crime scene specialist, I had a pretty clear idea of what had happened.

Which didn't stop Oliver asking, in his most authoritative tone, "What do you think you're doing?"

I just thanked the parenting gods he hadn't ended with *young lady*.

"Roasting a chicken," replied Jaz. "What's it look like I'm doing?"

Honestly, what it looked like Jaz was doing was impromptu redecorating. It wasn't just that there was red hair dye on the walls, floor, and sink; it was that our marble bathroom organiser had somehow fallen into the toilet, where, on account of being marble, it had cracked the bowl, meaning ominous beads of slightly reddish water were now forming on the outside of our recently cleaned loo and there were little chips of white stuff all over the place that could have come from the bowl, the lid, or the bathroom organiser itself.

"Don't worry," I said, "it ha—"

Trouble was, Oliver wasn't in a 'Don't worry, it ha—' mood. "What *possessed* you to try dyeing your hair without asking us, without supervision, using *our* bathroom supplies, in the middle of a dinner party?"

I'd expected Jaz to shrug, but she didn't. And honestly, that slightly scared me. "Fancied a change."

"*Look*"—Oliver was giving real rubbing-the-puppy's-nose-in-it energy—"at the damage you've caused."

Jaz looked at it. "Get a plumber."

"Is that all you can say?"

I'd seen malicious compliance faces before, but Jaz's was practised to the point of exceptional. "Get a plumber. Please."

Oliver opened his mouth. Then Oliver closed his mouth. Then Oliver opened his mouth.

"Going to send me to my room again?"

Oliver said nothing.

"Already grounded, so you can't do that."

I could see Oliver taking deep, steadying breaths.

"You gonna hit me?" Jaz smiled, although whether that was because she knew it was off the table or because she didn't, I wasn't sure.

"Certainly not," said Oliver very firmly. "But you are going to clean all of this up. By yourself."

Jaz looked at Oliver like she could not imagine hating anybody more. "Course I fucking am. I know how to fucking clean up after myself."

"Language, Jasmine."

"You forgotten that I've heard how your friends talk?"

"What's appropriate for adults isn't appropriate for children."

Without even bothering to reply, Jaz pushed past him and into the corridor.

"Jasmine, come back here."

She turned. "Getting the cleaning things, aren't I? Isn't that what you wanted?"

"You will *not*"—Oliver was setting a personal record for tense—"walk away from me while I am talking to you. You will not speak back to me. You will not do anything like"—he gestured at the bathroom floor—"like *this* ever again. Or else—"

I knew I wasn't a great parent. Jaz had told me multiple times that I wasn't a great parent. Okay, she'd told me that I was an actively shit parent. But if there was one thing I knew for *certain*, it was that you never dropped an *or else* unless you had something to back it up. Because you were definitely, definitely going to get...

"Or else what?"

"Or else," said Oliver with the fakest calm I'd ever heard him fake, "I will be forced to contact the agency and tell them that unfortunately, while Lucien and I have tried to be supportive of your needs, we are unable to provide you with the care you require."

And in Jaz's eyes, I saw something. A look I recognised far too well. The self-destructive comfort that came from proving that you'd lived down to somebody's expectations. And then she walked into her room and slammed the door behind her.

"That was *fucked*, Oliver," I stage-whispered as I followed him into the hall. With Jaz upstairs and guests downstairs, there was kind of nowhere we could safely have a row, but a row was coming whether

I liked it or not. "You do not get to make decisions like that without consulting me."

Oliver stopped by the front door and looked at me in genuine confusion. "Decisions like what?"

"Like what?" I was still keeping my voice low, but I felt like it was mostly making me raspy rather than stealthy. "Like 'threatening to send Jaz back into the system' is like what."

The look in Oliver's eyes was infuriatingly, almost *hideously*, calm. "I was just stating the facts as I saw them. We won't be able to keep Jasmine if she doesn't learn to—"

"You know what," I interrupted, "I feel like this is going to be a long conversation, and we still have a dining room full of Millennials who used to like each other. How about we stick to one crisis at a time?"

At least Oliver didn't say, *Well, you're the one who brought it up*, although I was pretty sure I heard him think it. He nodded, and we went back through to see what we could salvage from the remains of the dinner party.

It turned out that there wasn't much. Brian and Amanda had gone, as had the James Royce-Royces, leaving Peter and Jennifer in the front room waiting for a cab and Bridge and Tom in the dining room waiting for us.

I was barely through the door before Bridge was on her feet and hugging me.

"I'm sorry I ruined dinner," she told me with such sincerity that I felt like a shithead.

"You didn't ruin dinner," said Tom for what I strongly suspected wasn't the first time or the fifth. "James did."

I tried to make a conciliatory face over Bridge's shoulder. "I don't think anyone did, really."

"Although Jasmine's antics didn't help," added Oliver, with a sourness I really disliked.

"Can you lay off Jaz. Please," I pissy-begged, peeling myself out of Bridge's arms.

"I fear laying off her is what brought us to this situation in the first place."

For a conversation we were going to be having later, this seemed a lot like now. "Oliver, stop it. Seriously. I know you're stressed, but…but…" Utterly but-less, I ran out of steam.

Bridge glanced between us with the kind of concern you didn't want your friends to be showing you. "Is everything okay? Is Jaz okay?"

Oliver and I eyed each other in a how-big-a-lie-do-we-tell-here way.

"Yeah," I said, finally. "She was trying to dye her hair and managed to knock a bunch of shit over."

"It does happen when you're that age. When I was fourteen I tried to dye my hair pink because I thought it would make Andy Whitwell like me. But I didn't read the instructions properly, so it came out snot green and ruined my parents' best towels."

We stood there for a little while, nobody quite able to say, *How about we never do anything like this ever again*, and then Peter stuck his head through the door.

"Our taxi's outside." He paused, and I recognised the sort of cognitive dissonance a certain kind of nicely brought up middle-class person got when they were socially obliged to be grateful for something that had made their life objectively worse. "Thanks for dinner."

"Actually," said Tom, "can we split the ride with you?"

Peter made *sure* noises, and Bridge and Tom, with another round of goodbye hugs and a heartfelt "I love you" from Bridge that I was, just then, not quite in a place to reciprocate, followed them out the front door into the waiting cab.

Which left me and Oliver alone in our house. Just me, him, a conversation we needed to have, and a lot of uneaten shish barak. With a despairing look at what was left of the food, Oliver slumped into a chair and put his head in his hands.

"This," he said, "was a terrible evening."

And my feeling-bad-ness didn't know where to go because here was Oliver, the man I loved, clearly falling apart at the seams. But also everything that had been low-key bothering me pretty much since Jaz had arrived had now gone beyond high-key bothering me into actual fucking crisis. And, you know, maybe that was my fault. Maybe I should have said something more or differently or better. Only, chump that I was, I'd kind of been working on the assumption that, with time and patience and support and encouragement, Oliver would keep on acting like the man I loved. Not like a man who would throw a vulnerable teenager out of his house for doing teenage stuff.

"Look," I said, "I'm sorry to do this now. Because, you're right, this was a terrible evening. We've had a terrible evening. This is a terrible time to do anything. But…but I really need to know, did you mean what you said to Jaz?"

Except then I realised this wasn't going to help anything. Because if he didn't mean it, then it had just been an unbelievably cruel thing to say, and if he did…

Who was I kidding? Oliver always meant everything.

He looked up, all hollow and tormented. "She clearly has complex needs. We aren't necessarily best placed to meet those needs."

"And who is?"

"I don't know," he conceded. "Possibly she needs to be in a specialist home."

"Because she's traumatised?" I wasn't sure when I'd picked up Jaz's habit of weaponising her labels.

Oliver nodded. "Ultimately, yes. It isn't a kindness to keep her in an environment she won't thrive in."

This was twisting my heart even more than I'd expected it to. "She's not a fucking corgi, Oliver. Besides, what would her thriving actually *look like*?"

And it probably said something bad about where we'd got over the last couple of months that I assumed Oliver would shoot that down. When, instead, he seemed genuinely taken aback by the question. "I will admit, I hadn't considered that in detail. But not like this."

"Oh right. So thriving teenagers are like porn? You can't say what they are, but you know them when you see them?"

Oliver fully scowled at me. "Don't be cute, Lucien. This is important."

I fully scowled back. "I *know* it's fucking important and I wasn't being cute. I was being pissed off. You're not the only one who gets to have takes on important things."

"Then"—one of his eyebrows twitched upwards—"what's *your take*?"

And hearing my own words, repeated back to me in that superior tone, fucking broke me. Until that exact moment, I'd never doubted that no matter how much I joked about Oliver being cooler and smarter and more successful and just generally better than I was, he truly did see me as an equal. As a partner. As someone whose thoughts and beliefs and *takes* mattered.

"My take," I said, shocked at how icy I could apparently sound, "is that she's fine. She's not always happy, but why would she be? She's been taken from her family and shunted from stranger to stranger, school to school, since she was twelve. My take is that now she's here, she's doing her homework, she's cooking with us, she's only got in one fight, she's started learning guitar and is taking it seriously. My take is that Mum and Spud both love her—"

"They both love anybody," cut in Oliver.

"That's not a fucking failing," I yelled.

"I never said it was."

"Fucking hell, Oliver. This is not a debate. I'm trying to tell you how I feel, and I want you to just...I don't know, fucking listen? Not cross-examine me. And I'm sorry if you think the fact that Mum and Spud both love Jaz isn't admissible in court. But I love her too. And..." I broke off, discovering I was perilously close to tears and, while I was normally fine to cry in front of Oliver, now was not normally. "And," I finished, "I love you. And I want to spend my life with you and have a family with you. But how can I when...when..."

Oliver's eyes went their coldest, most ruined grey. "When what?"

"When..." I felt trapped. I felt like I was trapped in a cold, dark place and slowly running out of air. "When it's like...God, saying 'It's like I don't know you' is such a fucking cliché, but...you come home from court with these stories about your clients and how even though they've broken the rules, they're still human beings and... and I don't get how you can have so much empathy for all those pickpockets and shoplifters and so little for our own fucking kid."

This was going to be a *firstly* situation. Oliver was going to say *firstly* and then list a bunch of reasons why I was wrong, and a tiny little piece of me was going to hate him for it.

"Firstly," he said, "Jasmine isn't our child. She's our foster child. She still has a mother who she should, if things go well, eventually be able to go back to. Secondly, yes, all those pickpockets and shoplifters as you call them are indeed human beings. My duty to them is to represent them at trial, and I do that. My duty to Jasmine is to..."

And for once in a lifetime of having an answer for everything, Oliver...didn't.

"Is to *what*?" I demanded, trying not to sound triumphant.

In this case, though, the lapse had been only momentary. "Set a positive example and, with compassion, hold her to high standards."

"Okay, but *whose* standards? Because when I signed up for this, I thought I was going to be doing it with you but"—*don't say it, don't say it, don't say it*—"ever since Jaz arrived, there's been times"—*don't say it*—"I've felt like I'm living with your fucking dad."

There was a frankly terrifying lack of visible reaction. "That seems needlessly hyperbolic."

And I broke a little bit more. "Oh fuck off, Oliver. I'm not in a mood to think big words are sexy today. I *mean it.* You have been a judgemental, high-handed, closed-minded, borderline fucking *heartless*—"

"My, my," he drawled, "how *have* you put up with me?"

"Stop being a dick. I'm fucking serious. I'm not saying you've been a monster—"

"You just called me *borderline heartless*."

"Well," I pointed out, "you did threaten to ship Jaz back to the pound."

His eyes widened. "I did no such thing."

"I was right there. I heard you."

"No." Oliver was beginning to fray, very slightly, around the edges. "She asked what the consequences would be if she continued to act inappropriately, and I explained."

"You can't explain to a child you're going to send them away."

"What was I supposed to say?"

"Literally anything else." I threw my hands in the air. "Look, I realise I'm not great at this, either, but if there is one thing I know about, it's feeling like you have to reject people before they can reject you. It's so, so, *so* obvious that Jaz has been waiting for the day we say, 'Sorry, you're not worth it, here's a bin liner.' And now we've said it—"

"We haven't said it."

"She *feels* like we've said it, and frankly, *I* feel like we've said it. And that's the same fucking thing."

"Then I'm sorry I misspoke. But perhaps I wouldn't have if you'd had my back. Just once."

I stared at him in disbelief. "I've had your back, Oliver."

"You have sometimes refrained from actively undermining me. I wouldn't call that having my back."

"Well...well...your back has been doing shit I don't agree with."

"You mean disciplining our foster daughter?"

"I mean acting like that can only mean one thing."

"It means quite a limited set of things." Oliver ran a fraught hand through his hair. "None of which you seem to want to do. I didn't ask to be the strict parent. You forced the role on me."

"Bullshit," I exploded. "You jumped into that role with both feet because that's what you think parenting *is*. Because you were raised by arseholes, and for some reason I honestly can't begin to understand, you've decided you want to follow in their arsehole footsteps."

There was the sort of silence you got when you said something terrible to someone you really cared about. Of all the sorts of silence, it was the absolute suckiest.

"Oliver," I tried, feeling sticky and messed up because part of me wanted to take back everything I'd said, but also...I didn't? Because it was, like, true? Or close enough to true that I needed him to hear it.

And then, because I didn't know how to get past the sorry-not-sorry-but-sorry of it all, the sucky silence continued until Oliver said "I see" in this quietly devastated voice. Followed by, "I...I'm not sure there's anything more we should say to each other right now. I...I think I might go to bed."

Once again, I was left in that dithery confused state because what I wanted more than anything was to go upstairs with Oliver and lie in his arms and pretend none of this had ever happened. Except it had. So I couldn't.

"I..." The word hung there like a loose thread from a sleeve. "I might not?"

"Then...I'll see you in the morning?" He sounded uncertain. The same way I felt uncertain. Like neither of us knew how badly we'd fucked this.

"Yeah," I replied.

That was when I realised that this would be the first time I'd watched Oliver go to bed without me in...maybe in ever. And I couldn't bear it, so I followed him to the foot of the stairs, and then when he went up I went past and into my study, where I found Spud still curled up in his pen. We should have let him out after the guests had gone, really, only we'd got distracted stabbing each other in the emotional liver.

"Well," I said to him as he skipped up to me with oblivious puppyish happiness, "it's just you and me again tonight."

"Ruff," said Spud.

And it turned out, that was exactly what I needed to hear.

CHAPTER 37

I'VE ALWAYS BEEN A HEAVY sleeper. Probably because my sleep patterns—like most of my lifestyle—were extremely unhealthy. So when Oliver came down a few hours later, I didn't wake up until he was physically shaking my arm.

I made totally dignified blurgling noises and swatted at something I might have been dreaming about but instantly forgot. "Wharaugh?"

"Do you really think you couldn't raise children with me?"

"Wur?"

Oliver was sitting on the arm of the sofa wearing his stripiest pyjamas and his most serious, most introspective expression. "Do you really feel that if it doesn't work out with Jasmine—"

That woke me straight up. "Hold on, don't turn Jaz into some kind of...dry run."

To my surprise, Oliver looked immediately apologetic. "Of course not. And you're right. I just mean—do you think that... because of the way that things have gone with Jasmine. Because of—have the last few weeks really made you so convinced that I... that I can't be a good father?"

Sometimes when somebody asks you a really horrible question, the best answer you can give them is the time it took you to think of one. And I was beginning to suspect this was one of those situations.

Still, since I'd used the thinking time already, I did my best to use some actual words as well. "It's more—I don't know if the kind of dad you're trying to be and the kind of dad I'm trying to be are the kinds of dad who can dad together." Then I very quickly added, "Butthatdoesn'tmeanIwanttobreakuporanything."

"Are you sure?" asked Oliver. Which made me taste bile and possibly blood. "Because…because if I'm honest, I'm not sure I'd want to stay with me if I felt the way you said you feel."

This was getting dangerous. Losing-things-you-loved dangerous. "How do you think I feel?"

"You've made that very clear, Lucien. You as good as said—no, you *did* say—I was turning into my father."

Okay, there was that. "Yeah, but not all the time. Just, like…"

"Just when I'm around Jasmine?"

With the stakes being so high, it might have been a bad time to call him out, but this was kind of the whole problem. "Her name," I told him, "is Jaz."

I could see him mouthing out the word, rolling it around like a Werther's Original. "I suppose that *is* rather indicative."

"Yes," I said. "Yes, it is."

Oliver looked down at his hands. He was perched on the arm of the sofa only inches away from my head and he looked small. Really, really small. And then he went on, in the quietest voice I'd ever heard, "I don't know what to do."

That was so unexpected that I had no idea how to handle it. If it was good or bad or both or neither or anything. "About what? Jaz? Us? The leftover shish barak?"

He was breathing very deliberately now, like he was worried he might forget how. "I…I didn't expect this to be easy."

We'd just come off the worst and biggest argument we'd ever had, including some of the really big ones from back when his dad had been at his worst, so I didn't want to escalate. But I'd also *noticed* something. "Oliver," I said as gently as I could manage. "You said that in the pub too. Is it...is it at all possible that you're saying it because deep down, there's a little part of you that sort of...y'know. Did. Expect it to, I mean."

Oliver blinked. "Credit me with some self-awareness."

He could, on the whole, have had much worse reactions. "No, seriously, think about it. If you're totally, completely, one hundred million percent honest with yourself—"

"Lucien"—he was trying to sound playful, but I could see I'd hit a nerve—"criticise my parenting all you like, but *please* never cite a percentage greater than a hundred."

"If you're totally honest with yourself, didn't part of you think this would be...easier for you than it is for other people?"

"Because I have such an unbelievably high opinion of myself?"

"Because you're really good at stuff. You've been really good at stuff your whole life. And I know you've always had your issues and there's always been things you've struggled with, but it's always been, like, internal stuff. Not stuff other people can see and judge you on."

Oliver had gone very quiet, and I tried to pivot into a more positive direction.

"You did great at school, and at university, then went on to do a very cool job that you also do great at. You're an amazing cook. You're good in social situations. Dogs love you. Even Next Door's Kid at least *pretends* not to think you're a cock. I'm not saying either of us have covered ourselves in glory over the last few months, but I think part of the reason I've handled things better is because I'm *way* more used to fucking up than you are."

For a little while, Oliver was silent, unable to manage more than a weak smile. "This has been so hard," he said at last. "More than hard—terrifying. And not just the fostering, but all of it. You've probably already noticed this, Lucien, but we're...we are actually building a life together, and that's—that's probably the most difficult, most frightening thing I've ever done."

"Hey, I'm not *that* difficult to live with."

It had been a joke, but Oliver was in a sincerity space, so it didn't quite land. "Sorry. No," he stumbled. "I didn't mean it like that. I just mean we have so much to lose now. Not just the simple fact of each other. But everything we are together."

That was, honestly, kind of meltingly romantic. But I wasn't totally sure I wanted to let the romantic meltiness of it distract me from the fact that things were still in a kind of a fucky place, coparenting-wise. So I stayed silent, and let Oliver continue.

"I think..." he went on, far more uncertainly than I was used to him being, "I know you said that teenagers resent everyone, but I don't think I was emotionally ready to be so consistently rejected."

"Pretty sure teenagers reject everyone too."

"She doesn't reject you."

I tried not to burst out laughing. "She does. Of course she fucking does. She's constantly going on about how I'm a shit parent who can't drive, and she obviously wants to go back to her mum."

"With you," Oliver insisted, "she's coming around. With me, she isn't. You called this a learning process, but where I'm concerned, she isn't learning."

Oh. Yeah. I'd dodged this last time because I didn't want to make Oliver sad. Only now he was sadder. It was almost like emotional cowardice wasn't a good idea, long term. "The thing is," I said, "I didn't actually mean a learning process for *her*; I meant a learning process for *us*."

"And what am I supposed to learn?" he asked despairingly. "To put up with her insulting me—insulting *us*—and ignoring us and occasionally sabotaging us until she turns eighteen and leaves?"

It said some weird things about where I was emotionally, at least as far as Jaz was concerned, that even expressed in Oliver's most cynical, most rational terms, it didn't sound like the worst thing in the world. "Maybe? That's basically what we'd do if she was our own kid."

"If she was our own kid, we would have had fourteen years of setting positive examples, so she would hopefully be a lot more reasonable."

"Okay," I said. "Two things. Firstly"—apparently I could *firstly* with the best of them—"if you really think that, you'll be in for a massive shock if we ever do adopt. I'm pretty sure all kids are nightmares one way or another. Secondly, this is about *family*, Oliver. Family isn't about rules and boundaries and best practices. Kids or no kids, you're my family, and I'm not with you because you're setting me *positive examples*. I'm with you because I love you."

He looked over at me, conflicted in a way that made me feel conflicted, committing us both to one big confliction loop. "And I love you. But while William Morris might have had a point about romantic relationships, I don't think even he would have applied the same principle to parenting."

My face sagged. "You're going to make me ask who William Morris is, aren't you?"

"He wrote a poem called 'Love Is Enough,' which allegedly once received the three-word review 'It is not.'"

"Okay, but it *is*, though, isn't it?"

Oliver gazed at me. "For us, of course. But we're grown men and largely responsible for our own well-being. Where a child is involved, there are—"

"Fuck me, Oliver." I flopped my head against the sofa cushions in exasperation. "Will you please wake up and smell the…the William Morris. I mean obviously when you're looking after a kid you need to, like, make sure they don't starve or join a gang or get hooked on smack or whatever. And that shit is probably harder than it seems. But after that, love is, like—fucking hell, it's not just *enough*, it's *everything*."

"That's a nice sentiment, but—"

"Do you think that I've gone from being a miserable twentysomething fuckup who hates himself and lives under a pile of abandoned pizza boxes to a very happy thirtysomething fuckup who you're building a life with because you *set me clear boundaries*?"

His face grew just the tiniest bit pinched. "Well no, but—"

"You changed my world," I told him, breathless and only partly from all the swearing, "because you loved me. Just loved me. For who I was, with all my weird bits and my shit bits and my socks all over the floor. I didn't change because you tried to change me—"

"That would have been difficult to achieve and counterproductive."

He was so close to getting it I was practically furious. "Right. So why would Jaz be any different?"

"Because she's a child."

"She's a *person*. And she needs the same thing I need, the same thing *you* need, if you'd just fucking admit it. She needs to know we care about her no matter what, that we're here for her no matter what. That we're on her side, even if she really did murder an evil racist."

Oliver might have been with me up until that last one. "Murder a what?"

"Sorry. Book thing. Very out of character for me, I know."

"Are you talking about *To Kill a Mockingbird*?"

"We did it at school. Leave me alone. The point is that she needs to know we've got her back. Even if she wrecked the bathroom. Even if she put meat in your lentils. Even if she smashed next door's greenhouse, which by the way she *definitely* didn't. That doesn't mean we can't do boundaries and whatever. It means"—I was running out of words and feels at about the same time—"it means we just have to love her, Oliver. You can do it for me. Do it for her."

For a moment, Oliver just sat there, processing. And then in a small, quiet voice, he said, "What if I can't?"

"You can."

"I don't think that's an answer."

Crossing my legs, I swivelled around on the sofa to face him. "If you can't, you keep trying."

Oliver's breathing was getting slower and more deliberate again. He moistened his lips and said, still quiet and still small, "It's not that simple."

"William Morris, Oliver. Remember William fucking Morris."

"I'm not sure he's an authority."

Reaching out, I took hold of both his hands. "This is as simple as we make it. It's as complicated as we make it. Just try, Oliver. Basic, primary-school-level, one-foot-in-front-of-the-other try."

Oliver was blinking back tears. "I'll—saying you'll try to try seems facile, but it might be the best I can do in the moment."

"You know what?" I said. "I'll fucking take it."

"Ruff," agreed Spud, who had scampered back into the living room at some point while me and Oliver were spattering our hearts all over the floor. Maybe he thought they were dog treats.

I scooped him up onto my lap. "Hello, boy. *You* know Daddy Luc is right about this, don't you?"

"Ruff," he replied. But he was squirmier than he normally was when he got lap time, and he jumped back onto the floor. "Ruff. Ruff."

This was my fault. I'd messed up his cirwhateverian rhythms, and now he thought it was walkies time, which was why he was dashing back and forth between the sofa and the front door like little Timmy had fallen down the well. Only the well was in our front drive and Timmy was, like, his need to wee or something.

"Should I take him out?" I asked Oliver.

With what I suspected was a conscious effort to respect my skills as a dog owner, Oliver replied, "If you think he needs it."

Rising with the grace of a man who had slept on a sofa, I did the dog-summoning thigh pat. "C'mon, boy, let's go into the garden."

Normally that would have worked. But instead of bounding over to be rewarded for a bowel movement, Spud plonked his arse in front of the front door and said, "Ruff," and then, "Mruff?" and then, "Aroou?"

"Sorry," I called through to Oliver. "He seems a bit…off rhythm? I might need to take him to the park or something."

"I'm sure he'll calm down," Oliver called back. "But it really is up to you."

Partly from guilt, partly because sometimes a late-night walk could be nice, especially if your head needed clearing, I hooked Spud up to his lead and took him out into the street, hoping he'd stop acting weird after he'd been able to run around for a bit.

He kept acting weird. He yanked the lead taut running to the end of the drive, then sat down. Then ran back. Then did it all over again, yapping as he went.

Still pyjamaed and weary, Oliver appeared on the front porch. "Is everything okay?"

I looked down at Spud. He didn't *seem* okay. He seemed agitated. And not just Daddy-Luc-used-me-as-an-emotional-support-animal agitated.

And while I was puzzling over that, Oliver asked, "Lucien, what's happened to the car?"

I looked at the car. Or rather, I looked at Spud, who was sitting where the car should have been, his tail hammering on the floor as if to say, *Why are you humans so dense*. And I was suddenly, horribly certain that I knew exactly what he'd been trying to tell us.

"Fuck the car," I said. "Where's *Jaz*?"

CHAPTER 38

PERHAPS IT WAS JUST A defence mechanism, but Oliver slid right back into rational-and-calm-in-a-crisis mode. And that was a relief on so many levels, not just because it was always a relief when Oliver was rational and calm in a crisis but also because it was so typically *him* that it meant he was back to being Oliver. *My* Oliver, the Oliver I knew and loved, instead of the weird authoritarian stranger who'd been paying random unscheduled visits for the past six weeks.

"I'll check her room," he said calm-in-a-crisisly.

"Won't that be a bit pointless?"

Oliver shrugged. "Yes and no. I agree she's probably gone, but we'd look like fools if we ran into the night looking for our missing foster daughter and it turned out she was upstairs asleep and the car had been stolen quite independently."

"That seems pretty unlikely."

"I'm trying to avoid jumping to conclusions. Besides, even if she did abscond with our motor vehicle, we'll learn something from what she left behind."

If Jaz had left anything behind, it was probably a note saying "seeya suckers, p.s. Luc you were a shit dad," but that aside, Oliver was right.

We trooped upstairs, and he rapped smartly on Jaz's door.

"Jaz," he called out. "We're concerned that you might be missing, so unless you tell us not to, we're going to come into your room."

Silence.

"Jaz," he repeated. "I'm sorry if we're waking you, but we're coming in now."

It had been nice and polite, and also completely unnecessary. The room was empty.

No. Not empty. The *bed* was empty and—I noticed—made, but everything else was still there. Her laptop, her clothes, the guitar my mum had stolen from Brian May.

"We can at least assume she intends to come back," Oliver murmured. "That or she planned extremely badly."

I still didn't know Jaz anywhere near as well as I wanted to or thought I should, but she didn't seem the sort to plan a runaway badly. I mean, hell, she'd made the bed before leaving. "That's good?" I ventured.

"Relatively. Still, we'll need to contact the police."

And just like that we were back in the stop-being-your-dad space. "Fuck me, Oliver, she's a kid. Do you really think getting her arrested for grand theft auto is the best thing for her?"

Oliver's expression was that very specific hurt-but-acknowledge-I-deserve-it face that I was way more used to doing myself when he, say, suggested I could sometimes be unreliable, flaky, or lacking in motivation. "I didn't mean about the car, although I understand why you wouldn't give me the benefit of the doubt. I meant about her."

"About her?" I asked, feeling slower on the uptake than I would have liked.

"She's a missing child. She almost certainly wasn't abducted, but it's the small hours of the morning, she's in a car she might not know how to drive, and she's fourteen. I don't want to be alarmist, but literally anything could happen."

I tried my best not to imagine quite how long a list *anything* covered. My best didn't do great. "Isn't there, like, a twenty-four-hour thing with reporting people missing?"

"That's a myth," Oliver told me, and it was weirdly comforting being back to a world where Oliver told me things were myths instead of one where we had gut-splaying arguments about our values, assumptions, and emotions. "For any missing person but *especially* a child, the first twenty-four hours are the most important. A rule that said you had to wait twenty-four hours would, a lot of the time, be equivalent to a rule saying you had to wait until the person was dead."

Fuuuuuck. "Thanks for that."

"Which is why we're not going to wait twenty-four hours. Or any hours. I suggest you call Jaz. She's more likely to pick up if it isn't me. Then, if that doesn't work, we'll go to the authorities."

"But what about"—I shuddered—"like the whole grand theft auto thing?"

"Twocking," Oliver replied.

I wasn't in the mood for jokes. And that sounded a whole lot like a joke. "What the hell are you on about?"

"Taking without owner's consent. Or just taking without consent, or simply twocking. If the car is damaged, it could be aggravated twocking."

If our kid hadn't been missing, I'd have had something to say about how weird it was that we gave crimes such cutesy names in this country. But time was of the essence, so I pulled out my phone and tried calling Jaz.

And I heard a ringing.

From the dining table. Where Oliver had left her phone after he confiscated it.

"Fuck."

I really needed Oliver to be calm right then, and he was.

Perturbed, but calm. "Then I suppose," he said, "we try the police and cross the twocking bridge when we come to it."

Only we didn't, because his phone rang before we got the chance.

"This is probably mixed news," he said, answering it. Then there was a "Yes" and then a "Was there by any chance a teenage girl with the car?" followed by a long silence and then "Her name is Jasmine Johnson, she has a right to the presence of an appropriate adult; my partner and I are her legal guardians."

"Let me guess," I said, once he'd hung up. "Twocking."

Oliver nodded gravely. "Possibly aggravated twocking."

"Fuck."

He went back to his phone. "I'll get a taxi. We need to be in Dagenham."

Just-long-enough-to-change-out-of-pyjamas later, the taxi arrived. And, barely twenty minutes after that, we were getting out in front of a squat brick building that looked so much like the first thing you'd imagine when you heard the phrase "a police station in Dagenham" that I was briefly worried the driver had dropped us off there from sheer power of suggestion. Fortunately, it turned out some places are exactly what they look like. We hurried inside, and behind the desk, we found a duty officer whose boredom and tiredness were fighting for control of his face, with no clear winner.

"I'm Oliver Blackwood," said Oliver. "I'm here for my car, and to speak with Jasmine Johnson."

The duty officer spoke into an intercom. "Blackwood, here for the twocker."

"Alleged twocker," Oliver corrected. Then he followed up with, "I'll need a room where we can speak privately."

That seemed like a stretch to me, and it must have seemed like a stretch to the officer, too, because he gave Oliver a shifty look. "Not sure we can do that."

"You have a legal obligation to," Oliver told him. Because of course he did. Oliver wouldn't have brought it up otherwise.

"Says who?"

"Your code of practice under the Police and Criminal Evidence Act 1984," replied Oliver smoothly.

I'd seen this a few times now, and it never stopped feeling like magic. There was just something about a well-dressed man confidently citing legislation that made people in general and the police in particular get very compliant, very quickly.

Not long after, we were sitting in a spare interview room, completely unsupervised, with Jaz. And this time she wasn't even in handcuffs. Although she *was* glaring at us both like she actively resented our being in the same room, building, city, country, or planet as her.

"Have they explained your rights?" Oliver asked.

Jaz shrugged.

"Jaz"—I still wasn't wild about Oliver doing his I'm-being-calm-and-in-control tone with Jaz, but at least he'd stopped calling her Jasmine—"I know we've had an argument, and I do apologise for my part in it, but right now, it's very important that you listen to me."

She shrugged again.

"Have they tried to photograph or fingerprint you?"

There was just the tiniest shake of her head.

"Good. They can't without my or Lucien's permission, and we won't give it to them. They're also not allowed to take hair or saliva samples."

Jaz said nothing, and she was still looking at Oliver like she hated him, but I could tell when she was paying attention, and this was one of those whens.

"What have you told them?"

She shrugged.

"Nothing?"

A head-twitch that could have been a nod.

"Good," said Oliver again. "At some point, there is going to be an interview. I am going to accompany you." He took a deep breath and got very, very rigid. Then he shot a meaningful glance at a security camera. "Shall I tell you what I remember happening this evening?"

At last, Jaz's ice-girl facade cracked. "Go on then, this ought to be good."

"We had a fight," he said, his voice soft and cool and level. "It became very heated."

"Oliver," I half whispered, "I don't think this is helping."

Jaz was half grinning. "No no, this is fantastic. Come on, Oliver, tell me how inappropriate I was."

"I lost my temper," Oliver continued. "And I told you to get out of my house. I think, although of course it's hard to remember these things exactly, that I said something like you could take the car and go for all I cared. I didn't mean it literally, of course, but you *clearly*"—he gave Jaz his most no-seriously-you-have-to-fucking-trust-me look—"didn't realise that, which means you *sincerely believed that you had my permission to take the vehicle*."

Jaz nodded. She might not have been Oliver's biggest fan, but she was sharp. "Yeah. Sounds about right."

I had to admit, this did not seem like a fantastic idea. I mean, I knew twocking was bad, but this felt like it was just moving the bad around. Like there was crummy parenting and then there was telling a teenage girl to get in a car in the middle of the night and drive away with it. My one faint consolation was that Oliver probably knew what he was doing.

Fuck, I hoped he knew what he was doing.

When they came to collect Jaz for her interview, she was only allowed to take one adult with her. And obviously that adult was Oliver. Which meant I was left filling in paperwork and worrying while Oliver and Jaz tried to pass off a case of aggravated twocking as a simple misunderstanding.

Eventually, when I was about halfway through the checklist of "ways this could go horribly wrong" that my brain had handed me without being asked, Oliver and Jaz came out into the reception area. There were a couple of officers with them, and they shared a few words with Oliver that I didn't catch. And then Jaz was getting her stuff back, such as it was, and a few moments after that we were being ushered out the door by a cluster of Dagenhamian cops who clearly regretted having ever met any of us.

Our car had been brought around from the lot they'd been storing it in, and it looked *mostly* fine. One taillight was out, but otherwise it seemed drivable. So we drove it.

Well, Oliver drove it. And we stayed pretty silent until we were out of Dagenham, because it felt really luck-pushy-fate-tempty to say, *Hey, good job perverting the course of justice* right in front of a police station.

"Did it go all right?" I asked.

Oliver seemed to be giving Jaz room to answer first, but when she didn't, he stepped in. "They concluded that the case wasn't worth the Crown's time to pursue. Especially because we both maintained that Jaz thought I'd given her permission to take the vehicle." His lips twitched. "Twocking cannot exist if there is reasonable expectation of consent."

"Yeah but..." I rubbed my eyes because I'd had barely any sleep and what I did get was on a sofa. "Would it have been simpler to just tell them we didn't want to press charges or whatever?"

"On an American television show, yes. In real life in Britain, no."

I groaned. "This is going to be one of those 'That thing isn't a thing' things, isn't it?"

"Yes. I'm sorry to inform you that that thing is, indeed, not a thing. Private citizens do not press criminal charges in this country. The Crown does. Technically speaking, had Jaz stolen our car, the crime wouldn't have been against us; it would have been against the king."

"Hang on," I protested, "it's a car, not a swan."

"It's the king's law."

"But it's our car."

"We'll make a republican of you yet, Lucien."

"Also," Jaz added, only slightly sarcastically, "I didn't steal it. I took it reasonably, believing myself to have consent."

"Oi," I said, parentally. "Don't..."

"Don't what?" asked Jaz.

"I'm not sure. But don't do it."

It was dark and I was facing the wrong way, but I could feel Jaz rolling her eyes at me. "Oh, I feel so secure and reformed now you've set these firm boundaries for me."

And Oliver, the fucking traitor, laughed.

"Look." It was rare for me to be the adult in the room, even if the room was an average-size car, but here I was. "If you can both come down from the criminal high you're on, isn't this going to kind of fuck up the whole fostering situation? It can't reflect well on us that we apparently encouraged our kid to drive off in our car in the middle of the night."

"It's certainly nonideal," admitted Oliver.

My heart had taken something of a battering over the past couple of the days. So it tried to pound, failed, and just kind of flurped sadly. "How nonideal, nonideal? Like, 'You've been bad parents, don't do it again' nonideal or 'We no longer trust you with children or vehicles' nonideal?"

"Honestly, it could be either."

In the back seat, Jaz let out a single, explosive "Hah." Then, when I pivoted to look at her, she said, "I fucking *knew it*. This is just you trying to get rid of me."

I saw Oliver's hands tense on the steering wheel. "Jaz," he said. "I am truly sorry for saying that we would send you away if your behaviour didn't change. But"—I could hear him searching for a less Olivery way to express himself, but in the end, he must have decided that Olivery was best, as long as it was the right *sort* of Olivery—"you're an intelligent young woman, and you know the system better than Lucien or I do. Do you really think if I wanted to get rid of you, I'd need to be...economical with the truth to a police officer to do it?"

As unwilling as Jaz was to accept that either of us could be right about anything, she couldn't quite pretend that Oliver was wrong on that one.

"I say this," he went on, "purely for information, and without in any way prejudging how you choose to feel about it. You were at serious risk of being charged with a crime. A petty crime, but it would have given you a record, put your biometrics into the system, and—while community service was more likely—could even have landed you in a young offender institution. My first priority was to protect you from that. If, as a result, Lucien and I are deemed inadequate parents and you're sent to another family, that is..." He was looking for words so, so carefully. "That isn't what I want, but it's better than the alternative."

Jaz folded her arms and slumped back in the seat with intense sure-whatever energy. And I did my best not to flip the fuck out.

Because as much as I loved Oliver's analytic streak, all my instincts said no, the version where we lost Jaz would be worse than any other version. Even if—and it was the *even if* that put me and my instincts into a kind of uncomfortable conflict. Because *even if it was worse for her* was clearly a selfish thing to think, but also I couldn't stop thinking it and also it seemed selfish to *not* think it as well.

It occurred to me that this was a very tiny, very distant echo of what Jaz's mum must have been feeling basically every day, for years. And it fucking sucked. *If you love somebody, set them free* was incredibly easy to say, but as words to live by, they were horrible.

Except that was the thing about Oliver. He didn't pick his values by what was easy, or by what sounded good on a motivational poster. He actually lived them. Whatever the consequences.

Oh shit. Consequences.

"Hang on," I said to him. "Isn't this going to be incredibly bad for you? You know, with your job and everything."

I shouldn't have been surprised that, while the thought had hit me like a custard pie in the face, Oliver had followed it through to its logical conclusion long before he'd opened his mouth at the police station. "Being officially branded a bad parent doesn't matter to the bar one way or another. And, as for any…misstatements I may have made to the Dagenham Constabulary, that's not wonderful, but"—he shot me a sideways keeping-his-eyes-on-the-road look—"you can't really believe this is the worst thing anybody has ever done and still practised law?"

"So everything will be fine?" I asked, in my most hopeful voice.

"Almost certainly."

The *almost* was doing a lot of heavy lifting there. It might not have meant much to Jaz, but I knew what Oliver's career meant to him, and being *almost* certain he wouldn't fuck it all up wasn't a position he'd put himself in lightly. And on top of that, the one thing I knew he cared about more than his career—apart from, like, me—was his principles, and I was pretty sure they at least discouraged lying to law enforcement. But when it mattered, when the choice had been Jaz's future or Oliver's ethics, he'd chosen Jaz's future.

It wasn't what Atticus Finch would have done, and I was really, really glad about that.

I gave Oliver a long, slightly soppy look. And then I looked past him and out of the window and into the night, and I noticed we were taking kind of a funny route. The trip from Havering to Dagenham was less than twenty minutes, but Oliver seemed to be building in a whole lot of meandering time.

"Jaz," he began, as we turned into an obvious-if-you-were-looking-for-it detour. "Where were you going tonight?"

She didn't answer. She didn't answer for a really long time. And Oliver just let her not answer until eventually it was like not answering got too much for her and she said, "Home."

"To your mother's?" Oliver clarified.

Jaz made a vaguely affirmative grunt.

For a while Oliver let that hang. Then, "But you didn't ask the police to call her? You had a right to."

He was playing this cagey, but I knew from experience that Jaz had a healthy mistrust of authority figures—and an unhealthy mistrust of everybody else, which made trying to get information out of her risky. "She's got a lot on her plate," she muttered.

"A lot in what way?" asked Oliver.

And once again there was silence, and once again Jaz finally broke the silence with half an answer. "She has bad days."

Oliver just echoed her. "Bad days?"

"Got nobody to look after her. Not now."

"And who..." I tried very carefully, hoping I wasn't about to crack something fragile, "who used to look after her?"

"Me," said Jaz, matter-of-factly. "My nan until a few years ago, but it got worse after she went."

I did the maths in my head. Obviously *a few* wasn't a specific number, but it was usually more than two. Which tallied with what we'd been told in the pre-fostering briefings. But the problem with briefings was that they were clean and impersonal. Even when they had details, they were about times and dates and exactly when a particular woman had tried to kill herself. They weren't about what it all looked like from the viewpoint of her then-twelve-year-old daughter.

Oliver kept driving. He was taking us in circles now and seemed to be sticking to quiet streets.

"She didn't want me to call the ambulance," Jaz continued, after another, longer silence. "When I found her. Said they'd take me away."

"You did the right thing," Oliver replied exactly the right amount of immediately. No hesitation, but not so fast it sounded rushed or like he was protesting too much. And that's how it was with him. He was so fucking rigid and ethical and forthright that when he said you'd done the right thing, you knew for an absolute fact that he meant it.

Even Jaz knew. "Still took me away, though, didn't they?"

I froze in the front seat, knowing I needed to say something like *Well, at least she's not dead.* Only much, much less crap. Except I didn't know how and I was too scared to try.

But one of the things that made me and Oliver work, and keep working, was that his too-scared-to-try and my too-scared-to-try were in very different places. "They did. Which doesn't change the fact that you probably saved her life."

When we got home, Jaz went straight to Spud's pen, picked him up, and took him to her room. And, while it probably wasn't best dog practice or best parent practice, I didn't say anything, and neither did Oliver. We just flopped straight into bed. Well, I flopped straight into bed. Oliver, even post-crisis, took a moment to put his pyjamas back on.

"Fuck," I said, rolling into his arms. "Fuck."

"It's okay." He drew me closer. "Everything's going to be okay."

I breathed in the scent of fabric softener and Oliver. "You were, like, so cool today."

"If you recall, I was deeply uncool for most of it."

"I'm shallow, though. I get my head turned easily."

"Well, as long as it keeps turning towards me."

"Always," I said embarrassingly. "Seriously, though, I don't know what I'd have done without you."

"Without me, Jasmine—Jaz—wouldn't have run off in the first place."

"Maybe. Maybe not. I'm getting the impression we both have our distinct ways of fucking up parenting."

I heard Oliver swallow hard in the dark. "I don't want to be like my father."

"You're not. David Blackwood wouldn't have done anything you did tonight."

"No," Oliver agreed. "He wouldn't." He sighed, his fingers drifting lazily down my spine. "I keep wanting to find something… good…positive…meaningful in the way I was raised. To think that maybe it taught me discipline or built character or, in some unhelpfully nebulous way, made me the man I am today. But I think—" He broke off, self-consciously. "I'm sorry, I should probably be saving this for my therapist."

What I wanted to say was *You can tell me anything and I'll never judge you or let you down or reject you because I love you more than anything in the world*. But I'm an emotionally cowardly arsehole, so what I said was, "Call it a dress rehearsal."

And, hearing what I really meant, Oliver kissed me deeply for a long, long moment that became long, long moments. Finally, we broke apart, a little breathless, staring at each other through the grey light of what was now definitely Sunday morning.

"I'm going to do better, Lucien," Oliver whispered.

If anyone else had said that to me—and many people had, Miles and my dad included—I'd have dismissed it as bullshit. But this was Oliver. Perfect-imperfect Oliver Blackwood, my boyfriend-for-life, the best person I knew. Who always sorted the recycling and kept his socks in ordered pairs. Who saw the good in me I could never see in myself.

Which meant I'd always see the good in him back.

CHAPTER 39

SUNDAY—OR TECHNICALLY THE REST of Sunday—was quiet. Not totally the *good* kind of quiet. Jaz spent literally the whole day in her room, but if we were judging success on a spectrum from "stays in her room" to "steals the car and drives to Dagenham," then things were definitely moving in the right direction.

Downstairs, the wreckage of the previous night's dinner lay congealing in the good crockery, and Oliver set about diligently collecting it all up, scraping what could be scraped into the bin, and then loading the rest into the dishwasher. I followed him, diligently picking up the occasional fork and trying not to look or feel too utterly useless. Then I realised I could do something *genuinely* non-useless and went upstairs, turned the water supply to the toilet off to stop it leaking all over the floor, and arranged for an emergency plumber.

Around noon I got a text from Bridge that read IS JAZ OKYA?

I texted back Long story, and my phone rang three milliseconds later.

"It's Bridge," I yelled through to Oliver. "I might take it upstairs."

Oliver made "Of course" noises from where he was still slightly distractedly cleaning, and I vanished into the bedroom to explain the previous night's events to the woman who, while she wasn't my token straight friend anymore because I'd picked up loads of those when I got with Oliver, was definitely still my *best* friend.

"Oh *Luc*," she sympathy-wailed when I was done. "That's so *sad*."

Sad was certainly one way to put it. "I think she's okay now. Well, okay-ish. She's in her room."

"I meant more it was sad in general. Imagine being so desperate to see your mum that you had to steal a car."

I didn't have to imagine very hard because I'd seen it play out in front of me, but I knew what she meant. As somebody whose mum had only been downgraded to second-most important person in his life relatively recently, the thought of being forcibly separated from her, especially at such a young age, was horrifying. "Yeah," I agreed. "Yeah, it's kinda"—I made a noise that I hoped encompassed the enormity of the concept—"when you think about it."

"I *know*," replied Bridge, who used *I know* as a sort of all-purpose expression of support.

"So, how're you holding up?" I asked her. Because while the Jaz thing had been intense, it hadn't been the only intense thing that had happened yesterday evening, and the first intense thing had been quite Bridge-centred.

In all the years I'd known her, it had never taken more than a "How're you holding up?" for Bridge to tell me with unflinching honesty exactly how she was feeling. And today was no exception. "Oh, Luuuc." Bridge was the only person I knew who could produce audible emojis. "I feel *terrible*. I ruined everything."

"I really don't think you did."

"I'm the one who made a scene. I should never have even *started* showing baby pictures, and I *certainly* shouldn't have jumped all over poor James like that."

"Poor James," I reminded her, "is a grown-arse man who can take care of himself and who has been winding us all up for months.

Like there's 'proud of your kid' and there's 'won't shut up about your kid' and then there's whatever James was, which is worse."

"But it was coming from a place of *hurt*." Bridge sounded like she was about to burst into tears for our mutual very annoying friend. "I'd never have been upset with him if I'd realised he was coming from a place of *hurt*."

That was Bridge all over. But Bridge being Bridge all over and me being me all over was kind of what made our relationship work. "Take it from somebody with a lifetime of firsthand experience," I told her, "you can be coming from a place of hurt and still be acting like a dickhead."

"I should apologise to him," declared Bridge, whose belief in the power of apologies was as unshakeable as it was unfounded.

"You probably should," I said. "But also remember, he should probably apologise to you too. Honestly, we should all probably apologise to each other. I don't think any of us exactly came out of that looking good."

Bridge went quiet for a moment. And then came back with a plaintive, "Oh, why does it have to be so *hard*?"

"I think it's part of being an adult?" I told her. "If it's any help, I'm not happy about it either."

From the other end of the phone, I heard the sounds of movement. The kind of sounds of movement I heard when Bridge was about to set off at no notice to do something noble and foolish.

"Bridge," I asked, hesitantly, "are you putting your shoes on?"

"I'm going to see James. Then I'm taking James to see Jennifer."

"Are you one hundred percent certain that's a good idea?"

"Yes."

That had been a silly question. "Okay, but are you sure the fact you're one hundred percent certain it's a good idea actually makes it a good idea?"

"Well, I don't see how it can make things worse."

The beautiful thing about Bridge was that she genuinely didn't. And I suppose I didn't see how it could make things worse either. Only that didn't stop me from having the clagging, all-pervading feeling that it definitely could anyway. Except that was the difference between me and Bridge. Well, that along with gender, sexual orientation, taste in Christmas movies, and whether or not Tom could stand going out with us. She really, truly believed, deep down, that people were good and the world was good with them.

"Tom," I heard her calling in a muffled, hand-over-the-microphone kind of voice, "I'm going to see James." Tom's reply was too distant to hear, so I just got, "That's what Luc said." Then, "No, he isn't. And I'm going to see Jennifer afterwards."

"You know," I said. "You don't have to do this alone. I can come with you if you want."

I thought I heard Bridge making *hang on* noises in the background. "You think you should ditch Oliver to come running around our friends' houses with me the day after you threw the world's worst dinner party and your foster daughter slipped lamb into his vegan main course, trashed your bathroom, and stole your car, forcing him to compromise his professional ethics to save her from a criminal record?"

I thought about that for the half a second it took me to realise how right she was. "Okay yeah, good point." Then I said, "But, fuck, it feels weird not to be coming with you."

Bridge sighed wistfully down the phone. "I think we might have to accept that our days of being there every time something interesting happens to one of our friends are behind us."

That sucked. "That sucks."

"In a way." I heard the click of Bridge's door opening. "But it's not all bad. Yes, you probably won't be here when Autumn says her first word, and I won't be with you when Jaz gets her GCSE results—"

"Honestly," I said, "*we* probably won't be with Jaz when she gets her GCSE results. It seems really unlikely that we'll be able to keep her after the whole car-stealing thing."

This bounced off Bridge's bulletproof optimism. "The fostering people will understand. Very few people are evil, Luc."

"I don't think it's about being evil," I told her. "I think it's more about being, like, busy and part of a big bureaucratic system?"

"My point *is*"—I heard another door open, a car door this time—"even if you're not here to share every moment with me and Tom and Autumn and I'm not there to share every moment with you and Oliver and Jaz, we're still part of each other's lives. And our lives are *bigger* now than they were when we were in our twenties because we're older and we have more important jobs or larger families or just *other friends* we've met over the years." I heard a seat belt and an engine. "Hang on, I'm putting you on speaker."

I hung on.

"And I don't just mean," Bridge went on, "because some of us have got children. Brian and Amanda have more going on than they did ten years ago too. So do Priya and Theresa and Andi. You pick stuff up as you go, and if you don't put any of it down, you just get...stuffed. I suppose."

The way she put it, it almost sounded comforting. "I suppose," I echoed, noncommittally. Then I added, "Anyway, I should let you go. Being on hands-free is almost as dangerous as talking on a mobile normally."

Bridge laughed. "Oliver really did change you, didn't he?"

I couldn't do *little bit* fingers down the phone, so I just said, "Yeah. Yeah he did," and left it at that. Then, once Bridge had safely hung up—only, I was sure, to immediately call somebody else because Oliver and I were probably the only people in the world who took the no-hands-free-while-driving thing seriously—I schlumped downstairs to see how Oliver was doing in the kitchen.

And also to see what had happened to that bloody plumber.

Which meant Sunday ended very much as it had begun, apart from the slight inconvenience of an emergency tradesman charging us way too much to whack a bit of sealant on a cracked toilet and tell us we should arrange to get a new one installed sooner rather than later. By the evening, Oliver and I had curled up downstairs in the front room in our usual me-on-Netflix-him-on-laptop configuration. I'd heard no more from Bridge, at least not directly, but Are the Straights Okay (Dinner Party Remix) had been renamed Dinner Party Survivors' Club, which I thought was a good compromise between whimsical, not sweeping things under the rug, and also not overly reminding everybody of a deeply upsetting argument about our various friendship circles' overlapping traumas, marginalisations, and identities.

"I think things'll shake out," I told Oliver idly between episodes of *Perfect Match*.

Oliver glanced up from his laptop. "I very much doubt it. I have no idea what Francesca sees in Damian, and he seems somewhat threatened by her bisexuality."

"No," I said. "I mean, yes. Clearly that. But I was talking about our actual friends we know in real life."

He got that *I'm teasing and you haven't noticed* smile. "Ah. Then yes. I'm sure it will shake out. It wasn't the first time any of those people have fought with each other, and it won't be the last either."

"It feels like the first time we all fought each other *at once*."

Putting his laptop aside, Oliver replaced it with me. And it was never going to be particularly dignified for me to sit in my boyfriend's lap, but I was never stopping. "I think, in this regard, found families can be much like any other kind of family. Sometimes special occasions end in massive rows."

"Wow, that's going to be fun for the next forty years."

"I said *sometimes*. Not all the time. And, while I'm aware this is deeply saccharine, what matters isn't whether we fight; it's whether we can move past those fights with love and compassion."

"God, you're right," I said. "That *does* sound saccharine."

"The truth sometimes does." Oliver gave me a rueful look. "It's one of the nicer things about reality."

CHAPTER 40

IM SOOOOO SORRY EVRYONE, BRIDGE messaged the following morning as I was logging into my Zoom meeting. Which I took as a sign that her in-person conversations with Peter and Jennifer and the James Royce-Royces had gone non-disastrously.

To which Priya replied I can't believe the one I skipped was the one where things finally got interesting.

> THEY WERNE T INTERESTING THEY WERE VERY URTFUHL WHICH IS WHY IM SO SORRY

I'm sorry too. That was James Royce-Royce.

So am I. That was James Royce-Royce.

Alex popped into view with a cheery, "Hullo, Luc! Marvellous technology this, isn't it?"

We'd been using it for literal years at this point. And he made the observation at least once a week. "Yeah," I said, "amazing."

Stop being mature, Priya was saying on my phone. I want fucking blood. Polyamorous childfree lesbians repre-fucking-sent.

We're not childfree. That was Andi. We have stepkids.

> Adult children don't count.

They fucking do. That was Theresa.

"Okay," I said to Alex, looking away from what I *really hoped* wouldn't be another your-life-choices-are-bad-and-you-should-feel-bad conversation. "What cheese is made backwards?"

"Edam," he replied at once.

"Oh, you've heard that one?"

Alex looked blank. "No, just good at word puzzles. Have you got a joke for me?"

The joke, as always, was on me. "Not today, I'm afraid."

Barbara Clench, who had popped up two seconds earlier, wasted no time in giving me a disapproving look. "Good, we're meant to be having a meeting, and don't think I can't tell when you're stalling."

"This isn't stalling," I told her, "this is just regular wasting time. It'll become stalling when the rest of the team get here."

Still a bit concerned where things stood after Saturday, I glanced down and sent a Yeah I'm sorry too message to the chat followed by a No more dinner parties for a while maybe?

"I can see that you're texting, Luc," Barbara Clench told me. "You aren't being subtle about it."

"I would *never*," I protested.

"Your phone is plainly visible on camera."

Shit, this was why I needed one of those background things that made everything blurry.

Conversation in Dinner Party Survivors' Club continued to be pretty amicable, with Jennifer sending Peter and I are also sorry, and Brian following up with Amanda and I realise we might have said some things that didn't come across how we meant them to. Which, from what I knew of the two of them, was about as close to an apology as they were going to get. And you know what, that was fine. I was past the age where I could be arsed to police the way other people said sorry for stuff.

Besides, Dr. Fairclough had just logged in, which meant I should probably actually start doing my job.

Especially because her greeting—as was pretty typical for Dr. Fairclough's greetings—went, "I've budgeted seventeen minutes from my afternoon for this, and if we go over, I'll be late with my samples."

I didn't want to know what they were samples *of*. "Okay," I began. And I was suddenly beginning to wish I *had* been stalling because this was going to be a horrible conversation and having a good bit of stall set up in advance would probably really help me. But I'd never been one for planning in advance, so I just had to launch into it. "I don't want to do the good-news-and-bad-news thing—"

"Then don't?" suggested Barbara Clench, with the hostile playfulness that had become our relationship.

"But I've got good news and bad news," I finished.

"What kind of news?" asked Rhys Jones Bowen, who'd just appeared that second. "Sorry I'm late, got my dongle trapped in the hoover."

Alex looked pained. "I say, how did you manage that?"

"Oh, you know, I was just cleaning up around the back of the old workstation and wouldn't you know it, my dongle popped out, and before I could put it back in, it had shot up the hoover like a mouse up a skirting board."

"You mean your Wi-Fi dongle?" I clarified, "which is why you couldn't connect until now?"

Rhys Jones Bowen looked confused. "Well, what else would I mean?"

"Honestly," replied Alex, "I thought you were talking about your old chap."

"No." Few people could give a drawn-out *no* like Rhys Jones Bowen. "My old chap wouldn't fit."

"Doesn't do to brag, Rhys," Alex chided him.

And once again, Rhys Jones Bowen looked confused. "I'm not bragging. Just saying my old chap wouldn't fit up a hoover. He's not an especially large man, although he's put on a bit of weight since he retired, but the nozzle isn't that wide."

"You might be thinking of *old man*," I told him.

To which Dr. Fairclough said, "Twelve minutes."

"Right, right." I tried to force myself back to professionalism. "So the bad news is that Saint's band didn't want anything to do with him, which means he isn't going to keep funding us and we'll probably lose our jobs."

"That does seem like *quite* bad news," Alex observed.

"So the good news," added Barbara Clench, "better be pretty spectacular."

"I know," I said, a little meekly. "And if it's any consolation, I really did try to keep Saint on board. I took my foster kid on an impromptu tour of the country to keep Saint on board. Hell, I nearly got fucking *arrested* to keep Saint on board."

"Language, Luc," said Barbara Clench.

Alex, on the other hand, seemed less bothered by the swearing and more inclined to gee me up. "Still," he said, "chap does his best, that's to a chap's credit, eh what?"

"You tried," Rhys Jones Bowen agreed, "and that's the most important thing."

"The most important thing," said Dr. Fairclough, "is this country's declining population of dung beetles. But I do agree it was irrational to expect Luc to reverse that trend single-handed."

"Anyway," continued Alex, with the air of a sunflower about to get shafted by a snap frost, "things could be worse. Luc has good news for us, don't you?"

"Yes," I said, suddenly aware that the good news sounded way less good in the context of *You're probably all still redundant* than I'd hoped. "The good news is that my mum has agreed to use CRAPPstonbury to launch her comeback tour, so we should actually have a good final year. Plus, it's not *completely* impossible that we'll do well enough that we won't need Saint's money at all."

"Not completely impossible?" asked Rhys Jones Bowen.

"Not *likely*," I admitted. "But in a lot of ways, it's the best shot we've had since the earl died."

"Wait a minute," replied Alex, completely and utterly predictably, "when did the earl die?"

"Last year?" I reminded him. "You were at his funeral?"

Alex frowned. "I'm sure I'd have remembered something like that. Old Hilary's a friend of the family, you know. Although I hear his son's a *fearful* oik."

"Well," I said, "then the good news is you'll never have to deal with his fearful oik of a son again."

Something attached to Dr. Fairclough's computer, or possibly just to Dr. Fairclough, beeped. "Zero minutes," she said. "I'm deeply sorry that we were unable to preserve the Coleoptera Research and Protection Project for future generations, but I take some comfort that when the inevitable mass extinction event eradicates humanity, the Blattodea at least are likely to outlast us."

"I don't think that's *very* comforting," I pointed out.

"It probably is if you're one of the Blattodea," replied Barbara Clench.

"True," I conceded. "But the thing is, *I'm not.*"

Rhys Jones Bowen was looking contemplative. He usually looked at least a bit contemplative, probably as a result of being so infuriatingly secure in himself. Or having a beard. "Well," he said, "I can't say I'm not sad to see it go. But I *also* can't say it wasn't a laugh while it lasted."

Alex bowed his head solemnly. "Fare thee well, C.R.A.P.P. We shall not see thy like again."

"I mean, there's still about four months left until CRAPPstonbury," I pointed out.

"Fare thee well, C.R.A.P.P.," Alex corrected himself. "We shall carry on seeing thy like until around the middle of June, and *then* we shall not see thy like again."

Dr. Fairclough had, of course, already gone, which meant it was up to me and Barbara to officially call things to a close. And it felt weirdly final, even though it strictly wasn't. Even though we'd be back in the office the next day, and the day after, and the day after that.

But it was getting really close to being over. And I wasn't sure how I felt about that.

Not that I had much time to feel anything. Because I had a social worker's visit to prepare for.

"You said *what*?" asked Esther at the emergency post-letting-your-foster-daughter-get-arrested meeting.

"Somewhat rashly," replied Oliver, "and to my deep regret, I said something approximately along the lines of 'Take the car and go for all I care.' It was foolish and I should have realised that at her age, Jasmine would take me literally. But unfortunately, I had lost my temper and wasn't thinking clearly."

Esther flipped her notebook shut and frowned. "You know a more cynical woman might point out that it's a bit of a coincidence how you said almost *exactly* the minimum amount you could have said for Jaz not to be guilty of twocking but also for you not to be guilty of child endangerment."

One of Oliver's eyebrows curved into an arch. An arch presumably aimed at the nonexistent more cynical woman. "Now you mention it, that is quite the happy accident, isn't it?"

"Still"—Esther gave both of us a don't-fuck-it-up look that

RuPaul would have been proud of, or possibly would have failed to recognise the value of and kicked off the show in episode three—"I hope we're agreed that you're never going to say anything like that ever again."

Oliver gave a slightly exaggerated headshake. "Absolutely not. I have learned my lesson and will be far more careful with my language in future."

"Well then." Esther put her notebook in her bag. "I think that's everything."

I was so relieved that we'd got away with the whole twocking incident that when Oliver said, "Actually, there is one more thing," I thought I was having an auditory hallucination.

And from her expression, I got the impression Esther was feeling similarly. "Why do I get the feeling you're about to push your luck?"

Oliver was sitting bolt upright with the kind of posture you saw in office diagrams about how to sit with good posture. "I think now is an appropriate time to talk about Jasmine visiting her mother."

From the look on Esther's face, she did *not* think now was an appropriate time. "You think directly after she stole—"

"Took with reasonable expectation of consent."

I'd never seen somebody put quite as much grudging into an expression of grudging respect as Esther did. "—after she took your car with a reasonable expectation of consent is a good time to talk about changing the terms of her placement? Because in my professional opinion, this is guilt talking."

In my have-been-with-him-for-five-years experience, she was exactly half right. Oliver clearly did feel incredibly guilty about how things had gone with Jaz, and not just the whole car-stealing thing. But he would also never, ever, ever suggest a course of action he didn't sincerely believe in.

"Okay," I said, "but *I* didn't give her a reasonable expectation that we consented to her taking our car, so *I* don't feel guilty. And I think it'd be a good idea for her to see her mum too."

"Noted," said Esther, "but you *are* an inveterate people pleaser."

"She went to Dagenham last night," Oliver went on, "which is where her mother's flat is. Lucien tells me she was deeply upset when Ms. Johnson didn't attend their first meeting at the school."

"She was," I confirmed. "And you know that because you were there."

"I was there," agreed Esther. "Ms. Johnson wasn't. And, as you point out, Jasmine found that upsetting."

"From everything I've seen," Oliver continued, "her relationship with her mother is profoundly important to her. I think she'll benefit from being able to maintain it."

Esther didn't say, *Why does everybody think they're a fucking expert*, but she didn't need to. "Jasmine's mother," she said, "is highly resentful of the foster system and passes that resentment along to Jasmine when she's allowed contact with her. She has complex mental health needs which Jasmine is not emotionally equipped to deal with, and those needs, amongst other things, make her extremely unreliable, so on top of that she makes Jasmine feel abandoned when, like she did last time, she simply fails to appear."

"I mean," I said, "that sounds like my dad, only he doesn't have mental health as an excuse. He's just a prick."

Oliver, though, took a different tack. "Might I ask when contact was last tried?"

"When Jasmine was first put into care," replied Esther.

"So two years ago? That's a long time for a fourteen-year-old."

Esther narrowed her eyes at Oliver. "I'm beginning to think you're a *very* good lawyer."

"I do my best."

"If you think this will make things easier"—Esther's voice was a low tone of warning—"I'll tell you for free. It won't."

That made me shift uncomfortably in my seat, but Oliver just nodded his most I'm-completely-on-top-of-this nod. "I'm not concerned about making my life easier," he said. "I'm concerned about making Jaz's life better. I'm very aware that those are different propositions."

Sometimes, all I really wanted to do was point at Oliver and say, *Yeah, what he said*. This was definitely one of those times. Although in the end I went with an even cleaner, even simpler, "Same."

It was pretty clear that Esther still had Concerns. The kinds of Concerns where you could hear the capitalisation, but it was hard to say no to Oliver when he was in the mode where he said things like *I'm very aware that those are different propositions*.

And so she reluctantly agreed.

It felt good—really, really good—to be on the same page with Oliver again. I just hoped the page we were on didn't have *This is a gigantic fucking mistake* scrawled over it. But, even if it did, it was our page and our gigantic fucking mistake, and we'd figure it out together.

Getting Esther on board with letting Jaz see her mother more often had been tough, but in a lot of ways it wasn't the most important thing. The most important thing was making sure Jaz was on board with it.

After the meeting, I'd gently pointed out to Oliver that maybe we could have saved ourselves a lot of bother by asking Jaz first and then just dropping the whole thing if she hadn't been cool with the idea. But then he'd gently pointed out back that if Jaz had been in favour—and it seemed likely she would be—and then Esther had said it was impossible, it would have meant we'd got Jaz's hopes up for no reason and would probably have been another mark on her long list of "reasons never to trust those two arseholes again."

Okay. He didn't use that exact language.

But however he'd expressed it, we remained as joyously same-page dwelling as ever, and that evening, when Jaz got home from school and, with teenage predictability, slunk into the kitchen to grab herself two slices of bread, we were waiting for her.

"Jaz," said Oliver as casually as he could manage, which, honestly, wasn't very, where Jaz was concerned. "We've—there's something we've been meaning to talk to you about."

Jaz froze. She looked like she trusted Oliver about as much as the global community of beachgoers trusted sharks immediately after the first *Jaws* movie was released. "Is this about my hair?"

Now she mentioned it, her hair being half dyed, and *badly* half dyed at that, did make her look a bit like I'd put her head in the washing machine with a pair of my red silk boxers. "We can probably book you in at a salon," I told her. "Or if you'd rather do it yourself, one of us can help you."

Still wary, Jaz stood there eyeballing us with one hand lightly, and slightly self-consciously, resting on her head.

"But actually," said Oliver, "we wanted to talk about something else. We had a meeting with Esther today about...about what happened, and we were wondering..."

Jaz was getting increasingly tense. Not stealing-the-car-and-driving-to-Dagenham tense, but quite possibly running-out-the-room tense.

"We can't make any promises," he went on, "because unforeseen problems do arise. But if you would like, Esther has said we can try to arrange for you to meet more regularly with your mother."

We'd had Jaz too long to expect her to go all Little Orphan Annie, to leap in the air and be all, "Gee whiz, misters, *would I*?" During our discussion with Esther, we'd run a range of scenarios, and the one we got was close to our best case. Which was that she said, "Y'what?"

"We thought," I chimed in, because this needed to be a both-of-us thing, "that if you were okay with it, we'd start seeing if we could arrange for you to visit your mum more often."

She shrugged. "Whatever."

Yeah, that had also been part of our best-case scenario. "Right," I said. "Thing is, we do actually need a bit more than that. I *know* you're sick of everybody telling you how fucking *child-centred* they're being, but we aren't going to do this unless we're really sure it's what you want. And that means you're going to have to, um, tell us."

Jaz made a kind of shudder that suggested having a sincere opinion about anything Oliver or I suggested was unthinkable to her, unless that opinion was *It's shit and you're both shit.*

"Let's try it this way," said Oliver. "Lucien and I intend to reach out to Esther and your mother to start making arrangements first thing tomorrow morning. If you *don't* want us to, just say literally anything that isn't *whatever*."

Jaz glared at Oliver like she was hoping she could spontaneously turn into the Ark of the Covenant and melt his face off, Indiana Jones–style.

And then she said, "Whatever."

But when she said it, she smiled.

PART FOUR

SPRING/SUMMER

CHAPTER 41

WHEN ESTHER HAD SAID THAT arranging for Jaz to see her mother wouldn't make our lives easier, she wasn't kidding. She wasn't on the same street as kidding. She and kidding had met once at a party six years ago and then moved to separate continents.

It soon became clear Jaz's mother, Maisie Johnson, had the kind of depression that, well, that gets your kids taken away by social services.

The first visit we'd arranged, at Esther's suggestion, had been on relatively neutral ground close enough to Maisie's house that it wasn't an onerous distance for her to travel but not so close that we were concretely on her turf.

Eventually—and this had been a very Oliverian choice, now I think about it—we'd opted for a nearby park which, according to its website, had been opened in 1995 to give local residents a taste of the countryside. It had a tearoom and nature walks, and it wasn't a pub so didn't raise tricky questions of dog-and-child-appropriateness.

Just nailing down the details of the first meeting had taken over a month, which meant that whatever goodwill we—and especially Oliver—had earned for making the initial effort had evaporated in the interim. Which, on one level, we understood was to be expected when you were dealing with somebody for whom a month was still a sizable fraction of their conscious life, but on the other hand was a bit of a pisser.

As we got closer to the actual day, Jaz got increasingly agitated. I'd love to be able to say she got increasingly *excited*, but *agitated* is definitely the right word. She got antsy, snappish, and surly. Which made the atmosphere in the O'Donnell-Blackwood-Johnson household honestly kind of unfun.

Not that we were doing this for fun, of course. Which Oliver reminded me. Daily. He hadn't quite hard-pivoted away from being Mr. Boundaries and Examples, but he seemed to have taken the lesson about being On Jaz's Side to heart, which meant he was now On Her Side with the same unwavering intensity with which he was on the side of honesty, justice, veganism, and me.

Two days before our first scheduled meeting, there was a banging at the door. Oliver and I answered it to find Next Door's Kid, Next Door's Kid's Dad, and Next Door's Kid's Mum standing on our doorstep, looking irate. Irate even by the standards of Next Door's Kid's Mum and Next Door's Kid's Dad, which was very, very irate indeed.

"Jacqueline," said Oliver. "Richard."

"Oliver," said Next Door's Kid's Dad back. "Luke." I could always, always tell when people put a *ke* on the end. "Your guest—"

"Foster daughter," Oliver and I replied, simultaneously.

"Your foster daughter set a bloody *dog* on Colin."

My first instinct was *She would never*. My second instinct was *She might, actually*. My third instinct was *Good*.

Oliver looked down at Next Door's Kid. He was doing his serious face again, and for a heart-squashing, stomach-twisting moment, I thought we were right back where we'd been six weeks ago. "Tell me what happened, Colin," he said.

Next Door's Kid met Oliver's gaze with tears glistening artfully in his eyes. He looked like a Dickensian orphan about to meekly ask for a second bowl of gruel. "Mr. Blackwood," he began, lip all atremble, "I was in the park, feeding the ducks."

"What with?" asked Oliver.

Next Door's Kid looked momentarily confused, but only momentarily. "Bread."

I had nothing like the skill set necessary to work out whether he was telling the truth or not. It's not like he had a convenient bag of Hovis poking out of his pocket or crumbs all up his lapels. He *did* look wet, dirty, and extremely bloody around the knees, but that could have meant anything.

"You should be careful with that," said Oliver, playing it completely straight. "Bread isn't bad for ducks *per se*, but they benefit from a varied diet."

"Oh," said Next Door's Kid, who seemed a touch concerned that things were going off-script.

"They like sweetcorn."

This wasn't going in the direction that Next Door's Kid had been expecting, but he did his malicious best to get back on his bullshit. "I was feeding the ducks," he repeated, "just minding my own business, when the girl from next door pointed at me and was all, 'Get him, boy,' and the dog ran over and tried to bite me. And I was scared, so I tried to get away, so I fell in the lake."

For a moment, Oliver said nothing.

"Well?" demanded Next Door's Kid's Dad.

Oliver raised an eyebrow. "I'm rather flattered you think Spud is so well trained."

I honestly thought Next Door's Kid's Dad was going to have some kind of haemorrhage. "Oliver, this is serious."

Oliver nodded. Then he looked back down at Next Door's Kid and said, almost casually, "Do you know what I do for a living, Colin?"

"Banker?" offered Colin. I couldn't help assuming he'd wanted to say a different *-anker* word but remembered at the last minute that he was currently mask-on.

"I'm a lawyer. People lie to me a *lot*. I don't like it, but it's usually very easy to spot." He half smiled. "It's not that I have any special technique, you understand. It's simply that some things are just very, very obviously not true."

"Are you calling my son a liar?" demanded Next Door's Kid's Dad, still looking like his blood vessels were in for a bad time.

"Just making conversation." And now Oliver went from half smiling to full smiling. Full, it-was-so-lovely-of-you-I-shall-be-sure-to-write-a-thank-you-letter, nicely-brought-up-middle-class-boy smiling. "You see, the thing is, when people tell me these stories that are very, very obviously not true, I can never really blame them. People don't start out bad, after all. Sometimes they're victims of circumstance, or they've been let down by the system." He looked at Next Door's Kid's Parents, still smiling. "Or they just have bad parents. Thank you so much for bringing this to my attention, Richard, Jacqueline," he said, nodding. "You can rest assured I'll give it the attention it deserves."

Before they could say anything, he shut the door in their faces.

"Okay," I said, "I'm pretty sure that counts as using your powers for evil."

"I'm trying extremely hard," Oliver replied, "to avoid using either Jaz or Colin as playing pieces in petty games of status with our neighbours. But I *suspect* that in this context, the fastest way to end that particular game is to win it."

I gave him a supportive nod. "Also. Fuck them."

"And also that."

One of the bad habits I'd picked up during the dark days of my mid-twenties was leaving off counting my chickens until they'd not only hatched but also grown up and been carried off by foxes. And Oliver wasn't the only one trying to do better, so I let myself believe that this really was Team O'Donnell-Blackwood-Johnson getting back together at last. "You're hot when you're laying the middle-class smackdown."

Oliver's lips twitched. "You should see me in Waitrose."

"Oh really?" I pushed him back against the wall. "Are you like, 'These carrots aren't even heritage.'"

His breath was coming a little more quickly as he struggled to strike a balance between bantering and letting me blow him in our hall. "Very much so. The last time I was there, the free coffee they gave me didn't even have oat milk in it. I was livid."

There was a clunk as I whipped off his belt and a *zzzzp* as his zipper came down.

"Lucien." One of Oliver's hands curled in my hair, half tender, half commanding, just the way I liked. "Is this a good idea?"

I was already on my knees. "It's a great idea."

"But—"

"She's out with Spud. We've got at least ten minutes, and we know I can do this in five."

"Does that reflect well on you or poorly on me?"

"I think," I said, "it reflects the fact we're often quite busy and I really want to suck you off." I shot him a lovingly frustrated look. "Do you mind if I get on with it?"

"What if we get a delivery?"

"Then they can leave it with a friend or neighbour."

"I've just made our neighbours hate us."

I nipped at his still gym-honed thigh, well aware that, for some reason, raising prissy objections to getting off was a kind of Oliverian foreplay. "And, as you've pointed out, they're too repressed to admit it."

"Good point." There was a tremor of laughter alongside the desire in Oliver's voice. "Commence."

So I commenced. I commenced the house down.

And, by the time Jaz came home with Spud, both her foster parents were sitting innocently on the living room sofa, like they totally hadn't done it in the hallway.

"Just so you know," said Oliver when Jaz stuck her head through the door to let us know she was back, "I think Colin was trying to get you in trouble again."

Ever since Oliver had started working tirelessly to make something happen that Jaz really, really, really wanted to happen, she'd... been pretty much the same to him because at the end of the day she was still a teenager. "He's a prick."

"Not disputing. Just, if there was anything you wanted to tell us..."

There wasn't. She went straight to her room, taking Spud with her.

But she went calmly. And we let her go out of trust rather than fear.

We'd arranged to meet Maisie at noon on Saturday. Between them, Jaz's impatience and Oliver's punctuality outvoted my general lethargy, and we made it to the tearoom for quarter to twelve and settled ourselves into a nice window seat to wait.

The first fifteen minutes passed quickly, me and Oliver sipping our coffee while Jaz picked listlessly at a muffin and stared out the window.

The next fifteen minutes passed slower. Honestly, I didn't think any of us, even Jaz, had expected her mum to be there bang-on twelve, and so when the coffees ran out, we just ordered another two and carried on waiting.

After a half hour, I started surreptitiously checking the time. Oliver, having a sense of self-discipline, did better. But when it got to ten past one, he very gently pulled his phone out and said, "I'm just going to give Maisie a call to make sure everything is still going to plan."

"She'll be here," replied Jaz. She'd eaten hardly any of her muffin, but she'd worried the rest of it into crumbs between her fingers.

Without comment, Oliver slipped outside. And while we waited, I tried to lighten the mood with casual conversation.

"Perhaps she's stuck in traffic," I suggested.

Jaz glared at me. "You actually think that?"

Lying to children was bad. Telling children you thought their mothers had flaked on them was worse. "I think there's all kinds of reasons to be late."

"You mean like maybe she's tried to kill herself again."

I didn't want to touch that one with a barge pole. But I was probably going to have to. "I'm sure she hasn't," I said. I had no idea if that was true, but it seemed like the kind of thing Jaz might need to hear.

"Oh right. So she's just"—Jaz gave a surprisingly expressive shrug—"ditching me for the fun of it. Because she's a shit mum. Because she's a shit mum who got her kid taken away by the socials."

That was what Oliver would have called a false dichotomy. But *That's a false dichotomy* seemed like a fucking awful response, so I hesitated.

Fortunately, by that point, Oliver had come back in, which meant he could take over. "For what it's worth," he said, "I believe that your mother would be here if she could, but the reality of her situation is that she might not be able to. And that isn't a reflection on her or on you."

Unfortunately, Jaz wasn't in the mood to be reassured, and I couldn't exactly blame her. "What'd she say?" she asked.

Oliver was radiating calm in a way that Jaz still didn't quite trust. "It went straight to voicemail. I can try again in a little while if you like, and we can wait as long as you want, but there's a good chance your mother won't make it. Not today, at least."

Jaz just glared.

"If she doesn't turn up," Oliver went on, putting way more faith into that *if* than I'd have been able to, "we'll reschedule."

Jaz continued glaring.

She basically continued glaring for four straight hours, because we waited there, the three of us, until closing. All the way back she sat in silence and all Sunday she stayed in her room, not even letting Spud in, which I took as a really bad sign.

She was just as bad on Monday, and, on Tuesday, I was called into school for a meeting, because she'd been fighting again.

CHAPTER 42

OLIVER HAD FOLLOWED UP AFTER the first, failed meeting to reschedule and to quietly check that Maisie was at least immediately safe. The rescheduled meet-up had, unfortunately, been an almost complete repeat of the first, with an almost complete repeat of the fallout to go along with it. Jaz managed to avoid getting suspended, only because she managed to avoid actually beating people's heads against solid objects, but she got some pretty stern talkings-to, and her regular meetings had progressed through "concern" into "warning," with an implication that "final warning" was on the horizon.

"How many times are we going to try this?" I asked Oliver very, very quietly when I was very, very sure that Jaz was out the house. "Because I'm beginning to think it might have been a really bad idea."

He gave me one of his most determined looks. "I'm not going to say that we'll keep trying until it works, because there *may* come a point where we're doing more harm than good. But that point isn't now."

"Isn't, like, the definition of insanity doing the same thing over and expecting different results?"

"Perhaps," Oliver conceded. "Sometimes. But sometimes it's the definition of not giving up on people."

So the third try went ahead. We went back to the tearoom in the park in Dagenham, we bought two coffees and a muffin, and we waited.

We waited for two hours.

And then she showed up.

Maisie Johnson was a short woman, barely taller than Jaz, and carrying the kind of weight that was a common side effect of some antidepressants. Her hair was the exact same shade of dirty blond as Jaz's—or as Jaz's had been before she'd dyed it—but that was the only similarity between them I could see. And I looked. I looked for a good while.

I wasn't sure what I'd been expecting. From Jaz or from her. But somehow I think I got it anyway. Because although I'd spent a whole lot of time telling myself—and Jaz had spent a whole lot of time telling me—that I'd been doing a terrible job of parenting her, I knew Jaz pretty well. So I wasn't at all surprised that she was more relaxed and more affectionate with her mum than she was with me and Oliver. But I also wasn't at all surprised that *more relaxed and affectionate* meant "actually gave her a hug but was still mostly quiet" and not "turned into a completely different person."

The guidelines for this meeting had been quite specific. We could give them their space, but Jaz and her mum were on no account to be left alone together, and we were to firmly but politely challenge any attempts Maisie made to undermine the foster system.

Not that she did. Oliver and I sat at a nearby table doing our best to look like we weren't listening in, even though everybody there knew that we were obliged under the terms of our placement to be listening in.

Not that there was much to be listening in *to*. It would've been easy for me to put that down to Jaz's perennial teenage uncommunicativeness, or to Maisie being out of practice talking to her daughter. And sure, maybe those things were factors, but they weren't the main point. The main point was that some things were bigger than words.

So Maisie and Jaz sat opposite each other, Maisie drinking her tea and Jaz still picking at her muffin, and they said basically nothing to each other that wasn't *Fine* or *Y'know* or *The usual*. And then when we went home, Jaz brought the silence with her. And she sat in her room with Spud the whole of Sunday.

Oliver made sandwiches and took them up to her.

To my surprise, she ate them.

We had a couple more Saturdays like that, and then the fourth—or sixth, if you counted the two when Maisie hadn't been able to make it—was different. It was full spring now, and the—I don't know tulips or daffodils or whatever, the flowers you get around that time of year—were in full bloom. It was also, it turned out, close to the anniversary of Jaz's grandmother's death.

Until we'd been making plans for meeting four-slash-six, it hadn't really occurred to me how young Ms. Johnson Senior must have been when she went. She couldn't have been far north of sixty. I hadn't really known any of my own grandparents—I never met any of Dad's relatives, Mum's father wasn't in the picture, and her mum was off somewhere in France, living what I assumed was her best life—but I'd always had a pretty clear idea in my head of what a gran looked like. Somebody ancient and silver-haired, who talked about the blitz and rationing and when all this was nowt but fields. Not somebody who'd spent her late twenties watching *The Simpsons* and listening to Nirvana.

As always on visit days, Jaz was subdued that morning. Only extra subdued because "We're going to see your mum" was a way nicer pitch than "We're going to see your mum in the cemetery where your grandparents are buried."

"Are you not wearing a coat?" Oliver asked her as we gathered in the hall.

Jaz looked at him like she thought he was the third-worst human being who had ever lived. "Not cold."

"The weather might turn."

Sullenly, Jaz pulled her coat off the peg and folded it over her arm. "If it gets nicked, you're buying me a new one."

Oliver gave her the kind of smile she still didn't appreciate. "That is, indeed, one of our responsibilities."

"Also," I added, "who'd steal your coat from a cemetery?"

Jaz shrugged. "There's some right scumbags about."

I was very slightly proud of Oliver for not pointing out that it was unhelpful to think of people who stole as scumbags and that in fact, anybody who found themselves reduced to stealing clothing from graveyards had probably lived an extremely difficult life to that point.

We got into the car and set out for Dagenham. And I was *also* very slightly proud of Oliver for not saying anything even resembling "I told you so" about the coat when—as you'd expect for Britain in spring—it started drizzling miserably while we were only halfway through Romford.

"What was your nan like?" I asked Jaz as the windscreen wipers made their first halfhearted swipes at the equally halfhearted rain.

Like always when questions started shading towards personal, Jaz let that sit for quite a while before finally saying, "Nice."

After a not-too-long drive, we arrived at a little cemetery in the borough of Barking and Dagenham, and Oliver fished the umbrellas out of the boot. Jaz made no comment about putting her coat on.

The final resting place of Jaz's grandparents was a pretty unremarkable bit of ground that, under the grey sky and in the generally grey surroundings of that not-quite-London-not-quite-Essex part of the world we were in, felt the drab kind of peaceful.

As we walked along paths I thought Jaz knew far better than a teenager should, we saw memorials going all the way back to the First World War. Whole families laid out together. Babies who died in the thirties. A German pilot shot down in 1940. Parents and grandparents and way more children than I wanted to think about.

Fuck, I hated cemeteries. I think I might have hated them even more than parties.

Maisie was already waiting by the grave, holding an incongruously bright umbrella. I say *grave*, but it was *graves* really. Two of them side by side. *Deborah Johnson, died 2020* and *Second Lieutenant Mark Johnson, died 2004.*

"Covid," said Maisie, nodding at her mum, "and an IED." She nodded at her dad. "Rotten fucking luck, right?"

Jaz walked calmly over to stand by her mother and, without saying anything, took her hand.

"Y'know"—Maisie gazed at her daughter with a cocktail of emotions so curdled that it almost gave me a headache—"I weren't much older than you when he went. Looking back, I reckon it fucked me up more than I realised."

"These things do," said Oliver.

Things had been thawing between us and Ms. Johnson for a couple of weeks now, but that frosted them right back up again. "And what would you know about it?"

"Not a lot," Oliver admitted. "I was nearly thirty when my father died, and while I've found that very difficult to process, I can't imagine what it would be like to go through the same thing as a child."

Maisie frowned. "Sorry for your loss."

"Thank you."

For a while we just stood there and let ourselves get drizzled on. Then Maisie asked, "What was he like then, your old man?"

"He was a complicate—" Oliver stopped, looked at me, looked at Jaz, and then said, "Honestly. He was kind of an arsehole."

"Oi." Jaz glared at Oliver, seeming genuinely offended. "You can't say *arsehole* in a graveyard."

"He can, love," Maisie told her. "Anyway, some people just are, and there's no point pretending they weren't. Your dad was a right piece of shit, and I'd say that anywhere. To anyone."

And whether this was the right anywhere, or these the right anyones, Oliver continued. "He was… He was the kind of parent who mistook discipline for affection." Oliver looked at Jaz very deliberately. "Actually that isn't true. He was the kind of parent who *pretended* discipline was affection, when he knew the difference perfectly well. He drummed the idea that his way was the right way into me and my brother so hard that I think we both grew up simultaneously terrified of turning into him and of *not* turning into him."

"Grandad was a hero," replied Jaz, a little defiant. And very confident about the life of a man who'd died years before she was born.

"That's what Mum said," Maisie clarified. "But he was just a soldier. Died in a war he shouldn't have been fighting for a cause he didn't believe in, is what I reckon. But I suppose he done it for us in a way."

"Good pay being a squaddie," Jaz added, sounding like it was something she'd been saying her whole life.

There were already fresh flowers on both graves, and I felt like a bit of a dick for not thinking to bring some ourselves, although I suspect Oliver would have had sustainability concerns. Still, for a moment we just stood with the drizzle beading on our hair while we stared at those two bright pops of colour against the parched grass and packed dirt of the Johnson family graves.

"She did her best," Maisie continued after a while, "with me. Better than I did with her." She half nodded towards Jaz.

Jaz gave her mother a look of not-quite betrayal. "Don't say that."

"I'm still your mother—you don't get to tell me what to say.

Mum looked after us both, and without her, I can barely look after me. It's shit, but it's how it is."

Despite our umbrellas, the damp was soaking its way in through my trousers. Which meant every silence was an exercise in clammy misery.

"I may be speaking out of turn," Oliver said at last, "but I suspect that there might be support you're entitled to that you aren't currently taking advantage of."

Maisie had that not-sure-if-I'm-meant-to-be-offended look people sometimes got around Oliver. "You what?"

"He always talks like that," explained Jaz. "Don't take it personal."

"In my experience," he went on, "it isn't in the state's interest to actually advertise the services it has available, because then people use them and that costs money. Which means a lot of people don't claim support they're entitled to. There are also charities who—"

"I'm not a fucking charity case," snapped Jaz, "and neither's Mum."

I hoped now was the right time for Oliver to get all *Well, technically*, because he had that *Well, technically* vibe. "*Eton* is a charity case," he replied, and I silently congratulated myself for calling it. "If it's okay for a school full of rich men's rich sons to accept help when it's offered, it's okay for you too."

Maisie looked deeply, deeply suspicious. "What're you saying?"

"I'm saying"—Oliver spoke very carefully and very softly—"that the system could work better for you than it currently is. I don't know exactly what you need to do to get Jaz back, but I know a lot of people who *should* know. Several of my friends are family lawyers. I don't want to overstep, but...but I think I can help. And I'd like to. If that's what you want."

That was a lot. It was especially a lot because this wasn't something we'd particularly talked about, and while it was probably the right thing to offer, I didn't entirely *like* the idea of working towards a post-Jaz future, as inevitable as it was. But, given the choice between an Oliver who was kind without consulting me and one who was an authoritarian dick without consulting me, I liked the first one way, way more.

Jaz and her mum just kind of stood there, not *quite* knowing how to respond. Honestly, I wouldn't have blamed either of them for telling Oliver to fuck off because while the system had put him and the Johnsons together, he was still near as damn it a stranger to Maisie. And Jaz still, as far as I knew, thought he was a prick.

But the *Fuck off* never came.

Instead, Maisie, in the cagey tones of a woman who has been let down way too often, just said, "Keep talking."

And Oliver did.

He was cautious, because of course he was cautious. And he didn't make any guarantees, because of course he didn't make any guarantees. But he *cared*. And I loved that he cared. And I loved that he could show he cared through the highly specific language of being able to navigate the British legal system because, fuck me, was that useful sometimes. And as I listened to him talking through the Children Act 1989 and evidence-informed frameworks for return home practice with the Johnsons, I was struck with a clear, bright-light certainty that this would work. That I was watching the start of something that would, at some point, end with Jaz getting taken away from us.

I don't think I ever really understood the word *bittersweet* until then.

CHAPTER 43

"WHAT," SAID PRIYA. "THE FUCK. Is this?"

What the fuck was me, Mum, Judy, a trailer filled with professional-grade music-performing shit, an open-topped car that had been built in the last century, and a ditch.

"I blame the dogs," Judy insisted.

Oh yes, me, Mum, Judy, a trailer filled with professional-grade music-performing shit, an open-topped car that had been built in the last century, a ditch, and all of Judy's dogs. I should have seen this coming. Or should I have seen this coming? I'd offered to arrange transportation to CRAPPstonbury, and when Mum had said Judy was taking care of it, I'd assumed she was going to take care of it by literally any other method other than hitching a large wagon to the back of her tiny car and driving it too fast down roads that were too narrow on surfaces that were too skiddy around corners that were too tight. After ten minutes of that, the ditch had come almost as a relief.

The window of the truck rolled down, and Jaz stuck her head out. "Why did you even bring the dogs?" she asked.

"Never mind the dogs." I glared at Priya. "Why did *you* bring my foster daughter?"

"She wanted to come," Priya told me. "Said she could help."

"I wanted to see how badly you'd fucked this up," Jaz clarified. "I think the answer is *loads*?"

Walking the fine line between parental and professional, I approached the truck. "Jaz, you were meant to stay with Oliver and your mum."

"I know. But it's really boring right now. It's just portaloos and people setting stuff up."

I felt a weird tug of pride that, in the last few months, Maisie's visits had got routine enough that Jaz felt comfortable bailing in the middle of one to watch me humiliate myself.

"For your information," Mum was saying, still in the ditch, "this is not a *fuckup*. The legends of the rock 'n' roll, we do not have *fuckups*. We have *stories*."

Jaz jumped down from the truck and ran to help Mum back onto solid ground. I, meanwhile, did my best to wrangle dogs and instruments and bits of cable I didn't understand out of the half-overturned trailer pile and into a more sensible vehicle.

"You know," I told Jaz as she and Mum took charge of kit-shifting, leaving me with just the dogs, "I didn't want you down here for a reason. You helping with my job, my actual job I get paid actual money for, is really…child-labour-y. It isn't going to look good at our next review meeting."

She didn't seem especially impressed at that. "If they was going to take me away, they'd have done it by now. Reckon you're stuck with me."

"Okay, but it's also probably, like, exploitative and shit."

Priya dumped the remains of a broken guitar into the flatbed. "No, she's earning valuable work experience. This right here"—she made an expansive gesture covering the chaos around us and the idyllic, if lightly manure-scented, countryside around that—"this is a future in events management."

"I mean," said Jaz, "if *he* can do it."

"Hey. I worked very hard on this and used a lot of valuable skills I've earned over my years as a professional fundraiser."

Jaz was giving me an *I call bullshit* look.

"And also, I made a lot of it up as I went along and had a ton of support from my much more competent friends."

"Fucking right." Priya helped Mum into the back of the truck. "By the way, so we're clear, not taking the dogs."

Judy, who had been standing by the side of the road through all of this with the same placid, slightly detached air I saw a lot in Alex, snapped back to earth. "Hmm, what? Oh no, shouldn't think so. If you're sorted for transportation, I'll probably walk up to the field. It'll do the girls good to stretch their legs." She glared at one dog in particular. "*Won't it*, Camilla?"

"Are you sure, Judy?" asked Mum. "It is a very long way, and although I do not like to be saying it, you are not as young as you used to be."

"Pish posh." Judy took a deep lungful of bracing country air. "Been doing longer walks than this my whole life, and I won't stop until they put me in a box. In fact"—she started climbing over a stile with her dogs gathering behind her—"I'll race you. You take the high road and I'll take the low road and all that."

Priya leaned on her truck with her arms folded. "You know the low road is death, right?"

I paused, arms full of amp. "Hang on, what?"

Priya turned to me. "It's like, you try to come back alive, but I'll get killed fighting the English and then I'll get brought back and buried in Scotland and I won't care I'm dead on account of how my girlfriend dumped me up by Loch Lomond."

"How do you even *know* that?" I deposited the amp in the back. It might not have been an amp. It was a box with knobs on it.

But Judy was already stomping across fields and calling over her shoulder, "That high road is looking longer all the time."

"Do not get killed fighting the English," Mum yelled after her. "Vive the Auld Alliance."

With Mum's musical paraphernalia packed, those of us who weren't taking the low road that was possibly death back to CRAPPstonbury clambered into the truck, and we set out on the higher, less fatal, but longer and windier roads through the little country lanes of Surrey.

"I'm just saying," I insisted to Priya on the drive, "it sounds made up."

"What else would the low road be?"

"I don't know. The M6?"

"Google says it's death," Jaz said from the back seat.

Mum, who was sitting beside her, made a wise older-lady noise. "All folk songs are about death, Luc. Or fucking. Sometimes both."

"'All Around My Hat'?" I tried.

"The willow is a symbol of mourning," replied Mum. "Also in some versions, she leaves her true love for another man, so there is fucking in it too."

Jaz looked up from her phone as if she'd had a very important thought. "What about 'My Old Man's a Dustman'?"

"That," Mum told her sternly, "is not a folk song. It is a comic song by Lonnie Donegan."

"Folk songs've got to start somewhere," Jaz pointed out.

But Mum wasn't letting that one slide. "When it becomes about death or fucking, then it becomes a folk song."

"Mum," I pleaded. "Don't encourage Jaz to try and make 'My Old Man's a Dustman' about death or fucking. Also, let's all stop saying *about fucking* in front of my fourteen-year-old."

"What if the dustman," said Priya, who, like Oliver, was annoyingly good at the whole keeping-your-eyes-on-the-road thing, "is actually Charon?"

"Then," Mum conceded, "that would make it a folk song." And just when I thought I'd got away with it, she added, "Especially if Charon is fucking."

The CRAPPstonbury site was already buzzing, even though technically nobody should have been arriving for another few hours. The stages had been set up, the bands—and a lot of bands had come out of the woodwork now that this was also the start of the Odile O'Donnell Comeback Tour—were messing with instruments and bickering, both of which I understood to be pretty normal parts of the creative process.

Oliver, Maisie, and Spud met us as we piled out of Priya's truck into the venue field. Spud bounded over happily and, indeed, yappily, but Maisie looked honestly dazed.

"Oh my God," she said, "you're Odile O'Donnell."

Jaz literally cringed. "Mum! Don't embarrass me."

I was pretty damned stressed with all the CRAPPstonbury chaos, but I glanced up at Oliver then, and we took a moment to share how much it meant that Jaz had got to the point where her mother was an embarrassment, instead of something lost and locked away from her.

Mum—who was looking more like Odile O'Donnell now than I'd ever seen her, with dark eyes and big hair that had come through the ditch experience looking intentionally dishevelled—patted Jaz on the shoulder. "Jas, you did not tell me your mother was a fan."

Grinding one toe into the dirt, Jaz made didn't-think-it-was-important noises.

It was weird, unsettlingly weird, seeing somebody interacting with my mum like she was an honest-to-shit famous person, but Maisie seemed straight-up starstruck. Looking slightly downwards, she said, "*Welcome Ghosts* got me through a really hard time in my life."

"That is a coincidence," said Mum, "because it got me through a hard time in my life too. I am going to need to go and get ready for my set soon, but if you and Jas would like to come with me..."

"Mum," I said, "child labour laws are a thing."

She waved a hand. "Not when you are famous."

"I think yes, even when you're famous."

"I'm fine," said Jaz. "You want me to carry something?"

"Actually"—Maisie stuffed her hands in her pockets—"I might...I might bail."

I'd sort of been expecting this. Maisie had been doing better recently, but there was *better* and there was *able to cope with a festival crowd*. Still, it hit Jaz hard, and, while she tried to hide her disappointment, she didn't quite manage it.

"That's completely understandable," Oliver Olivered into the breach. "I'm finding it quite overwhelming myself, and it's only going to get more hectic as the day goes on."

Maisie shrugged. "Yeah."

"And," he added, "we'll see you next week?"

"Yeah," Jaz echoed. "Next week?"

"Of course," replied Maisie. Who meant it every time and who was sticking to it a lot more these days. "And I'll be okay for a bit longer. Just...not sure for how long."

"You can go sit down in the refreshment tent if you need a breather," I offered. "They know you're with me, so it won't be a problem."

"I was actually going to head that way anyway." Oliver gently brought Spud to heel. "If you'd like me and Spud to accompany you?"

Maisie nodded. "That'd probably be good. A bit of shade, you know."

"Okay." I did my best to appear cool, calm, and in control of the situation. "Civilians and Spud to the refreshment tent. Mum, head backstage. I'll get someone to get the truck unloaded. Someone who isn't a child."

"Not a child," muttered Jaz.

"Legally," said Oliver, "you very much are."

She half smiled in that way she got when she was gearing up to take on Oliver, like she wasn't sure yet if she was baiting him or playing with him. "Legally, it's okay for security blokes to put kids in handcuffs."

"Fair point. Although I personally like to think I'd avoid exploiting underage workers even if it were legally permissible."

I watched them wending through the gathering crowds, wishing I could join them. Because this was shaping up to be an okay festival, and it would have been nice to sit under the marquee, drinking craft beers on a summer afternoon and hanging out with my, y'know, my family. Except the okayness of the festival relied on me not doing that. And, instead, doing my job.

I activated the walkie-talkie I had clipped to my collar. "Alex, can you—"

"Twaddle here," returned Alex. And then after a long enough pause that I was just about to reply, he added, "Over."

I sighed. "One, you don't have to do the *over* thing. Two, you're doing the *over* thing wrong."

"Over," said Alex.

"Stop saying *over*."

"Stop saying what? Over."

"Over."

"Didn't hear that. Just got the *over* part. Over."

"I want you"—I spoke very clearly and very slowly—"to stop saying the word *over*, by which I—"

"Which word? Over."

"Alex, I need you to get a truck unloaded."

"So I should stop saying *truck*? Please confirm? Over."

"No."

"No, don't say *truck*? Or no, do say *truck*. Over?"

"Alex," I tried again, wondering—as I always did—if this was somehow my fault. "I need you to get someone to unload a truck—"

"That's going to be bally difficult to do if I can't say *truck*. Over."

"You can say *truck*," I yelled. "You can say everything except *over*."

"Everything except what? Over."

The channel crackled. "I've got someone on it," said Barbara Clench, from wherever she was. Which, unlike every other member of the team, was almost certainly where she was meant to be.

"Thanks, Barbara," I said.

"Over," said Alex.

"How are sales looking?" I asked.

"No idea," said Alex. "Over."

"Cautiously healthy," said Barbara Clench. "Between pre-sales, the gate, and CRAPP's other sources of income, we should get another year, maybe eighteen months. But obviously we'll know more when it's all over."

"When it's all what?" trilled Alex. "Over."

There was a long silence. "Out," said Barbara very deliberately.

I sank down on another knobby box that may or may not have been an amp, and sucked in a deep, anxious breath. That was probably the best news I could have received that didn't quite qualify as good news. I hadn't sunk us, but I hadn't saved us, either, and I didn't know how to feel about that. Like, did I really want to spend the next however-long of my life jumping from scheme to scheme, desperately trying to keep a failing charity alive? On the other hand, walking away or just letting it die seemed shitty. Still, it could have been worse. At least since Saint had dropped out, I didn't have to deal with—

"Luc Fleming!" Saint's voice rang across the field. "Why the fuck am I not on the set list?"

I should have known. Of course he'd show up. Of course he'd expect to be playing. "You told me you weren't coming," I pointed out.

"That's just industry talk. Where's Odile?"

"Setting up. Look, the thing is, Saint—"

I didn't get any further because there was yet more yelling. The other two living members of Rancid Sputum were tromping across the field towards us, Rik Jism currently shouting some very rude things at a security guard who was trying to make him leave.

"I *told you*," Saint bellowed at his former bandmates, "you're not *welcome*."

MagiMix had dragged out his old—very old, judging from the fit—punk rocker gear and was now bearing down on us in ripped jeans and a leather-jacket-over-bare-chest combo that was a lot harder to get away with on a primary school headteacher. "You think we just come and go when you tell us to?"

"I think you had your chance," Saint replied, "and you fucking blew it."

I quietly explained to the security guard that Rik and Mix were—if you really stretched the point—with me, which freed up Jism to join the party. Because after all, what party didn't need more Jism? He'd also repunked himself for the occasion, his hair spiked and his piercings—of which there were many—back in. Thankfully, he did have a shirt on. "*We* fucking blew it? You fucking blew it, mate."

"The fuck I did."

I confronted the Rancid Sputum reunion with what I hoped was an "in charge" face rather than a "screw you" face. "For the last time, what are you all doing here?"

"*They*," replied Saint immediately, "are trying to horn in on my big moment."

"And what big moment is that?" I asked, even though Saint was immune to sarcasm.

He just stared at me. "Opening for Odile."

"Why would you think you're opening for Odile?" It felt weird calling her that instead of *Mum*. "The last time we spoke, you told me to shut down the whole festival, and I told you to fuck off."

Rik Jism was glancing between us like a squirrel at a tennis match. "Hang on. What he said to me was that Odile was playing the shitbug festival, and she'd asked him to open for her and he was going to do it without us."

"Why would my mum even have heard of you?" I exploded at the same time Saint spread his hands in an infuriating gesture of *oops* and drawled out, "What I actually said was, she'll want us to open for her."

"Well, she'll won't." I shut that down with more gusto than grammar.

Saint was still refusing to believe he hadn't got his way. But MagiMix hadn't got to be the deputy headteacher of Celvestune Primary School by being slow or stubborn. "Oh, of fucking *course*. I should have fucking *known*."

While MagiMix was reserving his anger for Saint, Rik Jism wasn't so discerning. He got very, very up in my face and poked his finger into my chest. "So there's no gig?"

I stepped just slightly out of poking range. "No, there's no gig. You didn't *want* a gig."

"I didn't want a gig when there was nothing in it for me," Rik Jism corrected me. "Opening for Odile is something for me."

"But apparently," added MagiMix, who I realised was still wearing his glasses, making the old-school rocker-boy look even less convincing than it could have been, "not something we're getting. Which is a shame because I was really hoping to be able to put this in the newsletter."

"You want to put a punk gig you played shirtless next to a guy called Jism in a primary school newsletter?" I asked.

MagiMix looked down at his bare torso. "Maybe I should put a top on."

Saint turned around and put a hand on MagiMix's chest. "Hold on. The Mix does *not* put a top on."

"As far as you were concerned, the Mix wasn't playing the gig at all ten seconds ago," Rik Jism pointed out. "Neither was I."

"Also, there *is* no gig," I added.

Sometimes I wondered how Saint didn't give himself whiplash with how quickly he changed direction. "Hey, we're here," he said, "and we are *Rancid fucking Sputum*. If we're going to do this thing, we do it *hard*."

"Not too hard," clarified MagiMix. "I *am* still needed in school on Monday."

Rik Jism rolled his eyes. "Fuck me, when did you get to be such a lightweight?"

"When I joined an industry that doesn't run on cocaine and sexual harassment?"

"Hey, I dropped out of the music business too," Rik Jism replied.

"I wasn't talking about the music business. I know what those big-city firms are like."

It looked like Rik Jism was about to protest, but in the end he said, "You know what? Fair."

"Nobody is *doing* anything," I tried to explain. "Hard or other—"

"Obviously"—Saint had jumped headfirst into a lake of delusion and seemed to be taking his bandmates with him—"we'll open with 'Fuck the Man, Fuck the System.'"

"Actually," said MagiMix, "this might wind up online, and parents from my school might see it, so I'd rather like to limit the number of f-bombs if at all possible."

Rik Jism coughed into his hand in a way that sounded a lot like *Pussy*.

"Could you change it? To perhaps 'Eff the Man, Eff the System,'" suggested MagiMix.

I privately bet myself that Saint would tell him radio edits were for sellouts.

"Radio edits are for sellouts," Saint told him.

Rik Jism patted Saint on the back. "Saint, mate, it's not selling out if you're not being paid."

"How about 'Shit in Thatcher's Mouth'?" Saint tried.

"Not *super* topical," pointed out Rik Jism. "And if Teacher Boy here has a problem with *fuck*, he probably also has a problem with *shit*."

"'Wanking to Picasso'?"

MagiMix gave a thoughtful nod. "Yeah, we can do 'Wanking.'"

Saint smiled. "'Paradise in a Nun's Gash'?"

"Quite a lot of religious students." MagiMix sounded very apologetic. "Might be hard to explain."

"'Come on Eileen.'"

"No!" That time the *no* had come from Rik and Mix simultaneously.

I shouldn't have been getting involved, especially because this was a hypothetical list for a set that wasn't going to happen, but I also couldn't help myself. "What's wrong with 'Come on Eileen'? It's a disco classic, isn't it?"

"You're thinking of a different 'Come on Eileen.'" Rik Jism's voice had a note of warning in it.

"Fucking Dexys stole the title from us," explained Saint.

MagiMix folded his leather-jacketed arms over his otherwise exposed nipples. "With a time machine," he added, "because that's the only way they could have released their song in 1982 when you didn't write the Sputum version until 1987."

Saint sneered. "That Kevin Rowland's a tricky bastard."

Before they could drift any further down memory lane, I cut them off. "I'm going to say this one last time. There is no gig. You are not playing. Rancid Sputum will not be opening for Odile or for *anybody*."

Saint finally heard me. And he didn't like what he heard. "Hold on. This is my fucking festival."

I'd really hoped telling him to fuck off once would be enough. Then again, Rik Jism and MagiMix had hoped that too. "It's CRAPP's festival. The money to set it up came from your dad and other doners; the money it's making belongs to the charity and not to you. You don't have any authority here, Saint."

"Hey," Saint protested, "I'm not into institutional power."

I tried to adopt an assertive posture. Then realised I looked like a wanker and stopped. "Good. Then this situation shouldn't be a problem for you." Having made my point, I glanced at Jism and MagiMix. "Richard, Michael, sorry you had a wasted trip."

"You could've told us before we got into the set list," complained Rik Jism.

"I think he sort of did," said MagiMix.

Rik Jism, who, for an accountant, seemed to have a worryingly poor eye for detail, considered this. "Okay, yeah I suppose he might. Besides"—he glared at Saint—"it wouldn't be the first time he'd got us invested in something that never happened."

"Oh my God," said Saint in the aggrieved tones of somebody who was definitely in the wrong but would never admit it, "you can*not* still be angry about that."

"I hitchhiked," said Rik Jism, "from Kettering to fucking *Prague*."

"There was a mix-up," Saint protested. "Also, it was in 1992. Get over it."

MagiMix gave me an apologetic look. "As you can see," he said, "these things tend to happen a lot with Rancid Sputum." He stroked his chin contemplatively. "There's probably material for an assembly here."

"What's the lesson going to be?" Annoyingly, my brain decided to think about that. "'Don't count your punk rock concerts before they hatch'?"

"I think I might go with 'Sometimes your friends will try to get you to do things you don't think are a good idea, and you should listen to your instincts and/or parents.'"

Saint groaned heavily. "Fuck me, Mix. When did you get so fucking square?"

"At the exact point"—MagiMix drew himself up with a surprising amount of dignity for a man in his sixties with his nipples on display—"that I got confident enough to stop caring what other people thought of me." His eyes alighted on something past my left shoulder. "Ooh, is that vegan pop-up?"

As MagiMix set off for Bronwyn's tent, Rik Jism hesitated for a moment and then followed him, leaving me, Saint, and something that was probably an amp standing in ankle-deep mud in the middle of a field.

"They'll be back," said Saint. "They always come back."

"Maybe they will," I told him. "But let's be clear: I don't care. I don't care what they do. I don't care what you do. You can stay, you can go. It doesn't matter. But I have a festival to run." I glanced across the field, where the first attendees were starting to grab food and stake out the good spots. "A festival, I might add, that's going pretty fucking well and—"

"Jones Bowen One to O'Donnell." Rhys's voice crackled breathlessly over the walkie-talkie. "Jones Bowen One to O'Donnell."

Oh, for fuck's sake. "Yes?"

"Are you receiving me?"

I'd been told walkie-talkies were a really useful thing to use if you were running a big event. And that was probably true—if you weren't working with the kind of people who thought the moment you gave them a radio you'd inducted them into the French Resistance. "Clearly I'm receiving you."

"Thank goodness. You need to come at once. There's a terrible problem."

"What kind of problem?" I asked, with a sense of doom settling over me like an unfashionable cagoule.

"Well, it's a bit hard to explain," said Rhys Jones Bowen. "But it involves two male voice choirs, some chains, and an awfully large number of portable lavatories."

CHAPTER 44

I THOUGHT I'D DONE PRETTY well on the lavatorial front. The number of portaloos I'd booked—very *nice* portaloos, for what it's worth, the kinds of portaloos you wouldn't mind using if you were also the sort of person who donated money to extremely middle-class conservation charities—was definitely adequate for the expected crowds, even with the late rush we'd experienced after the announcement of the Odile O'Donnell Comeback Tour. Or at least they would have been if at least two dozen of them hadn't been chained shut, with the beautifully rich but currently very angry voices of a Welsh male voice choir yelling from inside them.

"Alan Bowen," a tall, thin man was saying outside the central toilet, "you are not coming out of there until you and your group of rebels and apostates relinquish all claim to the title of Skenfrith Male Voice Choir."

"I will not, Bill Thomas," Rhys's uncle Alan replied, somewhat muffled, from within the confines of his portaloo. "You are a traitor, and I will *never* let a man like you sully the good name of the Skenfrith Male Voice Choir. Why, we've been on *Songs of Praise*, you know."

"Oh, you and your *Songs of Praise*." Bill Thomas threw his hands in the air. "That's all you ever talked about. There's a reason we all despised you in the end."

We'd tried to stop the Skenfrith Male Voice Choir politics from boiling over. We'd even booked both of them to avoid either one taking it as an insult. Apparently, that had been a mistake. "Hi!" I crashed to a halt next to an extremely flustered Rhys Jones Bowen. "Can I help anybody with anything?"

Bill Thomas turned to me with a look of outrage that, frankly, I didn't think a man who'd just locked a whole male voice choir in a row of portaloos had any business adopting. "You can," he declared. "You can strike these *pretenders* from the lineup."

"You can strike those *usurpers* from the lineup," countered Uncle Alan.

"You see the impasse I'm at here," I told both of them.

And both of them replied, "I do not."

"It's bad enough that they're here *at all*," Bill Thomas continued. "But they have the *gall* to be performing under the name the Original Skenfrith Male Voice Choir, when quite clearly the original choir is the version led by its duly appointed director, not the schismatic version led by a disgruntled former officeholder."

Uncle Alan wasn't taking that lying down. Partly because he was stuck in a portaloo, so he didn't have room. "The Original Skenfrith Male Voice Choir is the one made up of its *original* members under the guidance of its *original* director. The true travesty here is that you're letting his lot perform under the name of the Real Skenfrith Male Voice Choir."

"The Real Skenfrith Male Voice Choir," Bill Thomas shot back, "is the one led by its real director elected under its real charter that meets every week in the real church hall it's been meeting in for forty years."

Uncle Alan wasn't taking that lying down either. "We meet in the same church hall."

"But on a Tuesday. The Real Skenfrith Male Voice Choir has *never* met on a Tuesday, and it never will."

I cast my eyes over at Rhys Jones Bowen. "Help me out here?"

He looked a little surprised that I'd asked him. Probably because although I'd been working on myself very hard for the past several years, I was still in a lot of ways the same bellend he'd always known I was. "Are you sure?" he asked. "You're primary festival organiser."

"I'm sure," I said. "This seems like it's way more your area than mine."

So Rhys squared up to the Real Skenfrith Male Voice Choir. "Well, isn't this a pretty pickle?"

Bill Thomas folded his arms. "It's your uncle's fault. He should have taken his defeat with good grace."

"Good grace?" called out Uncle Alan from inside the stall. "How much good grace can a man have when he's locked in a portaloo?"

"You know as well as I do," replied Bill Thomas, "that this portaloo has been a long time coming."

Rhys Jones Bowen shook his head. "Gentlemen," he said in tones of abject disappointment. "Is this any way for self-respecting choristers to behave? Why, in my view, you're bringing shame on the whole institution of the Welsh male voice choir, and that, you will know, is not a thing I would say lightly."

Uncle Alan's reply, when it came, was more than a bit huffy. "I don't see what *I've* done wrong."

"Oooh, Uncle Alan." It turned out that Rhys had a better not-angry-just-disappointed voice than I did. "We all know that you've been needling Bill Thomas for years. Is it any wonder he went off the deep end?"

Bill Thomas didn't quite say *hah*, but he did look ill-advisedly triumphant.

"And as for *you*." Rhys Jones Bowen fixed him with a cold stare. "Chaining other choristers in toilets. Why, I've never seen the like in all my days. Let them all out at once, and we'll talk about this like reasonable people."

Somewhat chastened, the Real Skenfrith Male Voice Choir grudgingly unchained the Original Skenfrith Male Voice Choir from their lavatorial prisons. When they were done, Uncle Alan and Bill Thomas stood next to each other, and Rhys Jones Bowen addressed them with such fierce disapproval I found myself slightly wilting.

"Will you two look at yourselves," he declared. "I ask you"—here he stared at Uncle Alan—"what would Auntie Mabel say?"

Uncle Alan looked down. "Mabel doesn't understand choir politics."

"You may say that, Alan Bowen," said Bill Thomas, "but your wife has a better head on her shoulders than you'll ever have."

"And I suppose"—Rhys Jones Bowen turned the same disappointed glare onto Bill Thomas—"that your Beryl would be extremely proud of the way you've conducted yourself today?"

The spectres of their spouses had brought the duelling choirmasters down slightly to earth, but not so far down they'd get their feet muddy. "I'm not having his lot go on first," said Uncle Alan. "It's demeaning."

"And the same goes for me," said Bill Thomas. "Only, you know, the other way around. And I'm not going on the little stage if he's on the big one."

"Nor me him," added Uncle Alan. "But once again, with us being in the opposite positions."

I closed my eyes for two seconds and hoped that I wasn't missing something. "Okay, so you're refusing to be on different stages?"

Bill Thomas and Uncle Alan both nodded. "Yes."

"And you're also refusing to be on the same stage if the other group goes before you."

"That's right," they both confirmed.

"You're being very difficult," Rhys Jones Bowen told them.

"Okay," I tried, "so if you won't go on different stages or the same stage at different times, what if we put you on the same stage at once?"

"That wouldn't work," protested Bill Thomas.

"No," agreed Uncle Alan. "We're doing completely different set lists."

If I was lucky, this would be typical CRAPP bullshit. I knew how to deal with typical CRAPP bullshit. "And what are those set lists, exactly?"

"Well," said Bill Thomas, "we're going to open with 'You Raise Me Up,' then do 'Men of Harlech,' 'Myfanwy,' and 'Cwm Rhondda,' and finish on 'Hen Wlad Fy Nhadau.'"

Uncle Alan frowned. "Whereas we were going to start with 'Men of Harlech,' then do 'Myfanwy,' then do 'Cwm Rhondda,' and finish on 'You Raise Me Up,' leading into 'Hen Wlad Fy Nhadau.'"

"Are those," I tried, "not the exact same songs?"

"Well yes," conceded Uncle Alan, "but in different orders."

I looked at Rhys for support, in case I was about to make a massive faux pas. "Can you not just *change* the order?"

"Suppose we did," said Bill Thomas. "What then? I suppose you'd want us to both be on stage singing the same songs at the same time. With two different choirs. Nobody's ever tried such a thing. What would it even sound like?"

"Won't it sound like one *big* choir?" I suggested hopefully.

There was a long pause.

"You know," Bill Thomas said eventually, "the bellend *might* have a point."

"Think of it," put in Rhys Jones Bowen, "as a sort of Super Group."

Uncle Alan seemed to be rolling this idea around in his brain. "You mean, the Real Skenfrith Male Voice Choir and the Original

Skenfrith Male Voice Choir together in concert?" He turned to Bill Thomas. "What do you think?"

"I think," Bill Thomas said, a smile beginning to spread across his face, "that we'd take over the bloomin' world." Then he took a moment to reflect. "Well, take over northeast Monmouthshire at least. Which is a good start."

"But what would we *call* ourselves?" asked Uncle Alan.

Rhys Jones Bowen nodded sagely. "Funny you should ask that. How about the Real Original Skenfrith Male Voice Choir?"

Having, with Rhys's help, resolved the Great Male Voice Choir Feud, I had a precious thirty-five seconds to myself before Alex walkie-talkied me with the next crisis.

"Luc, Luc," he babbled. "There's a strange man hanging around the refreshment area. I'm pretty sure he's homeless and he definitely has a knife." He paused. "Over."

My instinct was always to assume that the more certain Alex was about something, the less likely it was to be actually true. So I felt pretty confident that investigating this mysterious intruder wouldn't get me stabbed.

And sure enough, when I got there, I found myself in a completely knife-free zone. I also seemed to be in a completely Alex-free zone, but then I realised that he was hiding behind a speaker like a cartoon spy.

"You see!" He pointed at the hunched, leather-jacketed figure sitting on a log just outside one of the refreshment tents. How he'd thought a homeless man could afford those clothes or that much hair product I wasn't sure. Then again, Alex might have thought *homeless* meant *had to let out one of his mansions*.

"That," I told Alex, "is the Earl of Spitalhamstead."

Alex boggled. "But he looks like such an oi—"

I didn't let him finish. "You okay, Saint?" I yelled out.

To my surprise, he didn't yell anything back. He just sat there with his head down and his hands clasped one inside the other.

I approached him the way you might approach a normally aggressive dog that you'd found vomiting in the corner of your garden. "You okay?" I tried again.

"The guys are off eating jackfruit hot dogs," he said. "You were right. They hate me."

Yeah, they do seemed unnecessarily mean. "*Hate*'s a strong word—"

"Okay, but they really, really don't like me." An almost hopeful look crossed his face. "Hey, do you think there's a song in that?"

"Already was one."

He frowned a frown of utter defeat. "Fuck. Why does that always happen to me?"

"Have you considered," I began very, very cautiously, "that perhaps original music production isn't your single greatest strength?"

As down as he was clearly feeling, Saint still gave me a challenging look. "And what *is* my single greatest strength?"

"You're...very passionate?"

He looked away, and then said, half addressing me and half addressing fate itself, "You mean I'm a talentless piece of shit who's lived his whole life on Daddy's millions and never built or done or achieved anything?"

That pretty much summed it up. But, once again, it felt unnecessarily mean to say so.

"That's a...that's a very negative way to put it."

Slowly, he swivelled his head back towards me. "So how would *you* put it?"

"I suppose...we're all dealt a particular hand in life. And you, well, you happened to get dealt a..."

"A really good one?" Saint replied. "One that I could have used to do anything, and in the end all I used it for was to piss around pretending to be a musician hoping that one day, maybe one fucking day, my old man would put his *fucking* bugs down for five seconds and—"

"Notice you?" I didn't like to interrupt. Especially when it was the putting-words-in-somebody's-mouth kind of interrupting. It would have been the last thing I'd do with Jaz because she was my kid—my foster kid—and I needed to let her grow and flourish and be her own person. But Saint was nearly fucking seventy. He was as grown and as flourished as he was going to get.

Besides, I'd been right.

"Yeah," he said. "Fucking stupid, right? Fucking stupid and fucking clichéd and not at all fucking rock 'n' roll."

I shrugged. "I don't know. I reckon probably quite a lot of rock 'n' roll is just people trying to get their dads' attention. Or their mums'. Or some boy or girl they liked at school. I mean, I don't think you spend your life standing on a big platform shouting *Notice me* if there isn't somebody you want to notice you."

In my own humble opinion, I'd handled that one pretty well. Not that you'd know it, because Saint was totally ignoring me.

As was his right. Little flourishing flower that he was.

"Just once," he said, kind of past me, "just *once*, I'd have liked him to say, 'You know what, Hilary my boy, that song you did about Norman Tebbit's ballsack, I was offended by it, but I respect you for having the guts to sing it anyway.'"

"Yeah." I shrugged again. "I think all sons, in a way, want their dads to say something like that." That was almost certainly untrue—I knew a whole range of men with a whole range of different relationships to their fathers, but I didn't think Saint was the kind of guy who was much interested in discussing the spectrum of modern masculinity. He was way too sigma. "I mean, not *exactly* like that," I clarified. "Like the Norman Tebbit's ballsack thing is pretty specific."

"Wouldn't even need to be the music," Saint went on and went on ignoring me. "'Good job bagging that grouse, Hilary.' Wouldn't even need to be about something I'd *done*. Could have been, 'Hey, Hilary, haven't seen you for a year, how was Eton?'"

And that…that felt a whole lot more universal. I knew people who didn't give a shit what people said about their accomplishments. But being abandoned sucked. Though the jury was out on whether it sucked more to be abandoned by somebody who'd left, or by somebody who was still there.

"And now"—he heaved a deep, tragic sigh—"the bastard is fucking dead. And he'll never say, 'By the way, just in case you were wondering, you aren't a complete fucking disgrace to your ancestors.' Fuck me, he'll never even say, 'Pass the sugar.' He'll never even have sugar. Because he's fucking *dead*."

And out of nowhere, he slumped sideways onto my shoulder and started crying. "He's fucking *dead*, Luc. My fucking dad is fucking dead."

This was not where I thought this day was going to go. I reluctantly gave him a pat and a platitude. "He had a good innings."

"He's fucking *dead*," Saint repeated, like he'd only just realised. "Do you know how hard it is to stay angry at a man when he's fucking *dead*?"

I'd find out when my own dad went. Except, actually, I wouldn't. Because I wasn't angry at Jon Fleming. I hadn't been in a long time. "Well," I said, "you do seem like you're giving it a good go?"

Saint gave a wet snuffle. "I've spent nearly a *year* trying to…I don't know…with the beetle charity and like… *Fuck*, I hated that beetle charity."

"CRAPP," I reminded him. "That's the charity I work for."

"Fuck," he said for the I'd-honestly-stopped-countingth time. "And you did all this"—he looked around at CRAPPstonbury—"for me?"

"I mean if I'm honest," I admitted, "I did it in a vain hope that I could trick you into thinking that your dad's interests and yours remotely overlapped, which I don't think they do."

Saint pulled his teary, snotty head off my now teary and snotty shoulder. "Still, you *did it*." He looked at me the way I think in his head he imagined he wished his father had looked at him. "You're a man who *does things*, Luc Fleming."

"O'Donnell," I reminded him. "My name is O'Donnell. Like my mother."

"My mother was a good woman," Saint told me. "She'd be disgusted with the way I turned out."

"No, she wouldn't," I said. And I was surprised at my own conviction.

"How do you know?"

"Because...because good people are never disgusted by somebody just...being themselves. You've not done anything *wrong*, Saint." Okay, that was a lie; he'd done a whole lot of things wrong, and if he hadn't been a peer of the realm, there'd probably have been arrest records to prove it. "You've lived a life that's a bit...different, is all. Different isn't bad."

Nodding a little distractedly, Saint got to his feet. "Thanks," he said, and he seemed to actually mean it. "You've...you've given me a lot to think about."

"No problem."

"And..."

I didn't know what I was expecting from that *and*. But I got a fucking miracle.

"And you know what?" Saint went on. "I think I'll keep the fucking beetle charity. At least until I can work...you know...work my shit out."

"That's very kind," I said, only partly insincerely. "I think your mother would be proud."

For a moment, it was like Saint didn't know what to make of that. But in the end, he decided to believe it. "You're a good man Luc Fl—Luc O'Donnell."

Smiling at me, he threw up the devil horns one last time.

And he walked away.

Seven hours later, CRAPPstonbury was in full swing, and honestly, I was more stressed than I'd been at any point over the whole process. Previously, my biggest concern had been that the whole thing just wouldn't happen. Now my biggest concern was that I had ten thousand people standing in a field, all of whom had paid a decent amount of money to get in, all of whom would want to be fed, entertained, and not trampled to death because I'd missed something on a health and safety briefing.

But apart from that, it was a good atmosphere.

As the Real Original Skenfrith Male Voice Choir made their way onto the stage to a much warmer reception than I'd have expected from a crowd who mostly hadn't been following CRAPP events for half a decade, I took a moment to slip backstage—okay, backfield—and take a breather.

I sat down on one of those square boxes with knobs on that I was beginning to suspect might not be amps actually and reminded myself, very firmly, to breathe. I'd got the reminder bit down, the breathing bit not so much, when Oliver stepped out from behind a different big box with knobs on whose level of ampness I couldn't even begin to guess.

"There you are," he said, resting a soothing hand on my back.

"Fuck. What's gone wrong now?"

"Nothing. I just meant that I've been looking for you because you're my boyfriend and I wanted to see you."

"Oh." That made sense. "Where's Jaz?"

"With our dog and our friends. She's fine."

"And Maisie?"

"Left some time ago. Also fine."

"Oh," I said again. Honestly, without something to panic about, I had nothing.

After a moment or two of dealing with my nothing, Oliver sat down beside me, which made things a bit bum-over-the-edgy but was worth it for the closeness. "You've done a good job, Lucien."

"Thanks. I guess I did, huh? And Saint might even let us keep running."

"I'm glad to hear it. But you know it was never your job to save the entirety of C.R.A.P.P.?"

"Wow. I wish you'd told me that months ago, before I did all this."

He laughed. "If you recall, I encouraged you to explore opportunities in the fast-growing field of Dogstagramming."

"Don't tempt me. Spud's not safe from the sailor suit yet."

"He will be if Jaz has anything to say about it." We both fell silent for a second or two, or as silent as you could be with a Welsh male voice choir belting out "Men of Harlech" in the background. Then Oliver said, "You know I'm very proud of you, don't you?"

"For doing something that wasn't my job?"

"There are a lot of things that are nobody's job but still need doing. And if more people stepped up and did them, the world would be a better place."

"Like recycling and fostering and shit, right?"

"Particularly recycling. The other day, you put a paper bag full of orange peel into the general waste."

"I was busy," I protested. "I was busy stepping up and being the change I want to see and whatever."

"It was a compostable inside a recyclable. The definition of adding insult to injury."

"You can punish me later."

"Don't get my hopes up. You're bound to be exhausted this evening."

"Then you can punish me, like, slowly and tenderly."

His eyes shone their softest grey. "It's a date."

Leaning in, he kissed me in that Olivery way I never got tired of. Like there was nothing in the world more important than me, and him, and us. Except then my arse slipped off the amp and I went straight down into the mud, dragging him on top of me.

And, honestly, it didn't make much of a difference.

We just kept on kissing. Because, sometimes, it didn't matter how old you were, or how many grown-up things there were to think about; you just needed to be with the person you loved.

Eventually, both of us slightly the worse for wear, we went to join our friends.

"Fucking hell, you two," said Jaz. "What have you been up—actually, don't answer that. I'm too traumatised already."

"It was very romantic," I insisted.

Jaz clapped her hands over her ears. "Fuckofffuckofffuckofffff."

"She's great, isn't she?" said Priya. "James, I'm expecting Baby J to be able to swear at least as well as this by the time he's nine."

James Royce-Royce, who was looking after Baby J while James Royce-Royce was running his Gourmet Street Food Experience, looked sceptical. "Not sure James would like that."

"He would"—Priya smirked—"if you told him most kids only start dropping f-bombs at eleven."

There was a ripple of slightly nervous laughter. We'd mostly got to the stage where James Royce-Royce's compulsive need to treat babies like Top Trumps was an in-joke, but we were still working on it.

Sophie was lounging on a picnic blanket wearing dark glasses, a white sundress, and shoes that were way too expensive for the ground, the weather, or the whole overall vibe. "If you've got a thing for terrible children, *please* consider taking the twins off our hands. I've become quite bored of them."

Ben looked glum. "I really don't think we can just give them away. There's probably laws about it."

"Who's the barrister?" asked Sophie, raising an eyebrow. "I'm sure I can find a loophole somewhere."

Bridge, who had for some reason decided that because it was a music festival, she had to go full Woodstock, with a caftan and flowers in her hair, took Autumn to sit next to Sophie on the picnic blanket. "Auntie Sophie pretends to be mean," she said to Autumn in the universal talking-to-babies voice, "but deep down she's made of chocolate and marshmallows, isn't she? Is-n't-she?"

"She's fucking not." Unlike his wife, Tom had chosen to dress like a sensible person.

"He's right," agreed Oliver. "Sophie has always been pure evil and will always be pure evil."

From across the way, Brian and Amanda were wandering back from the Royce-Royce Experience with supplies for the group. "Don't tell James," Brian called out from slightly too far away, "but these pasties are fucking brilliant."

"Actually," said James Royce-Royce, watching his son plundering sausage rolls from Amanda's bag, "could we keep the *fucks* down a bit in front of the kids? Baby J's mirroring a lot."

"Fuck," said Amanda. "Sorry."

"Fuck," said Baby J.

"Ruff," said Spud.

"Hey." Priya put up her hands. "I'm an artist. I have to be allowed my free expression."

"You're a visual artist," Oliver pointed out. "I don't think swearing in front of children translates much into sculpture."

She shrugged. "Art's mysterious."

Realising I hadn't eaten all day, I pounced on one of the slow-roast pork sandwiches and stuffed it slightly embarrassingly into my face. "Is everybody having a good time?" I managed to ask between bites.

"The twins aren't here," said Sophie, "so yes."

"Also," chimed in Brian, "you got a fu—a blooming Bolt Thrower tribute band. I don't know how you managed to dig them up."

Honestly, neither did I. I'd mostly just taken anybody who looked available. "I'm mysterious too," I explained. "Also I think they were cheap."

"Undervalued," Brian corrected me.

I looked at Jaz across the group. She'd tucked a carefully wrapped pork pie into one pocket but otherwise wasn't eating anything. "So," I said very gently, because this was going to some very her-mum-related places, and that was still a fine line to walk, "Odile"—still felt weird—"is going to be up really soon and, well, if you wanted to come watch from the wings, I think she'd like it and—"

Jaz gave a shudder I thought was exaggerated. "She won't drag me onstage or make me sing with her or anything, will she?"

I could say, with absolute certainty, that she wouldn't. "No, she's way too kind and way too vain."

Having made sure somebody was looking after Spud, Jaz wandered over to join me and Oliver.

"I'm sorry your mum couldn't stick around for this," I whispered to Jaz as we approached the stage and the closing strains of the Real Original Skenfrith Male Voice Choir's rendition of "Hen Wlad Fy Nhadau" began to die away.

I'd been shooting for compassionate. I worried I'd hit crass. But Jaz seemed fairly chill. "For the best. She'd have loved the music, but the crowd's too much."

Jaz, Oliver, and I mounted the stage and lurked in the wings, out of sight of everybody but the techs and the backup singers. I could see Judy on the other side, her dogs lying at her feet, probably because they were exhausted after the walk from Pucklethroop-on-the-Wold. In front of us, my mum—my actual mum, looking younger, more alive, and, in ways I didn't like to think too much about, more *herself* than I could ever remember seeing her—strode out in front of the festival crowd, who cheered the way only ten thousand genuinely excited and moderately well-catered-for people can cheer.

"Hello, CRAPPstonbury!" she called out, with the effortless confidence of a legend of the rock 'n' roll. "My name is Odile O'Donnell. I was going to say it's good to be back, but really"—she put her hand over her heart—"I never went away. I am here. I am here for *you*. And I am never leaving."

In that moment I'd have bet good money that every single human being in that crowd felt like she was saying those words to just them, directly and personally. But to me they hit different. Because I'd lived them. And I knew they were true in every part of me. And I wanted more than anything else to pass them on to the people I cared for.

I laid one hand on Jaz's shoulder, and Oliver slid his arm around my waist.

And the music started.

EPILOGUE

JAZ WAS SIXTEEN WHEN SHE left us.

She did…okay at her GCSEs. I think. Ever since they'd started being numbers instead of letters I'd kind of lost track of what they meant, but she got an 8 in music, which Mum was pretty made up about. Oliver had been more excited that she'd got a 6 in maths, because she'd been having trouble with that the whole time, and it had taken ages for her to let him help her with it.

The morning Jaz's mother was due to collect her, I got up early. I'd been getting up early a lot lately. I was never going to become a morning person, but between a dog and a kid, I'd got weirdly used to having stuff to do before ten, and while I still didn't *like* it, my brain was gradually accepting that it was the new normal.

"Coffee?" offered Oliver as I stared blearily into the toaster.

"Hmm?"

"Would you like some coffee?"

I didn't quite have it in me to answer, but Oliver made me some anyway. Which was one of those things that felt like real love.

Putting his arms around me, Oliver kissed me gently on the back of the neck. "We prepared for this."

"We *talked* about this," I replied, "we didn't *prepare* for it. You can't."

"No," agreed Oliver.

And for a while we just stood there like that, him holding me and me resting against him, like there was nothing but the two of us in all the world. I tried not to think about how in a bit over an hour, that would be one step closer to being true. At least there'd be only the two of us in all the house.

Well, us and Spud.

We were interrupted by a sound of disgust coming from Jaz. Disgust of the older-people-I-live-with-are-showing-affection kind. Not the homophobic kind. "Are you two finished being shit?"

Oliver turned his head fractionally towards her. "No."

I disentangled myself from him and tried to avoid bursting into tears. "And we never will be."

Jaz pushed past us, grabbed a couple of slices of bread, and popped them in the toaster. She'd been out of the yoink-two-slices-and-vanish habit for at least a year. When her toast popped up, she buttered it, then retrieved a packet of Maldon Sea Salt from the cupboard and sprinkled a few flakes artfully over the top. "So," she began. There was an edge in her voice that, even after all this time, I didn't think I'd ever heard. "This is weird, right?"

I suddenly had no idea what to do with my hands. "I'm *trying* not to be."

"We're very glad that Maisie is able to take you back," said Oliver more levelly. "But that doesn't mean we won't also miss you."

Jaz looked very fixedly at her toast. "Yeah, well. You said. Yesterday. And the day before."

"And we still mean it today," replied Oliver.

I didn't reply anything. I was beginning to find it a bit difficult to get words out.

Scuffing one foot on the floor, Jaz lapsed into a still-characteristic silence. "Yeah," she finally repeated. "Well."

We sort of avoided talking from then until the doorbell went.

Spud ran to it, yapping, and I spared a thought for how much he'd miss Jaz as well. In some ways, he'd been closer to her than any of us.

Holding out a faint, desperate hope that this would actually be Next Door's Kid's Parents popping up with some last-minute complaint, I rested for a second with my hand on the latch. Oliver and Jaz lined up behind me, and Spud scampered around my feet, totally oblivious about what was going on. And then, when I couldn't delay any longer, I opened the door.

It wasn't Next Door's Kid's Parents. It was Maisie. Which meant it was over.

"Hi," she said, in that very specific tone people got when they knew they were happy about something you were sad about.

Oliver and I hi-ed back, and Jaz—who I didn't think was *trying* to give the impression that she was desperate to get rid of us—started gathering up all the bags she'd packed in advance. The suitcase she'd taken on her year eleven geography field trip. The laptop bag we'd got her for the laptop we'd got her to replace the one she'd had from Bellefield when it inevitably broke. The guitar my mum had stolen from Brian May. The sports bag Jaz no longer had to use for her PE kit because she was somehow starting her A levels already and so would never have mandatory football ever again.

It was terrifying how many memories you could build in just a couple of years.

"Thanks," Maisie went on, only slightly awkwardly. "For, y'know, looking after her."

"It's fine." It was the most not-falling-apart tone I could manage. "Literally the job description."

"It was our pleasure," added Oliver.

Jaz turned and gave him a *the fuck it was* look. "The fuck it was."

"Jasmine," warned Maisie. It had taken me a while to get used to the fact that Maisie actually did always call her daughter by her full name, and that Jaz didn't seem to mind it from her. But it made sense when I thought about it. "Don't be a prick."

Thankfully Oliver, always ready with a slightly-too-formal response to anything, just smiled. "It's fine." Then he turned to Jaz. "I hope this won't be too sentimental, but I assure you, these last two years have been the most rewarding of my life."

"And he has, like, a super-rewarding job," I chimed in uselessly.

Stepping lightly over our threshold, Maisie hugged me and said in a soft voice, "I know how hard this is."

Then she hugged Oliver, and he hugged her back and replied, "Just so you know, Jaz will always have a home here if she...if she needs one or if she wants one or..."

"Or if she just wants to visit," I added, not at all desperately. "You will visit, right?"

Jaz made the most noncommittal sound I'd heard her make in two years of hearing her make extremely noncommittal sounds. Which was the closest she was ever going to get to a yes.

"Of course we will." Being a grown-up, Maisie was slightly more willing to be reassuring.

And then we all lapsed into a horrible silence.

"We know this is for the best," said Oliver in that what-matters-is-what's-right way of his that, honestly, we all really needed from him just in that moment. "And we know she's not ours. But..."

"But we're hers," I finished for him. "Always. Or as long as she wants us."

From the look on Jaz's face, *as long as she wanted us* ended about eight minutes ago, but her face was sometimes deceptive. Especially when feelings were involved. It was one of the many things we had in common. Or, possibly, one of the many ways I was still worryingly like a teenager.

Maisie picked up the last remaining bag. "Well."

"Well," I echoed.

And then I said "I guess you should..." at the exact same time Maisie said "I guess we should..."

"We shouldn't keep you," cut in Oliver firmly.

Which was, unfortunately, true. On many levels.

We shut the door and were just retreating, full-on-no-shit heartbroken into our front room, when there was another knock.

Spud fucking lost it.

"I *suppose*," said Jaz when Oliver and I opened the door again, "that, all things considered, what with one thing and another, in the overall scheme of things you weren't *completely* shit foster parents."

Oliver put his hand on his heart. "Thank you, that means a lot."

"To be clear," I added, "he's pretending to be sarcastic, but we both totally mean it."

I got the impression that Jaz was already one-third regretting this. "*And*," she added, "I might actually maybe miss you sometimes maybe." She dropped into a squat and ruffled Spud's fur. "And I will *really* miss *you* because *you* are the *best boy, aren't you*?"

"Are we in the way?" I asked.

Jaz glanced up, half smirking. "A bit, if I'm honest."

"To be clear," said Oliver, with the sternness that Jaz had long since stopped taking seriously, "you don't get to keep our dog."

"Yeah." Jaz continued commiserating with Spud. "Not fair, isn't it, boy?"

"Arooou," agreed Spud, the little fluffy traitor.

Once our foster daughter—former foster daughter—had finished ignoring us in favour of our pet, she stood back up. And finally, with a don't-you-fucking-dare-say-anything look on her face, she hugged me.

Then she hugged Oliver.

Then she crouched back down to pat Spud again.

"Right," she said. "I'm out. But I'll be back to check in on Spud so…behave yourselves."

We promised that we would. We shut the door behind her.

And then she really was gone.

"Aroou?" said Spud, somewhat anxiously, as we walked back into a suddenly much emptier, much quieter house.

I followed Oliver into the living room, where he was looking round like he didn't recognise it.

"You know," he said, "I can't remember the last time we hoovered behind the sofa. We should probably pull it out and—"

Then he shaded his eyes with a hand and burst into tears. Which was almost a relief because it gave me something to do that wasn't bursting into tears myself. I drew him gently onto the sofa that we definitely weren't hoovering behind that evening.

He made a slightly futile attempt to wipe his eyes. "S-sorry."

"Yeah," I told him. "How dare you express emotion."

"Well, this is a little undignified."

"Fuck dignity, Oliver. Our kid just left."

"With her mother. Which is the right thing for her."

I knew Oliver would have a handkerchief, even if he'd temporarily forgotten. I took it out of his pocket and gave it to him. "Things can be right and still suck."

"I know. But it's particularly complicated when the right sucky thing is a right sucky thing you've been working to make happen for two years. And then it finally happens, and it feels a lot suckier than it does right."

"Is it possible," I asked, "you're overthinking and actually we're both just sad?"

He shot me a teary look. "And you're not… I know how you… You don't think it's my fault she's gone?"

"What? No. Where is this coming from?"

"I suppose I'm just aware that if I'd let things be, she'd probably have stayed until she was eighteen."

"Or she might not have. Anything could have happened."

"I still might have expedited something that—"

"Oliver." I kissed him in an *I love you but shut up* way. "Stop. Everyone in this situation was a grown-up. Well, everyone except Jaz. Well, everyone except Jaz and Spud."

"Ruff," agreed Spud, who was sitting at Oliver's feet, giving dog comfort.

"Maisie wanted her daughter back. Jaz wanted her mum back. You helped make that happen. And I love you for helping make that happen. Even if..." I sighed. "We're both hurting because of it."

Oliver closed his eyes for a moment. "Sorry," he said again. "Not for the emotions. For...for being silly."

"Eh." I waved that away. "I like it when you're silly. Makes me feel useful."

He managed a watery smile. "There are more important things in a relationship than being useful. You taught me that."

"Yeah, but I've got those things nailed."

"You do," he agreed, clearly meaning something totally different and a lot more flattering. He half turned towards me. "I don't know what I'd do without you, Lucien."

"More hoovering, probably?"

"Actually, we should probably dust the top of the television as well."

"Oliver, you're still crying. Why are you talking about dusting?"

He gave a weepy, self-conscious half laugh. "Because I'm...I'm at a loss, I think."

"So am I. Let's just be at a loss for a while? Maybe take Spud for a walk in a bit?"

"Ruff," said Spud. And then, seeming to remember Jaz was gone, added, "Aroou."

"That doesn't seem..." Oliver broke off. Then tried again. "Adequate?"

"Is anything going to be?"

"One would hope so. Eventually."

"Okay," I said. "But eventually's ages away. I'm trying to get through now."

Oliver drew me closer, half protective, half needy. "We're going to be all right."

"Of course we are."

"It's just...hard to think. About anything."

"That's okay."

"Or to imagine what we'll do next."

I was quiet, the seconds and minutes slipping away, as I snuggled deeper into Oliver's embrace. "I guess," I said finally, "we don't have to?"

"Isn't that a little nihilistic?"

"I don't think so. I think it might be the opposite of...of that."

"You aren't totally certain what nihilism is, are you?"

"I mean, is anyone? Like, something something abyss, something something monsters, something something God is dead."

Oliver opened his mouth, then closed it again. "Actually, that's pretty much it."

"I think," I went on, leaving the dead God in the abyss with the monsters, "I just meant that it doesn't matter that we don't know what we're doing today. Because we'll always have tomorrow?"

"You," murmured Oliver, "are the only person I know who can make procrastination sound romantic."

I shrugged. "Well, maybe that's because I can't imagine anything more romantic."

"Than procrastination?"

"Than being so sure of someone, so completely in love with them, that you can stop worrying about the future on account of how the most important thing about it is already sorted."

Oliver blinked, crying again, but more gently this time. "Oh, Lucien," he said.

And when he kissed me, there in our under-hoovered living room with its under-dusted television, he tasted a little bit of coffee and a little bit of crying, but mostly of forever.

Our forever.

Whatever that looked like.

ACKNOWLEDGMENTS

As ever, my heartfelt gratitude goes to my agent, Courtney Miller-Callihan; my editor, Mary Altman; the wonderful team at Sourcebooks; and my amazing assistant, Mary.

ABOUT THE AUTHOR

Alexis Hall writes books in the southeast of England, where he lives entirely on a diet of tea and Jaffa Cakes. You can find him at quicunquevult.com, on Instagram @quicunquevult, and on Facebook at facebook.com/quicunquevult.